SMOLDERING PASSIONS

"Kissing is ugly and sinful, is it?" Gerrick leaned closer, but the beautiful girl held her ground and glared at him, making him doubly angry. "Tell me, miss, have you ever been kissed? Do you know what pleasure is to be found in kissing—and other intimacies of the flesh? Or do you simply condemn what you know nothing about? Embracing ignorance, rather than holiness."

"That, sir, is none of your business!"

Gerrick grinned, for the long-lashed eyes had gone wide, and the soft, tender lips were trembling. A bit more goading would crack her tedious self-righteousness. He was beginning to enjoy himself immensely. He leaned even closer to her.

From the corner of his eye, he saw her hand rise, but before he could react, she struck his face a stunning blow.

Acting on instinct, he grabbed her and pinioned her struggling body against him so she couldn't strike again. Clawing at his arms, she arched her back in a futile effort to free herself.

His own dizzying upsurge of desire caught Gerrick unaware. Bending over her, he nuzzled first her neck and then her white throat . . .

ZEBRA'S GOT THE ROMANCE
TO SET YOUR HEART AFIRE!

RAGING DESIRE (2242, $3.75)
by Colleen Faulkner

A wealthy gentleman and officer in General Washington's army, Devon Marsh wasn't meant for the likes of Cassie O'Flynn, an immigrant bond servant. But from the moment their lips first met, Cassie knew she could love no other . . . even if it meant marching into the flames of war to make him hers!

TEXAS TWILIGHT (2241, $3.75)
by Vivian Vaughan

When handsome Trace Garrett stepped onto the porch of the Santa Clara ranch, he wove a rapturous spell around Clara Ehler's heart. Though Clara planned to sell the spread and move back East, Trace was determined to keep her on the wild Western frontier where she belonged — to share with him the glory and the splendor of the passion-filled TEXAS TWILIGHT.

RENEGADE HEART (2244, $3.75)
by Marjorie Price

Strong-willed Hannah Hatch resented her imprisonment by Captain Jake Farnsworth, even after the daring Yankee had rescued her from bloodthirsty marauders. And though Jake's rock-hard physique made Hannah tremble with desire, the spirited beauty was nevertheless resolved to exploit her femininity to the fullest and gain her independence from the virile bluecoat.

LOVING CHALLENGE (2243, $3.75)
by Carol King

When the notorious Captain Dominic Warbrooke burst into Laurette Harker's eighteenth birthday ball, the accomplished beauty challenged the arrogant scoundrel to a duel. But when the captain named her innocence as his stakes, Laurette was terrified she'd not only lose the fight, but her heart as well!

Available wherever paperbacks are sold, or order direct from the Publisher. Send cover price plus 50¢ per copy for mailing and handling to Zebra Books, Dept. 2388, 475 Park Avenue South, New York, N.Y. 10016. Residents of New York, New Jersey and Pennsylvania must include sales tax. DO NOT SEND CASH.

RUBY ORCHID

KATHARINE KINCAID

ZEBRA BOOKS
KENSINGTON PUBLISHING CORP.

Katharine Kincaid is also the author of
  Crimson Desire
  Crimson Embrace
  Defiant Vixen
  Violet Smoke

ZEBRA BOOKS

are published by

Kensington Publishing Corp.
475 Park Avenue South
New York, NY 10016

First printing: July, 1988

Printed in the United States of America

For Florence, my friend and mother-in-law,
With special thanks for everything,
Especially for watching the children
While we researched this book in Hawaii.

Prologue

Newport, Rhode Island, 1833

"Madeline, love, don't. We've got to talk." Gerrick rose up on one elbow and pushed away Madeline's hand, which had wandered below his navel.

"Not yet," the dark-haired young woman whispered huskily. "The night is still young. Later, we can talk."

"You witch. Does it please you to control me like a puppet dangling from a string?"

Gerrick rolled his nude body on top of Madeline's and held her pinioned against the ivory silk sheets. Outside, sleet from an early spring storm was slashing against the windowpane. Inside, a cozy fire burned on the grate and cast flickering shadows upon the wall. It was all the light Gerrick needed to see the wicked smile curving Madeline's lips. Gazing up at him through gold-tipped lashes, she tilted back her head and arched her body, thrusting her pointed breasts into prominence.

"Surely, you aren't finished," she purred knowingly, rubbing her knee against his inner thigh.

With a deep groan, Gerrick fell on her. He doubted he'd ever be finished with Madeline Barrows; of all the women he'd known, only she possessed the power to make him beg—even grovel. He never seemed to tire of her; back he came, again and again, and when he wasn't with her, he dreamed of her—dreamed, finally, of owning her and making her his wife. Though many had tried, no other woman had succeeded at turning his thoughts toward marriage—only Madeline, with her long, shining brown hair, sultry eyes, and sinuous body.

Deliberately, he pushed from his mind the important discussion they must have this night. Quelling the ugly memories that plagued him waking or sleeping, making his life a living hell in which Madeline was his only comfort, his only hope, was more difficult. But with her help, he finally succeeded. Yes, the night was still young, and the woman he loved was eager for him.

Afterward, Gerrick slept, and when he awakened, Madeline was sitting in the huge armchair beside the fire, watching him with a cool, detached air, almost as if they were strangers. She had donned a lace-trimmed velvet dressing gown, the color of wine, and he disliked not being able to see her body. After they married, he would insist that she always go naked in their chambers—and if she became cold, he himself would warm her.

Grinning, he stretched leisurely, savoring these few, precious moments when his worries were held at bay, and his big body was as sated and content as a tomcat's after a night on the prowl. Sleet still rattled the windowpane, but the wind had died down, making conversation easier. "Ready to talk?" he queried. "Come sit by me—and take off that damn robe. You know it irritates me when you wear clothes."

Rising from the chair, Madeline said not a word, but neither did she remove the gown. She came only as far as the foot of the bed, and there she stood, still as a stone, making him uneasy with her chilly silence.

"Miss Barrows," he said formally. "Will you do me the honor of becoming my wife? Before you answer, let me explain. I'm not asking you to marry a penniless man."

"You're not?" Surprise flickered in the cool depths of her obsidian eyes. "And just what has happened to change your present circumstances?"

"I've thought of a way to recoup my family's fortunes—*and* to gain revenge on Amos Taylor. Tomorrow, I'm going away. But when I return, I shall be rich—even richer than I was before. Money can't bring back my mother and sister, of course, nor can it make a whole man of my poor, crippled father—but it *can* ensure the destruction of the bastard who destroyed my family. . . . And it can keep you, my love, in the manner in which you've grown accustomed."

"That is . . . admirable," she said carefully.

Gerrick waited for her to say more—to ask questions—and when she did not, he felt a prickle of grim foreboding mixed with his irritation. "Don't you want to know where I'm going and when I'll be back?"

"If you care to tell me . . ." Her voice trailed off like that of a bored acquaintance. Growing alarmed, he sat up. Where was the eager, supportive lover of only an hour ago?

"Damn it, Madeline, I'm not talking about strolling around the block, but of sailing halfway around the globe! And I'm asking you to *wait* for me, to marry me as soon as I return!"

"Which will be—when? Years from now? In several years, you *may* return a rich man?"

So that was what was bothering her, Gerrick thought. She doubted he would ever be rich again. Well, what did he expect? For a time, he himself had doubted it. The string of tragedies that had befallen his family had almost destroyed *him*, as well. If he had not had Madeline to turn to, he *would* have been destroyed.

"Not *may*, my love, *will*. I *will* be rich, again. The Scotts have always been rich. We're the leading family of Newport, remember?"

"Were," Madeline corrected. "You *were* the leading family. But Lady Fortune has now deserted you, and you're nothing, Gerrick. You're asking me to marry a nobody . . . and that I cannot do."

This last was spoken forcefully; even so, Gerrick wasn't certain he had heard aright. "You're refusing? After all these years, you don't want to marry?"

"Oh, yes," she said, toying with the sash on her dressing

gown. "I want to marry—but not you. Tomorrow evening, at a small dinner party at my aunt's, I am announcing my betrothal to Enoch Breckenridge."

Gerrick leaped off the bed, scattering bedclothes left and right. "Who the hell is Enoch Breckenridge?" he shouted, towering over her as he tugged on his breeches. "Tell me where to find him, and I'll leave immediately to call him out."

"He doesn't live here." Eyeing him coldly, Madeline retreated a step or two behind the armchair. "He's a wealthy landowner from Philadelphia."

"Where did you meet him?" Gerrick thundered. Advancing toward her, he shrugged on his shirt, tearing the fabric in his haste to be dressed.

"That is not your concern. What does concern you is that I'm going to marry *him*, not you. The wedding will take place next month, right here at the inn, though we plan to live in Philadelphia. So you see I cannot possibly wait until you return. You can't seriously expect me to wait."

"And when were you going to inform me of all this—on your wedding night? Would you have welcomed him into your bed only minutes after I had left it? You're marvelous between the sheets, Madeline—but not that marvelous! Two besotted lovers in one night might be more than even you could handle!"

"I . . . I was going to tell you, tonight. This was going to be our last night together. I'm sorry. . . . Don't you realize how sorry I am?" Haughtily, she lifted her chin. "I can't marry a poor man, Gerrick. And I can't sit patiently waiting while you regain your fortune and chase after your father's business partner . . ."

"You think I should just forget that Amos Taylor, not only my father's partner but his best friend, embezzled us out of every dollar we owned? Should I, perhaps, forgive the man responsible for the deaths of my mother and my sister, and for leaving my father a helpless, broken old man?"

"I've heard all this before, Gerrick," Madeline cut in coldly.

"Then maybe you'd better hear it again!" Gerrick knocked aside the chair and seized Madeline by the shoulders. "Amos Taylor set fire to the warehouse in which my mother and my sister were innocently inspecting a new shipment of silks. God help them, they were picking out fabrics for Abby's trousseau! Amos never even checked to see if someone was inside; all he cared about was destroying the evidence in his office, evidence of his embezzlement that my father already had in his possession."

"I'm sorry for your mother and sister, Gerrick. And I'm sorry for your father. He should have killed Amos with that bull whip, instead of almost being killed when Amos shot him. . . . But I can't help anything that's happened. Maybe if you'd gotten to Amos before he fled, maybe if you'd stopped him from stealing what cash you had left . . ."

Losing all restraint, Gerrick shook her. Her head snapped back and forth like a ragdoll's, and her silken hair flew in all directions. "How could I have stopped him when I didn't know anything about it until it was too late? Have you forgotten? I was here, with you—working up my courage to propose!"

"Stop it, Gerrick, you're hurting me!"

He stopped shaking her, and she backed away from him, one white hand clutching her throat. "Why did it take such courage to finally propose, Gerrick? Haven't I always been here for you—welcoming you into my arms even when you reeked of the perfume of other women? Wasn't I always willing to do anything you wanted? Haven't I satisfied you more than any woman you've known?"

"Y—yes," Gerrick choked. "But marriage . . . it's a big step. And you weren't—you aren't—the sort of woman my family wanted for me."

"You mean I wasn't . . . I'm *not* the blue-blooded brood mare who could bring suitable class to the Scott line of thoroughbreds."

"No, you're not," Gerrick flatly admitted. "But I had already decided to marry you despite my family's objections. I'm offering marriage now, this very minute. If you

11

prefer, we could marry *before* I leave—and I won't be gone for years. The most time this adventure will take is one year—maybe two, at the maximum.''

"How very kind of you, Captain Scott! Only I no longer need or want your kindness. I've found a rich man who will marry me regardless of my lowly station as the daughter of a mere innkeeper. Of course, he's pleased that I've acquired all the polish you've so kindly taught me— and he's also pleased that I come to him with such expertise in bed. His first wife was a prude and a dullard; in his second, he wants youth, beauty, and experience—all of which I possess in abundance, especially the latter, thanks to you.''

"I'll kill him!"

"No, you won't, Gerrick. Before I see you harm him or try to stop our marriage, I'll kill *you* first.'' Seemingly out of nowhere, a small pistol appeared in Madeline's hand. It must have been hidden, Gerrick realized, in the pocket of her dressing gown.

"You haven't the nerve to shoot me," he taunted. "Not after all we've meant to each other.''

"You mean what I've meant to *you,* Gerrick. To me, you were nothing but a chance to rise in society. Now, you can't even offer that.''

"Then why during these last few weeks have you continued to welcome me into your bed—risking your already somewhat tarnished reputation every time I came?''

Still aiming the pistol at him, Madeline smiled a slow, provocative smile. She loosened the sash at her waist and allowed the wine-colored dressing gown to fall open. "Because no man will ever please me as you've pleased me, my darling. If it's any consolation, I'll never forget you. You're every woman's dream of the perfect lover—the handsome, lusty stallion who knows a dozen ways to satisfy a woman—and who, in a single night, can outperform even the biggest and healthiest of studs.''

Gerrick bowed stiffly, concealing his raging hurt and disappointment with a tight-lipped grimace. "Thank you, Miss Barrows. I always did aim to please."

The smile never left her face as she parted the gown, giving the firelight free access to her gleaming white flesh. Slowly, her fingers stroked the outline of her breast. "We needn't part enemies, Gerrick. There's time before morning for a tender good-bye . . ."

For a moment, he was tempted, but a hot, sweeping bitterness held him in check. "Tender? You've no tenderness in you, Madeline, just as there is none in me. I don't know why I didn't see that before now. One day, you'll see it, too; one day, you'll regret the choices you've made this night. Tonight, we could have begun anew, changed for the better . . ."

"Perhaps . . ." She cocked her head, her mouth turning down in a childish pout. "Since you won't stay until morning, I'm already regretting it, Gerrick."

Gerrick felt sick. His head had begun hammering, and his stomach churned with pain, hatred, and revulsion. Nevertheless, feigning indifference, he picked up his remaining things and headed for the door of her chambers.

"Gerrick?" She padded after him in her bare feet. "What time will you be sailing—and where? Before you go, you can at least tell me that."

He paused before opening the door. "Have you changed your mind?"

"No . . ."

"Then you wouldn't be interested. Except to know that my destination is about as far away from you as I can get."

Mindful of the inn's other guests, Gerrick went out quietly and shut the door behind him.

Chapter One

Hanalei Bay, Kauai, 1834

Captain Gerrick Hadley Scott did not ordinarily waste time gaping at the moon. This moon, however, stirred his senses in a way he hadn't allowed himself to experience for almost a year. It was a full moon, incredibly large and luminous, riding high on the crest of lush, cumulus clouds unlike any clouds he had ever seen back home in New England.

Here in the Sandwich Islands, or the Hawaiian Islands as they were now being called, everything was larger, more vivid and spectacular, as if painted by a half-mad artist drunk on wine and the scent of plumeria. The sunsets in these tropical waters took Gerrick's breath away, and from what he could view of the nearest island, the vegetation grew taller, greener, and more profuse than any to which he was accustomed. Palm trees waved their lacy fronds like exotic dancers, flowers rivaled precious jewels in the brilliancy of their color, and the beaches were carved from sugar—all of this painted against a backdrop of majestic, cloud-draped mountains and steep cliffs rimmed by the bluest of blue waters.

A man would have to have one foot in the grave not to respond to the sensual possibilities throbbing in the sweet, moisture-laden air. And since Gerrick hadn't held a woman for months while at sea, and every woman he'd seen since they dropped anchor in the afternoon had been either partially or fully naked and as beautiful as a mermaid cavorting in the turquoise waters of the sheltered bay, he would have to be an intimate of Saint Peter himself not to feel a rush of heady excitement.

And I'm certainly no saint, Gerrick mused ruefully as he leaned on the ship's rail and contemplated the beauty of his surroundings.

Soon, the natives would be coming to escort them ashore for a torch-lit banquet, the preparations for which were already under way beneath the swaying palms. And soon, Gerrick would have to decide whether to join his eager crew members in their drunken revelries beneath the moon, or to remain aboard, sequestered in his cabin, alone with his bitter memories and brooding on his plans for vengeance.

"It's everything they say it is, isn't it?" a voice asked from behind him.

Startled, Gerrick turned to see his closest friend and now his partner in this adventure, John Reynolds. "What is?" he asked bluntly, refusing to openly acknowledge the effect the moon was having upon him.

"This island . . . this moon . . . this sea . . ." John replied amiably, undeterred by Gerrick's cold attitude. He grinned, his swarthy, round face fully visible in the bright-as-day moonlight. Beneath the cowlick of dark hair that hung perpetually across his forehead, his brown eyes sparkled with irrepressible good humor. "They say that if a man spends any time at all in the Sandwich Islands, he'll never want to go home."

"They say that about Tahiti, too, and the Fijis, and the Marquesas, and just about anyplace where palm trees grow," Gerrick scoffed.

Looking carefully at his friend, he noticed something different about him: John had shaved his shaggy beard, donned clean clothing, and apparently dived overboard for a bath in the crystal clear waters. John's black hair still glistened wetly, and from a nick on his chin where the razor had cut him oozed a single drop of blood that

15

threatened to fall and spot his immaculate, open-to-the-waist white shirt.

"You're looking quite the dandy, John. Planning a big night in the arms of some dusky island beauty?"

John glanced toward shore, his teeth gleaming. He flexed his powerful shoulder muscles and thumped his fists on his massive chest. "It'll take more than one woman to satisfy *me*, tonight, Gerrick, my boy. I'm as randy as an old billy goat put to pasture a long time with no ewes."

"Poor old fellow," Gerrick mocked. "Had I known this voyage would have imposed such hardship upon you, I'd have left you at home to bedevil the young ladies of Boston."

"And it's not been a hardship for you?" John asked, suddenly serious, his eyes probing Gerrick's face.

Abruptly, Gerrick turned back toward the rail. "None that I've noticed," he denied coolly.

Despite his best effort to ignore them, unbidden and unwanted memories suddenly flooded his mind's eye—lovely, laughing Madeline, her nakedness hidden beneath her long, rippling brown hair, her slender, supple body as eager for him as he was for her. The pain of remembering cut like a knife, and helplessly, he grimaced.

"Let her go, Gerrick," John said softly, compassionately. "She wasn't worthy of you—nor of your family. All she wanted was your name and money. And when you lost that—at least, the money part—she proved what she was by marrying the first rich dandy who came along."

"Don't," Gerrick warned, his anger rising. Even though he knew John was right, he couldn't bear to hear Madeline reviled. Not his lovely, sensuous Madeline, the first woman he had ever really cared about in all his thirty-two irresponsible, skirt-chasing, devil-may-care years.

"She was no better than a whore," John persisted. "She sold herself to the highest bidder."

"That's enough!" Convulsively, Gerrick's hands balled into fists. He jerked toward his friend, ready to deliver a stunning punch to John's smooth-shaven chin.

The shorter man gazed at him almost pityingly, then

quietly folded his arms across his huge, hairy chest. His calm refusal to fight was a devastating blow to Gerrick's already-battered pride. Though Gerrick towered over John by a full head, John could easily have bested him, and they both knew it. Not for nothing had John been called "The Bull" during their years at school in Boston, and later, at countless county fairs where Gerrick—young, brash, and fast-talking in those days—had made wagers that John could take any man who stepped into the ring with him.

Gerrick's sobriquet had been "The Brain," and the two of them had schemed, fought, drunk, and wenched their way across all of New England before they finally settled down to fulfill their family obligations, John in Boston where his family built ships, and Gerrick in Newport, Rhode Island, where his family had owned a far-flung shipping empire that bought goods from all over the world and sold them at stunning prices.

Had. His family *had* controlled such an empire, and that was the other tragedy he couldn't bear to discuss, not even with his closest friend, John Reynolds.

"She wasn't worthy of you," John repeated stubbornly, appearing not to notice when Gerrick clenched his fists even tighter. "Take it from me, old friend: It's time you stopped mourning her and remembered that a man's lusty appetites can be satisfied by any woman with a willing heart and body."

"Not *my* appetites, John. You've never been in love. You can't possibly know what it's like to have the woman you worship cast you aside like an old bonnet she no longer fancies."

After so long a time maintaining his silence, it was suddenly a relief for Gerrick to talk about it, and his anger ebbed as he searched John's compassionate face for answers to questions he'd been asking himself for months. "Why did she do it, John? I trusted her. I needed her . . ." Gerrick swallowed hard, the bitterness of it almost choking him. "For the first time in my life, I wanted to shelter and protect a woman—to *give*, instead of

17

just take."

John frowned and put a consoling hand on his shoulder. "You aren't the first man to be taken in by a pair of flashing eyes and a comely figure, my friend, and I doubt you will be the last. Had you married the hard-hearted vixen, she would have made you miserable."

Gerrick slammed his fist down hard on the railing. "Damn her! And damn Amos Taylor! If it wasn't for him . . ."

John's hand suddenly clamped down hard. "Gerrick, you've got to stop brooding and let go of the past. What's done is done. It's over and finished."

Gerrick jerked away. "No! For me it will never be finished, not until Amos Taylor pays for his crimes. As soon as I regain my fortune, I'm going after the bastard. First, I'm going to ruin him financially, assuming he hasn't yet squandered the money he stole, and then I'm going to kill him—slowly and agonizingly."

Silence greeted this statement, and Gerrick turned to look at John. "Does that shock you? It's what I've been planning all the months of this voyage. It's what I've been doing in the silence of my cabin—plotting how to make Amos Taylor suffer, just as my mother and sister suffered, as my father suffers still, and as I'm suffering. Before I'm through, Amos Taylor will wish he had never heard of the name *Scott*. He'll wish he'd managed to get rid of every last one of us."

John's swarthy face was unreadable but his eyes held a measure of censure. "And after you've destroyed him, what then?"

"Then?" Gerrick shrugged. He had no idea what he'd do afterward. It didn't seem important. "Then, I'll come back here and chase island maidens with a vengeance. I'll be the old Gerrick you once knew—the lighthearted, reckless, utterly stupid son of a bitch you've known all your life."

"The Gerrick I knew would never have given his life to the cause of vengeance," John said stiffly. "That Gerrick was a fighter, yes, but in his own way also a high-minded soul. He lived hard, fought hard, and loved hard. Like all the redheaded, hot-tempered Scotts, he was bigger than life, brasher and bolder than ordinary folks, but also something of a dreamer and an idealist. Indeed, he was generous and forgiving to a fault. He never brooded on wrongs done him, never thought ill of men or believed the worst of them. And for that reason, he always got their best—their trust, their loyalty, their—''

"The old Gerrick was a fool," Gerrick snapped. "My father trusted Amos Taylor, and look where it got him—his wife and daughter dead, his fortune gone, he himself half-blind and living confined in the shell of his big house, all his furnishings sold, his servants let go, and only one old manservant to care for him for the remainder of his days. No, I'll never again be the fool that my father was!"

There was a short, awkward pause, and then John cleared his throat and asked quietly, "Does that mean you don't trust *me* anymore, Gerrick? Is that the reason you haven't yet told me *why* we've come to these beautiful but godforsaken islands?''

Slowly, Gerrick turned to face the broad-shouldered, thick-muscled man who had been closer to him than a brother all his life. Once, without a moment's doubt or hesitation, he would have entrusted his life to John Reynolds. Now, he felt confused and discomfited by John's question; he even half wished that he had come to the islands without him, that he had not gone running to Boston to persuade John to join him on this venture. If they *did* find what they had come for, if the rumors were not all false, then he and John would be the joint possessors of a fortune worth as much as either of their families had ever obtained in their lifetimes. Could John be trusted not to turn on him, as Amos had turned on his father?

"I don't know," he answered honestly. "All I do know is that from now on, I'll be more careful than my father was.''

The words hung between them in the air like some

19

alien, noxious odor, and John's eyes bored into Gerrick. "I see," John finally said. "Then I, too, have been a fool."

"You?" Gerrick asked sharply. "Nothing so bad has ever happened to you."

"Not so bad, no—but in its own way, just as devastating. I've been fool enough to accompany a man halfway around the world on a mysterious business venture, the nature of which he refuses to reveal except to tell me that it's one in which I might lose a great deal of money and possibly my life. Now, I learn that he's not sure he trusts me. *I* certainly don't need a fortune as desperately as you do, my friend, but still, I came for the sake of friendship, because I thought you needed me, and for that, I am a fool."

"It's not like that, John . . ." Gerrick protested, but his friend's knowing expression stopped him cold. It *was* like that. He hadn't trusted John enough to tell him why they had come to the islands. All he'd told him in Boston was that his mother and sister were dead in a fire, his father injured in an accident, and his family fortunes reversed. Would John join him in a fund-raising expedition to the Sandwich Islands?

And John, true friend that he was, had asked no questions—not even how and why he had decided upon the islands to regain his lost fortune. For John, it had been enough that Gerrick needed him, and he had accompanied Gerrick on this long, danger-fraught voyage. And while Gerrick had brooded in his cabin, often remaining there for days on end, drinking himself into a stupor, John had managed the ship and kept the uneasy, mutinous crew from revolting. Gerrick had heard him one night, calming the irate first mate, Erasmus Mockensturm:

"Just give him time, Erasmus. He'll soon be back to his old self. He's a Scott, by God, and the Scotts stand head and shoulders above other men. He'll overcome his recent tragedies and make rich men of us all."

"I'll make you rich," Gerrick promised coaxingly, remembering John's faith in him. "I'll make you rich beyond your wildest dreams."

"Rich," John repeated in an insulted tone. His black eyes snapped. "I thought I was rich before, in friendship if nothing else. . . . Am I permitted to ask how? I've little taste for whaling, and while there's money to be made in it, it's a dirty, stinking business that fouls your entire ship. Surely, you didn't drag me all the way out here to carve whale blubber. This ship isn't even properly outfitted for whaling."

"No . . ." Gerrick answered, still hesitating but feeling more ashamed by the minute. "No, I brought you to the islands because here, on this very island, high up in the mountains is something that men would cheerfully die for—or at least, *kill* for—something that everyone thought was long gone and therefore is even more valuable than it used to be. And it used to be worth its weight in gold . . ."

"What?" John growled. "Damn it, man, tell me straight out!"

Gerrick glanced about to make certain none of his crew was within earshot. Most had already gone ashore, except for the watch who stood a discreet distance away. Even so, Gerrick lowered his voice and half whispered his answer.

"Sandalwood . . ."

"Sandalwood!" John exploded.

"Lower your voice!" Gerrick exclaimed. "The whole damn ship needn't know about it."

"Sandalwood," John repeated, shaking his head. "I'm no merchant, Gerrick, nor even a tradesman or well-traveled sea captain like yourself. But I do build ships, and in that capacity, I know something about fine woods—including sandalwood. That boom is over. It only lasted until the sandalwood forests were cut down, and no more trees were left. None had even been planted for the future. The men who pass for kings in this part of the world never thought to preserve any; they simply cut down the trees and sold or gave the wood away, as whim or stupidity prompted them. Within a decade or two, the sandalwood trade was over. You should know all that—didn't your father make part of his fortune in sandalwood?"

"My father *did* dabble in the trade," Gerrick conceded.

"But he came in too late, after it was well established, and prices had gone sky-high. Indeed, he lost money underwriting voyages here, because by the time he took an interest in it, the wood was already seriously depleted, and what was left, Kamehameha refused to sell to him."

"Kamehameha?" John stumbled over the foreign, strange-sounding name. "*Which* Kamehameha? I understand there's been more than one."

"The first one, the patriarch and king of all the islands at the time. My father tried bribing him, begging him, and conspiring to topple him, but the old man was too strong and wily—and the competition against my father too keen from other quarters. Not long after, Kamehameha the First died, and one of his weak sons took over, but by then, my father had invested in other commodities closer to home. And besides, the vultures out here were stripping the islands faster than he could have acted."

"So why are we here? How did you find out about this supposedly overlooked treasure?"

Gerrick paused and wearily passed his hand over his face. He hoped John wouldn't think he was crazy when he heard the entire, strange tale. "A few years ago, Captain Moses Nottingham, one of the sea captains who first tried to negotiate with Kamehameha on my father's behalf, stopped at Newport for a visit following a successful trade voyage to Canton and told us an incredible story. While wintering in the islands, Captain Nottingham met a missionary right here on Kauai. The man was ill, and Nottingham took pity on him and transported him and his daughter to Maui, where there was another missionary, a doctor, who could help him. On the voyage, a storm blew up, and the missionary worsened. In his delirium, he raved about an undiscovered stand of sandalwood, high up in the mountains, the location of which was known only to himself. Apparently, the poor fellow couldn't decide whether to keep the whole thing secret or negotiate a sale of the precious wood, cutting in Kamehameha the Third and the king of Kauai for their share, on the condition that a fine new church of wood planking be built on Kauai to replace the old thatched-roof hut that had blown down in a hurricane.

"Unfortunately for us, the man's condition improved along with the weather, and Nottingham could learn nothing more about the matter. The missionary even denied he knew anything of sandalwood still remaining on the island. Nottingham himself returned to Kauai and searched for it, but was unable to find any—nor would the natives help him. Frustrated, and needing more time and money to investigate, Nottingham returned home. My father dismissed the story when he first heard it, but afterward, whenever business was slower than usual, he and Amos discussed the possibility of my sailing here to prove or disprove the rumor."

"Amos? Amos knew of the rumor?" John's heavy eyebrows arched in disapproval, and Gerrick hastened to reassure him.

"It was Amos who kept talking him out of it, calling it a 'wild-goose chase,' and pointing out that half of the poor bastards sent out here as missionaries are crazy as loons. It isn't likely they'd know a sandalwood tree if it bit them. If they did recognize one, they'd probably destroy it because, as you've probably heard, they have as little respect for free trade as they have for whaling."

John nodded. "Yes, I'd heard that. At our shipyard, one of the things most often demanded in a new whaling vessel is that it be strong enough to withstand the prayers of the missionaries to consign it to the ocean floor."

"Well, Amos finally convinced my father not to sink any money into such a risky venture, but it was only after all of our problems occurred that I realized why he'd been so set against it."

"Amos himself wanted to go after the sandalwood?" John queried suspiciously.

Gerrick grimaced. "No, Amos hates the sea. What he didn't want was for my father to discover how little cash we actually had. On several occasions, my father was ready to sign up a crew and outfit a ship immediately."

"So after you realized Amos's true intent, you decided to

investigate the rumor yourself, on the off-chance that it might be true."

"What choice did I have?" Gerrick demanded angrily. A renewed sense of desperation flooded him. "I was lucky to get out of Newport with the clothes on my back. That rumor represents my one opportunity to return home a rich man, able to hold up my head and take my rightful place in the community."

"And able to prove to Madeline Barrows that she made a terrible mistake." Censure and disapproval flickered once more in John's expressive dark eyes. "I'd hardly say it was your *only* hope, Gerrick. With what little money you had left, you could have bought a share of Reynolds Shipyards, and combining your talents and mine, together we could have made a fortune convincing merchants like your father to build and sail their own fleet of ships, instead of leasing them."

"I . . . I wanted to make it on my own," Gerrick stammered. "To prove that I could do it. I didn't want to take advantage of our friendship."

"Advantage? And just what the hell do you think you've *been* doing?" John roared.

A hot flush crept up Gerrick's neck. "I apologize, John. For my selfish bull-headedness and mistrust, as well as for bringing you here. It was a mistake; I admit it. I've indeed dragged you on a wild-goose chase, and you've every right to be furious."

Caught off guard by the sudden apology, John studied him a long moment. Then, he sighed. "On the contrary, Gerrick. Your instinct for making money in unlikely places has always been excellent. I haven't forgotten that when your father and mine refused to pay for our youthful exploits, you always found a way—but somehow, I was always the one who got bloodied, while you got the prettiest women."

Gerrick's mouth began to twitch in a faintly familiar manner; he had almost forgotten how to grin. "This time, John, I promise you—*you* can have the women, and if there's any bleeding to be done, I'll do it."

Considering, John cocked his head, and Gerrick grinned more widely. His grin had always proven to be extremely persuasive, among men as well as women, and he was gratified now to see John softening as in the old days.

"All right, Gerrick," said John finally with a sigh. "Once again, I'm your man. I'll help you search the whole damn island for that sandalwood, if necessary. If it's here, we'll find it. But first, before I scale mountains and dangle from precipices, I demand to know your plans—all of them. You do have plans, I presume."

Elated, Gerrick clapped his friend's shoulder. "Of course! All we have to do is find the daughter of that missionary who told Captain Nottingham about the sandalwood."

"The daughter? Why don't we just find the missionary? Perhaps if we offer to help him rebuild his damn church— out of sturdy planking, this time—he'll lead us straight to the sandalwood. That is, if he hasn't already sold it to someone else and *built* his precious church."

"I did make a few inquiries before coming here..." Gerrick said drily. "There's no record of any recent sandalwood shipments out of the islands—and no record of any wooden churches yet constructed on Kauai. The missionary died soon after his encounter with Moses Nottingham.... But his daughter is still very much alive."

"And probably as ugly as sin and as close-mouthed as a broom handle."

"No matter. I'm sure I can handle an innocent like Caitlin Price."

"Caitlin Price . . . her name, I take it."

Gerrick nodded. "A stiff-necked New Englander herself so at least we have something in common."

"Hah!" John snorted derisively. "If you're thinking of charming her, I'm afraid you're sadly out of practice."

"Me? Out of practice?" Gerrick was startled. "What do you mean?"

"Come ashore with me, lad, and I'll show you," John

said slyly. "Odds are I can tumble three women while you're still wooing one."

Gerrick regarded his friend with exasperation. He knew what John was about; but suddenly, he didn't mind. His gaze returned for a moment to the moon—glowing blue-white with sensual promise. Yes, he thought, it was time to stop grieving over Madeline and his family, to pull himself together, and to start living again. There would be a time and place for dealing with Amos Taylor. But right now, he was here, alive, anchored offshore from the greenest, loveliest island on earth, and it was time simply to be a man, with a man's needs and appetites.

"You're on, my friend. What do you bet—a bottle of rum? A handful of coin?"

"No," John said. "A picul of sandalwood. That *is* how it's bought and sold, isn't it? By the picul, which is, I believe, a bundle of wood weighing one hundred and thirty-three and a third pounds."

Gerrick stared. "You knew more about this than you ever let on, didn't you?"

John shook his massive head. "Not about why we were coming. But I did browse through all those reports on the history of the islands that you had in your sea chest. I thought *one* of us should study them."

It was a reproof, but a kind one. "I'm glad it was you," Gerrick said sincerely, and to his surprise, he discovered he really meant it. "Yes, I'm glad it was you, John, the best friend a jackass like me ever had."

Chapter Two

Caitlin Price finished packing her uncle's things in a small battered trunk and turned to reiterate her arguments one last time. "*Why* must you leave immediately? The morning would be soon enough. Besides you know what will happen as soon as you go; the sailors from that newly arrived schooner out in the bay will—"

"Really, Caitlin. Must we review this to the point of tediousness?" Her uncle had his back to her, but he sounded as if he were addressing a wayward child, rather than a full-grown woman. His large, heavy hands never paused in stuffing food for the journey into a knapsack.

"But what could be so important that—"

"I've already told you all you need to know, Niece. The Missionary Board requested me to come as soon as humanly possible. Their letter was in the schooner's mail packet. Tonight, the moon is full and the sea is calm, a perfect night for sailing. I've an outrigger waiting on the beach. If I don't leave tonight, by tomorrow the weather could change, closing the channel for weeks."

"And they mentioned nothing about my accompanying you? I simply can't believe that I, too, wasn't—"

"With all due respect, Niece, you are *only* a woman."

Uncle George irritably tightened the drawstrings on the leather pouch. Then, he drew himself up to his full, impressive height, straightened his claw-hammer coat, and adjusted his carefully tied stock. Placing his tall, high-crowned hat on his balding head, he picked up the knapsack and stared down his enormous, blue-veined nose at her.

Caitlin studied him helplessly and with choking irritation. Uncle George's imposing figure—he was thick of chest and jowly of jaw—and his pale gray eyes, piercing and closely set, were nothing like her gentle father's. Nor did he possess the distinctive, pale blond coloring and fair skin of the Prices. Caitlin could see no family resemblance whatever, yet her own dislike and petty jealousy aside, wasn't this scant reason to doubt his claim of being her father's long-lost brother?

His arrival on Kauai four months ago had come as a complete surprise; suddenly, he had appeared on her doorstep to assume her father's duties. Once she got over her initial shock, she had found it easy to understand why her father had never mentioned him. Uncle George had been the black sheep of the family, disowned and excommunicated, until he finally saw the light and reembraced the faith with a fervor equal to or even surpassing that of his older brother, William.

Now, he was the new resident missionary—and also, to her dismay, her guardian. It mattered little that she had been managing very well on her own, and had, in fact, been running the mission even before her father's broken body had been found at the bottom of a steep gorge. No woman was considered bright enough or capable enough to order her life without male interference; since she didn't yet have a husband, Caitlin owed unquestioning obedience and respect to her uncle.

She understood her duty—only her heart twisted at the thought that she hadn't been included in the invitation to come to Maui for this mysterious, important meeting. Uncle George was still a newcomer to the islands, and in many things, their opinions differed.

"You will tell them how things are with us," she said stiffly. "How desperately we need a new church—a sturdy structure built of planks, not grass matting."

"Of course, I'll tell them, though I doubt it will do any

good. This not being Oahu or Maui, we can't expect the same support as the islands with the biggest ports of call."

"I know, but we can keep trying." It was one of the few things on which they both agreed—the need for funding in order to build a new and better church. "And will you please inquire as to whether there's been any reply to my father's request to find a suitable husband for me? Surely, by now, they've received word of someone in New England who's willing to wait until he arrives at his new post before taking a wife. Remind them that I speak the language fluently; that facility alone should be an asset to a neophyte."

Uncle George frowned disapprovingly. "You needn't remind me of my duties, Niece. You are far too forward—not an admirable quality for the future wife of a man of the cloth."

Caitlin bit back an angry retort. Her forwardness was the thing on which they most disagreed. "When shall I expect you home?"

"As usual—when I reappear. I have in mind stopping in Honolulu on the return trip from Maui, so I can't really say. Your little friend, Pikake, can keep you company while I am gone."

"My father never found it necessary to spend so much time traveling. There's too much to be done right here."

"Well, my dear Caitlin, that is why I have you . . . to keep the mission running smoothly while I attend to more important matters."

Flushing at his insulting tone, Caitlin wondered what *did* occupy her uncle's time. He was always going somewhere. Her father had traveled about the island, too, ministering to the farthest villages, but never to the same extent as Uncle George. Perhaps he had some other purpose besides preaching and teaching—or maybe he just had itchy feet, a feeling with which Caitlin had grown distressingly familiar. Quite often lately, she felt bitterly dissatisfied with her present life and achingly longed for some change or excitement—anything to break the monotony of a once-cherished routine that had somehow gone stale.

"I assure you that all will be well, Uncle. Please inform Brother Bingham, when you see him, that he may rest easy while the mission is in my keeping."

"Just attend your duties, Niece. If you do that, you'll have no need for unseemly praise or flattery. Your reward shall come in the hereafter."

Uncle George effortlessly hoisted the small trunk onto one shoulder and slung the knapsack over the other. "No need to follow me down to the beach. Better stay out of sight until that schooner departs."

"As you wish . . ." Bristling inside, Caitlin watched him as he walked to the door. She didn't need to be reminded of the danger from carousing sailors; it was *he* who needed reminding. "Wait a minute. Your Bible . . ."

Spying the book lying forgotten on a nearby shelf, she rushed to get it. How could he go off without his Bible? Her father would *never* have forgotten so important an item.

"How fortunate you remembered it before I left." Neglecting even to say thank you, Uncle George plucked the heavy volume from her hands and carelessly jammed it into his knapsack on top of the food.

"You're welcome!" Caitlin snapped.

Her uncle gazed at her a long moment, his gray eyes coldly calculating, and Caitlin suppressed a shiver. When he looked at her like that, so deadly serious and disapproving, she couldn't help wondering what he was thinking. Unlike her father, there wasn't a shred of humor in the man; if anything he exuded menace. He was secretive and judgmental, and though she'd never witnessed him really losing his temper, she knew that if he did, he might become violent. At times, he seemed ready to explode.

"Good-bye, Uncle. Have a safe journey." She leaned closer, experimentally giving him the opportunity for a peace-making embrace, but he rudely stepped around her and tramped out the door.

After his departure, Caitlin prepared for bed. As she

changed from her plain, worn daydress into her night-gown, she guiltily tried to analyze her feelings toward her uncle. It was a relief to have him gone; yet it was depressing, too. She felt ashamed that she could summon no tenderness or affection for the man who was her only living relative. Surely, she ought to feel something other than loathing and vague suspicion; of what exactly did she suspect him?

"Tutu Caitlin!" a female voice called gaily. "May I come in?"

Caitlin paused in brushing her long, unbound hair. Glad of the interruption, she left her bedroom, passed into the main room, and smiled at the pretty, slender Hawaiian girl standing in the doorway leading out onto the front *lanai*.

"Pikake, I'm so glad you've come! Uncle George is off on another one of his mysterious journeys, and in the morning, I had planned to ask you to stay with me while he is gone."

"I see him leaving. That is why I hurry here. See? I already bring my things. Tonight, maybe I stay."

As the smiling Hawaiian entered the house, Caitlin's spirits lifted. Pikake set a small bundle down on the floor, and the two grinned at each other then flew into each other's arms. Laughing and hugging, they embraced affectionately until suddenly it dawned on Caitlin what her friend had just said. Leaning back, she frowned. "What do you mean 'maybe'? Have you other plans for tonight?"

When Pikake sheepishly dropped her gaze and chewed her lower lip, Caitlin sighed. Her little friend was up to something, and Caitlin suspected what it was, but if she hoped to talk her out of it, she'd have to use tact and diplomacy. Like most Hawaiians, Pikake still saw nothing wrong with the old ways, despite having been taught new and better ones.

"Well, no matter. We'll talk about it later." Instead of launching into an immediate tirade, Caitlin smiled and held out the brush. "I was just brushing my hair. Would

31

you like to finish it?''

Amazed that she wasn't being scolded for wearing *hau* or hibiscus blossoms, both on her head and encircling the slim ankles peeping out from under her long, otherwise decorous *holuku*, Pikake's face lit up. Her brown eyes sparkled, and her perfect white teeth flashed in the glow of light cast by the whale oil lamp on the table. "Oh, yes, Tutu Caitlin!"

Pikake's fingers eagerly closed around the brush, and Caitlin turned around and faced the unshuttered opening that passed for a window in the large, roomy thatched hut, her home for the past twelve of her twenty-two years. Through the window, Caitlin could see the huge, silvery moon shining brightly. Probably, the moon, as well as the afternoon arrival of the schooner in Hanalei Bay, were providing a temptation almost greater than Pikake could resist.

"So we have visitors to the island, do we not?" she gently prodded. Without looking, Caitlin knew that Pikake's smile had faded; there was less enthusiasm in the way the girl tugged the brush through Caitlin's waist-length tresses.

"Visitors, yes, I think so," Pikake admitted. "Though I have not seen them with my own eyes, Tutu. It was one of the other girls who told me."

"What other girl?" Caitlin pressed, closing her eyes and leaning her head back in response to the luxurious pull of the brush.

"Ilima," Pikake said reluctantly.

"Ah, yes, Ilima, always the first to shed her *pa'u* and swim out to a ship wearing nothing but a smile and flowers in her hair. Ilima, the devil's own handmaiden."

"Yes, Tutu Caitlin," Pikake agreed in a subdued voice. "One of the devil's own."

For a few minutes, Caitlin said nothing so as to allow the seriousness of her pending rebuke to sink in. Pikake was also silent, her brushing becoming less eager by the moment. She did not even bother making her usual exclamations over Caitlin's silver-gold hair, nor did she

32

try to talk Caitlin into leaving it loose and unbound in the Hawaiian manner. Pikake knew where the conversation was heading, and like the child she was, hoped to avoid any unpleasantness by maintaining an uncharacteristic silence.

"You aren't planning to go down to the *luau* on the beach, are you?"

"Oh, no, Tutu Caitlin!" Pikake exclaimed too quickly. The brush paused in midair. "I know *luau* to welcome ship is bad thing. Sailors will make plenty of *pilikia*, trouble, and God will weep in his heaven while the devil rubs his hands and laughs at poor island girls who lose their virtue."

"That's right, Pikake," Caitlin said approvingly. Turning, she took the brush from the girl's slender fingers. "If you consort with the sailors, at best you'll get a terrible disease, and at worst, you'll lose your immortal soul to the devil."

Pikake gazed at her forlornly, furrowing her brow in sadness and confusion. "But I still no understand why Christian God no want man and woman enjoy each other. If he no want, why he put big, smiling moon up in sky?"

So Pikake *had* felt the temptation inherent in the moon's provocative, silvery glory. Drawn by feelings she feared in herself as much as in her friend, Caitlin went to the window and gazed up at the huge, drifting clouds over which the moon held majestic dominance. The very air seemed to throb with temptation, and Caitlin, half shivering in awareness of it, stroked her arms through the thick linen nightgown concealing her body from neck to wrist to toe.

"God put the moon there to test and challenge us," she answered. "He wants a man and woman to enjoy each other only when they are lawfully married, and then only for the purpose of creating children. Even after marriage a man must exercise restraint, and a woman, of course, must simply close her eyes and endure. She is the vessel in which the seed must grow, but on no account must she indulge in wicked thoughts and impulses. A God-fearing woman

33

must rise above such things, and because she is the stronger of the two sexes in these matters, she must help her husband to rise above them also."

"I no understand your god," Pikake pouted, her full lower lip curling over her upper one. "Full moon is good. *Panipani* is good. Make both man and woman happy. Make Pikake very happy someday when handsome *kane* stick his big *ule* in my *kohe*."

"Pikake!" Shocked by the girl's frank language, and even more surprising, struck with an odd sort of anguish, Caitlin whirled upon the startled Hawaiian. "You should be ashamed of yourself to—to say such things, to *think* such things! Those are the devil's own thoughts, and you must cast them aside. Before, you didn't know any better, but now, after all I've taught you these many years, you do."

Pikake's large, velvet eyes swam with remorse. "I'm sorry, Tutu Caitlin. You good friend, and I no want to make you angry. If you say don't go to *luau*, Pikake won't go."

"But it isn't for *my* sake that you mustn't go!" Caitlin put down the brush and slipped an arm about her friend's shoulders. She looked deep into Pikake's eyes, compelling her to listen carefully. "It's for the sake of your own soul. Do you understand? And for your safety and self-respect. . . . One day, you will marry, and you will want to give your husband the gift of your innocence, and a body that is pure and unsullied."

Pikake gazed at her doubtfully. "What is 'unsullied'?"

"Not dirtied. Not *used*." Caitlin groped for the right words. "A strong, healthy body, seen and touched by no one else, that will be his and his alone."

"Why his alone?" Pikake queried. "Hawaiian man not mind if woman choose her own lovers before she marry. That way she learn how to give and receive pleasure. He not even mind if she lie down beneath moon with another man *after* she marry. He just go find other female to make *panipani*, and everybody be happy."

"But, that's *wrong*, Pikake! As I've been telling you all

along!" Losing patience, Caitlin pulled away from her friend and began pacing the floor in her agitation. "The old ways are wicked and evil. They contradict the laws of God. Your people must now marry in the Christian manner and be faithful to their spouses for as long as they both live."

"White men not faithful to wives they leave back home," Pikake argued. Her jaw set stubbornly, but her eyes followed Caitlin as she traversed the pandanus mats from one end of the large airy room to the other. "And maybe white women not faithful either. This I do not know, because I no see enough white women to judge. But *haole* men, married or not, always very willing have *panipani* with Hawaiian women. How come they no keep God's laws?"

Caitlin stopped pacing and gritted her teeth in exasperation. What Pikake said was true: Even men inclined to be pious back home seemed able to shed their scruples as quickly as they shed their clothing. Indeed most of them, immediately upon arrival, began parading about half-naked, embracing heathen customs as if they'd been born to them. This abandonment of restraint, above all else, was the source of bitter conflict between the missionaries and the whalers and traders.

"They don't keep God's laws, because they have succumbed to the temptations of the Evil One," Caitlin explained more patiently, though it seemed as if she was repeating herself for the thousandth time. "Not all white men, of course, are bad, but *most* of the ones who come to the islands are. Whalers and traders—*opala haoles*—are bad to begin with because their only interest in life is to earn filthy lucre and . . ."

"Filthy lucre?"

"Money—to purchase luxuries and to support their vile habits and way of life."

"Is good thing Hawaiians no need filthy lucre," Pikake asserted with a broad, relieved smile. "Hawaiians have sea to fish and swim in, coconuts to pick from trees . . . only work is to plant taro and vegetables. And also if king commands something like when he used to command cutting of sandalwood. Then, Hawaiians oh-so-sad because must work all the time like *haoles* and never have time to play."

"Yes, well, it's a good thing the sandalwood is all gone. The traders, like the whalers, have caused nothing but grief and trouble. I can still remember how your people almost starved to death because they'd had no time to plant or cultivate taro and sweet potatoes. They were kept too busy searching for sandalwood on Mount Waialeale."

Pikake was silent for a moment, her brown eyes searching Caitlin's face. "But, sandalwood *not* all gone," she countered softly. "Don't you remember, Tutu Caitlin? One time, you and I sneak away from mission and follow your father on journey deep into—"

"Hush, Pikake! Don't ever mention that! No one but you and I know about that sandalwood, or it would have been discovered and cut long ago. And since my father is dead—and I sometimes wonder whether his death had something to do with it—we must *never* mention the sandalwood he found to anyone. I haven't even told my Uncle George about it."

Pikake wrinkled her nose. "If he knew about it, *Makuakane* George would send us into mountains to cut it down, and then he would sell wood to traders and live like rich man."

"Pikake! He would *not.*" Caitlin was not just shocked, but angered. "Uncle George's ways *are* different from my father's, but he is still a good man, as pious and God-fearing as my father. He, too, would want to protect the islanders from all the bad men who'd come here looking for more sandalwood if word got out that some still existed."

"Then, why you no tell him about sandalwood?"

Pikake wasn't being contentious, just curious. And Caitlin had to wonder why she *hadn't* told Uncle George. He was as desperate as she herself to build a new church to compete with the ones being built of stone or imported piece by piece from New England by the missionaries on

36

Oahu and Maui. They often discussed possibilities for raising the necessary funds on their own, without help from the Missionary Board. Still, because of the mystery surrounding her father's tragic death—he'd been missing for weeks before his body was finally found—she'd said nothing.

Men had been looking for the wood, she knew, and questioning her uncle about it, but when they hadn't found any, and her uncle had been unable to help them, they'd finally sailed away. Twice since then, her uncle had questioned *her* about it, but both times, while she hadn't lied, she *had* steered the conversation to something else. In the face of their need for a proper church, was it right to keep the find a secret?

"You no trust *Makuakane* George?" Pikake asked, precisely echoing her thoughts.

"Of course, I trust him! It's—it's just that I don't know him very well, yet." Caitlin's loose hair whipped about her shoulders as she tossed her head, remembering the past. "All those times when Father told me about his family in New England, he never breathed a word about Uncle George. But then, I suppose if he thought that his younger brother had sold his soul to the devil . . . Oh, Pikake! If only Father had lived long enough to learn that George has repented the wicked ways of his youth and embraced religion—even to becoming a missionary himself. How happy and proud Father would have been! Finally, at long last, he would have had someone to help him. He and Uncle George together could have found a way to build a new church—*without* the sandalwood and all the problems it could cause."

Pikake came to her, her lovely face puzzled. "But your father have you. Why he need *Makuakane* George? You kind and understanding—friend of all islanders. That is why we call you *tutu*—grandmother—because you are wise and respected like old person. But *Makuakane* George not so kind, not so wise. He have mean eyes and big, thundering voice. Make islanders tremble. He not like you and *Makua* William."

Makua William—*Father* William, the name that Kauaiians had called her father. He had, indeed, been a father to them. A vision of her father's pale, lined face, his kindly blue eyes, and sun-bleached hair rose in Caitlin's mind, and a spasm of grief shot through her. Her father had preached the same things Uncle George now preached—that the islanders must clothe their nakedness, repent of their sins, and reform their wanton ways. But he had also preached God's love and forgiveness. He had encouraged and cajoled—while Uncle George only threatened, making the Christian God sound every bit as harsh and vindictive as the Hawaiian war god, Ku, to whom human sacrifices had once been offered.

"No, Uncle George is not like us, Pikake," Caitlin sadly conceded. "But he's a man of God, sent here to rescue and save God's children from eternal damnation. And as such, we must help him all we can."

"If you say so." Pikake sniffed. "But I no like *Makuakane* George. He can go back mainland anytime."

"You just don't like him because he disapproves of your wearing flowers," Caitlin scolded. "And so do I. Women should dress simply and plainly, so as not to arouse the base natures of men."

The flutter of Pikake's long lashes betrayed her displeasure at being reminded of the continued error of her ways. "At least, I no swim out ship naked like Ilima."

"Yes, at least you don't do that." Smiling, now, Caitlin hugged her friend. She didn't know what she would do without Pikake's company, especially now when her father was gone and there was only scowling Uncle George to talk to—and most of the time, she didn't even have him. Sometimes, the burden of being her father's daughter was almost too much to bear. Living alone in the thatched-roof house, except for Uncle George or, in his absence, Pikake, she couldn't avoid loneliness.

Her days were no problem, filled as they were with Bible lessons, housekeeping chores, and ministering to the health needs of the natives, but her nights—sometimes during the warm tropical nights she thought she would scream with loneliness. One could only spend so much time praying and reading the precious, well-worn books that arrived all too infrequently from the mainland. One could only ignore the temptation of the moon and stars for so long.

Again, hardly aware that she did so, Caitlin padded to the window in her bare feet. Pikake followed, and the two of them stood side by side, listening to the rustle of the palm fronds stirred by the tradewinds and straining their ears for other night sounds. Somewhere in the darkness, laughter sounded, followed by scurrying footsteps. Caitlin frowned, and Pikake giggled, then hiccuped in an effort to suppress her giggle.

Then, the drums began—a slow, sensuous, throbbing that vibrated first in Caitlin's chest, then in her belly, and finally, in her entire body. Torches flared in the distance, illuminating figures running toward the beach. "They're all going down to the *luau*," Caitlin snapped. Anger and disapproval swelled in her breast as she watched a girl wearing a brightly colored *pa'u* knotted low around her hips run past the window.

The girl's upper body and breasts were bare except for a chain of *ilima* blossoms that concealed nothing, and she was laughing in her excitement. "Isn't that Ohai's daughter?" Caitlin asked, leaning out the window and looking after the girl whose flesh flashed in the patches of bright, dappled moonlight.

"I think so," Pikake said. A note of longing had come into her voice, and it didn't escape Caitlin's notice.

"Only this morning, she was in Bible class!" Caitlin fumed. "And so were you!"

"Yes, Tutu Caitlin."

With growing fury, Caitlin watched as several more of her students raced past. One even had the affrontery to stop, look up at the window of the house which stood above the ground on stilts, and wave to Pikake. "Pikake!" she called in lilting Hawaiian. "Aren't you coming to the *luau*? The *kanes* from this ship are as tall and handsome as gods. You won't want to miss seeing them, and who knows how long the ship will stay?"

"I can't come," Pikake responded sadly, her eyes flicking in Caitlin's direction.

"We'll miss you during the *hula*," the girl called before running on her way.

"The *hula!*" Caitlin demanded of Pikake, who would not meet her glance.

Truly angered now, Caitlin left the window and stormed out onto the *lanai*, or balcony that was actually a wide porch, with a thatched roof to keep off the frequent rain showers. The house stood on a slight rise, and the *lanai* offered a breathtaking view of the crescent beach through the palm trees. Caitlin's father hadn't been able to afford having a real house from New England brought over, but he'd done the best he could to provide for his daughter. His wife, Caitlin's mother, had died before the three-room structure was built, but it was she who had chosen the spot for it, and Caitlin could never come out onto the *lanai* without thinking of both her parents.

Flowers bloomed in profusion around the porch, and palm trees, ironwoods, and pandanus shaded it, providing a place of great beauty and tranquility—until tonight. Tonight, Caitlin paced the *lanai* with anything but peace and tranquility in her heart. Down on the beach, within sight of the very house designed by her saintly mother and built by her equally saintly father, a wicked, pagan ritual was taking place.

The serpent was loose in the Garden of Eden, endangering the souls of God's children, and also their good health, for the sailors invariably brought diseases among them, to which the islanders had little or no resistance.

Caitlin paced back and forth, pausing now and then, hands on hips, to watch the unfolding scene of drunkenness and debauchery on the beach. At some point, she noticed that Pikake was no longer watching with her.

"Pikake!" she cried, but the only sound was the beat of the drums and the rhythm of men's voices as they chanted the ancient hula songs or *meles*.

"Pikake, where are you?" Caitlin ran into the house and searched its three rooms—the large one for living and the two smaller ones for sleeping—and not finding Pikake, ran to the back door and threw it open.

It was a door of pandanus mats, and it flapped in the gentle wind. Caitlin pushed past it and stood on the smaller *lanai* that faced the misty mountains, rather than the sea. Pikake was nowhere to be seen. A cloud swallowed the moon, and all was darkness for a moment, reminding Caitlin of the darkness of sin and evil into which Pikake, tempted past her endurance, had no doubt fallen.

"Oh, Pikake," Caitlin wailed, feeling more alone than she ever had in her life.

She ran back to the front porch. Just then, the moon reappeared, and there, down on the beach, in the mass of bodies swaying to the *hula*, stood a slender, familiar figure: Pikake. Her long, high-necked *holuku* stood out in sharp contrast to the near-nakedness of the other girls.

"Pikake, how could you?" Caitlin murmured, and without another hesitation, she raised the hem of her heavy nightgown and hurried down the steps toward the beach.

Chapter Three

Long, shining black hair, sparkling brown eyes, wide generous mouths curving in happy smiles, and wonderful, supple bodies surrounded Gerrick on every side. And the men were as strong, straight of limb, and well favored as the women were beautiful. He was glad he had come ashore; for the first time in months, he felt tinglingly alive.

John's big arms already encircled two bare-breasted beauties. Looking back over his shoulder and winking, John shouted, "What did I tell you, my friend? If this isn't paradise, I don't know what is!"

Amid the din of laughter and native chatter, Gerrick could not understand a word being said to him. But the flirtatious smiles and bold glances needed no translation: He could have his pick of any one—or two or three—of the half-naked, flower-bedecked women accompanying him down the beach. His jaws ached from grinning.

Beneath flaming torches, a feast had been laid out for their enjoyment. Savory smells taunted Gerrick's nose, and the thud of drums filled his consciousness. He felt transported to another world—where the past no longer existed and the future barely mattered. There was only the present and its tantalizing pleasures awaiting his discovery.

With the eagerness of a man half-starved for laughter and human companionship, Gerrick cast aside his remaining hesitations. Tonight, he would eat, drink, and be merry—and Amos Taylor, Madeline Barrows, and his own lust for revenge be damned. Other lusts were rising in him now, and he quickly seized the nearest smiling maiden and planted a long, passionate kiss on her full, sensuous lips.

She giggled and laughed, playfully rubbing noses with him, and did not pull away when he held her imprisoned along the length of him. Amazed, he leaned back and studied her. The tender, budding breasts suggested that she was little more than a child, but the way she moved her body, clad only in a hip-hugging, brightly colored cloth, was all woman. Her hips swayed in time to the drumbeat; never had he seen a woman move her hips that way—but then he'd never seen a woman wearing a circlet of flowers in her flowing hair and more flowers about her neck, wrists, and ankles, as if they were the finest of jewels. And indeed, the flowers set off her golden-brown skin to perfection, better even than diamonds or rubies.

Still laughing, the girl darted away from him, to be replaced by another sloe-eyed beauty, who offered him half a green coconut shell from which to drink. Gerrick drank deeply of the cool, pungent liquid; he'd rarely tasted anything so refreshing. His senses leaped in anticipation of the feast to come, and eagerly, he allowed himself to be led to a place of honor on the woven mats spread out across the sand.

Gerrick seated himself, and John sat down heavily beside him, his round face flushed, his black eyes shining. "No one will ever believe this back home. And I'm not sure I want to tell them about it or they'll be coming here by the boatload."

Chains of fragrant, pink and white blossoms criss-crossed John's massive chest, and looking down, Gerrick discovered that he, too, was wearing flowers though he had no recollection of how they had gotten there. "It's like a dream," he agreed. "And I hope I don't wake up for a long time."

Long, woven grass mats had been laid end to end, and

every available inch held a delicacy awaiting his ravenous appetite. He saw platters of fruit, heaped as high as his head, highly polished boards filled with exotic vegetables, both cooked and uncooked, and fish broiled whole and garnished with more fruits and vegetables. Great calabashes filled with a thick, purplish substance lined the mats on both sides, and over all hung the smell of roasting pork, which Gerrick surmised was coming from a steaming pit a short distance away where a knot of Hawaiian men were gathered.

A smiling girl pressed a smaller calabash into his hands, and Gerrick drank. He choked as the fermented liquid stung his nose and throat with a fire akin to whisky or rum. "What is this?" he gasped, but John was busy drinking from a calabash of his own.

Afterward, John wiped his mouth with a grin. "This is something called *awa*—what passes for spirits in these parts. I read about it in those reports of yours."

"I wish I'd read the damn reports." Gerrick took another long swallow from the calabash. This time, the fiery liquid went down more easily, and warmth curled in his stomach and eddied outward along his nerve endings.

If he drank much more of this before eating, he'd be drunk within the hour. Gerrick glanced about for members of his crew and saw every man-jack of them similarly seated or lounging on the mats beneath the smoking torches. Each was surrounded by beautiful women, and each looked dazed, as if he'd suddenly awakened to find himself in paradise.

Gerrick had to suppress a snort of laughter. Even his fierce-looking first mate, Erasmus, wore a bewildered expression as he opened his mouth to accept a tidbit of food being offered by a plump, grinning woman who had evidently marked him for her own. "Look at Erasmus," Gerrick urged, but John was too busy draining his second calabash of *awa*.

Without further ceremony, the women began passing food to the dazzled seamen. In lieu of plates, large green leaves were placed before them, and on these, the women heaped generous portions of fish, fruits, and vegetables. They then passed the huge calabashes, and one girl showed Gerrick how to scoop out the purplish substance with two fingers and then suck the pudding-like mass into his mouth.

It tasted both bland and slightly sour, but not wanting to offend her, he ate heartily of it. The Hawaiian men distributed the pork, which had been cooked to succulent tenderness so that it fell off the bone and melted in the mouth. It was the first fresh meat he'd eaten in a long time, and Gerrick gorged himself on it. When his stomach began feeling uncomfortably full, he stopped eating, despite the protests of the smiling women, and again studied his surroundings.

It was his custom to make careful observations of whatever place in which he happened to find himself. Now, belatedly renewing this old habit, he relished studying the natives, his own men, and the exotic, colorful setting. This was exactly what he needed: a complete break from everything he'd heretofore known.

He noticed that while the men, whites and Hawaiians alike, were stuffing themselves, most of the women ate little or nothing. They seemed to pick and choose their food with care, many avoiding the pork altogether and nibbling abstemiously at the fruits and vegetables. Beneath his lashes, Gerrick watched the woman next to him gingerly select a piece of fruit from the nearest platter. Her hand paused over a slice of banana, and then, as if she feared taking it, moved to the breadfruit.

He was intrigued. Reaching past her, he took the banana and offered it to her, lifting it to her lips. She raised her eyes to his, hesitated, then smiled and shook her head.

"Go on, take it," he urged, breaking off a piece and eating it himself to show her that it wasn't harmful. He'd eaten bananas in other parts of the world and never suffered any ill effects.

Still, the girl refused. *"Kapu,"* she explained. *"Kapu,"* and Gerrick resolved then and there to learn the islanders' language so he could understand what they were saying.

45

He also resolved to read every one of the reports in his cabin, reports his father had amassed from sea captains, missionaries, and anyone else who'd ever traveled to the South Seas.

In what still remained of his father's extensive library at home were handwritten, eyewitness accounts of travelers to all parts of the world. Gerrick's father, Matthew, and his grandfather, Hadley Scott, had been students of the universe, acquiring an awesome knowledge of customs and trade goods from China to India to Europe and almost everywhere in between.

Gerrick had inherited the family trait of desiring to learn everything there was to know about a place, but he didn't usually feed that desire until he actually arrived at a new destination. Then, his curiosity became insatiable. Now, having finally arrived in the islands after months at sea, he was ready, and the hunger to know Kauai, conquer its secrets, and make it his own rose strongly within him.

"John," he hissed, elbowing his friend in the ribs. "Do you know what *kapu* means?"

"What?" John licked pork grease from his fingers before answering.

"In those reports you read, did you learn any of the local language?"

"Not much," John said. "I'm afraid we'll have to find an interpreter first thing tomorrow. Maybe that missionary's daughter will help us."

"It would be better if we ourselves learned to speak Hawaiian," Gerrick countered. "Before you get too drunk, start memorizing words and phrases."

"Words and phrases!" John blinked at him incredulously. "The only words and phrases I'm interested in learning tonight are the ones having to do with you-know-what. Shall I ask the women what they call their titties and their sweet, little, round behinds?"

"You might as well start somewhere," Gerrick drawled. "Remember, we didn't come here on a picnic."

John gaped at him a moment, and then determinedly wrapped his arm around the waist of the comely young

46

woman between them. "If you think I'm working tonight, my friend, you're crazy. Have another drink of *awa*—or go on back to the ship if you want. If it's the only way to get you out of my hair, I say—go back to brooding. I'm not starting work until tomorrow."

Something touched his lips, and Gerrick saw that it was a brimming calabash. The girl who'd refused the banana was holding it to his mouth. Smiling, she urged him to drink. Conceding his defeat, Gerrick grinned, shrugged his shoulders, and drained the calabash in one gulp. John was right. Tomorrow would be soon enough to start work; the night was still young, and only *half* his appetites had yet been appeased.

As if on signal, the drums suddenly changed beat, and the women rose as one body and departed the feast. "Hey, where they all goin'?" one man cried, and another hastened to reassure him. "Oh, they'll be back soon. I heard about this. Now, they're gonna dance one of them wild, pagan dances . . . and after that . . ."

A hush fell over the ship's crew as all the men, including Gerrick and John, sat waiting for the women to return. Gerrick's eyes sought the musicians, sitting off by themselves under a separate ring of torches. He craned his neck to see their musical instruments. One type of drum was made from a single, huge gourd, and the other resembled a large kettle. Some of the men held rattles, and still others were playing a kind of stringed bow, held between the lips and strummed with the fingers.

The music picked up in tempo, and the drums beat faster. Gerrick heard a long sigh, his crewmen expelling their breaths in a collective expression of awe and excitement as a long line of young women, their bodies oiled and gleaming, danced into the clearing beneath the trees. Gerrick's heart thudded, and beside him, John murmured, "My God, just look at them! I didn't know humans could move like that."

In perfect unison, the women's bodies swayed to the beat of the drums, and their hands and arms waved in a storytelling gesture. Every movement was graceful and

47

compelling, and Gerrick longed to know the meaning of the strange, stirring dance. Then, the drums beat faster still, and the blood raced in Gerrick's veins as the women's hips gyrated faster, defying bodily limitations.

Gerrick's eyes were drawn to a small slender maiden who stood out from the rest, because she alone of the bare-breasted women wore a garment faintly reminiscent of New England. It covered her from neck to ankle. However, she was anything but a prim New Englander. Seemingly mesmerized by the haunting rhythms, she danced oblivious to everything and everyone. Her head was thrown back, and her eyes closed as if she were lost in some ancient, mist-shrouded moment before the world began.

Stirred by her intensity, her total loss of awareness of her surroundings, Gerrick held his breath. Primitive longings swept him, and he pictured himself leaping to his feet and joining her in this abandoned dance, and then throwing her over his shoulder and carrying her away with him.

You're a civilized man, he reminded himself, not some heathen—and besides, you've never danced like *that* in your entire life.

"That one's mine," John whispered, and Gerrick shot him a startled glance. Thankfully, John was looking at another girl—one whose physical endowments reminded Gerrick of a milk cow belonging to a farmer friend of his father's.

"You can have her," Gerrick whispered back. "I want the little one who's hiding all her treasures beneath that long, proper gown."

"What little one? What gown?"

"Over there . . ." Gerrick nodded in the girl's direction, but to his surprise, in the few moments he'd been distracted, the girl had removed the confining garment and was now dancing completely naked, except for the flowers encircling her neck and ankles.

"Lord Almighty!" John exclaimed, and Gerrick, too, was shocked.

The slender girl—hardly more than a child—was dancing without any qualms whatever about her nudity.

Trailing her gown in one hand, she seemed unaware of what she had done. Her skin glowing with a soft bronze sheen and her eyes still closed, she shook her long, shining, black hair and gyrated her hips in a near frenzy. Her concentration on the dance was so total that she appeared almost in a trance.

"Dance over this way, sweetheart!" one of Gerrick's men called. Long arms reached out to snatch the girl, and Gerrick unthinkingly leaped to his feet.

"You can't have her, Henderson," he shouted. "I've already chosen her for myself."

"Aw, Cap'n," Henderson complained, darting Gerrick a look of surprising hostility. "There's plenty of other women."

"Then *you* choose one of them."

Henderson scowled, and from behind him, Gerrick heard John clear his throat. "She's too skinny anyway, Henderson. I would have thought you'd have better taste."

Henderson glanced back toward the girl, who had abruptly stopped dancing and was now looking about in confusion, not quite knowing where she was. "Yeah, I guess you're right . . ." he conceded. "Beggin' your pardon, Cap'n. If you want 'er so bad, you can have her."

"I would have had her with or without your permission," Gerrick snapped.

"Yes, sir," Henderson said, but Gerrick suddenly realized, with a stab of shame, just how much of his authority he'd lost on this voyage. In the past, though Henderson tended to be a troublemaker, he had never dared speak to Gerrick in such an insolent manner.

And he'll never speak to me that way again, Gerrick vowed. If he *never* found the sandalwood or Amos Taylor, he would at least retrieve his manhood and the respect his men had once given him. He had wallowed in self-pity long enough. From now on, he'd be the man he had always been—confident, authoritative, and irresistible to women.

This latter thought made the corner of Gerrick's mouth twitch in wry humor. The slender Hawaiian girl was watching him now, her eyes wide and hesitant, almost as if she were trying to make up her mind whether or not she liked him. Walking toward her, he smiled encouragingly. The dancers parted to give him room to pass, and wide-eyed, she gazed up at him.

To her, he must seem like a giant, he realized, for her head only came as high as the center of his chest, and she had to tilt back her head to look at him. Taking his time, he looked her over carefully, while she did the same to him. Her boldness and lack of self-consciousness delighted him—so also did her delicate beauty. She was daintily made—her breasts and hips childlike—and he would have to be gentle with her, but her eyes and her shy smile held a clear invitation. When she suddenly stepped closer and leaned her body into his, never taking her eyes from his face, he knew that *she* knew exactly what he wanted.

Still smiling, he traced the line of her full, soft lips with his index finger. She had a mouth made for kissing, and he intended to do plenty of that before this night was over. Pausing just long enough to give John a long, triumphant glance, he tucked the girl's hand beneath his arm and steered her toward the dark shadows cast by the palm trees.

"Good luck, Cap'n!" one of his men called good-naturedly. "If ye've forgotten how t' do it, come back here an' one of us'll show ye'."

Recognizing the voice of Erasmus, his first mate, Gerrick responded in kind. "The day I need *your* help, old man, will be the day they stitch me into a canvas sheet with a cannonball for company and bury me at sea!"

His men laughed and hooted, and Gerrick heard another say distinctly, "I knew whatever ailed the cap'n would be cured once we got t' the islands."

"Hush, or he'll hear you," someone else growled.

Having already made up his mind to mend his ways, Gerrick ignored the comments, though they still stung him, and he walked faster. When he and the girl came to a patch of darkness far enough away from the beach to afford privacy, Gerrick stopped and drew the young

50

woman into his arms. Her soft, supple flesh excited him, and the fragrance of the flowers in her hair enticed him to nuzzle her neck and breathe deeply of her clean, sweet smell.

"It's been so long since I held a woman," he murmured as his heart started to pound. "Little one, I'll try not to hurt you, but I don't know how gentle I can be when I feel this way."

He tilted back her head and covered her lips with his mouth, almost gasping at the sweetness he found there. She allowed him to kiss her, rubbing her nose alongside his in return, which he surmised must be the native manner of showing affection, since she was the second one to rub noses with him. As he held her tighter, he became achingly aware that her nipples, in tantalizing contact with his chest, were already budding. Even so, he suddenly sensed a slight resistance.

"What's wrong?" he wondered aloud.

To his utter amazement, she answered in English. "Not here. Pikake no want make *panipani* here. We go private place where no one see us. Come, I take you there."

She held out her hand to him, and Gerrick was so stunned that she had spoken in his own language, he placed his hand in hers without a single word. She stood on tiptoe and brushed an experimental, feather-light kiss across his open mouth. Then, she giggled.

"You big handsome *kane* Pikake been waiting for long time. I take you very special place. Not bad, not wicked," she assured him. "Is good thing man and woman enjoy each other."

Gerrick had no breath to argue or even ask questions. Am I dreaming this? he asked himself as he followed her deeper into the palm forest. His only link with reality was the moon peeping through the lacy fronds, as huge and beguiling as ever.

Where was the girl taking him? And did it really matter? With the promise of pleasure shimmering before him, he would gladly have followed her anywhere.

Chapter Four

Halfway to the beach, Caitlin tripped on her nightgown and sprawled in the sand. Sitting up, she rubbed the grit from her eyes and, with an unladylike snort of indignation, pushed back her long hair and struggled to rise. The twisted nightgown hampered her efforts. Even worse, her right ankle buckled under her, and she collapsed, forced to admit that she'd hurt herself.

"Oh—*drat!*" she muttered, wishing she dared say something even stronger.

For several moments, she sat massaging the throbbing limb. No bones appeared to be broken, but she had given the ankle—and her self-esteem—a good twist. How like her to fall on her face the first time she sought to fill her father's shoes! It was just as she'd always been taught: Women should stay out of the business of men.

That dictum had always sounded shortsighted and unfair to her, but she had never really rebelled against it. Her father's yoke had been a loving and gentle one, and it was only since the arrival of Uncle George that she'd begun questioning the rules by which she'd been raised. Now, she wondered if perhaps God Himself wasn't sending her a message: Go back to the house and stay there. Curb your temper until morning when you can discuss this rationally with Pikake.

Bracing herself against a palm tree, she finally managed to regain her feet. Gingerly, she leaned her weight on the ankle and was relieved to discover that it *would* support her. She could still walk, but the pain was such that her hesitations were intensified: Pikake was four years younger than she herself but clearly of an age to make up her own mind about her actions.

Not only that, but Caitlin wasn't even dressed. She would appear ridiculous if she arrived on the beach in her nightgown, barefoot and with her hair tossed about by the tradewinds. What would the men from the schooner think? Would they jeer at her efforts—making unseemly comments, or even worse, propositions?

Her father had always insisted that she stay near the house while ships were visiting the island; he hadn't wanted her to be exposed to coarse-talking, hard-drinking seamen, though she'd seen plenty of drunken sailors on the streets of Honolulu at Oahu, and Lahaina, on Maui. But there, of course she'd always been in the company of other missionaries. Now, she was alone and had no one but the promiscuous islanders to protect her.

I really shouldn't do this, Caitlin thought. I'll make a spectacle of myself, preaching good behavior to creatures bent on sinning.

Peering in the direction of the beach, she tried to see what Pikake was doing now. The smoke from the torches obscured the scene, but as a light, fretting wind blew it aside, what she saw shocked and dismayed her. Pikake, naked as the day she was born, was kissing a tall, broad-shouldered *haole* with reddish-colored hair.

A moment later, they stepped apart, and the man took Pikake's hand and began leading her beneath the trees a short distance farther up the beach. This was every bit as bad as Caitlin had feared: Pikake had surrendered herself to the devil, in the form of a handsome *haole* who would probably give her a dreaded disease even as he destroyed the girl's innocence.

Dressed or not, injured or not, barefoot or not, Caitlin must save her. And thus decided, Caitlin wasted no more time pampering her ankle and agonizing over her decision. Changing direction, she limped after her friend, determined to catch up with Pikake before the *haole* had his way with her.

At first, it was hard-going, but gradually the throbbing in her ankle diminished, and Caitlin was able to concentrate on Pikake's trail. Occasionally, she caught glimpses of the two figures in the moonlight as they moved farther inland, with Pikake now in the lead. Since she'd lived here for most of her life, Caitlin knew the area as well as any islander. Still, she wondered where Pikake was headed. Suddenly, the answer came to her.

Not far from the location of the *luau* was a lovely, quiet spot where a waterfall tumbled down into a pool surrounded by lush, tropical growth and orchids that bloomed the year round. Caitlin herself often bathed there in the warm waters or stood beneath the tinkling waterfall to wash her hair. Afterward, she liked to lie upon the rocks or soft mossy ground to doze and dry herself. If she was completely alone, as she usually was since Pikake preferred swimming in the ocean, she sometimes shunned clothes like the natives did and lay naked upon the black lava rocks, her hair spread out like a lady's fan.

It was a place where one could enjoy unequaled privacy, and Caitlin had never revealed its existence to anyone—not even her father. Had he known that she swam or sunbathed there, he would not have approved. Of course, she had always atoned for her misdeeds by praying or reading the Bible before she left, and had found a sense of peace and communion with the Almighty that she rarely experienced in more organized devotions in church.

That Pikake should lead a *haole* to the spot, for such evil purposes, seemed to Caitlin a kind of blasphemy. Yet, there could be no doubt where Pikake was headed. The land had begun to rise steeply upward, and away from the breezes on the beach, Caitlin grew warm in her coarse linen nightdress. Her long hair weighed heavily on her neck, and she wished she had at least taken the time to confine it in her usual severe braided knot.

She was panting by the time she finished the climb to the hidden pool. Her hair fell about her shoulders in tangled disarray, and her gown, having caught in vines and roots, was torn in two places. As the soft murmur of a woman's voice drifted toward her, she paused to catch her breath and listen; it was Pikake talking to the *haole*.

Caitlin edged nearer to a clump of tall, concealing ferns and peeked around them. Not six feet away stood the tall *haole*. His broad back was to her, but as he turned, the moon illuminated his profile, and Caitlin got her first good look at him. The view transfixed her, for the man was stunningly handsome. Moreover, he already had removed his shirt, and his splendid physique drew her eyes like one of the spectacular, scenic vistas so common to the island.

Struggling to remain cool and collected, she observed that he was taller than her father had been, and even taller than her Uncle George. Indeed, she knew of only two or three Hawaiians whose height equaled his—and many Hawaiian men were tall. Whereas her father had been lean and stringy, and her Uncle George was thick-set and somewhat paunchy, this man had a well-shaped, muscular body that might have belonged to a young Hawaiian king or one of the old island gods. Sleek muscles sculpted his bare chest, gilded now by the moonlight, and cords of muscle in his thighs strained against the cloth of his trousers.

Yet for all these unseemly bulges, his waist and hips were narrow, and his hands curiously graceful as he tossed his shirt to the ground. Caitlin's glance flew to his face. Yes, he was as handsome as a Hawaiian god, with a straight, chiseled nose, a strong jaw and chin—clean-shaven with no beard—and thick-lashed eyes whose color she could not ascertain. Only the color of his hair was apparent; the moonlight struck red sparks from the thick, unruly curls—curls that were repeated in the hair on his chest.

In the moonlight, in this romantic place with water splashing in the background and the air redolent with the scent of plumeria, this man was the very image of masculine grace and power. A *haole* who looked as he did, especially one with copper-colored curls, could have his pick of the island women; so why did he have to choose Pikake? Why not Ilima or one of the other girls whose souls were already lost?

As she watched, his teeth glinted in a smile, and his hands dropped to the wide belt at his waist. But before he could unbuckle it, Pikake uttered a soft little moan and pressed her naked body into the *haole*'s arms. Immediately, his arms crushed her to him, and he lifted the girl off her feet and captured her mouth with his.

Caitlin's whole body flushed, and she felt alternately hot, then cold. What would it feel like to have a man embrace *her* like that? To tilt her head and devour her mouth with long, smoldering kisses?

Shivering breathlessly, Caitlin marshalled all her fading willpower to recall who and where she was. Praying her voice wouldn't quiver, she stepped from behind the ferns and called Pikake's name. What came out was a hoarse little cry that she herself did not recognize. At the sound of it, the man stopped kissing Pikake and turned in her direction. A long moment passed as he stared at her, a frown creasing his handsome brow and a startled expression on his face.

"Pikake . . ." she finally got out. "I've come here to save you from yourself."

The *haole*'s eyes narrowed, and the force of his all-encompassing gaze made Caitlin feel strangely weak-kneed. The sky seemed to tilt, and the moon spun wildly. For the first time in her life, she feared she might faint. "Pikake, did you hear me?"

Why didn't her friend say something? And why was the tall *haole* staring at her with such penetrating concentration, as if he were seeing a ghost?

Gerrick could not believe his eyes. He blinked, but the white-robed figure with the flowing silver hair did not disappear. With the mountain at her back, she remained standing among the gigantic ferns, resembling a painting he had seen in a book as a young boy. The painting had been entitled "The Avenging Angel," and in it, the beautiful, stern-faced figure had been holding a spear in one hand and a Bible in the other.

Searching for weapons, Gerrick's eyes swept the incredible apparition, but this angel bore none. Nor did she have the huge silvery wings he remembered so distinctly. Nevertheless, he half expected a ball of fire to hurl down from the clouds. Clearly, the angel was angry, and just as clearly he had drunk far too much *awa;* this ethereal creature could not be real.

"Pikake," the angel repeated. "Come home with me. Come home with me, now."

Pikake? Gerrick had no idea to whom she was referring until the girl beside him stirred and came to life. "No want go home, Tutu Caitlin. Pikake stay here. You go home and I come, later."

"Pikake, what you came here to do is wicked and evil. This man is the devil's own spawn who will drag you down with him to eternal fire and damnation. Look at you. You're no better than Ilima. In fact, you're worse. You *know* this is wrong."

Beside him, the girl bowed her head. Her slender shoulders drooped. Gone was the seductive woman, and in her place stood an errant child. Even her flowers seemed to wilt. "Yes, Tutu Caitlin." Shame and defeat underlined each word, and Gerrick couldn't help feeling sorry for her and angry with her tormentor. He opened his mouth to say something, but the angel beat him to it.

"Come home with me, Pikake," she entreated, holding out her hand. "Don't be stubborn. In the morning, you'll thank me for this."

"*I* won't thank you!" Gerrick exploded. "Just who in hell do you think you are?"

His voice ricocheted off stone, and both women jumped. Then, the Avenging Angel straightened her shoulders, came closer, and seized the girl's hand. "My name is Caitlin Price," she said haughtily. "And you should be ashamed of yourself."

57

"Ashamed!" Gerrick bellowed. In his anger, her name scarcely registered. "Why, in God's name? I haven't done a damn thing except steal a few kisses from a girl who was enjoying them until *you* came along!"

"You intend to do much more than just kiss her, sir." The angel's voice was icy, raising goose flesh along his shoulder blades. "How would you feel if she were your sister—or your daughter? Would you want some rutting boar to endanger her immortal soul, not to mention infecting her body with a filthy disease?"

"Disease! I assure you, miss, that I'm perfectly healthy and not in the habit of spreading disease. Nor am I a—a rutting boar."

"Then what would *you* call a man who sows his seed to the four winds, not even knowing the name of the young woman he's bent on getting with child?"

"With child!" Gerrick realized that his repetitious exclamations were beginning to make him sound dull-witted, but he was so stunned that for a moment he couldn't answer more intelligently.

"Have you other children back on the mainland?" The angel pursued relentlessly. "And do *their* mothers have names? Perhaps you have descendants in every port you've visited. Likely you don't even *know* if you do or not. A man with your loose, indiscriminate morals can hardly be expected to keep track of his bastards. *Or* of the spread of disease. Go home, sir! You're not wanted. The islanders deserve better than what you have to offer . . ."

Her accusations struck like whip lashes, and Gerrick reacted violently and indignantly. "And just what is it *you* have to offer? This lovely young girl"—he gestured to the Hawaiian still standing silent and shamefaced between them—"was—until a few moments ago—perfectly happy, carefree, and—and giving. . . . But now look what you've done to her. Why, you've humiliated her! Made her ashamed of her beauty and her—her generosity of spirit. Before, she was childlike and innocent. Now, she's . . . degraded. And I don't see why she should be!"

The eyes of the Avenging Angel shot sparks. Were her

58

eyes blue, or gray, or green? Gerrick could not be certain. He only saw that her lashes were incredibly long, brushing her cheeks like silvery moth wings as, slowly, she looked him up and down, her flashing eyes condemning him as the lowest creature on earth. His glance dropped to her mouth—such a tender, sweet mouth! It should *never* be spewing such venom and leveling such unfair, ridiculous accusations.

"A child's first brush with evil is always a sobering experience," the angel said primly. "The child can't help but feel tainted. It is only after long exposure to evil—after wallowing in it like you, sir—that one loses the capacity to be ashamed."

"How *dare* you judge me?" In his astonishment and irritation, Gerrick's voice shook. "You don't even know *my* name, yet you dare purport to know the state of my soul and the condition of my character."

"I know what I *see* . . ."

"And kissing is ugly and sinful, is it?" Gerrick leaned closer, but the angel held her ground and glared at him, making him doubly angry. "Tell me, miss, have *you* ever been kissed? Do you know what pleasure is to be found in kissing—and other intimacies of the flesh? Or do you simply condemn what you know nothing about? Embracing ignorance, rather than holiness."

"*That*, sir, is none of your business!"

Now, Gerrick grinned, for the long-lashed eyes had gone wide, and the soft, tender lips were trembling. A bit more goading would crack her tedious self-righteousness. Beginning to enjoy himself immensely, he whispered, "Just *who* do you think put the pleasure in kissing and fornication? And *who* do you think made the sexes want to engage in such shameful activity anyway? If the whole damn thing is so wrong, then why does it feel so right?"

Gerrick inclined his head and leaned even closer, so that he was almost nose to nose with her. Maybe her eyes were silver, he thought distractedly, gazing into them and exerting all the force of his well-honed charm and magnetism. From the corner of his eye, he saw her hand rise, but before he could react, she struck his face a stunning blow. His head reeled from the impact, and he straightened in astonishment—the silver-haired angel in the long white gown had hauled off and belted him a good one!

Acting on instinct, he grabbed her and pinioned her struggling body against him so she couldn't strike again. For a split second, she ceased struggling and gazed up at him in horror. Suddenly, he realized what had stunned her into near paralysis: his full arousal was pressing hard against her thighs. Holding her tightly, he increased the pressure of his loins, rubbing slowly and deliberately. Her eyes widened even more. Then, clawing at his arms, she arched her back in a futile effort to free herself.

His own dizzying upsurge of desire caught Gerrick unawares. Bending over her, he nuzzled first her neck and then her white throat. Her full, soft breasts eluded his attentions but momentarily distracted him so that he loosened his grip. In that instant, she escaped.

"You beast!" she cried, sounding as wounded as if he had raped her. "You wicked, whoring devil! Come, Pikake, we must get out of here!"

And suddenly, she was gone, dragging the Hawaiian girl after her. They disappeared into the thick, tropical undergrowth faster than he could bellow, "Wait a minute, damn it!"

His voice echoed and bounced off the rocks. After that, the only sounds were of the gentle splashing of water and the breeze sighing through the palms, carrying with it a faint odor of roasting pig intermingled with the perfume of flowers.

Too stunned to move, he rubbed his still smarting cheek and attempted to digest what had just occurred. As full sanity returned, he groaned in anguished realization. "Damn my soul, that was *Caitlin Price*. Dear God, what have I done?"

Dismay flooded him in a cold drenching wave. This was the worst thing that could have happened; he had alienated the one person on the island who could have helped him find the sandalwood. Obviously, Caitlin Price would never consent to help him now, not after all the names she'd called him and the sins she thought he had committed—and especially not after he'd almost forced himself upon her.

How would he ever explain all this to John? John would think he'd gone crazy. John would . . . John! John would have to be the one to approach her, to gain her confidence and cooperation. He, Gerrick, would have to stay well out of it. In fact, the less she knew about his and John's friendship . . . or even about their association . . .

Slowly, as he paced back and forth by the pool, Gerrick formulated a plan. It wasn't the *best* plan, or the easiest or most desirable—but considering the way he'd ruined his chances of charming Caitlin Price, he had no other options. This wouldn't be the first time he and John had employed deceit in one of their schemes, but somehow, this time seemed worse than all the others. He really would *much* rather have won the support of the intriguing, silver-haired beauty. After all, he mused, of all the women whose charms he'd enjoyed over the years, not one had been a missionary. Caitlin Price presented a unique challenge, but one, alas, that he must pass to John.

Now all that remained was to convince John to go along with his plan—and John, he suspected, wasn't going to be wild with enthusiasm, even though a beautiful woman was involved. At least, not when he heard the details.

"No!" John cried. "Absolutely not. I refuse to even consider it."

John shoved a yellow glob of breadfruit in his mouth and chewed stubbornly, while Gerrick gazed off into the distance, giving his friend time to adjust to the idea. They were having breakfast under a palm tree—the cold, cooked fruit, left over from last night, furnished by a giggling group of native women standing a short distance down the beach. Aboard his ship, still anchored in the bay, Gerrick could see members of his crew moving about their morning duties.

The hour was late for these routine tasks, but his men hadn't returned to the ship until almost dawn, and some, he suspected, hadn't made it back at all—another example of the laxity into which they'd fallen. It was a laxity he intended to do something about, just as soon as he'd won John's wholehearted cooperation.

John, as Gerrick had anticipated, was *not* enthusiastic. Nor did he appreciate being torn away from the arms of four island maidens. But as soon as he recovered from his throbbing headache, caused by drinking too much *awa*, he might be ready to listen to reason. Patiently, Gerrick waited, feigning great interest in the brilliant turquoise water lapping the white sand beach. The vivid colors of sky, water, sand, mountains, and palm trees were unreal, and Gerrick still could not assimilate the natural beauty surrounding him. He wanted to explore and discover more of this enchanting place and was suddenly filled with impatience to begin his search for the sandalwood.

"Caitlin Price is a real beauty, John—everything you could want in a woman. All you need do is play to her prejudices, and she'll fall into your arms like a piece of ripe fruit."

"I've got all the fruit I want right here." John scooped another yellow glob out of the huge shell in front of him. "Besides, I doubt she's my type, Gerrick. Why should I go running after some frightened little virgin when there's any number of experienced beauties at my fingertips who can't spread their thighs fast enough—for me or for you?"

"There's no one like this one, John. She has waist-length silver hair, a face like an angel's, and a body that would tempt a saint."

John spat out a large seed. "I thought you said she was wearing a long white nightdress when you saw her."

"She was, but I can assess a woman's body no matter what she's wearing—and this one is shaped like Venus." Remembering the softness of Caitlin's sweetly rounded contours as she struggled against him, Gerrick felt his blood stir. "Trust me, she's a Greek goddess."

"She's also a missionary, which means she has scruples. It may be weeks, even months, before I can thaw her out. What am I to do in the meantime? Live like a monk?"

Gerrick shrugged. "Isn't a bit of abstinence worth it if we come out of this adventure rich?"

"I doubt it." John wiped his mouth on the back of his hand and leaned on one elbow. "What makes you think she'll ever trust me enough to tell me about the sandalwood? She may not even *know* about it."

"That's a chance we have to take, John," Gerrick insisted patiently. "Right now, Caitlin Price is our only hope. We've *got* to get her cooperation and assistance—as an interpreter, if nothing else."

John's brows dipped in a ferocious look that had intimidated many an adversary, but which Gerrick dismissed as mere quibbling. "I don't like it, Gerrick. I'm no actor, for God's sake. She'll *never* believe I'm a fellow missionary. I don't look, sound, or act like one. From the start, she'll know it's a lie."

"Then don't claim you're one. You can say you've recently converted and now want to atone for your past wickedness by bringing salvation to the natives." Gerrick snapped his fingers. "Now, why didn't I think of that sooner? It's the perfect story! You can say you want to build a church here, but you'll need her help to do it."

John scratched his stubbled chin and regarded Gerrick skeptically. "And if she happens to know the whereabouts of an undiscovered stand of sandalwood, it would obviously be God's will if she told me about it, right?"

"Right! You're willing to sink every last coin you have into such a noble undertaking, but alas, you don't have quite enough coins. However, if *she* could just contribute something . . ."

"What if she can? What if she has money stashed away for just that purpose?"

"Then, you'll just need *more* money—for the church organ, the church bell, the Bible school for the natives . . . the *sewing* school so all the island girls can learn to fashion nightgowns to cover their nakedness. . . . Come on, John, you'll think of something."

"But what if there isn't any sandalwood, after all?" John growled, unconvinced.

"Then after we search the island thoroughly, we'll simply sail away and never be heard from again."

"That's my whole point! I won't even have fond memories of nightly orgies on the beach with which to console myself." John sat up, pushing the remaining breadfruit to one side in the warm sand. "No, I don't think much of this plan of yours, Gerrick. Once again, I'm the one who has to make all the sacrifices. While you're plucking little grass skirts left and right, I'll be lucky to steal a kiss or two from a New England spinster with ice water running through her veins."

"Now, John, it won't be that bad, I promise you."

Glancing past John's shoulder, Gerrick saw an amazing sight. Coming down the beach toward them was the very person they'd just been discussing: Caitlin Price. It had to be her; what other woman on the island would be dressed as if for a fall outing in New England—wearing a long skirt, long sleeves, high neck, a poke bonnet, and even a shawl about her shoulders despite the day's growing heat?

"Get up and start lecturing me!" he hissed at John.

"What?" John asked, startled.

"*Lecture* me! Preach to me about my wanton ways— and hurry up about it. Caitlin Price is headed in our direction."

"Now? She's coming here, now?" Twisting his thick neck this way and that to catch sight of her, John scrambled to his feet.

"I don't care what you think, my friend!" Gerrick shouted, rising and grabbing John by the shoulders. "What I do with my life is my own business, and neither you nor anyone else has a thing to say about it. . . . Go on, argue with me," he urged under his breath. "And make it sound convincing, damn it!"

For a moment, John looked panic-stricken, but then he cleared his throat, scowled disapprovingly, and shook his finger at Gerrick. "Gerrick Scott, we've been friends for a long time. But if you don't mend your ways, I'll count you as one of my worst enemies. . . . Why, you—you're a disgrace to your sainted mother! God rest her soul. What would she think of your present activities—whoring among innocent women! Throwing your life away on—on drink and wild living! Squandering your family's fortune on the evils of the flesh!''

Even Gerrick was taken aback by John's boisterous, impromptu attack. John actually *did* seem sincere. Winking at him and warming to his task, John continued his tirade, his brown eyes snapping, his voice thundering, making Gerrick's skin prickle.

"You've become an instrument of the devil!" John cried. "And I urge you—nay, I *plead* with you—to mend your ways before it's too late. Why don't you do something *good* for the natives, instead of despoiling them?''

"Why, what should I do, John, build them a church?" Gerrick drawled, becoming inspired now himself. "Should I waste my entire inheritance converting a bunch of pagans, just because *you* intend to play the fool? I may have brought you here, because I was coming anyway to—to search for my brother, but I have no intentions of refusing the hospitality offered by beautiful, half-naked women.''

"Your *brother?*" John whispered, panic flashing in his eyes again. "What are you talking about?''

"My brother, Hadley, is surely here somewhere . . .'' Gerrick said loudly. He gestured toward the mountains rimming the beach and valley. "Off studying his beloved plants, I'll warrant, with nary a thought for his frantic relatives. I do intend to find him, of course. But I also intend to relax, first, after our grueling voyage. And that means happily sampling the charms of every woman who appeals to me. I'm not a saint, like you, John—and frankly, I liked you better when you were a sinner. You weren't so damn self-righteous then.''

"Self-righteous!" John thundered, taking his cue with a roll of his eyes at Gerrick's inventiveness. "I'm not self-righteous. I've simply come to realize the sinfulness of my

65

life thus far The only way to heaven is through conquering the devil within—and I'm damn well going to conquer *my* devils whether you do or not. It's just that—as your friend—I feel compelled to warn you of the error of your ways . . ."

"This man is incapable of seeing the error of his ways," a new voice said, and Gerrick feigned surprise as he turned to see Caitlin Price, standing only a step or two away from John and him.

She had approached almost soundlessly, but her faded, tattered parasol now cast a cooling shadow over him, shielding his eyes from the dazzling sunlight. And her face as he eagerly studied it was even more beautiful in the light of day than it had been in moonglow.

"Ah, Miss Price . . ." he said coldly over the sudden wild thumping of his heart.

In order to still it and compose himself, he allowed his glance to sweep slowly over her. Her dowdy brown dress had only a hint of ruffle at the wrist to soften the long, severe sleeves, and her glorious, silver hair could not be seen beneath the plain poke bonnet hugging her head. In all respects, she was dressed in a manner he found ugly and depressing—but as his eyes focused on her face with its delicate cheekbones, tender pink lips, and clear blue-gray eyes, he was thunderstruck by her beauty; it was not in the least marred by her icy, disapproving expression.

"J—John," he croaked. "Here is someone you'll be glad to meet—Miss Caitlin Price, a female whose views of my character identically match your own."

"Miss Price . . ." John said, his surprise evident on his round face as he, too, perused the young woman's astonishing, aureate loveliness. Darting Gerrick a glance of stunned pleasure, John took Caitlin Price's hand and bowed low over it. "I am enchanted. Somehow, in this godless place, I never expected to meet a true lady like yourself."

Though John's reaction was exactly what Gerrick wanted, he was oddly annoyed. Gerrick elbowed his friend aside and smiled grimly at Caitlin Price. "May I ask why you've come here, Miss Price? Surely, it isn't to apologize for your rude behavior of last night. I would have thought your kind *never* apologizes, even when apologies are definitely called for."

"Apologies!" Livid indignation rosied Caitlin Price's delicate features. "If anyone should apologize, it's you, sir!"

"Me? Why whatever for? As I recall, *I* was the one who took the beating. Do your religious beliefs countenance violence? If they do, I am amazed. As a Christian myself, I've always been taught to abide by peace and gentleness—even to offering the other cheek when violence is done me. Here, Miss Price"—Gerrick leaned toward her—"is my other cheek. Belt it, if it will make you feel better."

"I believe I shall, for you deserve it!" Caitlin Price raised her hand, but as Gerrick only stood there, neither flinching nor defending himself, her cheeks reddened, and she suddenly whirled on her heel and stalked a short distance down the beach. Behind the nearly transparent parasol, her shoulders were shaking, but as Gerrick watched with avid interest, she gradually regained her composure.

"Stick around, John, this should be interesting," he whispered. "And it's also the perfect opportunity for you to gain her good graces."

"I have an idea. Perhaps *I* should belt you," John suggested blandly, his gaze riveted to Caitlin Price's slender, indignant figure.

"You better not try it!" Gerrick replied irritably. "I mean . . . Oh, forget it. Here, she comes again."

Chapter Five

Caitlin took several deep breaths and desperately tried to remember why she'd thought it such a good idea to come here and confront this man in the clear light of day. Her heart was thumping, her knees were wobbling, and butterflies were swooping her stomach. She was afraid to look at the bold, red-haired scoundrel who had held her so intimately last night. Her eyes might reveal what she still felt: outrage and confusion—and also something mysterious and terrifying to which she couldn't yet put a name. She knew only that her entire being still vibrated with the burning imprint of his body pressed against hers.

Oh, yes, she guiltily recalled, she was going to request that he weigh anchor and sail immediately for Honolulu. She was going to give him a made-up story of how he would be offending the reigning monarch, Kamehameha III, if he did not pay his proper respects before doing whatever he had come here to the island to do. The idea had seemed such a good one in the hazy, gray hour before dawn; now, it seemed so foolish that she was embarrassed for having thought of it.

You are buying time, Caitlin, she reminded herself. Before the troublemaking *haole* can return from Oahu, Uncle George will be here to take over the task of defending the islanders against this man's wickedness.

As Pikake had pointed out, Uncle George had a voice like thunder, and thunder just might work where a woman's pleas and scoldings had failed.

Squaring her shoulders to bolster her confidence, Caitlin stalked back to the two men on the beach. At least, she wasn't mistaken about the morals of the tall *haole;* the shorter man had confirmed her worst suspicions. Perhaps, if luck was with her, she might turn the dark-haired gentleman into an ally, someone who could help her shame the red-haired devil into leaving the island women—especially, Pikake—alone.

"Sir . . ." she said to the shorter man. "If I may, I would like to speak with you alone."

"Me? Alone?" The man appeared both surprised and delighted. The tall *haole* frowned, which was all the encouragement Caitlin needed.

"Yes. Would you mind strolling a short way with me, for it seems we share certain concerns. Indeed, you may be the answer to my prayers."

"Why—I'd be delighted! You'll excuse me, won't you, Gerrick? Our present argument is getting nowhere. Perhaps you need time to think on what I've already said. Besides, I could never refuse the request of such a—a fine, upstanding young lady. If you'd be so kind as to postpone our discussion until tonight at dinner, Captain Scott . . ."

Captain Gerrick Scott. Caitlin imprinted the name in her mind. And as she did so, she gave the captain a long quelling look, meant to dissuade him from attempting to intrude on her walk with his companion. Unfortunately, *she* was the one who felt quelled. Gerrick Scott had green eyes that fairly skewered her in their intensity. And his hair, she decided, wasn't really red, but a rich, burnished color—chestnut, it might be called. His brow and his jaw seemed carved from lava rock, and the only softness in his entire face was in his mouth. His lips were full, almost indolent, and they reminded her of kissing—a thought she quickly pushed aside.

"Actually, I came down to the beach to speak with *you,* Mr. Scott," she heard herself say. "But now, I know I was meant to meet you, sir"—she smiled at the shorter man— "and to overhear what you were saying."

69

"What was it you wanted to speak with me about?" Gerrick Scott interrupted.

"It isn't important—at least, not now that I've met your friend," Caitlin answered.

In order to avoid Gerrick Scott's penetrating green eyes, Caitlin studied the shorter man. In his own way, he, too, was attractive, with his cheerful, round face, soft, dark-brown eyes, and large—though not fat—body. He reminded her of the jovial, thick-muscled Hawaiian men among the commoners who were unfailingly kind and gentle in their manner—and also, not too bright. This man, she felt certain, would be easy to handle.

He returned her smile with a flashing grin and offered her his arm. Since he was barefoot and dressed exceedingly casual, as was Gerrick Scott, in thigh-hugging breeches and open-necked white shirt with rolled-up sleeves, Caitlin did not feel comfortable resting her hand on his forearm. Had he been wearing a claw hammer coat or cutaway, as most men of decency did, she would not have hesitated. As it was, she clasped her parasol tightly with both hands and proceeded ahead of him, leading the way and hoping he—but not Gerrick Scott—would follow.

He did, and after they had left the captain some distance behind, Caitlin turned to the man beside her and began pouring out her heart. "Sir, I hope you don't think I'm overly bold—since I don't even know your name—but from what I heard you saying to Captain Scott, I feel certain I can trust you."

The dark-haired, dark-eyed man smiled and, taking her elbow, discreetly guided her around a chunk of driftwood on the beach. "You can trust me with your life, Miss Price. Unlike my misguided friend, Gerrick, I am a champion and protector of beautiful women—no longer a predator, out to compromise their virtue."

Caitlin blushed at his frankness. "That is precisely what I wish to speak with you about, sir—your friend's loose morals."

"John. My name is John Reynolds."

"Mr. Reynolds, then."

"No, John. . . . Please call me John, for I strongly suspect that you and I are going to become close friends."

"Well . . . all right, then, John. I, too, have that feeling—for it's obvious we . . . we . . ."

"Love good and abhor evil?" John supplied helpfully. "Yes, Miss Price—Caitlin—there's no sense tiptoeing around the truth. We are kindred spirits, and Gerrick Scott is a prickly thorn in both our sides."

"I know he is a thorn in *my* side, John—but how is he a thorn in yours?" Caitlin relaxed slightly and allowed him to lead her into the shade of a palm tree.

"He, ah, mocks everything I've come to believe in, Caitlin. Last night, I begged and pleaded with him to leave the island women alone. I even went to the banquet in order to keep an eye on him. It was terrible—that banquet . . . such drunkenness, such abandoned revelries . . . such . . . such *wanton* behavior."

John shook his head in pained remembrance. "I was ashamed, Caitlin. Shocked to my soul. I don't deny that once I myself might have joined my shipmates in these, ah, nocturnal activities. But since my conversion . . ."

"Your conversion? Just how and when did you embrace the faith, Mr. Reynolds?"

"It was, ah, on the journey out here. We, ah . . ."

In the dappled shade, Caitlin faced him squarely. Something in her new acquaintance's manner struck her as false, and she tried hard to remember exactly what she'd overheard. Gerrick Scott had said something about John wanting to *help* the islanders, while *he*, apparently, wanted only to find his brother and amuse himself as much as possible in the process.

"What was your reason for coming here, Mr. Reynolds? What was Mr. Scott's? He mentioned he had a brother, but I know of no other man named Scott who's come recently to Kauai. You say you were converted enroute to the islands?"

John flushed, and his dark eyes brimmed with discomfort. "Ah, it's still so new and painful for me to talk about these things, Miss Price. Please . . . won't you sit

71

down with me, and I'll tell you the entire story."

Caitlin looked back down the beach. Gerrick Scott was in the center of a swarm of island women. He was laughing and gesturing in an effort to make himself understood, but as she watched, he caught her glance, and his easy grin changed to a scowl. Reaching out, he drew one of the girls—it was Ilima—into his embrace, and his eyes transmitted a challenge, daring her to stop him from doing anything he pleased. That decided Caitlin.

"Yes, I'll sit down with you, John. I'm most interested to hear your story—and Mr. Scott's, as well."

John smoothed out a spot in the sand beneath the tree. Then he waited until she had closed her parasol and seated herself. She sat stiffly and uneasily, for never in her life had she sat down alone with a strange man—for the sake of intimate conversation, no less. When she had arranged her skirts so her legs and ankles were discreetly covered, she smiled up at him, and as if that were the signal he'd been awaiting, he nimbly sat down beside her.

"Now, then, Miss Price—Caitlin. My story . . . It began before we ever left Boston. I, ah, lost my young wife and little daughter to fever some time ago . . ."

"How tragic!"

"Yes, well, their deaths started me thinking about the sort of life I'd led up until then. . . . It wasn't a very good life, I'm afraid." John bowed his head, then looked at her earnestly. "So when Gerrick, my best friend, urged me to come with him to Hawaii, it seemed the right thing to do. I . . . I needed time to, ah, decide what to do with the rest of my life."

"Mr. Price was coming in search of his brother," Caitlin prompted him, steering the conversation in the direction that most interested her.

"Yes, ah, his brother, Hadley, came out here last year to, ah, study plants. And, ah, his family was worried because they hadn't heard from him in a long time. So Gerrick . . . being the concerned older brother . . . decided to come in search of him."

Caitlin frowned, wondering why she had no knowledge

of such a person ever arriving on Kauai. "He was a botanist, you say?"

"Yes, that's right—a botanist!" John looked relieved. "And he apparently arrived here, for he wrote a letter describing his work, sent it home by a returning whaler—and, then, was never heard from again."

"How awful that must be for Mr. Scott."

"Oh, yes, the captain's had a hard time of it worrying about . . . Hadley."

"His brother . . ."

"Yes, Hadley Scott—also the name of his grandfather. Gerrick's middle name, too."

"My goodness. His family must revere the name Hadley."

"Oh, they did—*do*." John grinned, and Caitlin was swept anew with the suspicion that this man wasn't being truthful or that he was toying with her. What on earth could he be hiding?

"So what happened on your voyage out here?"

"We, uh, hit a terrible storm. Our ship almost sank. And during that storm, I, ah, decided, once and for all, that I must reform. My wife was always preaching religion to me, you see, but I would have none of it. I was too stubborn. It took a raging sea with waves as high as our masts to make me see the light . . . but Gerrick, alas, only laughed at the spectacle. He actually dared the Almighty to sink us. The man is beyond hope. Despite all my efforts to reform him, he continues to lead a life of blatant disrepute."

John Reynolds glanced away, his mouth turning down at the corners, and his sadness finally won Caitlin's trust and compassion. "You mustn't feel too badly, Mr. Reynolds. Perhaps, in time, he'll see the error of his ways. Instead of blaming yourself, you should rejoice—for *you* were saved, and God must have kept you alive for a purpose."

"A purpose, yes . . ." John suddenly grasped her hand. "I *do* have a purpose, now, Miss Price."

"Why, what is it, Mr. Reynolds?" In vain, Caitlin

73

sought to dislodge her fingers from John's huge paw.

"The natives. I've come here to help bring salvation—in whatever small way I can—to these poor, godless wretches."

"You—you intend to preach the Bible?"

"Oh, no! I would never presume to do that. I haven't the training. But I will put all my worldly goods at the disposal of the island missionaries. If you will point me in their direction, that is. Maybe, as Gerrick suggested, I'll even help build a church."

"Mr. Reynolds!" Caitlin gasped. For a moment, she forgot to worry about how tightly John was holding on to her hand. "My—my *uncle* is one of the island missionaries. He's away just now at an important meeting of the Missionary Board on Maui—but when he returns, I'd be most happy to introduce him to you."

"What a coincidence! I should have guessed you were the daughter—I mean the niece, of a missionary. How long will your uncle be away?"

"I . . . I really don't know," Caitlin admitted. "He may return in a week or two, or perhaps not for a month. At this time of year, the weather becomes uncertain, and the waters of the channel may soon be too rough for safe passage. You yourselves could be stranded here for the winter if you don't depart immediately."

"We could?" John did not look unhappy over the possibility. "We hadn't planned to depart until Gerrick found his brother—and it may be weeks before he can explore this entire island."

Caitlin's heart began to pound at the thought of Gerrick Scott remaining so long. "Mr. Scott could not explore it in its entirety in any event, Mr. Reynolds. This island has many inaccessible places. And I doubt whether his brother—if indeed he came here—would dare venture into dangerous hidden valleys that are known to only a few."

"But that's exactly where Hadley Scott would venture. Why, the lad liked nothing better than to explore off the beaten track. He lost himself on the Spice Islands for two years."

74

"He did?"

"Lived on roots and berries, and discovered plants no one had ever heard of until then."

"Gracious! How interesting! Then, you intend to stay here for quite some time."

"Only as long as it takes, Miss Price." Leaning toward her, John Reynolds squeezed her hand, almost crushing it. "And personally, I wouldn't mind a long sojourn here, now that I've found someone who shares my, ah, views. You *do* share them, don't you, Caitlin?"

Flustered by his nearness and the intensity of his gaze, Caitlin dropped her glance to her other hand and plucked nervously at her skirt. "How could I not, Mr. Reynolds? My own father was a missionary, and his fondest dream was to build a church—a *real* church—for the islanders. My father and mother are both dead, but I would do anything to achieve their life-long goal. I'm only a woman, of course, but my uncle has stepped in to fill the breach and . . ." Aware that she was prattling foolishly, she raised her eyes to his and asked the question that was uppermost in her mind. "Just how much money do you have, John?"

Looking startled, John dropped her hand, and Caitlin quickly snatched it back.

"Good lord, woman, but you are direct!"

Rubbing her bruised fingers, Caitlin turned her head so her bonnet hid her face. Had she gone too far in betraying her eagerness to obtain control of this man's fortune? She felt a stab of shame at what might be interpreted as greediness on her part. But it's for the *church*, she reminded herself. Belatedly, she recalled that her reason for coming to the beach this morning had been to get the *haoles* away from Kauai—and now, she wanted them to stay. Was it *only* because of the church?

Feeling distinctly unsettled, even guilty, she leaped to her feet. "I'm sorry, Mr. Reynolds. I should never have asked such a crass question." Nervously, she brushed sand from her skirt. "Please forget that I *did* ask it. It's only that I was momentarily carried away by the . . . the wonderful

75

fact of finally meeting a white man on Kauai who is interested in something other than debauching our young women and despoiling our land."

"Despoiling your land?" John rose also, and picked up her parasol.

"Stripping it of trees—sandalwood trees, so that some of the mountains are bare now, and ugly, where before, when I was a child, one could climb the highest cliffs and see and smell great stands of *iliahi*, filling the air with their rich fragrance."

"There's no more sandalwood left, I take it. Not even a little bit?"

"There's none," Caitlin lied. "Our women and our sandalwood—and now, our whales are what most *haoles* want. They have destroyed the sandalwood—but I and a few others are most determined that they shall not destroy our women. As for the whales—they'll have to find their own protector, because I can do nothing about them."

"I see . . ." John said thoughtfully.

"So now you can understand why I'm so very glad you've come." Caitlin broke into a smile. Then frightened by the leaping response in John's eyes, she quickly snatched her parasol. "When my uncle returns, I'll come and get you, John Reynolds. Please don't leave before then—even if Mr. Scott *does* find his brother. God has brought you to us in the hour of our greatest need; you *can't* leave before speaking with my Uncle George. Tonight, when I say my prayers, I'll ask the Lord to delay Mr. Scott's departure for however long is necessary."

Caitlin fell silent, fearing she was once again betraying an overdose of eagerness. Hazarding another smile, she whirled and strode away, not even pausing when she had to walk by Gerrick Scott lounging beneath the palm trees where Ilima was feeding him bananas.

"Ilima!" she snapped, switching effortlessly to Hawaiian. "In case you are interested, which I doubt, today's Bible class has been canceled."

"Oh, that's all right." Ilima smiled one of her languorous, sultry smiles. "Today, I would not have come anyway."

"God forgive you," Caitlin muttered, hurrying past.

"Good morning to you, Miss Price!" Gerrick Scott called after her. "Come visit us again when you can stay longer."

It will be a cold day in hell before I will, Caitlin thought. The last thing she wanted was another encounter with Gerrick Scott.

"What did you talk about all that time?" Gerrick inquired of John over dinner in Gerrick's cabin.

"Mmmmmph—what?" John was downing the contents of a pewter tankard filled with a generous portion of Gerrick's ale.

Gerrick raised his voice and repeated the question, trying to make himself heard over the drumming of rain on the deck boards overhead. Tonight, there was no moon to excite his senses, and the entire ship's crew was aboard, recovering from the excesses of the previous night.

"Well?" Gerrick shouted impatiently. "What did *she* say? What did *you* say?"

Slowly, taking his time, John lowered the tankard and grinned at Gerrick over its rim. "I'm not sure I can remember—at least, not word for word. But you were right, my friend. Caitlin Price is everything you said she was and more. I'm pleased as hell that the two of you didn't like each other the first time you met. Now, she's mine, and I can tell you about her or not as I choose."

Gerrick's fist came down hard on the table, rattling the plates and silverware. "Damn it, John! You've been playing games with me all day. Did she mention the sandalwood or not?"

"She mentioned it." John wiped his mouth with a linen napkin, suddenly fastidious, as if the mere mention of Caitlin Price's name was enough to make him mind his manners.

"Well?"

"She said there isn't any."

"She's lying."

John shot him an amused glance. "I doubt it. She'd go after the sandalwood herself if she knew of it. You should have seen her eyes light up when I mentioned building a church. Had I offered her a string of emeralds, she could not have been more pleased."

"Emeralds would not become her," Gerrick growled, disappointed. "Her eyes are blue, not green like Scott eyes."

"Blue-*gray*," John corrected. "And her skin is like cream—with a golden cast to it. And her lips . . . ah, how can I describe such lips!"

"Her lips are prim, like she is. They're thin, prim, and unappealing."

"To you, perhaps, not to me. A man could die for a taste of those lips."

"Is sex all you ever think about?" Gerrick pushed away his half-eaten meal. "After last night, your gross appetites should have been satisfied—at least, for a time. Long enough, anyway, for you to concentrate on business, rather than pleasure."

Sighing, John leaned his big body back into the wooden armchair. "Last night was a mere brief stimulus—like eating dainties before the meat. Caitlin Price, my friend, is the main meal . . . and one I shall savor at leisure."

"She'll never let you lay a hand on her." Morosely, hoping he was right, Gerrick toyed with his crystal wineglass. It was still more than half filled with ruby liquid. The wine was a special bottle he'd been saving to celebrate their arrival in the islands, but tonight, it tasted like vinegar. He wasn't in the mood for wine—and John, of course, preferred ale. He might as well dump the precious stuff overboard or send it down to the berth deck for Erasmus to portion out.

"In time—and with careful handling—she will." John leaned forward, his eyes shining in the lamplight. "Do you know what she actually said? She said she'd do *anything* to get a church built. *Anything.*"

Gerrick felt even worse. "Then you'll be able to

persuade her to act as an interpreter, at the very least."

"I think so. I even planted the seed for gaining her cooperation in that matter. Of course, I had to spin a few lies . . ."

"What lies? I hope you didn't say anything we can't live with."

John looked wounded. "Me? Why, all I did was corroborate *your* lies. I told her you intend to search the entire island for your mythical brother. She would *never* agree to help us if she knew the real object of our search, but for a brother—and for an opportunity to save your soul from the fires of hell . . . All you have to do is go on behaving like a perfect ass, and she won't be able to resist the challenge. Missionaries thrive on challenge."

Gerrick glared at his friend. John had done exceedingly well. Indeed, he'd done exactly as Gerrick had wanted him to do. Why, then, did Gerrick want to punch him in the mouth? Why these feelings of bitter jealousy? Caitlin Price meant nothing to him. She was pretty, yes, but hardly his type. And he certainly wasn't desperate for female flesh; he'd had his fill that afternoon.

Forcing his gaze back to his wineglass, Gerrick determinedly thought about the girl—girls—in whose arms he'd earlier found his pleasure. Only one stood out in his mind—the totally uninhibited young woman named Ilima. He remembered her because she was the only one of the bunch who knew any real English. She wasn't as fluent as little Pikake, whom he hadn't seen since his first night, but she did speak it—and she also stood out in his mind because Caitlin had spoken to her on the beach.

"Tutu Caitlin . . ." Ilima had said with a giggle, mimicking the way Caitlin Price walked down the beach with her nose in the air. "Tutu Caitlin no like make *panipani* with *kane*. When she lay down at night, only take Bible into bed with her."

The meaning of *panipani* and *kane* had been made clear with crude gestures, and all the other girls had laughed when Ilima repeated the coarse joke in her own language. Yet even though the girls laughed at "Tutu Caitlin," they seemed to genuinely like and respect her. When Gerrick had questioned Ilima further about Caitlin, Ilima had also said, "Tutu Caitlin good friend of all islanders. Have much wisdom and *aloha* in her heart. That is why she is called Tutu—Grandmother. Only in her head she mixed up."

Mixed up is certainly the right word for her, Gerrick thought disgustedly. Grandmother, indeed! She wasn't an old woman, *yet*. Why did she act like one? Didn't she realize she was human, like everybody else, with human needs and desires? Didn't she ever want to hold anyone close to her? Didn't she *need* intimacy?

The image of her striding down the beach haunted him. Her back had been so straight, her head held so high, her whole posture proclaiming that she—Caitlin Price— didn't need anybody or anything. Wasn't she lonely so far from civilization? Who did she have to talk to, to gossip with, to share those feminine mysteries that his mother and sister had always so much enjoyed?

"Well . . ." John stretched and yawned loudly, interrupting Gerrick's thoughts. "If you're going to ignore me, I'm going to bed."

"Sorry, John," Gerrick apologized. "I was just thinking."

"Hah! Envying me is more like it. Admit the truth. You can't stand the thought that Caitlin Price might actually prefer me to you in her bed."

"You're not in her bed yet, my friend."

"Time, Gerrick. It's only a matter of time. And like you said, she'll fall into my arms like a piece of ripe fruit."

John's certainty angered Gerrick. "I'll wager half my share of the sandalwood that I can win her first," he said impulsively.

"What?"

"You heard me, half. Take it or leave it."

John stared at him down the length of the white damask tablecloth. "Have you gone crazy? Has the tropical sun addled your brain? Caitlin Price is only a woman—an interesting diversion to break the monotony of our stay, but still a mere female. She's not worth losing a fortune over."

"My sentiments exactly. So what's wrong with a little bet to divert us even more? Or have you gone cautious in your old age?" Gerrick taunted.

He himself could not fathom why he'd posed such an extravagant, ridiculous wager. However, now that he had, he wasn't about to back down—which would make him appear more ridiculous. "Take it or leave it," he repeated stubbornly. "If you've got the guts. Half my share of the sandalwood says I can make her fall in love with *me,* rather than you."

"Oh, ho!" Grinning widely, John tipped back his chair. "So it's love we're talking now, is it?"

"That's the only way Caitlin Price will consent to go to bed with any man," Gerrick said uncomfortably.

"Hmmmmm . . . you've got a point. But won't she be hurt when we finally sail away?"

This was a complication Gerrick hadn't considered. He thought of his own hurt when Madeline Barrows had dumped him. Then, he thought of Madeline shamelessly giving herself to another man. Was her behavior so unusual? Or was it typical of most women? Yes, Gerrick thought, women were an unpredictable, uncaring lot, capable of smashing a man's dreams without a single qualm.

"So what if she's hurt?" he snapped. "She'll find herself another man in a hurry. Neither you nor I are good husband material anyway, and the next time she chooses, she'll be more careful."

John raised his dark eyebrows. "Grown cynical, haven't we? . . . Well, you're probably right. Unless *some* man thaws her frozen heart, she'll go to her grave a spinster— and a virgin, which is even worse. Seen in that light, we'd be doing her a favor."

"Hell, she might even thank us!" Gerrick quipped, closing his ears to his own callousness. He rose to his feet, leaned across the table, and extended his hand. "It's a deal?"

81

"Deal." John righted his chair, grasped Gerrick's hand, and gave it a hearty shake. "But I have to warn you, I'm so far ahead of you already, I don't see how you'll ever catch up. Caitlin Price thinks you're the devil himself."

"I am." Gerrick winked. "So be on guard; devils don't play fair."

Chapter Six

"And that concludes today's Bible class," Caitlin said. "Just remember, as you go about your business this afternoon, 'As you sow, so shall you reap.'" Caitlin looked pointedly at Ilima, but the girl only smiled vacantly, her mind far away from the small, open-sided grass hut that served as a schoolroom in lieu of a proper clapboard building.

"Ilima," Caitlin called, as her students—a dozen or so young women dressed in long, loose *mu'umu'us*—began chattering with each other while filing out of the hut. "Ilima, could I see you a moment?"

The girl nodded and rose gracefully. In an effort to redeem herself in Caitlin's eyes, she, too, had worn her *mu'umu'u*, which Caitlin had made for her, but Caitlin knew that as soon as she was down the path leading away from the schoolroom, Ilima would probably remove the concealing garment and go swimming out to the schooner to see if Gerrick Scott had released his men from their duties. The steady downpour of last night had ceased by this morning, and the day was a warm one—promising a pleasant evening and a repeat of the shameful activities that had taken place on the schooner's first night at the island.

Thinking of that night and the day following, Caitlin frowned at Ilima, but the girl approached Caitlin without a single hint of embarrassment or chagrin. Ilima simply

83

did not equate sin with her most recent, shameful behavior. If anything, she seemed more relaxed, more cheerful, and happier than ever—as if she found deep contentment in breaking the commandments Caitlin had labored so long and hard to teach her.

"Now, Ilima," Caitlin began, but just then, Pikake detached herself from the other girls and came running over.

"Tutu Caitlin, you want me go back house and prepare food for you? You are hungry?"

Since Pikake had come to live with Caitlin in her uncle's absence, Caitlin had been teaching her how to cook—a task normally performed by Hawaiian men. Caitlin wasn't hungry, but she wanted to keep Pikake occupied and far away from the schooner, so she nodded. "Yes, Pikake. Please do that, and if you find Inamoo at the house, tell him he *must* tend the garden today. The weeds are positively choking my poor vegetables."

Pikake wrinkled her nose. "I say let them choke. Missionary vegetables no taste good like *poi* and fish. If you learn eat island food, no need missionary food. Pikake and Inamoo feed you better—make you happy and smile all the time."

Caitlin sighed, wishing she *could* eat native-style. "Just boil some of the salt pork, Pikake, and get out some sea biscuit. I will have *that* for my dinner. It was good enough for my father, so it's good enough for me—and Uncle George would never approve of my turning up my nose at foods shipped to us all the way from New England."

"Salt pork—ugh! Tastes very bad and smells bad, too. Inamoo not going to like tending ugly vegetables either. He say *taro* and *uhi* better, and he have friend who be happy sell you some."

"I cannot afford it, Pikake, not at the prices your brother's friend can get for his sweet potatoes from passing traders. But tell your brother I *will* pay him for his services as a gardener. I will sew him a new pair of trousers."

"Inamoo no like trousers. He say too hot. But I tell him. When he come, he probably garden for nothing, just because he like you." Shaking her head at the strange ways of whites, Pikake departed, and Caitlin could finally give her full attention to Ilima. Studying the girl before her, Caitlin wondered what approach to take. Ilima was certainly a lovely specimen of island womanhood. Whereas Pikake was fine-boned and delicate—her beauty almost unnoticeable until you really looked at her or until she danced the wicked hula—Ilima's good looks were striking.

She was taller than Caitlin, and every inch of her was voluptuous—from her full lips, and huge, velvet eyes to her coconut-sized breasts and flaring hips. Her hair was black as midnight, and so untamed that it partially obscured her face, making it appear as if she were peering through a deep, jungle rain forest and enticing the onlooker to join her there. Caitlin never saw her without a pink or scarlet blossom tucked behind her right ear—proclaiming her availability as an unmarried woman.

"Ilima . . . where did you spend last night?" Caitlin asked bluntly, too upset even to bother switching to Hawaiian. "Did you go aboard the schooner and pass the night with Captain Scott?"

Ilima's long hair flicked across her face as she denied the accusation. "No, Tutu Caitlin. Captain Scott not allow females aboard his ship."

Well, that was an unexpected blessing. At least, Caitlin wouldn't have to worry about any of the girls being taken away from the island, which had happened before. She was aware of several girls who had never returned—even though the ships had, many long months later. One girl had died of a mysterious sickness, and two others had been left on islands far from home after the men had tired of them.

"Ilima, you simply cannot continue chasing after the men from the ships. Terrible things have happened to girls like you who don't know any better than to bestow favors on common sailors."

"Ilima knows better," Ilima said, smiling, and referring to herself in third person as the Hawaiians often did.

85

"You do? But just yesterday I saw you with Captain Scott."

Again, the sultry smile. "Captain Scott not common sailor. He a *captain*, very high born. In his own country, he royalty."

"Oh, I doubt that, Ilima. In America, no one is royalty. Only in England do they still have kings and queens—and here in the islands, of course."

"Captain Scott is king among Americans," Ilima insisted. "His family once owned many fine buildings filled with goods to trade."

"*Once* owned?" Caitlin queried, interested despite herself. "What happened to them?"

Ilima tossed her black mane. "Captain Scott not tell me. He say I ask too many questions and then he get mean look and send me away."

Good, Caitlin silently gloated. She avoided asking herself *why* she was so pleased that Ilima had been sent away. And she also did not dwell long on the amazing fact of Ilima's facility with English; obviously the girl had been practicing with others besides Caitlin. "From now on, you must stay away from Captain Scott, Ilima. He's a very wicked man, and I can assure you that he *isn't* royalty. Instead, think of him as the devil, and you will be far closer to the truth."

"Yes, Tutu Caitlin," Ilima readily agreed, but Caitlin knew that, like most Hawaiians, Ilima would politely agree and then do exactly as she pleased. The islanders were much like children in wanting to earn praise and avert displeasure, but every time Caitlin turned her back, they reverted to their old ways and then could never understand why Caitlin became exasperated. Even Pikake could not really be trusted, as the other night had proven.

"All right, Ilima, if you promise to behave yourself and stay away from Captain Scott and the other sailors—you may go now."

Ilima's eyes lit up at the dismissal, and she impulsively hugged Caitlin and then flew out of the schoolroom. With a sinking heart, Caitlin watched her go. "She'll have her *mu'umu'u* off within minutes," she lamented aloud, and then quickly gathered together her Bible and other teaching materials. If she didn't hurry back to the house, Pikake, too, might head for the beach, and Caitlin was determined that of all the souls entrusted to her care, Pikake's should be saved.

The walk home made Caitlin feel uncomfortably warm. She was glad to reach the coolness of the porch where she could then doff her shawl. Missionary customs dictated that the missionaries eat, dress, and live as similarly as possible to what they would have done back home in New England, and Caitlin maintained the customs partly out of respect for her father's memory and partly out of determination not to be found wanting by the Missionary Board or Uncle George.

Though island weather never justified wearing a shawl over already hot, confining clothing, Caitlin dutifully wore her shawl whenever she went out; in New England, the late autumn days were cold, and the snowy winter was on its way.

Untying the ribbons of her bonnet, Caitlin removed that as well, and pushed back a strand of damp hair that had somehow escaped her braids. This was the hottest part of the day, when she rarely went anywhere for fear of sunstroke. Once in a while, when she could stand it no longer, she would sneak away to the hidden pool and there indulge in a secluded swim, afterward feeling cool and refreshed—and smelling much better, too. Having grown up in the islands, she had come to value cleanliness, the one thing she'd learned from the natives, who swam in the ocean several times daily. Even the lowliest heathen Hawaiian smelled better than the most respected missionary, and Caitlin often wished that her own uncle would consent to bathe more frequently. Unfortunately, like most of his compatriots, Uncle George refused to set foot in the rolling surf. She, herself, could bathe only in a bucket or at her hidden pool.

How I would love a swim this afternoon, she thought longingly. Descending the steps again, she went round the side of the house to the small thatched cook house, to see if Pikake was obeying her instructions.

"*Aloha*, Tutu Caitlin." Pikake's bright smile gladdened Caitlin's heart. "Pork boiling good now. Is all right I go find Inamoo? He not here, but I think I know where find him."

"You're not going down to the beach," Caitlin stated, rather than questioned.

"No," Pikake denied, her brown eyes guileless. "Inamoo probably upriver. I go upriver and get him. Then bring him back to tend garden—if he come."

"What could he be doing upriver that's so important?"

"He and our cousin making new *papa he'e nalu*," Pikake responded reluctantly. She bent over the simmering pork and stirred it with a large iron spoon. "I hear them talk about it."

Caitlin could understand Pikake's reluctance to impart this information. What Inamoo was making was a surfboard, and the missionaries did not approve of surfing. When the surf was high, Hawaiians often ceased their labors and went off to play for weeks or even months. The problem was so bad that on Maui, the missionaries had confiscated a goodly number of the surfboards and made benches out of them for the church. Here, where there were fewer missionaries to exert their will, the sport continued unabated—much to the chagrin of Caitlin's father, and later her uncle, who had done their best to curtail the wasteful practice that lured men from honest labor.

"Do see if you can persuade Inamoo to come tend my garden," Caitlin urged. "Tell him God will bless him for it."

"I tell him," Pikake promised. "But he may not believe it."

Minutes later, Caitlin was alone. Climbing the steps and reentering the house, she walked into her bedroom and lay down on the four-poster bed. After several tense moments, she decided she was still too warm and sticky to be able to relax completely. You ought to go out and weed the garden, she told herself, in case Inamoo doesn't come.

However, the mere thought of weeding in her heavy garments was enough to make Caitlin feel faint; she could scarcely tackle the job like Inamoo, wearing nothing but a loin-concealing *malo*. Feeling weary and dispirited, she closed her eyes. Immediately, a disturbing image invaded her thoughts: Gerrick Scott's green eyes—gazing at her mockingly. It was almost as if the Devil was laughing at her failure to restrain the islanders from sinning. Faced with the first real test of her vocation as a missionary, all she could do was lie on her bed, bemoaning the heat and wishing for someone to rescue her—and her poor, lost lambs as well.

Unless she stopped them, tonight the Hawaiians would once again revert to their pagan ways. The rain had stopped them last night, but it wasn't likely to rain again tonight. What she needed was a miracle.

Oh, Uncle George, come home!

Immediately, she was ashamed to be reduced to such sniveling cowardice. Tonight, she'd go down to the beach, find John Reynolds, and get *him* to help her end the drunken revelries. She wasn't alone anymore; she had John Reynolds, a strong, brave man to assist and support her efforts.

Thinking of him, she sat up, her mood considerably lighter. *Of course.* If she and John together confronted Gerrick Scott and begged him to control his men, perhaps he'd do it. Perhaps he could be shamed into decency. At least, with John beside her, she'd not be facing those mocking green eyes alone. Just thinking of Gerrick Scott's eyes—and of his tall, muscular body, so blatantly masculine and powerful—made her knees feel watery. She longed to flee and run away, as far away from him as she could get. What was it about him that so unsettled her? She couldn't free her mind from vivid images of him kissing and fondling young women, first Pikake, then Ilima, and then . . . herself?

Only one thing was certain: Gerrick Scott was dangerous—*personally* dangerous, not just to Pikake and

Ilima, but also to her, though why she should feel so threatened, Caitlin didn't know. Other than that first night when he'd held her tightly and shamelessly rubbed against her, he hadn't shown the least interest in her as a woman. And why should he? Beautiful women surrounded him; how could *she* ever hope to compete with the likes of Ilima—or even Pikake?

Driven by a need to see herself as Gerrick must see her, Caitlin rose from her bed and crossed the room to the heavy wood chest that served as her dressing table as well as for storage. Above it hung a cracked mirror in a chipped wooden frame. The mirror had belonged to Caitlin's mother, and when her father had given it to her, he had warned her against the evils of spending too much time in front of it. A single glance would confirm the fact that her braids were securely fastened at the nape of her neck; she needn't spend a quarter hour gazing into her own eyes or pondering her appearance.

Now, however, that was exactly what Caitlin did. Peering into the mirror, she tried to see what others—especially Gerrick—saw. Were her blue-gray eyes beautiful—or were they too widely spaced, too large? And what about her nose? It wasn't crooked, but the slight uptilt at the end of it seemed childish and unappealing. Her mouth was her most deficient feature; Hawaiians had wide, generous mouths, made for smiling, laughing, and—and kissing, though Hawaiians expressed affection by rubbing noses, rather than joining mouths.

Her own mouth, by comparison, looked impoverished. To soften it, she smiled and was stunned to discover dimples in her cheeks that she had never before noticed—probably because she'd never before smiled at herself in the mirror. When she smiled, she *did* look beautiful—well, pretty anyway. Her teeth were white and even, and showed no signs of decay like Uncle George's.

Next, she studied her hair. Her braids did much to minimize its startling color, and the severe hairstyle also made her appear plain, if not downright dowdy. No man could possibly admire her hair—not when every other girl

90

on the island wore her hair floating free down her back and adorned with flowers.

Disappointed by what she saw in the mirror, Caitlin stepped back and considered her dress—and was even more dismayed and disappointed. She looked old and drab. The fabric of her hand-me-down dress, once the property of some unknown benefactress in New England, was so faded that its original color could hardly be ascertained. Even worse, the dress sagged unattractively, making it appear as if she had no waist and scarcely any bosom.

I'm ugly, she thought, an old, ugly spinster that no man will *ever* want.

Tears stung her eyes, and angrily, she brushed them away. Maybe her father had taught her never to look in the mirror because he didn't want her to know how truly ugly she was. Maybe Pikake only exclaimed about her hair out of pity. Everything else about her was plain, drab, and unappealing. To a man like Gerrick Scott, she must be a laughingstock. And John Reynolds was drawn to her only because they shared the same views about religion.

As a woman, she was a failure. Even the youngest, greenest maid on Kauai knew more about being a woman than she did. From their youngest years, Hawaiian children heard and talked about sex every day. Nothing was hidden from them, and to Caitlin's horror, they even played at sexual games, while Caitlin, at age twenty-two and living in a society where women married at fifteen or even younger, still had no clear idea of exactly what went on between a man and a woman.

Oh, she knew the biological facts, but the *feelings*—the emotions that made the act so tempting and irresistible—were mysteries of which she knew nothing. The vague, formless longings that swept her in the dead of night, the prickles of goose flesh she felt when she was near Gerrick Scott—terrified and confused her. And what terrified her even more was that she might *never* understand them, might *never* experience the glorious rapture alluded to in the Scriptures.

91

Even the Bible, Caitlin had long ago discovered, contained passages that stirred the heart and spirit in mysterious, passionate ways. In the grand scheme of the Almighty, passion had its rightful place, but Caitlin suddenly feared that, for her, there would be no passion, no leaping of the senses, no twining of heart, limb, and destiny. She would grow old and die a hollow shell of a woman—upright and praiseworthy—but lonely as a stick.

"You must stop this," she told her reflection. "You must stop this right now—feeling sorry for yourself and thinking such dreadful, dangerous thoughts."

Stabbed with a piercing anguish, she suddenly had to escape the drab figure in the mirror and the stillness of the empty house. Without pausing to grab her shawl, Caitlin fled to the *lanai,* descended the front steps, and began running up the narrow twisted path toward the only place she knew where she could feel free and unfettered: her hidden pool.

Only in that beautiful, secluded grotto with its musical waterfall and lush, blooming flowers could she unbraid her hair, shed her clothes, and be the happy creature she so longed to be. She quite forgot, as she hurried along the overgrown, fern-choked path, that anyone but herself had ever been there—or would want to return, for nearly the same reasons that she herself sought its solitude and privacy.

Gerrick swung his long knife, a machete he had borrowed from one of his crew members, and chopped down a thick fern. Somehow, he had gotten off the path, but he knew that the pool lay somewhere in this direction, and he intended to find it. He had spent the entire morning working alongside his crew as they holystoned the deck, began repairs on a storm-battered mast, and dove beneath the ship to scrape barnacles from her hull.

He had been setting a good example as well as exerting his authority. John had gone inland to bargain with the natives for hogs, chickens, and fresh vegetables, both to feed the men during their stay on the island and also to reprovision the ship at the time of their departure.

John had wanted instead to pay a visit to Caitlin Price this morning, but Gerrick had convinced him that feeding the crew was more important. Without an interpreter, it would take John a long time to line up the needed supplies, and during his absence, Gerrick himself intended to pay a visit on Miss Price. But first, he desperately desired a freshwater bath, for he wanted to be at his best when he set about wooing the challenging Miss Price.

After chopping through a small jungle of thickly overgrown pandanus trees, Gerrick finally came to a cleared area he hoped would lead to the path. It did, though he still could not be certain this was the same path he had trodden in the dark behind the little Hawaiian, Pikake.

Where was Caitlin hiding the girl? Where did Caitlin herself live? This afternoon, he intended to find out, and he also intended to apologize for his behavior and then to ask Caitlin's assistance in locating his fictitious lost brother. She would probably refuse, but he had thought of a way to persuade her. If she agreed to cooperate—albeit unknowingly—in his search for the sandalwood, he would agree to place a curfew on his crew. The men would resent a curfew, but Gerrick was willing to withstand their grumbles for the sake of winning Caitlin's cooperation.

Regarding Caitlin, John could pursue his own goals in any manner he chose. Gerrick grinned to himself in sheer, perverse exuberance as he chopped through another tangled mass of roots choking the path. John was right about one thing: Caitlin wouldn't be able to *resist* converting him. What fun would there be in converting John, who had already established himself as being saved? Gerrick would slyly offer Caitlin the irresistible opportunity to save his soul—and in the process, she would fall in love with him, invite him into her bed, and lastly, reveal the whereabouts of the sandalwood.

For Gerrick had no doubt that Caitlin knew where it was. He had an instinct for such things. It was an instinct

93

that had *always* enabled him to know just when a man was ready to wager a whole year's earnings on the outcome of a brawl. It had enabled him to raise his half of the money for this voyage, and to get John to agree to this fantastic bet. Only once—no, twice—had he been utterly wrong in his instincts about people; like his father, he, too, had trusted Amos Taylor, and he had also trusted Madeline.

He would *never* trust Caitlin Price—but he would use her. Her piety was a tool that could bend her to his will. She probably saw her religious fervor as her greatest strength; he saw it as her greatest weakness—because he could manipulate it to gain everything he wanted from her.

Poor John didn't have a chance! Magnanimously, Gerrick decided that instead of demanding *half* of John's share of the sandalwood following his winning of their bet, he would only demand one quarter. After all, John was his friend. He might even settle for a couple cases of rum—providing John didn't lose his temper too badly when he lost. When fully aroused, John's temper was terrible, and Gerrick had learned over the years to retreat when his friend's ire was directed at him.

John would be *very* angry when he learned what Gerrick had been up to this afternoon—but his irritation would be aimed more at himself than at Gerrick, for John would realize that he never should have allowed Gerrick an opportunity to see Caitlin Price *alone*.

His blood singing at the prospect, Gerrick broke into a half-run. The pool *had* to be just ahead. After a quick swim and a good wash, Gerrick would then go back down the mountainside and look for Caitlin Price's house or mission or whatever it was she called home. And his plans would finally be set in motion; Caitlin Price didn't have a chance.

Chapter Seven

Caitlin had bathed, splashed about in the pool, combed her sun-dried hair—whimsically entwining an orchid in it—and now was ready for a nap. The hot sun had made her drowsy, and she could scarcely keep her eyes open. Folding her dress to make a pillow, she selected a broad flat rock in the dappled shade, placed her makeshift pillow upon it, and lazily stretched like a contented cat. Aware that her skin could burn even in filtered sunlight, she rummaged beneath a fern until she found a stone jar containing turtle oil that she kept hidden there for just such an impromptu visit.

Pikake had furnished her with the oil, called *hino hono*, which was obtained by cooking the fat of the green sea turtle. The oil was extremely effective in preventing sunburn. Caitlin had also heard of another remedy, the crushed, gelatinous leaves of the aloe plant, which the missionaries had recently introduced to the islands.

Never knowing when her skills might be needed, Caitlin had made it her business to learn all she could of Hawaiian plants and medicinal remedies. As she learned of each one, she entered it in a special journal. She also corresponded frequently with the missionary doctor on Maui, seeking his advice for medical problems with which she was unfamiliar. The islanders set great store by her knowledge, but she herself knew just how limited her skills were. When her own father had become seriously ill several years ago, she had had no choice but to persuade a passing trader to take them both to Maui.

Remembering that voyage, she sighed. Shortly after their return home to Kauai, her father had met his untimely end, and she had been left to carry on without him. Smoothing the oil on her bare flesh, she was overcome by another surge of self-pity. How lonely her life now was! How barren and desolate were her days and nights—devoid as they were of all intimacy and close affection!

As she massaged herself, lavishing the oil on her breasts, a strange languor settled over her, a desire to be stroked and caressed by someone other than herself. Gerrick's image flashed in her mind, and once again, she relived the sensation of his hard body pressing against her, his muscled chest crushing her breasts. Then she imagined Gerrick bending over her and touching her breasts, as she had just touched them, only *his* touch lingered long in the valley between the twin mounds, and even longer on the peaks. When her nipples contracted at the mere idea of such intimacies, she hastily set the stone jar back beneath the fern. What was wrong with her, that at the least provocation, all her thoughts turned to forbidden acts?

Determinedly, she pushed the wicked thoughts aside and lay back on the stone, closing her eyes and willing herself to peace and silence. She would conquer the demons within herself inch by fighting inch; she would honor her father's memory and be the pure, virtuous woman he had always expected her to be. Loneliness was her destiny, the yoke she must bear in order to be saved, and bear it she would—even if it wasted the delicate blossoming of her womanhood.

Through lashes growing heavier by the moment, Caitlin gazed at the shimmering green undersides of gently swaying ferns and palm fronds. The blue sky arched overhead, and the waterfall sang a tinkling, merry tune. In such an enchanting place, no one could be sad for long, and Caitlin succumbed to sleep with a grateful sense of letting go—of floating into serenity. She heard a distant splash but paid no heed; the sound was lost in the splashing of the waterfall, and there was no other sound, save the soft sighing of the tradewinds.

Gerrick thoroughly enjoyed his swim. He had heard the waterfall minutes before seeing it, and by the time he got there, he was already undressed—having strewn his clothing carelessly along the path as he neared his long-sought goal. The pool was clear as glass, and he could easily ascertain that the water was deep enough for safe diving. Believing himself completely alone, he dove in, swam back and forth several times and, much refreshed, was finally ready to more closely observe the hidden site.

A plucked orchid lying near the water's edge on a shelf of black stone caught his eye. The large, lavender blossom appeared to have been left there, for no other orchids grew nearby, and Gerrick's ever-active curiosity prodded him to swim over and investigate.

At this end of the pool, the black rocks formed natural steps. His curiosity piqued, Gerrick mounted the first step and the second, his attention on the wet rocks, made slippery by moss. As he emerged from the water, he reached for the orchid—and it was then he saw Caitlin.

Startled, he straightened, but Caitlin did not move. Her eyes were closed, her body relaxed, and she appeared to be soundly sleeping. A wide grin took possession of his face as he quietly approached her; this was altogether a new Caitlin—a breathtakingly gorgeous, sensual creature who had wantonly stripped off her clothing and now dared to lie naked in the sun-gilded afternoon.

But as he gazed down at her, drinking in the sight of her creamy flesh gleaming gold against the black rocks, he felt no lust. Rather, he was seized by a sense of awe, a feeling almost of reverence. No artist or sculptor could have created a woman fairer than she. Her blond hair resembled spun gold in the shaft of sunlight penetrating the huge, green ferns that shadowed her. Her face was the serene, lovely mask of a madonna, and the lines and curves of her

97

body were pure poetry, inviting him to read them again and again—knowing he would appreciate them only after slow and careful study.

Even her toes entranced him; they were soft, pink, and delicate, reminding him of seashells. She might have been a nymph or wood sprite—a creature so ethereal as to make him fear she would suddenly vanish, leaving him unutterably sad and bereft.

Behind her right ear, she had tucked an orchid, and Gerrick knelt and gently disentangled it from her hair. He would not have expected Caitlin Price to adorn herself with flowers; was *this* the *real* Caitlin? Or was the real Caitlin the prim, proper spinster in her heavy, high-necked clothing? In more ways than one, he was trespassing upon her privacy. She would be devastated if she knew he had gazed upon her nakedness—and discovered a side of her that had heretofore been hidden.

Instinctively he knew that *no one* had ever seen her like this, her body oiled and inviting, her hair wild and strewn with orchids. His hands tingled with the desire to caress her soft, gleaming skin, to explore where no man had ever been. Lust began to rise in him, hot, thick, and strong. What if he were to seize her and kiss and caress her until she helplessly yielded to him?

He would not let her go from this spot until she gave him what he wanted. But just what exactly did he want—another wrestling match with an unwilling partner? Never in all his years of chasing women had he stooped to rape or overpowering a woman with his superior strength. In this case, even if he seduced rather than raped her, it would still be an unfair contest. He had the advantage of years of sexual knowledge and expertise, while Caitlin Price had likely never yet known a man's kiss.

Gerrick had dallied with virgins many times before, but they had always been virgins who'd gone about as far as they could go without committing the actual act. They had been practiced teases, bartering their doubtful virtue for a marriage proposal.

Caitlin Price was the first truly virtuous, innocent

woman Gerrick had ever encountered, and he did not know how to react. In this moment of indecision, he only knew he wanted her desperately—but he didn't want to hurt or sully her in the process. She plucked a chord of morality in him that he'd thought had long since died.

Damn! he swore in frustration, feeling like a newly fenced stallion resenting the curtailment of his freedom.

Entwining one finger in Caitlin's silken hair, he marveled at the softness of it and the brilliancy of its color. Golden-haired by day, silver-haired by night, Caitlin was an enchantress, and Gerrick longed to gaze into her eyes to see if they reflected back the blue of the sky or the green of the tall ferns. Careful not to rouse her from sleep, he lay down on the shelf of rock beside her and leisurely studied her from head to toe.

He couldn't find a single flaw—nothing to mar the perfection of her sweetly rounded breasts, flat concave stomach, and gently flaring hips. Her thighs, knees, and calves were fit enticements for a sultan, and he forcibly stopped himself from running a finger down the creamy flesh of her inner thigh—which he knew would be softer than any silk, satin, or velvet he had ever touched.

"Oh, Caitlin . . . Caitlin . . ." he murmured, swamped with desire for her.

She stirred and turned slightly toward him, her warm breath lightly fanning his face. Mesmerized by her nearness, he watched her parted lips. The very tip of her pink tongue was visible, and as he watched, she licked her lips, rimming them with a sheen of wetness that all but destroyed his self-restraint. With a groan, he succumbed to temptation and lowered his mouth to hers. Her lips were as tender as flower petals as he brushed them with his own tongue, willing himself to be gentle.

Sliding one hand beneath her head, he clasped her chin with the other, thereby holding her still while he plundered her mouth with soft, gentle kisses. For a moment, he felt no response, but then her lips began moving beneath his, and he knew she had awakened. He didn't give her time to resist, but began kissing her more deeply, exploring the inner sweetness of her mouth with his tongue and encouraging her to accept the intrusion.

Her breasts rose and fell more rapidly as she warmed to his onslaught. Her hands came up to clasp him—or was it to push him away? Lost in his own thundering response to the long, passionate kiss, he hardly knew what she was doing—until she suddenly succeeded in dislodging his tongue and struggled to turn her face away.

"Caitlin . . . Caitlin, don't!" he pleaded hoarsely, catching her hands before she could strike him.

To keep her from rolling to one side and escaping, he pinned her down with the upper half of his body. Growing more agitated, she whimpered and tossed her head from side to side, and he saw hysteria rising in her eyes.

"There's no need to scream. I won't hurt you," he soothed, just as she began screaming.

He clamped his palm across her mouth, and she used her freed hand to claw at his face. Wriggling, squirming, and trying to kick him, she fought like a primitive animal, and he feared she might hurt herself struggling with her back pressed against the hard rock.

"All right! I'll let you up," he promised. "Just stop fighting me. I swear I'm not going to hurt you."

He rose to his feet in a single, swift motion, and she scrambled away from him, sobbing, and searching frantically for her clothes.

"They're right here!" He scooped them up and held them out to her.

She snatched them from his hand and clutched her dress to her breasts as if the cloth were a shield.

"Go on," he urged. "Get dressed if it will make you feel better, and then we'll discuss this like two rational people. Nothing happened except that I saw you sleeping, got carried away by your loveliness, and kissed you."

Seeming not to have heard him, she jerked her gown over her head and tugged it into place with trembling fingers. Her hair half hid her face and most of her body— but she appeared too agitated to notice this. Gerrick considered whether to cover his own nakedness, but his clothes were on the opposite side of the pool, and he must swim back across it to find them. He didn't want Caitlin to run away while he did so. Then he noticed something he hadn't seen before: This rocky shelf, the interior of the grotto, was surrounded on three sides by steep, impassable cliffs festooned by hanging vines, ferns, and flowers.

On the fourth side was the pool. Caitlin must have held her clothes out of the water while she swam to these rocks. The only other means of egress was through the waterfall itself, which tumbled down from one of the cliffs to form the pool. Gerrick grinned. In order to leave, Caitlin would have to remove her dress again or risk wetting it. He sat down on a ledge and watched her, deciding that it didn't disturb him in the least to appear naked before her. Indeed, he hoped his nakedness would prompt her to have the most wicked, impure thoughts imaginable.

When Caitlin had dressed, she walked to one of the huge, lacey ferns dotting the outcropping, and snapped off a frond fully three feet long and at least two feet wide. This, she suddenly thrust at him.

"Cover yourself!" she snapped. "We are not Adam and Eve, and this is not the Garden of Eden!"

"What a pity," Gerrick responded. "I had hoped it was."

He covered his face with the fern and peeped through it at Caitlin. As she did not seem amused, but only glared at him all the more, he then lowered the frond to his lap where it concealed him more than adequately.

Hands on hips, golden hair afloat on the breeze, Caitlin Price glared at him. "You may find this all quite amusing, Captain Scott, but I do not! I have never been so—so *shamed* . . ." Her voice cracked, and tears threatened to spill from the shimmering, blue-gray eyes. "You—you have *ruined* me, sir!"

Gerrick stared at her, not able to believe what he was hearing. *"Ruined* you? By stealing a mere kiss, I *ruined* you?"

Not answering, she wiped away her tears as a small child

101

would—using the palms of her hands. Her cheeks had flamed to brilliant scarlet, and Gerrick realized that she really was ashamed. Her reaction to his unexpected presence was every bit as bad as he'd guessed it would be. "I'd hardly say I ruined you by admiring your beauty," he said softly. "As for the kissing, I couldn't help myself. I apologize for doing it without your permission. Next time, I'll ask first."

"There won't *be* a next time," she stated emphatically. "This time was bad enough. I—I can hardly bear the shame of it."

More tears seeped from beneath the silvery lashes and dribbled down the crimson cheeks. She turned away from him and helplessly wept, her hands clasped to her face. Gerrick felt terrible. He couldn't even go to her and comfort her, assuring her that it *wasn't* as bad as it seemed. He would feel ridiculous clutching a fern in front of him.

"Look. You didn't do a damn thing. I discovered you quite by accident, and overcome by your loveliness, I stole a kiss. That's all there was to it. I intended you no harm, and *you* obviously never intended to do anything wrong . . ." He paused, not at all sure what she had or hadn't intended. Of what exactly was she ashamed? That she had slept naked on the rock in the first place? That he had discovered her? Or that she had *enjoyed* his kisses and *wanted* him to continue kissing her?

She raised hate-filled, accusing eyes to him. "You have seen what you ought not to see, Captain Scott. You have taken what you ought not to have taken. And I, too, have seen what isn't mine to see. . . . Only when a man and woman are married, ought they to—to . . ."

"Nonsense," Gerrick snapped. "I've seen plenty of naked women, and they've seen all there is to see of me. There's nothing shameful about the human body. After all, it was created by God—in His image and likeness, so I've been told. The human body can be a thing of great beauty—as yours is, Caitlin. Don't make what happened here ugly and sordid."

"It *is* ugly and sordid! Sex is *sinful*—except when used

according to God's laws, for the purpose of creating children. We are commanded to be fruitful and multiply, but that doesn't mean we have to *enjoy* it."

Gerrick's patience was wearing thin. Did she really believe such claptrap? Many women did, he knew. He had heard husbands lamenting the coldness of their wives in the marriage bed. It was one reason why he'd held off marrying for so long; he didn't want to marry a whore, but neither did he want a cold, unresponsive virgin who thought that sensual pleasure was wrong and sinful.

He threw away the fern and stood up. Caitlin's eyes widened, and she quickly looked away. "What are you so afraid of, Caitlin? Am I really that ugly? Does your God create ugliness?"

He strode to her and stood before her. Then, he took her face in his hands and turned it so she must look at him. "Answer me, Caitlin! Do you find me ugly? Here stands a man, fashioned as his Creator made him. What is your opinion? Am I ugly?"

The long lashes fluttered open, revealing luminous, tear-filled eyes gazing up at him in dazed confusion. The tender mouth trembled. "No," Caitlin whispered. "I do not find you ugly. Indeed, I find you quite the contrary."

Elation surged through Gerrick, and he could not resist pressing her further. "And was my kissing so distasteful? Did you truly hate it when I kissed you?"

A single tear slid down her cheek. "God forgive me, I did *not* hate it!"

A tenderness such as he had never felt for *any* woman welled in Gerrick's breast. "Caitlin, my love . . ." he whispered, drawing her into his arms and intending to kiss her, again.

"No!" she cried, pushing him away. "This is wrong! This is shameful!"

"*Why*, damn it, if *you* want it, and *I* want it?"

"Because you're not my husband, and you never will be!"

"But I *could* be!" Gerrick shouted. "Damn it, I *could* be, if we both wanted it."

103

"We *don't* want it!" she shouted back. "You're a—a despoiler of women, a—a scoundrel and a rogue!"

"And you're a stiff-necked, sanctimonious missionary who doesn't know the meaning of the words *love* or *forgiveness!*"

Shocked by the intensity as well as the subject matter of their argument, Gerrick stepped back. One part of him wanted to throttle her and force her to admit her feelings of attraction for him—feelings he had sensed in her the first time he had seen her playacting the part of the Avenging Angel. Another part of him was deeply stunned and sending messages of retreat and danger; what was he doing discussing marriage with a woman he hardly knew and thoroughly disliked? Had he gone crazy?

"You're right," she said. "I don't know anything of love or forgiveness. The Hawaiians are very loving, gentle, and forgiving—but we missionaries . . ."

She stared at him a long moment, her beautiful eyes filled with such consternation and self-doubt that he wanted once again to hold and comfort her, to banish all her fears and worries.

"Caitlin . . ." He reached for her, but she suddenly bolted past him and fled in the direction of the waterfall.

At first, he thought she intended to run straight through it, but then he saw her dart behind it, step gingerly across a wet ledge he hadn't noticed, and disappear into the rain forest. Once again, she'd left him alone—more shaken and disturbed by their encounter than he cared to admit.

Marry Caitlin Price? he thought, still stunned.

Why not? a little voice asked. Think of what you'd gain if you married her. She'd swear to love, honor, and *obey* you. And Caitlin Price, being the daughter of a missionary, would *keep* her marriage vows—even to telling you where to find the sandalwood.

And more importantly, Gerrick realized with a heavy sigh of longing, her delectable, creamy-skinned body would belong to him and him alone.

Chapter Eight

Caitlin stumbled up the stairs to the *lanai* at the back of the house and went straight to her room. She had used the back stairs, rather than the front, because she didn't want to meet anyone. She could never explain her wild hair, disheveled dress, and flaming cheeks; she herself had still not assimilated what had happened to her this afternoon.

She, Caitlin Price, had been seen naked by a man, and that man had kissed her—was that really all he had done?—and she, too, had gazed upon his nakedness. She had gazed upon him and *wanted* him—wanted to touch the rippling muscles of his chest and powerful forearms, wanted to feel the texture of his curly chestnut hair, wanted to once again experience his body pressing against hers.

To be truthful, she had wanted to go even further, past the boundaries of all she knew to be decent and morally upright. Why had no one ever told her what a man's kisses would be like? How they would crumble all her defenses and leave her limp with longing? How the darting caress of his tongue would make her quiver and pulse with totally unmanageable feelings and sensations?

Now, at last, she knew why Pikake and Ilima had cast aside her teachings and sneaked down to the beach at night; the attraction between male and female was stronger and far more potent than any religious blandishments aimed at keeping them apart.

Shaken to her core, Caitlin sat on the edge of the bed and contemplated the devastating discovery of her need and desire for Gerrick Scott. Now, she knew why the Missionary Board insisted that all missionaries be married in New England before coming to Hawaii. The temptations of the flesh were awesome; a man or woman who had no sanctioned outlet for them was bound to slip and fall— especially if he or she met someone like Gerrick Scott, who could cast a spell with a single glance.

Gerrick Scott. If he had continued kissing her, if she hadn't escaped in time, she would have allowed him further liberties—nay, she would have *encouraged* them, even to the final, inevitable conclusion to which such liberties must lead. Today, she had discovered *passion*, and like a brushfire in the dry season, threatening to consume all in its path, this tempestuous feeling could well consume *her*.

What was she to do? What would her father have advised? Instantly, she recalled an incident in which her father had discovered a young unmarried woman, as naked as she had been today, in the arms of a young man betrothed to another. Her father had hauled the two wrongdoers before King Kaumualii, and there, insisted upon the two of them marrying each other, though each was promised to someone else.

At first, Kaumualii had tried to placate her father, pointing out that no real wrong had been done; none of the parties involved—neither the parents of the wrong-doers, their intendeds, nor the wrongdoers themselves— had been harmed. But her father had given such convincing arguments to the contrary, condemning the Hawaiians for their ignorance and lack of decency, that the king, deeply stung, had ordered the wedding to take place that very day.

Her father had presided over it, sonorously intoning the words binding the couple together as if he were God Himself blessing the union. Afterward, still trembling and fearful, the couple had embraced not each other but the ones they had promised to marry. These others had wept during the ceremony, but no one had dared challenge the king's royal edict or her father's arguments. Her father had been so filled with righteousness, so divinely inspired and so certain of what he was doing, that like children, the Hawaiians—even the king himself—had meekly acceded to his greater authority. It had been one of her father's grandest triumphs.

Remembering this, Caitlin *knew* what her father would do in this situation. Dressed as formally as possible in his thread-bare, claw-hammer coat, he would meet with Captain Scott and demand that Gerrick do right by his daughter. If possible, before the day was out, he would see his only child married to a man she scarcely knew—for marriage was the only honorable conclusion to what had occurred this afternoon.

I have no choice, Caitlin thought, horrified. But at the same time her heart began to palpitate, and her breath came faster. To become the wife of Gerrick Scott . . . to belong to him, body and soul . . . But what if he said no— or worse yet, what if he was already married?

"Miss Price?" a man's voice called, and Caitlin jumped to her feet.

"Yes? Who is it?"

"John Reynolds. I've gotten myself into a bit of a bind, and I wondered if I might see you a moment."

"Why, yes, of c—course!" Caitlin's hands flew to her hair. She couldn't see John Reynolds looking like *this*. "P—Please wait on the *lanai*, and I'll be out in a few moments."

Caitlin kept John Reynolds waiting a full quarter of an hour, but by the time she emerged from the house, she had every hair back in place, and every wrinkle smoothed from her gown. Only her cheeks, unfortunately, still held the stain of her shame caused by the earlier meeting with Gerrick Scott.

"Mr. Reynolds . . ." she said calmly, extending her hand to him. "I'm so pleased you've come to visit."

"Miss Price . . ." Smiling, John rose to his feet from her father's favorite chair. He took her hand and bowed over it, then straightened and grinned more widely. "It seems like months since I last saw you."

"Mr. Reynolds, it was only yesterday." Growing wary, Caitlin withdrew her hand from his and gestured for him to sit down again. She sat down in a ladder-back, wooden chair several feet away. "You said you had some difficulty. How may I help you?"

"Ah, Miss Price—as forthright as ever." John pushed a lock of dark hair out of his merry brown eyes. "I do have a problem—a serious one, I fear." He settled back in the chair, becoming more solemn and serious by the moment.

"Miss Price, this morning I set out in the direction of a village we had heard was in the valley."

"The Hanalei Valley," Caitlin identified it for him. "Yes, there is a village there. There are also many taro patches and a river winding through it. It's a very peaceful, beautiful place—quite lush and green from all the rainfall on this side of the island. But aside from enjoying its beauty, why did you go there?"

"I was going to barter for supplies," John explained. "We need provisions now, during our stay, and of course we'll need even more when we finally sail away."

"Of course," Caitlin said, her heart thumping in her ears. Would *she* be aboard the schooner when it sailed? Where would she be going? She knew *nothing* of Gerrick Scott's life—where he came from, where he'd be returning. Nor, she suddenly realized, did she *want* to leave the islands; they were her home.

"I never even got as far as the village," John continued. "On the way I was met by a group of men—one of whom, a fat old fellow, seemed of great importance."

"The village chief, one of the old *ali'i*. He's not the most important man on the island, but he *does* control the valley. It's part of a pie-shaped wedge of land running from the heart of Mount Waialeale to the sea, over which he has complete jurisdiction. I know him well. He converted to Christianity many years ago."

"You *know* him!" John exclaimed. "Then perhaps you can help me speak to him on our behalf. I think he wants our ship in exchange for provisioning us."

Shock, disbelief, and outrage mingled on John's round face. "I don't understand the language, but from his gestures and those of his advisors—the men who came with him—he seemed to be demanding the ship. I hurried back here to tell Gerrick, but I'll be damned if I can find him. The crew doesn't know where he went . . . and now that *ali'i* fellow is camped down on the beach and won't allow anyone to bring us food or fresh water."

Despite her guilt—for *she* knew where Gerrick had gone—Caitlin had to smile at John's frustration. "The traders and the whalers have made the people greedy, Mr. Reynolds. There was a time when the people gave all they had for little more than a smile from their guests. But the islanders have learned some hard lessons. Always, the traders *took*, and if they gave in return, they gave useless baubles—a string of beads or a broken-bladed knife. The chiefs then got wiser, and now even the lesser chiefs want what the greater chiefs and kings have succeeded in getting—iron implements, ships, guns, even cannons. The *ali'i* whom you met today has no ship, but on the other side of the island, the *ali'i* at Waimea does have one or two; a Russian even once built a fort there."

"We can't give him *our* ship!" John stood in astonishment. "Miss Price, you must come down to the beach and explain this to him. We *do* have tools, and Gerrick also brought rum . . ."

Now Caitlin stood. "No rum, Mr. Reynolds. I am shocked you'd even suggest it."

"I *didn't* suggest it, Miss Price. I begged Gerrick not to bring rum to trade, but he insisted. I don't want to barter the rum, but frankly, if we can't get this fellow to see reason, we'll have to leave immediately in search of fresh water. We probably should have stopped at Oahu first and made all our arrangements with King Kamehameha himself. But Gerrick—Captain Scott—was so anxious to begin looking for his brother . . ."

"You needn't leave *yet*, Mr. Reynolds. I believe I can persuade the chief to be more cooperative. My uncle has many times preached to him regarding the sin of greed and the amassing of private wealth—which the chief *learned* from the *haoles*. In my uncle's absence, the chief is simply succumbing to an old, recurring temptation. If I speak to him, however, and remind him of his Christian duties . . ."

"Miss Price, you are a treasure and a godsend!" John came toward her, arms outstretched, but Caitlin stepped behind her chair, keeping it between her and the big American.

"I don't know how to thank you, Miss Price," John went on. "As you can see, we are desperately in need of an interpreter, someone who knows the language *and* the people, and also has some influence over them. I know you detest Captain Scott, but if you knew his family and how they mourn the loss of Gerrick's brother . . ."

"What are you asking of me, Mr. Reynolds?"

"I'm asking you to *help* us, Miss Price. Not just today with the chief, but also afterward, when we begin searching the island."

"You want me to accompany you as an interpreter?"

"Exactly." John looked so hopeful, so entreating, that Caitlin again grew suspicious of his motives.

"I thought you were more interested in saving souls than in helping Captain Scott locate his brother," she stiffly admonished. "I thought your primary concern was for the spiritual well-being of the islanders."

"It *is!*" John protested. "But as Gerrick's friend, I must also attempt to save *his* soul. I can't simply abandon him. Between us, as we help him search, we could perhaps soften his hard, unrepentent heart."

"I—I don't know," Caitlin hedged. "It wouldn't be proper for me to accompany you alone, two *unmarried* men . . ."

"You could take along a companion," John prompted, unaware that by not correcting her, he was revealing something of desperate interest to Caitlin. "Another woman, perhaps? Someone you know and trust."

Caitlin immediately thought of Pikake, whose company she would enjoy even if she *was* married to Gerrick, and the matter of propriety was thus resolved.

"I—I'll have to think about it, Mr. Reynolds. . . . That can all be decided later. Hadn't we better do first things first? If you'll lead the way, I'll go down to the beach with you, and try and persuade the chief to accept something *less* than your ship in exchange for food and water."

It took Caitlin all of ten minutes to convince the chief of the Hanalei Valley to settle for the finely made chisels, hammers, and saws that Gerrick had brought aboard his ship, the *Naughty Lady*, the name of which reminded Caitlin yet again of the sort of man Gerrick was. She counted out enough items to purchase hogs, chickens, and fresh fruits and vegetables to feed the crew for a period of several weeks. The rest she held back, but only after displaying the tools—including a large, curved knife the chief fancied—and indicating that they were for future trade.

The chief, a tall, portly old gentleman with a childlike face but shrewd little eyes, greedily studied the remaining items, but then his glance strayed to the schooner anchored in the harbor. As he studied it, disappointment showed on his face. He twitched his shoulders in his short, feathered cape—a symbol of his royalty—tossed his head in its close-fitting, feathered helmet, and hitched up his *malo*.

"I will have that ship one day," he said to Caitlin in Hawaiian.

"You have no need of it," Caitlin responded. "When you wish to travel on the water, you have canoes aplenty to take you wherever you wish to go."

"I will have the ship," the old chief repeated stubbornly.

"What is he saying?" John asked beside her.

"It is nothing for you to worry about," Caitlin said. "Some of your crew must now get your water barrels and accompany the chief's men, who will show them where to

111

get fresh water."

"Of course. Right away!" John turned from her and began issuing instructions to Gerrick's crew members, who waited sullenly on the beach.

Many of the crew, Caitlin noticed, were armed with pistols and cutlasses; if she had not come, there might very well have been a fight. Another thought flashed through her mind: Had Gerrick been here, would *he* have requested her help? Or instead would he have countenanced fighting?

She smiled at the old *ali'i*. "Laanui," she addressed him by name. "Lately, I have missed you at Bible class. You used to come and watch and listen—and you were doing so well learning your letters. Had you not ceased coming, you would almost be ready to begin reading God's word for yourself."

Laanui shrugged his wide shoulders, his child's face wreathed in an apologetic grin, as he looked out at her from the depths of the tall, crowned helmet. "Tutu Caitlin, I am an old man still clinging to the ways of his ancestors. The old ways are dead and gone now, but still, I remember. . . . My head is so filled with memories there is no room for these new ideas. Teach the young ones how to read and write the *palapala*. When I die, I had rather go home to Kane and Lono, and to Ku and Kanaloa . . ."

At mention of the four major Hawaiian gods, Caitlin immediately took offense. "There *is* no Kane and Lono— nor a Pele, Maui, or Laka," she insisted, naming some of the lesser gods as well. "They are all dead, Laanui! When your great Queen Kaahumanu sat down to eat with King Liholiho, the old laws, the *kapus*, were broken, and the ancient gods were no more. You must now embrace the new."

"Not I, Tutu . . ." Laanui said gently. "Go and complain to Governor Kaikioewa, if you wish, but I will not resume the Bible classes. I am too old."

"You are not too old to covet that ship," Caitlin pointed out. "And you willingly accept the tools and other goods the traders bring you."

Laanui began to laugh, his laughter welling from his large chest like a rumble of thunder. "That is different, Tutu! Only my heart belongs to the old ways; my hands . . ." He stretched them out. "My hands enjoy what the traders bring. Next time I trade, I want that big knife—and I also want that ship."

"Is anything wrong?" Hearing the chief's laughter, John had hurried back to her side, his dark eyes worried.

"Nothing is wrong," Caitlin answered sadly. "Except the corruption I have helped to further."

John frowned. "What is it? Is he still demanding the ship?"

"He'll not take your ship," Caitlin assured him. "If he insists on the ship, I'll go over his head to the governor of Kauai, who serves at Kamehameha's pleasure. Neither the king nor the governor would allow him to have it—especially if they learned what *I* would tell them about Chief Laanui."

"Caitlin, we are deeply indebted to you. Where is this governor? Perhaps, we should go and meet him."

"He lives where the Wailua River flows out into the sea. By water, it isn't far. But I doubt that he is there now. Often, he goes to Oahu or Maui to confer with the king—and he is also a good friend of the missionaries."

Chief Laanui grinned. "Laanui—good—friend—also," he repeated haltingly. "Good—friend—of—missionaries."

"He understands English?" John asked, amazed.

"Only a few words. He doesn't wish to expand his learning."

"Oh, look! Here comes Gerrick!" John cried. "Now, when we no longer need him, he finally appears."

Caitlin whirled to see where John was pointing. Her heart had leaped into her throat at the mere mention of Gerrick's name, and as she watched him come striding toward her, she couldn't help devouring him with her eyes. He seemed surprised to find her there, and even more surprised to see John.

"What's going on here?" he snapped, and Caitlin desperately hoped John would explain everything, be-

113

cause she had suddenly lost her voice.

"Gerrick! Where have you been?" John exploded, and Gerrick was just enough taken aback by the question to pause before he answered.

"I don't believe I have to account for my whereabouts to anyone," he responded coolly, searching his friend's face for clues to what was happening.

His gaze slid to Caitlin. She had certainly wasted no time seeking out John; had she told him what had happened by the pool? Jealousy swept him in a hot, burning wave. He didn't *want* John speaking to Caitlin—and didn't want Caitlin thinking that John was a better man than he was.

"Gerrick, this man is the chief of Hanalei. He came here to trade with us. He wanted our ship, but I ran and got Caitlin and she talked him out of it. We've just concluded our bargaining, and everything is settled—satisfactorily, I might add." John grinned triumphantly, darting Caitlin an admiring look that set Gerrick's teeth on edge.

"I'll be the judge of how satisfactory the bargaining was." Slowly, Gerrick turned his attention to the big Hawaiian standing beside Caitlin.

The man was dressed in an outfit that Gerrick found both ludicrous and majestic. On his head, he wore a yellow-feathered helmet that looked like an ancient Roman centurion's, and encircling his shoulders was a glossy, red-feathered cape. Gerrick peered at the feathers—plucked from birds of which he had no knowledge—and conceded that great workmanship and skill must have been required to assemble and fasten the plumage together. Still, the big Hawaiian was only a savage, naked beneath his cape, except for the hip-hugging garment concealing his loins.

"Aloha," he said to the chief, using the Hawaiian greeting that Ilima had taught him.

Surprise flashed in Caitlin's eyes, and her lips tightened in faint displeasure. The chief, however, grinned.

"Aloha!" he boomed.

Caitlin whispered something to the chief, and Gerrick rounded on her. "What are you telling him?"

"That you are the captain of the ship in the harbor," she answered levelly, her cheeks reddening beneath his gaze.

The chief then spoke, gesturing and grinning, and finally pointing to Gerrick's ship. Gerrick raised his eyebrows at Caitlin.

"He says he is pleased by the outcome of today's bargaining, but next time, he will not trade unless you are here."

"Why is that?" Gerrick demanded, frustrated that he couldn't understand.

"Because next time, he will not settle until he gains your ship."

"He'll never have my ship. The idea is preposterous."

"That's why I went to get Caitlin," John interjected. "I couldn't make the fellow understand."

Gerrick smiled at the chief, but inwardly, he was seething. "Chief, I'll see you in hell before I'll trade my ship to you."

"I can't tell him *that*," Caitlin protested, her blue-gray eyes alarmed.

"Then, just tell him I'll think about it."

Caitlin spoke softly to the chief, and whatever she said seemed to please him, for he smiled and bowed, beckoned to his followers who stood a respectful distance away, and then walked past Gerrick without another word. His retinue of natives quickly began gathering the pile of tools that lay on the mat in the sand. Taking note of each item, Gerrick said to John, "I hope we've food for several days at least, considering how much you've given him."

"We have food for several *weeks*," John informed him gleefully. "Thanks to Miss Price. She has also agreed to serve as our interpreter when we go searching for your brother. At least, she's agreed to think about it."

"Oh?" Gerrick stared at Caitlin, who met his gaze for only a moment before she looked away. "And just how did you persuade her, John? Or perhaps I should ask that of

115

Miss Price herself."

Gerrick gave John his back as he faced Caitlin and waited for her answer. The girl was completely unfathomable; why would she even hint she might help them after her behavior earlier today? Distraught and half weeping, she had fled from him—only to respond to a request for assistance that must have come moments later, after she arrived back home. Or had John somehow encountered her on the path?

No, Gerrick decided. Her hair was neatly combed and secured in her usual, severe, confining braids, and her dress had obviously been smoothed and straightened. She *must* have returned home before John found her—and Gerrick's jealousy was again aroused. *He* still had no idea where she lived. Instead of pursuing her, as he should have done, he'd remained for an hour or more at the pool—debating what he ought to do and trying to sort through his vastly disturbed feelings.

"Miss Price?" he prodded. "Are you *really* considering helping us? And if so, *why*, when I know how much you despise me?"

She lifted her long lashes, and he saw the same turmoil in her eyes that he felt inside himself. "Captain Scott," she said breathlessly, "I must speak with you alone. I . . . I . . ."

Her faltering hesitation made Gerrick grasp her arm and begin guiding her down the beach, out of John's earshot. He had the feeling that if she didn't say now what she wanted to say, she might *never* say it. And he also had the feeling that something momentous was about to happen. Whatever it was, he didn't want to miss it. Where Caitlin Price was concerned, he didn't want to miss anything.

Chapter Nine

The last thing Caitlin saw before Gerrick began escorting her down the beach was John Reynolds's puzzled face, his questioning eyes. They passed other curious faces; Gerrick's crew members watched her with expressions that bordered on insolence. Their glances seemed to say—who *is* this brazen woman, and what business has she with our captain?

Caitlin knew a moment of faintness; a ringing began in her ears, and the late afternoon sun so bedazzled her eyes that if Gerrick had not been holding her arm, she might have stumbled and fallen. It was all so unreal—this walk down the beach. What was she *doing?* Was this really happening?

I must not be a coward, she counseled herself. I must embrace my duty.

It was the only clear thought to which she could cling. All her life she had been doing her duty. Never had she flinched from it. That John had sought her aid with Chief Laanui seemed like divine intervention. Once again she'd been placed in Gerrick's company, and before she could lose her nerve and flee trembling back to the house, she must do what her conscience dictated; she must insist that Gerrick Scott marry her.

"This is far enough," she heard herself say.

"Excellent," Gerrick responded. "Would you care to sit beneath a palm tree as you did with John the other day?

117

Or do you feel more comfortable standing?"

"Nothing would make me feel comfortable, Captain Scott—for what I have to say is . . . is most difficult."

Caitlin stole a glance at Gerrick, but his green-eyed perusal so unnerved her that she quickly looked away and focused instead on the frothing surf gently lapping the shore. Sea birds were calling in the sky, and the late afternoon light was pure and golden. Everything shone with a soft-edged radiance, the harsh glare of the sun diminished, so that colors gleamed less sharply, and she was achingly conscious of the island's beauty.

"I . . . I suspect that I am different from most women you've known, Captain Scott," she began, searching for just the right words.

"That's true," he agreed. "You are more beautiful than most."

"I . . . I don't mean my looks."

"Perhaps not—but you *are* beautiful."

"Please don't say such things," she pleaded. "They aren't true—and I—I *must* be truthful with you, today, and . . . and always."

Gerrick made no response to this, but only stood regarding her thoughtfully. Caitlin could *feel* his eyes boring into her. "I am a spinster, Captain Scott. My uncle has been trying to arrange a marriage for me with a missionary from New England, but so far, with no success. You see, most of the missionaries arriving here are already married, but before his death, my father had hoped to arrange a betrothal by proxy to someone still on the mainland, with marriage to follow immediately upon his arrival in the islands."

"You mean a marriage to some jackass you'd never have met?"

Gerrick's language shocked her, but Caitlin decided to ignore it—for now. "Oh, we would have corresponded—conducted our courting by mail as it were. There wouldn't have been much need for an extensive courting; it would

118

already have been determined how much we have in common. By that, I mean the same religious convictions, the same goals in life, the same morals, and the same expectations."

"Sounds extremely dull," Gerrick drawled provokingly.

"We would have been extremely happy!" Caitlin flared. "Our lives would have been based on mutual respect and trust."

"And now he would have no respect for you—and certainly no trust."

"That is correct." Caitlin boldly locked eyes with him. "I'm no longer a fit candidate to be the wife of a pious, God-fearing missionary. I could . . . I could never admit to my . . . my . . ."

"Your normal womanly instincts?"

"My *sins!* My c—carnal desires, which no missionary should harbor in his breast!"

"Or *her* breast—especially not in such a sweet, innocent breast."

"You *mock* me, sir!" Caitlin cried. Losing her nerve, she would have fled his odious presence, but Gerrick grabbed her by the shoulders.

"Stop it, Caitlin! You don't have to go through this. I *understand* that you cannot yet accept your sensuality. You believe that what you feel is not normal and healthy—but as God is my witness, it *is.* You are a beautiful, desirable woman with normal physical and biological urges. It isn't *wrong* to want a man. What is wrong is that you *deny* these feelings. They *do* have a purpose, you know!"

"What purpose!" Caitlin spat. "All they do is render me miserable!"

A gentleness crept into Gerrick's manner. Drawing her close, he slid his arms about her waist and would not allow her to pull away from him. "Your feelings serve the purpose of bringing together two stubborn idiots who otherwise might not have noticed each other."

Not wanting to accept this, Caitlin struggled to free

119

herself. "I *won't* fall into bed with you just because I want you!"

"I don't expect you to. A woman like you requires more from a man—and I'm prepared to offer more. For me, marrying will be difficult, a sacrifice of my long-cherished freedom, but not as difficult as never having you."

"What are you saying?" Caitlin gasped. "Speak plainly!"

"You *know* what I'm saying; I want to marry you, *now*, tonight—before either of us can change our minds."

"B—but . . ." Caitlin's mind spun with protests. This was what she wanted, but *tonight* . . . Tonight was much too soon!

Gerrick tilted her face to meet his. "Tonight," he repeated. "For if I cannot have you tonight, I'll take you here, right now, on this beach in front of everyone."

And with that he brought his mouth down hard upon hers and kissed her until she had no will to breathe, much less utter a protest. Only dimly, in the back of her churning brain, did she realize that he had just made it impossible for her to refuse. His entire crew must be watching, and the islanders—including Chief Laanui—were probably also watching. To save her reputation, she *had* to marry him, tonight. Indeed, the sooner, the better.

When at last he drew back, flushed and breathing hoarsely, echoing her own ravaged state, Caitlin gathered her scattered wits and seized the opportunity to mention something of which he might not be aware. She herself had only just thought of it. "There is no one here to marry us. My uncle is away."

Gerrick held on to her, the pressure of his hands continuing to send shock waves through her body. "Surely, there is someone."

She shook her head, and his brow furrowed. Then, suddenly, a light came into his eyes. "I'd almost forgotten. My own ship's chaplain can perform the ceremony."

"You have a chaplain aboard your schooner?" Caitlin queried disbelievingly.

"Of course." Gerrick grinned at her incredulity. "He is

also . . . my first mate. But from time to time, he serves as chaplain, trying like John to rescue me from the fires of hell."

"I . . . I didn't know that," Caitlin said humbly.

"There is much about me that you don't know, sweet Caitlin. The first days of our marriage will be a learning experience for us both. Indeed, I believe I should delay searching for my brother for a week or two—so we have some time in which to get better acquainted."

"We could sail to Maui!" Caitlin exclaimed, an idea shaping itself in her mind. "We could even delay our marriage until we find my Uncle George, and he could then marry us."

"No!" Gerrick cried with surprising vehemence. "I will not compromise your reputation by taking you aboard my ship as an unmarried woman. Your uncle would hardly approve—especially since you'd have to stay in my cabin, and there's no one suitable to act as chaperone."

"My friend, Pikake, could accompany me . . ."

"She is Hawaiian, and everyone knows how lenient Hawaiians can be. Pikake would gladly leave you alone, should I desire to creep in and sleep with you. *After* our marriage, we could visit Maui, if you wish."

A blush crept up Caitlin's cheeks. What Gerrick said was true. Pikake was the last person she could trust as chaperone. Even worse, Caitlin herself could not be trusted to maintain a safe distance from Gerrick. Besides, if Caitlin tried to explain to her uncle and the other missionaries on Maui just *why* she was marrying Gerrick, a man so far outside the fold, they would strongly disapprove. But if she went to them already a married woman, what, indeed, could they say? She was of an age to marry whom she would. While her uncle's blessing would be nice to have, it wasn't strictly necessary. Who was Uncle George anyway to say who, when, or where she might wed?

"But I'm not certain I can be ready by this evening . . ." she demurred halfheartedly, remembering suddenly that she had nothing suitable to wear and no time to plan a feast or celebration which the Hawaiians would all expect.

"You don't have to do anything but show up," Gerrick said with a grin. "I'll take care of everything."

Caitlin gazed up into his eyes—glowing like the green depths of the sea where the surf broke over the coral. She still felt that this whole meeting was unreal. She, Caitlin Price, was going to marry a man she'd only just met, a man about whom she knew nothing except that he was a rogue and a scoundrel, and somehow, it seemed so right. Was she bewitched? Had she gone mad?

"Don't fight it, Caitlin," Gerrick whispered. "Fighting is useless, when in the end, you know you'll only succumb. And you do know that—as well as I."

"I—I *came* here to beg you to marry me," she admitted. "After what happened this afternoon, my father would have insisted upon it—but tonight! There's so much I must do!"

His teeth flashed whitely. "Then go and do it, my love. For if you stand here gazing at me another minute with those lovely, haunting eyes, I cannot be held responsible for my actions."

Such a wild fluttering of joy began in Caitlin's breast that she almost hugged herself. "I must go and find Pikake!"

Gerrick nodded. "The wedding will take place at moonrise here on the beach. If it rains, we'll hold it in my cabin aboard the ship!"

"Yes, oh yes!" Caitlin cried, her head spinning with thoughts of all she had to do before then. "I'll be ready."

Gerrick seized her hand and pressed her fingertips to his lips. "You had better be, Miss Price. . . . Now, run along, for I, too, have much to do."

Gerrick watched Caitlin hurry back up the beach, past his men and the Hawaiians who had been watching from a distance. There was such gladness in her walk, such a lilt and sway in her eager step, that his men couldn't keep their eyes from her. John, frowning furiously and looking as suspicious as any missionary, immediately set out to meet him.

"What was that all about?" John demanded. "Kissing her in broad daylight—and in front of everyone, too. Have you no consideration for her reputation or her delicate sensibilities? She'll be mortified when she stops to think about it. How did you gain her acquiescence? What lies are you spouting, now?"

"I merely asked her to marry me," Gerrick said. "And she has agreed. The wedding will take place tonight."

Dumbstruck, John could only stare at him. "But you and she . . . you only just met! And she hates you!"

"Not anymore." Gerrick laughed at his friend's expression. "It's the old Scott charm, my friend. I said I would woo her to my bed, and I did."

"You're sacrificing a hell of a lot, just to win a bet." John's dark eyes held chagrin, mixed with admiration and envy.

"I'm not sacrificing so very much. . . . Erasmus will perform the ceremony."

"Erasmus! But how can he marry the two of you? He's no preacher!"

"Caitlin doesn't know that," Gerrick quietly informed John. "And I'd be obliged if you didn't mention it."

John's mouth dropped open. There was a moment of stunned silence, and then John exhaled a long, deep breath. "You son of a bitch! This . . . this is the most despicable thing you've ever done. It sets a whole new record—even for you."

Gerrick shrugged. Now that John mentioned it, he *did* feel guilty. But he couldn't allow Caitlin time to rethink this whole thing. If she did, she'd back out of marrying him. Even one night of reflection would be dangerous; she'd consider his character, along with all the things she *didn't* know about him, and by morning, the wedding would be off. Good-bye, Caitlin. And good-bye, sandalwood.

"I'll be kind and gentle to her," Gerrick promised. "She'll be happier than she's ever been in her life."

"Until she learns what you've done!"

"Why should she learn of it? When we find the sandalwood, I'll make up some story about the dangers of the voyage to Canton, and how she must remain here, instead of accompanying us. Then, after we get to Canton, you can write to her and tell her that I'm dead; a storm at sea washed me overboard. She can declare herself a widow and look for a new husband—one more suitable for a missionary."

"You've got it all planned, haven't you?"

"I didn't—until just now. What's wrong with my plan? I'm gaining a beautiful woman in my bed, one who's sworn to love, honor, and obey me . . . and when I ask her to help us find the sandalwood, as my wife, she can't refuse."

"What if I reveal this wonderful plan to her ahead of time?" John demanded belligerently.

"You wouldn't do that."

"No, I wouldn't," John admitted after a pause. "But it isn't right, Gerrick. Caitlin Price is a decent woman. She doesn't deserve this."

Gerrick cocked an eyebrow at his friend. "Weren't you planning to tumble her into bed at the first opportunity?"

"Well, yes, but . . ."

"But nothing! If you had, she'd have hated herself the next morning. This way, she'll *love* herself. I don't see that I'm harming her at all. In her mind, when she's loving me she'll be gaining grace and storing up treasures in heaven. And so will I. I'll be preparing her for the next man—the one who will marry and cherish her as she ought to be cherished for the rest of her life. When I'm through, she'll be a fit consort for a king. Only an experienced lover, such as myself, can be trusted with awakening the sensuality of an unnaturally reticent woman such as Caitlin. In the hands of a lesser man, she'd only be ruined."

"I'd not have ruined her."

"No," Gerrick mused "You probably wouldn't—but you didn't win her, did you?"

*　　　*　　　*

124

"Tutu Caitlin, you are as beautiful as any Hawaiian *wahine* on her wedding night! I still can no believe this is really happening." Smiling, Pikake stepped back from adjusting the wreath of feathery scarlet lihua and creamy-white plumeria blossoms encircling Caitlin's head.

The girl's face was glowing, her eyes radiating admiration and approval. "It is about time, Tutu. All us Hawaiians who love you have been much worried because you so alone . . . woman *need* man, and man need woman. It is just as I always tell you."

Caitlin said nothing. Her eyes were drawn past Pikake to the chipped mirror on the wall above her sea chest. In that mirror stood a creature Caitlin did not recognize. Her high-necked dress, the least-worn *holoku* she possessed, seemed transformed by the double lei of flowers Pikake had insisted she must wear, and her long, shining hair lay in soft ringlets on her breast, another change Pikake had convinced her was appropriate for this night.

"Pikake . . . do you think Captain Scott will find me . . . pleasing?"

"If he do not, he blind!" Pikake snorted. "You prettiest *wahine* on Kauai tonight."

"You're not jealous?" Caitlin queried, turning to her friend in sudden worry. "After all, Captain Scott was first attracted to you."

Pikake vigorously shook her head in denial, almost dislodging her own wreath of hibiscus blossoms. "No, Tutu. Is right tall, handsome *haole* man should marry beautiful *haole* woman. Besides, I like other *haole*."

"What *haole*?" Caitlin demanded. "Pikake, what were you up to this afternoon? I thought you went upriver to find Inamoo."

"I did. But on way I see *haole* with dark brown hair and eyes speaking to Chief Laanui. He no see me, but I see him, and I think he very handsome *kane*—even more handsome than Captain Scott."

"Pikake, you stay away from John Reynolds!"

"Why, Tutu? Is he bad man?"

"No, but . . ." Caitlin could not really think of a good reason for forbidding Pikake to speak with John. She

125

didn't want to mention the reason most missionaries would have given: whites and islanders should not mix. The Missionary Board strictly forbade marriages between the two races. They would especially disapprove of such a marriage between two Christians—and thinking of it, Caitlin shuddered. She wanted John to be liked and accepted by the board; if she and John maintained strong religious ties, quite possibly Gerrick would eventually yield to conversion.

"By his own admission, John Reynolds is an upright Christian," she hedged. "But one day he'll go back to the mainland and leave you here, alone. You mustn't set your heart on him, Pikake, or you'll wind up hurt and disappointed."

"Oh, Tutu," Pikake said dreamily. "Never have I seen a *kane* with such strength as he has. Maybe I marry him . . ."

"Pikake, you haven't even met the man—or *have* you?"

"No, Tutu." Pikake giggled. "But I know the minute I see him that he perfect *kane* for me."

"Nonsense!" Caitlin countered briskly, giving her gown a final smoothing. But she wondered if it really *was* nonsense; hadn't she known the minute she saw Gerrick of the irresistible attraction between *them*? She would just have to pray that John Reynolds saw nothing in her little friend. An intimate relationship between the two would be impossible; if they *did* come to love each other, only heartbreak awaited them. They would become outcasts; both in the islands and on the mainland, decent folks would probably shun them. A white man with a brown-skinned wife was unwelcome everywhere—except among the worst elements of society.

"We'd better be going now, Pikake. Take the lantern and lead the way. We mustn't be late; I've not yet had time to consult the preacher as to how this ceremony will proceed, and there are certain things I must ask him beforehand."

"How fortunate Captain Scott *have* preacher," Pikake exclaimed. "Or you and Captain Scott might have to wait long time."

126

"Yes, it *is* fortunate," Caitlin agreed. "I only hope he has *agreed* to perform the ceremony without a prior posting of the banns."

This *had* worried her when she first thought of it, but then she had remembered that many of the missionaries had married as precipitously as she herself. Some had married only an hour or so before sailing for the islands. In such cases, the banns were merely read three times in succession, and if no one objected, the ceremony was performed without further delay.

Doubtless, this preacher would do the same, with little or no argument. After all, she and Gerrick had the rest of their lives to get to know each other. Many marriages took place between people who were practically strangers. All that was needed was enough love and commitment to carry the couple over the rough spots. No matter what the revelations about each other in the weeks and months following the wedding, enough love could conquer all.

And I will be such a perfect, loving, kind, obedient wife that Gerrick will *never* have reason to find fault with me, Caitlin promised herself. As for finding fault with Gerrick, she could think of nothing that would diminish the overwhelming emotions he aroused within her; God must have *planned* for them to find each other. Gerrick Scott was her life and destiny.

And with that single thought in mind, she eagerly hurried after Pikake.

Chapter Ten

"Now, you're sure you know what to do, Erasmus?" Gerrick inquired of his collar-tugging first mate.

Erasmus glowered at him from beneath shaggy gray eyebrows. "This is the most damn-fool thing ye've ever asked of me, Cap'n. An' I don't know why I'm doin' it 'cept I'm glad t' see ye showin' some interest in a female 'stead o' broodin' in your cabin like you been doin' these past few months. I'd about give up on ye."

"You wouldn't have done that, Erasmus. Why, you've been rescuing me from my mistakes ever since I was a young, green cabinboy and got so sick my first voyage out that I wanted to throw myself overboard."

"Should have let you," Erasmus grumbled, again tugging on the high, confining collar that Gerrick had insisted he wear. "I've had my hands full with ye ever since—what with one fool escapade after another. I'd hoped once't you rose t' cap'n, you'd leave off gettin' yerself inta scrapes."

"Don't worry, Erasmus. This scrape is far less dangerous than some I've gotten myself into. Miss Price holds the key to making wealthy men of us all. She's also a *very* beautiful woman. I wouldn't mind marrying her in a real ceremony."

"Ye wouldn't?" The shaggy eyebrows lifted, and Erasmus's fierce blue eyes stabbed at Gerrick, rocking his composure.

Suddenly realizing what he'd said, Gerrick shook off his discomfiture with a jaunty shrug. "It's true. Though how long our marriage would last is another story. No woman will ever leg-shackle me for life, my friend. I'm too much like you. The sea is my only mistress."

"It remains t' be seen whether ye're like me or not, boy," Erasmus snorted. "As f'r whether or not I can fool the wench inta believin' I'm a preacher, that also remains t' be seen. I ain't never conducted no weddin' b'fore. Ain't never been to more'n two or three weddin's in me entire life, an' the ones I did attend, I was too drunk t' pay much attention."

"Brother Erasmus, you will be magnificent. All you have to do is read the proper words, pause to let us say *our* parts, and the thing will be done. Miss Price will never know the difference."

Erasmus opened the heavy black Psalm Book Gerrick had dredged from his sea chest. Like most sea captains, Gerrick always carried both a Bible and a hymnal though he rarely read either. Feeling a twinge of guilt, for his own father thought any man who didn't occasionally dip into the greatest book of all time was a dullard, Gerrick grinned encouragingly as Erasmus peered at the leather-bound volume in the smoky glow from the torches erected in a semicircle on the beach.

"I still ain't too good at readin', Cap'n." Erasmus silently mouthed his part.

"You can do it." Praying he was right, Gerrick stepped back and viewed his first mate critically.

Years ago, when he had first become a sea captain, Gerrick had forced Erasmus Mockensturm to learn to read. He hadn't wanted any officers who couldn't read and write—an important distinction between officers and ordinary seamen. Now, he was profoundly glad he'd made the blunt-spoken, fierce-looking, older man polish a few of his rough edges.

Dressed in a cutaway coat belonging to John and wearing boots, trousers, and shirt that were Gerrick's, Erasmus looked fairly civilized. A waistcoat and high collar with a painstakingly tied cravat completed his outfit. The colors were all dark and somber, as befitted a man of the cloth, and if the clothing didn't fit perfectly, Gerrick could only hope that Caitlin wouldn't notice in the smoky darkness.

Smooth-shaven for the first time in years, Erasmus had cheeks as baby pink as his bald spot. The crinkly silver hairs fringing his ears had at least been neatly trimmed, and Gerrick had ignored his threats and pleas that on no account would he stoop to bathing. Erasmus had not enjoyed undergoing the transformation from bearded, wild-haired, grog-smelling, salty old seaman to squeaky-clean, well-dressed minister, but for Gerrick's sake he had endured it with only a modicum of grumbling.

Too bad I can't do anything about that scar slashing his forehead or that pugnacious nose of his, Gerrick thought. *Without those, he'd be totally convincing.*

Glancing up from the Psalm Book and catching his eyes, Erasmus snarled, "Quit yur gawpin', Cap'n, or I ain't gonna do it."

"Don't be testy, Erasmus. I was just thinking how handsome you look."

"Huh! Ye want handsome, git somebody else. I can't hold a candle t' you or John. I ain't seed the two of ye lookin' better in years."

"John?" Gerrick surveyed the beach where his men were still bustling about, making certain everything was ready. He hadn't seen John since he had announced his intentions of staging the mock wedding. As John had already registered his disapproval, Gerrick wasn't too surprised. The losing of his bet was another reason for John to make himself scarce, though in the past, he had always shown amazing good grace and sportsmanship whenever he'd lost to Gerrick.

I'll let him sweat a bit, Gerrick thought, *before I tell him I'm not really interested in collecting on this particular bet.*

Suddenly, he spotted John headed in his direction. Erasmus had not exaggerated; John himself might have been the groom in his polished boots, fawn-colored pantaloons, and cutaway coat and waistcoat of deep chocolate brown. His waistcoat was shot through with gold threads, and Gerrick glanced down at his own attire and wished he'd brought something more festive than somber gray and cream. Despite what Erasmus thought, the colors Gerrick was wearing were more appropriate for a funeral than a wedding. Of course, when he'd left Newport, he'd never dreamed he'd be doing *this*.

"I was just looking for you, John," Gerrick informed his approaching friend. "Everything is in readiness—no thanks to you."

"Did you honestly expect me to assit you in staging this farce? I still think you are making a big mistake, Gerrick. And it's not just because I'm a poor loser."

"Spare me . . ." Gerrick held up his hand. "I don't want to hear any more of your objections. Tonight, when I'm closeted in my cabin with my new bride, you can ask yourself if I've made a mistake—and I'll wager you'll change your mind in a hurry."

John's dark brows drew downward. "For tonight, maybe. . . . When a man's thinking with his crotch instead of his brain, he can justify anything. Eventually, however, when passion fades, he has to face up to reality—and sometimes reality can be damned disheartening. You may discover you can't live with yourself after this."

"Now, John . . ." Gerrick clapped his friend's shoulder. You never *used* to take things so seriously. It's ironic; when I've finally recovered my sense of adventure and have begun to enjoy life again, *you* start playing the doom-crier. No matter what I do, I can't seem to please you."

"Perhaps I'm just jealous," John admitted with a sigh. "I *still* can't figure out how you wormed your way into her heart. I'm the one who should be marrying—or should I say, *deceiving* her. Once again, you get the lady . . ."

"There are other fish in the sea, my friend . . . and speaking of fish, I think I see one with Caitlin—yes! It's Pikake leading my lovely, unsuspecting lamb to her execution."

Gerrick pulled away from John and walked quickly down the beach toward the two women. For a moment, Pikake blocked his view of Caitlin, but Gerrick scarcely gave the petite girl a glance; his gaze was riveted to Caitlin—beautiful, breathtaking Caitlin, her radiant, silver-gold hair adorned with scarlet and cream-colored flowers.

She's the loveliest thing I've ever seen, Gerrick thought, a huge lump forming in his throat. His eyes devoured her, wanting to see all of her at once and wanting, at the same time, to savor every detail of her stunning beauty.

As usual, her dress was nondescript—not as badly faded as her brown one, but still, nothing to boast about. Though it lacked the full, Lady Gigot sleeves so popular back on the mainland, the pale blue color did bring out the blue of her eyes. The dress also fit her curves better, too, he noted, though it still strove to hide what he so much desired to see and enjoy. The thought rose unbidden: *When I get her home, I'll dress her in silks, satins, laces, and velvets that cling to her curves and accentuate, rather than conceal, them. Better yet, I'll keep her naked.*

The latter thought had a disturbing ring of familiarity, and he hastily brushed it aside, his gaze returning to Caitlin's glowing face, framed by the flowers and the long, incredible hair. She was watching him with a kind of mingled fear and excitement, her lips slightly parted, her cheeks flushed, and her blue-gray eyes luminous. Gerrick longed to crush her to him and bury his nose in her silken tresses.

Easy, man, easy, he cautioned himself. Don't frighten her any more than she is already. If you leap on her like a randy stallion, it may prove doubly difficult to overcome her inhibitions later on tonight.

As she came abreast of him, he fell in step beside her and proffered his arm. "Caitlin, my ravishing bride . . . I'm so glad you are prompt. The moon is rising; it's time to begin."

"It's rising already?" She lifted dazed eyes to study the star-studded sky wherein the moon had yet to make

132

an appearance.

Gerrick did not give her a chance to hesitate. Taking the torch from Pikake's small hand, he led Caitlin toward the semicircle of light in which Erasmus awaited them. John, he noticed with a stab of relief, was watching Pikake instead of Caitlin.

Good, he thought. I hope the little Hawaiian distracts the hell out of him.

"Come along," he urged. "Brother Erasmus is growing impatient."

Everything was happening so fast that Caitlin had the feeling she was being caught up in a whirlwind of hurricane force. Suddenly, she found herself standing in front of a scowling, pink-cheeked, scar-faced man who looked distinctly uncomfortable as he held his open Bible in front of his chest and kept glancing down at it nervously.

"Gerrick," she pleaded, pressing his arm, but when he turned to her, she half forgot what she was going to say.

In the torchlight, Gerrick's russet curls gleamed like polished copper, and his eyes glowed like emeralds. She was only dimly conscious of the quiet, elegant cut and fabric of his clothing, but all too heart-stoppingly aware of his potent masculinity. She yearned to feast her eyes on his handsome face, and she briefly pondered the mystery of why the harsh plane of his jaw always seemed so at odds with the mischief playing about his full lips. She wanted to memorize every inch of him, so she would always remember how he looked on this night of their wedding.

Oblivious to her surrounding, she barely noticed the shadowy figures drawing ever more closely to them. All she could sense and feel was Gerrick's commanding presence beside her, hurrying her onward, making things happen much too quickly for comprehension.

"Gerrick, what about the banns?"

"The banns?" His confusion was evident.

"Has Brother Erasmus agreed to waive the reading

133

of them?"

"What? Oh, yes, of course. Don't worry your pretty head about it."

My pretty head. He thought she was pretty. And hadn't he earlier called her "ravishing"? Caitlin's heart skipped joyfully, and she bestowed a grateful smile on the chaplain who had agreed to marry them on such short notice. The man returned her smile with a baleful glare from beneath bushy, gray eyebrows, and for a moment, he looked so fierce that she felt intimidated.

"I'm gittin' tired o' waitin', Cap'n. Are ye ready t' start or not?" Brother Erasmus gruffly inquired. "I ain't gittin' any younger, ye know."

Caitlin was startled. She had expected a minister to sound more educated, but perhaps this one had spent too long a time in the company of rough-speaking sailors.

"You may begin, Chaplain Mockensturm." Gerrick gave Caitlin a reassuring smile and, lowering his voice, added softly, "Don't mind if Brother Erasmus fumbles a bit. He doesn't get much opportunity to perform weddings."

Caitlin blushed beneath Gerrick's intent gaze. He laced his fingers through hers and squeezed her hand, and Caitlin only half heard the fierce-looking, old man clear his throat and begin the ceremony. She clung to Gerrick's hand, barely listening to the clumsily recited words of the wedding ritual. Suddenly, Gerrick turned his head and said sharply, "John! You wouldn't!"

Jolted from her inner musings, she realized that Brother Erasmus had just asked if anyone present had any objections or knew of any impediments to the marriage. John, apparently, had stepped forward to mention some.

John's serious expression communicated both apology and warning. "Forgive me, Caitlin. I merely wanted to remind you that you've known Gerrick for such a short time. He's a complete stranger to you. Though I've agreed to act as best man, I can't help suggesting that you wait until you get to know him better. In view of the great differences in your backgrounds, a longer courtship would not be amiss."

Caitlin smiled her appreciation of his concern—misplaced though it was. "If you are worrying about Gerrick's lack of religion compared to mine, please desist, John. Gerrick's salvation is now in *my* hands, not yours. You may be assured that I will daily storm the gates of heaven with my prayers that Gerrick one day acknowledges his spiritual needs."

She turned back to Brother Erasmus. "Please continue, sir. I know exactly what I'm doing."

After a reproachful look at John, Gerrick again squeezed her hand, and Caitlin was once more transported to some magical, mystical place. The rest of the ceremony passed in a blur, and she did not even realize it was over until Gerrick tilted her face to meet his and gently lowered his lips to hers in a breath-robbing kiss that made her feel so faint she had to clutch at his sleeve for support. Then, Pikake was throwing her arms about Caitlin's neck and wildly hugging her, and Gerrick was shaking hands with his men—even John, whose mouth was still thinned in grim disapproval.

Curious Hawaiians clustered about them—glad for any opportunity to celebrate. Caitlin saw all of her students and many of the older men and women who had been far friendlier in her father's time than they had been since her uncle's arrival. Some she hadn't seen since Uncle George had preached his first fire and brimstone sermon, accusing them all of the worst of sins. She was kept busy greeting the islanders and accepting their congratulations as they expressed their wholehearted approval that "Tutu Caitlin" had at last found herself a husband.

Finally, Gerrick firmly grasped her elbow and led her to a place of honor at the feast-laden mats spread upon the sand. With a start, Caitlin realized that she was about to participate in her first *luau*. Timidly, she knelt down, and Gerrick took his place beside her.

"How did you manage all of this on such short notice?" she asked, anxiously eyeing the sailors uncorking a cask that *had* to contain spirits of some sort.

"I managed," Gerrick responded smugly, then seeing her worried look, he bent over and whispered in her ear. "I trust your cursed religion doesn't forbid festivities to celebrate a wedding."

"No, but . . ." Not wanting to spoil his joyous mood, Caitlin chose her words carefully. "Even at weddings, spirits are never consumed, and dancing is not allowed either."

"Oh?" Gerrick quirked an eyebrow at her. "Then I'm glad Brother Erasmus is not as strict as your priggish missionaries. Surely, there's no sin in *moderate* drinking and dancing, especially on such a happy occasion. How else can one fully celebrate?"

"We do sing hymns," Caitlin suggested hopefully.

"Hymns? I hadn't thought of that. Later, perhaps, I'll suggest it."

But to Caitlin's dismay, Gerrick made no move to stop the sailors from passing around wooden mugs filled to the brim with the liquid drawn from the cask. One grinning man even brought a mug to Gerrick and then, turning to her, inquired jovially, "Shall I fetch a tote for you, Miz Scott?"

Caitlin was so taken aback at being addressed by her new name that for a moment, she couldn't respond, and Gerrick smoothly answered for her. "Mrs. Scott doesn't partake of spirits, Emmanuel. But you can have hers if you like."

"Gerrick!" Caitlin exclaimed.

Gerrick shot her an amused grin. "Relax, my lovely Caitlin. You must become accustomed to looking the other way when my men want to enjoy themselves. I have already instructed them to mind their manners tonight, but you cannot expect them to behave like pious children. They've been waiting a long time to see me get married; they are entitled to enjoy the spectacle."

"Does that mean you will allow the Hawaiians to perform the *hula?*" Caitlin inquired hoarsely, unable to keep from showing her disapproval.

Gerrick seized her trembling hand and carried it to his

lips. "Not if you don't wish it, my love. In that, I will indulge you." Pressing a kiss on her heated palm, Gerrick never took his eyes from her face as he lowered his voice to a cajoling caress. "If this marriage is ever to work, we must both learn to compromise, mustn't we?"

Caitlin swallowed any further arguments. She couldn't think straight with Gerrick enacting bold intimacies on her hand. His seductive voice, combined with his burning touch and gaze, seared her very soul with a white-hot intensity. Compromise. Yes, she *must* try and meet him halfway in everything—at least until he could be made to see the error in his thinking.

"Let us eat and drink, sweet lady," he urged provocatively. "I mean to take our leave as soon as politeness permits."

Caitlin ate little. What she did eat, she barely tasted, and when Brother Erasmus brought out a fiddle and began playing lively tunes which made the sailors leap to their feet and attempt wild jigs, she only glanced at him in faint surprise. Somehow, her disapproval had mysteriously trickled away. Gerrick had insisted she sample a pungent liquid in half a coconut shell that he claimed was a specially made refreshment for their wedding, and she wondered if he was mistaken in believing that the strange concoction contained no spirits.

As she had never tasted spirits, she herself could not judge, but Gerrick certainly should know. She wondered what made the drink so warming as it burned its way down to her stomach. And she wondered, too, why she felt so lightheaded. Beside her, Pikake was giggling at something John was saying, her face flushed and animated, and her voice pitched much higher than normal.

"Pikake, are you feeling all right?"

"Oh, yes, Tutu Caitlin!" Pikake trilled. "John Reynolds is telling me funny stories."

Smiling broadly, John leaned around Pikake and winked. "Not funny stories—*jokes*."

137

"Yokes!" Pikake repeated, in a gale of laughter. "So that is what you call them!"

Becoming alarmed, Caitlin frowned. Pikake was acting so strangely. After she and Gerrick departed, who would protect her friend from all the drinking, dancing sailors?

"John," she cried. "Will you look after Pikake? I—I'm worried about what will happen after we leave the party."

"Of course, Caitlin. You know I'll allow nothing bad to happen to your charming little friend."

Charming. John thought Pikake was charming. Caitlin looked at Pikake and saw that the girl was gazing adoringly at John. Then she looked closely at John and saw that the big, muscular man was grinning back at Pikake, his eyes amused and indulgent.

"Actually, it would be better if you went home immediately, Pikake. Didn't I see Inamoo here? Your brother should be the one to take you."

"I no want to leave *yet*, Tutu Caitlin," Pikake protested. "And Inamoo *not* going to want to take me." The girl's eyes fastened on John. "If John no want to come with me, I find my way home alone. Is no problem."

As Caitlin watched in growing consternation, John took Pikake's tiny hand in his huge ones. "I'd be honored to escort you home, my dear."

Pikake giggled. "What is 'escort,' John Reynolds?"

"I will explain it to you, if you will then teach me the Hawaiian word meaning the same thing."

"I don't think . . ." Caitlin began, but Gerrick was suddenly grasping her arm and gently turning her to face him.

"Have you had enough, Caitlin? I think we can leave now, without being rude about it."

"Already? But it's still so early, Gerrick!" At the thought of what was to come—her wedding night—Caitlin was terrified. She could not even remember what had occupied her attention only a moment previously. Nor did she have any idea where Gerrick meant to take her; they hadn't discussed where they would pass the night.

Gerrick's wide grin grew tender and teasing. "Don't look so afraid, sweetheart. It won't be as bad as you think. I'm the gentlest of lovers."

A scalding flush crept up Caitlin's neck. How could he be so casual about what lay ahead? And how could she have put off thinking about it until just this minute? She had been so pleased and happy about the wedding; she hadn't once considered that she'd actually be spending the night in Gerrick's bed.

Her throat swelled with sudden fear and shyness. Desperately, she sought to delay the inevitable, but her suggestion that they remain awhile longer came out as a mere squeek of protest. Still grinning, Gerrick lifted a coconut shell to her suddenly dry lips. "Here, you look as if you need this. Go on, drink. It isn't going to hurt you."

With two shaking hands, Caitlin grasped the coconut shell and drained its contents. Immediately, she began choking on the powerful concoction, and Gerrick burst out laughing as he patted her on the back.

"Gerrick, what *is* this you've been making me drink all evening?" she sputtered when she had caught her breath. "Are you *sure* it contains no spirits?"

She thought she saw him wink at John over her shoulder, but when she drew back to look at him more closely—his face was swimming before her eyes—he merely smiled at her and cocked his head. "Would I lie to you, sweet Cait? I assure you; the brew is perfectly harmless. You *do* feel more relaxed now, don't you?"

Caitlin swayed against him, trying with all her might to gather her scattered wits. "Yes," she said thickly. "I do. And my name is Caitlin, not Cait." Only her father had ever shortened her name to Cait—and then only when he was in a teasing mood. "Are you teasing me, Gerrick?"

To her horror, she heard herself giggle, and then the urge to laugh welled up in her throat until she could no longer resist it. Clinging to Gerrick's shirtfront, she gave vent to the overwhelming urge. Her laughter ended on a hiccup.

"You've given her too much," she heard John say.

"The effects won't last long—just long enough to alleviate her fears," Gerrick responded. Rising, he lifted her into his arms and cradled her as one would a baby.

The sensation was so soothing—so comfortable. She cuddled against his chest and sighed. "I'm not afraid of *you*, Gerrick. I'll never be afraid of you."

Chapter Eleven

Gerrick gently deposited Caitlin on his bed, and then lit a whale oil lamp hanging from a hook overhead. In its soft warm glow, he saw that his cabin was festooned with flowers and cleaner than it had been in weeks. Despite Erasmus's misgivings over posing as a minister, he had done a wonderful job overseeing the wedding preparations. Even the longboat that had borne Gerrick and Caitlin from the beach to the schooner had been draped with chains of flowers made by Hawaiians that Erasmus had enlisted. The gruff first mate also had issued dire threats to any of the crew so foolish as to question what was going on.

Gerrick made a mental note to thank all who had labored so hard to see that everything was done as properly as possible, given the short notice. Of course, any expression of appreciation would have to wait until morning; wanting Caitlin all to himself, he had given orders to vacate the entire ship. The whole crew, including Erasmus and John, would be spending the night ashore, a prospect sure to please everyone—except, perhaps, Caitlin.

Now, glad of the privacy, he bent over Caitlin with a feeling of great tenderness. She presented an enchanting picture lying so trustingly upon his big bed. A short nap would refresh her, he hoped, and then he could at long last make her his, as he'd dreamed of doing since their

141

first meeting.

With one finger, he brushed the silver-gold hair back from her rosy cheeks. The *awa* she had drunk had been thinned with guava juice; he didn't want her too inebriated to respond to his lovemaking—but she *would* be more relaxed and less likely to fully experience the pain their first joining would cause. Gently, he removed the wreath of flowers encircling her head, and when she didn't stir, he then lifted her slightly and slipped off the leis of fragrant blossoms she wore about her neck.

The scent of plumeria was strong in his nostrils, and he reflected that from this day forward, whenever he smelled the sweet scent of the creamy blooms, he would think of Caitlin. Her skin was as deliciously perfumed, as petal-soft and delicate, and as tinged with pink as the plumeria blossom, and he could not resist nuzzling her tender throat. She stirred and smiled, but didn't open her eyes— and Gerrick was loath to awaken her just yet.

For a little while, he would just enjoy her, as he had enjoyed her beside the pool, drinking in her intoxicating beauty without the complications of making trivial conversation. Perspiration filmed her forehead and upper lip, and he wondered if she was warm. Several large portholes cooled his cabin; still, it was stuffier than it had been outside. He hesitated only a minute before deciding to remove her dress. How could she scold him, her new husband, when he was only thinking of her comfort?

A tremor of excitement shook his fingers as he gently maneuvered her onto her side and began undoing the fastenings of her gown. He really was a scoundrel to take advantage of so sweet and innocent a creature. But as each layer of clothing came off, his sense of guilt faded, to be replaced by the same awe and wonder he had experienced beside the pool.

Without doubt, Caitlin was every man's fantasy of a delectable, luscious female. He could think of no way to improve upon the ripe contours of her body. Her breasts were high and full, her waist narrow and maidenly, and her hips and thighs perfectly fashioned for conjuring

142

erotic images of conquest and possession. Her skin had an inner glow of health and a softness that reminded him of the tender muzzle of a newborn colt. Nothing in the world was softer—not even velvet.

After he had removed her clothing, Gerrick stood looking down at her for several long moments. The looking was agony, when touching was what he desired. Gingerly, he sat down on the bed beside her—certain that if he took her in his arms, she'd awaken, badly frightened by his bold actions. So long as he remained clothed while she was naked, he had her at a great disadvantage.

Well, I can remedy that, he thought slyly, rising and soundlessly tearing off his own clothes and dropping them on the floor. When he was as naked as she, he eased himself down on the bed and stretched out beside her. She was still lying on her side, as he had left her, and he moved closer until he could feel her silken flesh resting along his length from chest to toe. With a soft sigh, he buried his nose in her hair and inhaled deeply of plumeria, enchantingly mingled with her own special womanly scent.

Unaware of the exquisite torture she was inflicting upon him, Caitlin was still breathing slowly and regularly—more deeply asleep than he would have thought warranted by the small amount of *awa* she had consumed. But then, since she had *never* imbibed anything alcoholic, perhaps he shouldn't be too surprised. Fortunately, it was a long time until morning; he needn't hurry the long-awaited pleasure of making love to her.

Gently, he began to stroke her bare arm and to nuzzle her earlobe, determined to enjoy her softness even while she slept. Then, he began tracing the outline of her ear with his tongue. Caitlin's even breath became a sigh, and she rolled over on her back, one hand drawn across her eyes as she settled once again in slumber.

Gerrick grinned his pleasure; now he had full access to her splendid body and could gauge the effect of his ministrations. With a touch as light as a feather—so light that he imagined she could scarcely feel it—he stroked the curve of her white throat and continued downward to her breasts. She had lovely, rosy nipples, with wide aureoles, and the sight of them set Gerrick's blood to pounding.

Leaning upon one elbow, he dipped his head to taste them, lightly running his tongue around one pink tip. Taking the bud in his mouth and laving it thoroughly, he was gratified to feel it hardening. A soft sound, almost like a purr, issued from Caitlin's parted lips, delighting Gerrick, for it meant that her body was responding to him even if her mind had not yet grasped the reality of her situation.

Emboldened, he continued his gentle assault. He licked and kissed both gleaming mounds until they became engorged, and her nipples stood erect. Only then did he trace a slow path of kisses down to her navel, while at the same time slipping his hand between her thighs and nudging them apart. She resisted nothing that he did, and he knew the exact moment when his loving finally intruded upon her dreams; a rosy flush spread across her body, and the tip of her tongue appeared between her lips.

Soon, she would awaken, but by then, he hoped to have her so thoroughly aroused that any thought of fear or resistance would slip away, banished by rising passion. Before she quite knew what was happening, he would push his engorged member deep inside her—destroying forever the maidenhead that stood as a barrier to her full enjoyment of their union. Once that was done he could teach her pleasure—how to receive it and how to give it.

Finding that thought so exciting that he could scarcely control his own responses, he nuzzled the curly, golden hairs that concealed her sex. They were already moist, and he knew that within her woman's mound, the flesh would be tender and pulsating. He pressed his lips to the treasured place, wanting to know her more fully and intimately than he had ever known any woman.

"Caitlin, open to me . . ." he whispered, forgetting the need for silence in his eagerness to possess her with tongue and mouth, if not yet with his throbbing organ.

*   *   *

Caitlin sighed in the depths of her wonderful, erotic dream. It's only a dream, she told herself. Therefore I can lie here and enjoy it because I'm not responsible for anything that happens.

But marvelous, wicked things *were* happening—things she had only guessed at, as well as things her imagination had *never* thought to conjure. Nor had she ever imagined the pure pleasure such wanton behavior would engender. Her breasts and her loins were afire—tingling and aching with need. Instinctively, she arched her back and thrust her hips; her need centered in a tiny, vibrating spot at the very apex of her femininity.

Someone was stroking—licking? sucking?—that spot, and she recoiled from the idea in shock even as she found herself helplessly straining upward. Surely, that someone wasn't Gerrick! But the wondrous feelings that now held her enthralled were hauntingly similar to the ones she had first experienced when he kissed her beside the pool. She would always associate this wild, spiraling excitement with Gerrick; he had the power to stoke her innermost desires and set her blood afire.

Am I going mad? she wondered. This *couldn't* be happening—not to her, of all people.

Warm hands cupped her buttocks and raised her lower body. Caitlin felt her legs falling wide apart. Her first instinct was to fight the burgeoning fullness and pressure between her thighs. But her second reaction was to lie still and allow what was happening to happen. Her arms and legs felt weighted down, incapable of moving, and her body trembled with pleasurable sensations far too delightful to willingly surrender. This was a dream from which she never wanted to awaken.

The image of Gerrick's hard-muscled body arose in her mind. Oh, how she yearned for his possession! So strong was her need that she *felt* him moving over her and lowering himself between her parted thighs. She lifted her arms to welcome and enfold him, then tilted her hips to grant him entrance to her body. When he slid deeply into her, she knew a moment of searing, unexpected pain, as if her insides were being torn asunder.

Her breath caught sharply, and she bit down hard on her lower lip. It wasn't fair! She couldn't lose the pleasure now, not when she'd been so close to fully experiencing it. Tears squeezed out from beneath her closed eyelids, and she heard Gerrick speaking to her softly.

"Easy, Caitlin. Don't fight it. The pain will go away if you just relax."

His voice caressed and cajoled her. A moment later, his lips found hers, and he kissed her deeply—plunging his tongue into her mouth and finding her tongue. The distraction of his kiss eased the agony in her loins, and while her body adjusted to his invasion, he kept her occupied with long ardent kisses in which his tongue alternately possessed and dispossessed her mouth—offering encouragement and teasing her into dazed compliance.

When she again felt her need spiraling, he began to move within her. The searing pain had disappeared, leaving only a tenderness that scarcely mattered. This was no dream; she knew that now—and knew also that she could reject Gerrick and deny herself in the process, or freely follow his lead on this blissful journey they had only just begun.

He is my husband, she thought. I am his, and he is mine.

The barrier of her doubt and hesitation quickly crumbled beneath the weight of reason and commitment. This man was now hers to love, and she would love him with her body, her mind, and her soul. There could be no holding back, no false modesty, no coy denials of the overwhelming emotions he aroused in her. She *desired* his possession and yearned to please and pleasure him, so that he would never regret marrying her in such haste and sacrificing the freedom he so obviously cherished.

"Teach me what to do, Gerrick!" she pleaded in a whisper.

"Wrap your arms and legs around me," he responded hoarsely. "Don't fight your instincts. Do what your body tells you to do."

Trembling, she obeyed. In a moment, she caught his

rhythm of thrusting and withdrawing, so that he speared her again and again, each time ever more deeply, each thrust urging her to more dizzying heights of surrender. Losing herself to all else, she began moving her hips in a counter-thrust, both astonishingly new to her and anciently familiar.

"Lie still a moment," he commanded thickly, rising above her on knees and elbows.

She opened her eyes and gazed at him through tear-spiked lashes. He was so very beautiful and powerful in his nakedness, but before she could savor the magnificent sight, he shocked her by reaching down and fondling her breasts. When he tugged sharply at her nipples, she nearly bucked him off in astonishment—and then moaned in helpless pleasure.

An invisible cord seemed to stretch between her breasts and her loins, so that whatever he did to them, she felt it down below. As if this wasn't torture enough, he then reached down and gently massaged the very spot where his lips had earlier conquered and won her.

Arching her back, she clawed at his chest. "Gerrick! What are you . . . ?"

Then Gerrick was driving into her, lifting her hips to meet his plunge. He fell on top of her, thrusting with such force and vigor that she could do nothing but clasp him to her as his wild frenzy ignited a similar urgency in her. A roaring began in her ears; higher and higher they soared—until all was obliterated save the frantic straining of their bodies to reach completion. When release finally came, it was shattering.

"Gerrick!" she sobbed on a strangled cry. Her body shivered and jumped, receiving the seed he was pumping into her with a final cataclysmic shudder. Shaken to the core, she collapsed back onto the bed, sighing his name in a throaty whisper.

"Good God, Caitlin," he breathed in her ear. "I . . . I never *dreamed* . . . I never expected such . . . such enthusiasm, such eagerness."

Worried that she'd somehow offended him, she opened

147

her eyes and scanned his face. His grin was both wicked and delighted. "It was . . . all right, then?" she queried timidly.

"Dear girl, it was spectacular!" He hugged her to him. "I just never anticipated such a thrilling response from you."

Happiness bubbled in her heart, giving her the courage to finally *say* what she felt. Pushing him slightly away, she again gazed deeply into his eyes. Tears trembled on her lashes, the truth of her admission overwhelming in its unexpectedness. If he was shocked, so was she; what had happened between them seemed not just surprising, but downright miraculous.

"I love you, Gerrick," she whispered, savoring each magical word.

Breathlessly, she waited for a similar revelation from him. In answer, he leaned down and kissed her, and though she would have preferred to hear him voice the words, she accepted the gesture without criticism. Perhaps Gerrick found it difficult to express his deepest feelings; if so, she wouldn't press him. Someday, his tongue would be loosened. Someday, he'd *shout* his love for her; she would see to it.

"Sleep now, my lovely Caitlin," he murmured, levering himself off her damp body and drawing the sheet across her nakedness.

"Where are you going?" she asked as he reached for his breeches. Already she felt lonely for him and longed to have his arms around her.

"Just up on deck to see that everything is secured for the night."

"Hurry back . . ." she whispered sleepily, suddenly unable to keep her eyes open.

Chuckling, he bent down and brushed her forehead with his lips. "You may count upon my speedy return, my sweet. Didn't you plead with me to teach you about loving? Your lessons have only just begun."

She blushed in embarrassment at her earlier behavior. "What else is there to learn?"

"Why, Caitlin. You've only mastered the basic rudiments of lovemaking. What lies ahead is even better. Get your rest while you can, for I'm a most demanding tutor who insists on practice day and night."

Caitlin couldn't help smiling as she nestled into her pillow. She could not imagine *anything* being better than what she had just experienced, and she could hardly wait for her next lesson in lovemaking. But first, she needed sleep. Gerrick was right; she must rest while she could.

"Good night, my husband . . ."

"Good night, sweet Cait . . ."

Gerrick took one last look at the beautiful woman now occupying his bed and then quickly departed his cabin. Hurrying up the companionway, he burst upon the main deck at a half-run, feeling pursued by demons, and he glanced over his shoulder to reassure himself that Caitlin hadn't followed.

He hadn't wanted to leave her—and yet he'd been seized with a need to escape. Her avowal of love had caught him by surprise; it was no less shocking than her complete physical surrender. He simply had not expected her to give of herself so completely. The blood-smeared sheets attested to her virginal state, yet her responses had been those of a thoroughly practiced woman who craved sexual union and shamelessly sought her pleasure.

Even the most experienced woman rarely surrendered herself so trustingly and willingly. That a virgin should do so was nothing short of amazing. Most women held back until the last possible moment, and even then, they often hid their pleasure, or worse yet, stifled it—as if it were a shameful thing. Not Caitlin. She had actually begged him to tell her what to do—and then, she had done it, withholding nothing, not even the innermost secrets of her heart.

Her lovely, blue-gray eyes had held such brimming love, such trusting adoration. *I love you, Gerrick.* Damn! She had made him feel like a rogue! Had she resisted him, pleaded tearfully, and squirmed in discomfort, he would not feel half so bad. It was a woman's place to submit to a man and service his needs, and proud, haughty Caitlin deserved to learn her place in the biological scheme of things.

What shamed him most was that she had made a beautiful gift of her body—and by doing so, had elevated something essentially earthy and basic to a plane of being sacred and spiritual. Not only that, but instead of being the possessor, he had somehow become the possessed. Even now, when he'd been so recently satiated, he yearned to return to her bed and burrow once again into her silken softness. He wanted to wrap himself in her silver-gold hair and inhale her womanly sweetness as a drowning swimmer inhales fresh air. She was all life, all beauty—all refreshment and repose.

You lovesick ass, he excoriated himself.

Remembering the last occasion when he'd let a woman sneak past his defenses and make him vulnerable, he paced the deck in cold determination. No woman would ever again hurt him; he simply would not permit it. Caitlin Price meant only two things to him: sandalwood and sex. He'd use her to get what he wanted and to satisfy his raging passions, but when he was finished with her, he'd toss her aside without a pang of conscience. She could save all her pretty, glistening-eyed declarations for the next man!

Firmly decided, he stopped pacing and headed back toward his cabin and his bed. In the morning, he'd get right to the point and order Caitlin to help him find the sandalwood. And if she refused, he'd turn her over his knee and beat her plump, succulent bottom until she begged for mercy and swore her cooperation. After all, he was a man, wasn't he? Not a damn mouse! No matter how sweet her surrender, Caitlin Price would *never* tame him.

Chapter Twelve

Caitlin awoke before Gerrick, and she used the few moments of precious solitude to study her new husband as he slept beside her in the surprisingly large bed. He was such an incredibly handsome beast—so very masculine and yet so *pretty*. His face and body fascinated her; in repose, he looked less challenging and forbidding, and she fancied she could see the mischievous boy he must have been in the softened corners of his full, sensual lips.

Even in sleep, he seemed ready to break into one of his wicked grins, and she wondered how it was possible that he could provoke and disarm at the same time. This morning, a chestnut-colored stubble roughened his jaw, and his hair was in curly disarray. The sheet was drawn only to his waist, and his broad, muscular chest sported an equally curly pelt in which she longed to entwine her fingers.

She wished she could study the lower half of his body as closely, but removing the sheet would be far too daring, so she had to content herself with what was readily visible. Watching him and remembering what had transpired during the night, she felt a shiver of acute embarrassment; had they really done all she had imagined? Or had she dreamt more than half of it?

Her cheeks burned with shame as she thought of him kissing and fondling her so intimately. She must have been more tired than she realized to have slept while he was undressing her. She couldn't recollect leaving the wedding feast—much less how she'd wound up sprawled naked upon the bed.

What must he think of her—she, a pious woman, the daughter and niece of a missionary? Unable to enjoy Gerrick's beauty any longer, she turned her attention to his cabin. The room was large and comfortable, filled with heavy dark furniture that was either built-in or bolted to the floor. Brass fittings graced the big square portholes—open to admit the breeze and a brilliant slant of morning sunlight, and brass also winked from doorknobs, sea chests, cabinets, cupboards, and what she supposed were navigational instruments.

Every inch of the room had been carefully planned to contain something useful. There was a large writing desk, a round table and several wide, comfortable chairs, a wash stand, and of course, the big bed that dominated an entire wall. She wondered why Gerrick needed so large a place to sleep. Even with the two of them in it, the four-poster, canopied bed could have held at least one more person—possibly two.

Gerrick wasn't one to stint on comfort, Caitlin decided. Idly, she noticed a rack holding an impressive array of decanters filled with sparkling ruby or amber liquids. It was easy to guess what they were; when Gerrick wasn't looking, she'd have to empty them. Next, her eyes sought the shelves of books, each with its own sturdy guardrail. Her interest aroused, she squinted her eyes to read the titles but could decipher none of them at so far a distance.

The cabin had everything—places to eat, work, and sleep, plus plenty of reading matter to provide diversion. One could be quite comfortable on a long voyage, she realized, and questions began popping in her mind: Would she soon have an opportunity to test the cabin's comforts? Where would she and Gerrick make their home? And what about Uncle George? He didn't even know she was married; what if Gerrick wanted to leave the islands before her uncle returned?

With dazzling clarity, Caitlin suddenly grasped the

difficulties—nay, the penalties—of having jumped so hastily into marriage. She had neither clothes nor toilet articles. Yesterday afternoon, she had assumed they would probably spend the night in her house—or if they didn't, she'd have time to at least move her things aboard Gerrick's schooner.

Raking her fingers through her long, blond hair, she discovered the worst: it was badly tangled—and she didn't even have a brush or comb to get out the snarls! Another thought struck: Wasn't a wife supposed to prepare her husband's breakfast? This was her first morning as Gerrick's wife, and already she'd failed him.

Throwing back the sheet, she sat up and swung her legs over the side of the bed, but a hand suddenly grasped her forearm. "Where are you going, lovely lady? And why are you scowling like an angry fishwife?"

Caitlin snatched up the sheet to cover her nakedness, but when she turned, she realized her error: Now, Gerrick was no longer covered—and he grinned wickedly, amused by her modesty, and not the least bit shy about displaying his own blatant nudity.

"I *never* come to bed with clothes on, Caitlin. And you would save us both some awkward fumbling if you also came to bed naked."

After what they had already done together in his bed, she ought to be beyond blushing, but somehow she couldn't help it. Holding the sheet between them like a shield, she averted her eyes and desperately sought the location of her clothing. Surely, he hadn't disposed of her dress; yet on reflection, she wouldn't put it past him.

"Put down that sheet, and come back to bed, Caitlin." Gerrick's tone held a note of command that greatly dismayed her. The last thing Caitlin wanted was to lie beside him naked in broad daylight. That's how she'd gotten into this trouble in the first place. It scarcely mattered that the lamp had been lit last night when they'd consummated their marriage; she hadn't known what she was doing. She had been bewitched. But this morning, she was her old self again—and too ashamed to do

153

what he asked.

"Caitlin!" Gerrick sounded angry, but she dared not look at him to gauge his mood. "No matter what the issue, it's a wife's duty to obey her husband. Do you intend to break your wedding vows so soon?"

Her head snapped up in shock. She hadn't considered she was doing anything so terrible, and it cut deeply to have Gerrick accuse her of it. "No, Gerrick," she answered evenly. "I intend *never* to break my vows. If it pleases you to see me naked, I'll go naked whenever you wish."

Though shivers ran down her back, she threw down the sheet and eyed him boldly. Gerrick's green-eyed gaze scorched across her flesh, warming her despite her embarrassment. He grinned his mischievous, little-boy grin. "That's better. I thought we'd already dealt the killing blow to your maidenly shyness; come on, *look* at me. It's all right; I'm your husband now, remember?"

Forcing herself to adopt a calm sophistication she didn't feel, Caitlin allowed her eyes to sweep slowly over him. Gerrick made no attempt to hide himself, and she discovered something utterly amazing: That part of him that fascinated her the most was growing, swelling in size and becoming more rigid, even as she watched in utter astonishment.

"Do you like what you do to me, sweet Cait? The very sight of you is more than Mac can take. Your loveliness makes him stand right up and take notice. He can't help himself, poor fellow."

"M—Mac?" she questioned, confused as to whom he meant.

Gerrick nodded toward the lower half of his body. "That's Mac down there, my overeager friend who wants to be *your* friend as well. Long ago, I discovered that this particular portion of my anatomy has a mind of its own. John has even accused me of *thinking* with my crotch. Actually, I can blame most of my weaknesses and failings on Mac. He's been my downfall more times than I care to count. Indeed, he's the main reason why I married you— though the rest of me wanted you as well."

154

Caitlin had a wild impulse to laugh; she had never heard anything quite so fanciful—or so shocking and depraved. "B—but why do you call him Mac?"

"Well, I had to call him *something*. He's part of me, and yet he's separate, completely unresponsive to reason. The moment I met you, he started clamoring for attention—*your* attention, sweet Cait."

Caitlin wanted to look away; her whole body had gone crimson. But her eyes seemed glued to Mac, who had indeed taken on a personality all of his own. "Your f—friend, Mac. Is he capable of keeping his vows—I mean, *your* vows?"

"Of course!" Gerrick frowned at the question. "He can't go anywhere I don't go—or do anything I won't let him. If you keep him well satisfied, he'll never want to stray from home."

"And where is *home?*" Caitlin finally found the strength to lift her eyes to Gerrick's face. She didn't need to be told that he'd bedded many women; she'd known that from the first. What was important was the present and future: did Gerrick intend to be faithful?

"Come here, and I'll show you. Mac *craves* to find a home at long last. He's visited all over the world; but all he really wants is a warm hearth to call his own . . ." Gerrick's voice dropped to a whisper, and his eyes glowed a brilliant green. "Both of us want someone who will love and cherish us forever."

Caitlin went to the bed. In Gerrick's glibness, she suddenly sensed his loneliness. He hid his vulnerability well, behind smart remarks meant to shock and keep people from getting too close. But this time, he'd opened the door a crack and allowed her to see the *real* Gerrick, the one who for reasons still unknown to her, was filled with deep hurt and a bitterness he couldn't even discuss—as he couldn't discuss his sins of lust but had to invent Mac to take the blame.

In that instant, she made her decision.

"I will be Mac's home," she whispered, kneeling down on the bed and taking Mac between her palms. "If you will

155

only show me how to please him . . ."

At her touch, Gerrick groaned aloud. "I fear to show you anything; Mac is already your slave."

And are you my slave, too? Caitlin wanted to ask, but didn't because she feared his answer. She bent her head, and her hair made a curtain around her and Mac, cloaking them in privacy. Clearly, if she wanted Gerrick's love, she'd first have to win Mac's. I married you, too, Mac, she whispered silently, and now it's time we got better acquainted.

Gerrick writhed ecstatically on the bed. He could not believe what Caitlin—his prim little missionary—was doing to him. Last night, she had surprised him with her wholehearted responsiveness; but then it had been fueled by *awa*. This morning, she was stone-cold sober—and even more the wanton lover.

What depths of passion her primness had been hiding! And how very lucky he was to gain such a marvelous treasure! Most men had to pay whores to experience the pleasure that Caitlin was so innocently bestowing; did she even know how perverted her actions might be considered —especially by her fellow missionaries?

Gerrick prayed that she never would discuss sex with anyone other than him. Why, she was as uninhibited as any Hawaiian! And he suddenly guessed the reason for it: Somehow, despite what she'd been taught, she had absorbed the Hawaiian lack of pretense, their delightful natural response to life. She may have believed herself a dried-up spinster, may even have embraced that grim vocation, but the bonds of matrimony had set her free— probably for the first time ever—to enjoy the passions she had thought to subjugate.

Oh, Caitlin! Caitlin! he thought, barely able to contain himself as she bent over him, using her lips, hands, and mouth in ways he'd *never* yet experienced, not even with the best and highest-priced whores. She was driving him insane with desire.

"Woman, cease! Do you think I'm made of stone?"

Caitlin lifted her head and pushed back her long golden hair. Undisguised lust blazed in her lovely blue-gray eyes; he, at least, recognized it for what it was. "Mac is just beautiful, Gerrick," she murmured throatily. "I had no idea a man could be so beautiful . . ."

"Stop it!" Gerrick grasped her arms and hauled her on top of him.

She lay perfectly still, her breasts flattened against his chest. "You . . . didn't like it? I'm sorry. It seemed so natural for me to . . . I mean, after last night, when you did the same to me, I thought . . ."

Her cheeks flushed scarlet, and Gerrick finally silenced her with a thorough kiss that left his self-control even more ravaged. "Of course, I liked it, you little wanton. But if you hadn't stopped . . ."

"What would have happened?" she inquired guilelessly, and Gerrick cursed himself for using the word *wanton*. Never did he want Caitlin to suspect that she'd done anything other than was considered normal and proper between husbands and wives during their first sessions of lovemaking.

Groaning, he clasped her to him. "Mac would have disgraced himself."

"Disgraced? Why, disgraced?"

"Because he wouldn't yet have had the opportunity to satisfy *you!*"

"But Gerrick . . . I thought a husband and wife only worried about whether or not the man was satisfied. Women aren't supposed to enjoy—"

"You thought wrong!" Before she could ask any more disturbing questions, Gerrick rolled over onto his side and pushed her off him. "Now, turn over and cease your chattering. Don't say another word. If you don't mind, I'd just like to hold you a minute while I catch my breath. And then, after that . . ."

He let his voice trail off seductively, but Caitlin seemed to miss the unspoken implication. Turning to face him, she demanded, "Gerrick, am I really a wanton?"

Her question would have been humorous had she not been so deadly serious. He could have kicked himself. "No, sweet Cait, you are not." He kissed the tip of her nose. "I was only teasing."

"Do all husbands and wives do what we do?"

He felt he was treading barefoot across an anthill. "I really don't know, Cait, because I haven't been in bed with them. But I *can* tell you this; I don't think anything that a man and woman do in the privacy of their own bed is wrong or distasteful. We were created to give each other pleasure—and the idea that a woman should lie passive, *enduring* rather than enjoying, is an insult to our Creator."

Caitlin appeared to be considering this, and he held his breath waiting for her reaction. "Then you think if it *pleases* us both, there's nothing wrong with it—nothing *bad.*"

"That's exactly what I think—and while we're on the subject, you must tell me if there's anything I ever do that doesn't please you."

Her lovely eyes alight, she sighed and cuddled closer. "So far, I can't think of anything. I love what you do to me, Gerrick."

Gerrick wondered if she could hear his heart thumping against his ribcage. She continued to astound him with her forthrightness and ready acceptance of sexual intimacy. He had expected that by this morning, she'd be pleading a headache, at the very least. "Turn over, Caitlin," he begged. "I want your back to me."

"My back? But why?"

"Because the only way I'll be able to make love to you is if you can't touch me for a little while."

"What are you going to do?" she questioned, instantly complying.

Presented with the creamy white expanse of her back and shoulders, Gerrick fitted himself around her so that his hands could fondle the front of her as she lay against him spoon-wise. "There," he sighed. "That's much better."

158

Snuggling closer to him, she wiggled her bottom, and Gerrick almost climaxed then and there. Every move she made was so damned seductive—while at the same time, so artlessly innocent. He had thought himself a seasoned veteran, but Caitlin made him feel like a young green boy again—hardly able to contain himself.

"Don't move around so much," he pleaded hoarsely. "At least, not yet."

"Yes, Gerrick," she responded obediently, but still, he could feel her plump, pink buttocks pressing against him, and the impulse to thrust was so strong he had to grit his teeth.

"When you want me to move, just say so," she instructed softly. "I'll do whatever pleases Mac the most— for I *want* to please him, Gerrick. Celia just *adores* him."

"Celia?" he croaked.

"Mac's home away from home. I always wished I'd been named Celia. It's such a warm and pleasant name."

"Warm and pleasant," Gerrick muttered. "Doesn't nearly do Celia justice."

"It doesn't? Then what does?"

"Velvet . . ." Gerrick whispered. "Or satin. Or silk."

"Those aren't real names," she protested, but his hands found her breasts, and he silenced any further comments she might have made by making her gasp with delight instead.

"Lesson Number Two . . ." he whispered in her hair. "And I pray you enjoy it every bit as much as Lesson Number One."

They spent all of the morning and most of the afternoon in Gerrick's cabin. Hunger finally drove them out; Caitlin felt starved by the time Gerrick admitted that man "did not live by love alone." His reference to "love" thrilled her. Though she had declared her feelings several times, Gerrick had never once said the words that would have made these hours together perfect—the most perfect and satisfying she had ever known.

"I'm so ashamed, Gerrick," she apologized. "I should have gone in search of food hours ago."

He pushed her back down on the bed. "Stay right here; I will bring us something to eat. After all, I know the ship, and you do not."

"But it's my job to wait on *you!*" She started to get up, and then thought of facing the knowing glances of his men and having to inquire of them where the ship's cooking quarters were located, and she lay back down again.

"I won't be long." He winked at her. "Mac is getting lonesome already. . . . You'll find water in the pitcher if you care to wash, and I also have some toilet articles in that cupboard over there."

When he started to go out the door stark naked, she stopped him with a startled cry. "Gerrick! Hadn't you at least ought to put on your breeches?"

"No! And don't you dress yet either. We have the entire ship to ourselves. I told John not to let anyone come aboard until I hoisted the flag. I've given them all a holiday."

"A holiday!" She suddenly realized what kind of holiday his men were surely having. The Hawaiians would celebrate for days, with *luaus, hula* demonstrations, surfing contests, illicit sex—and she wasn't even there to put a stop to it. "Gerrick, we must get dressed, now!"

"No, my dear, we mustn't." Before he went out the door, Gerrick snatched up the gown she'd worn yesterday and shot her a rakish grin. "Stay just as you are. I'll return in a few minutes."

As soon as he left, Caitlin jumped out of bed. Dashing to the washstand, she poured water into the china basin and was splashing her face with it when she suddenly realized that now she was Gerrick's wife, *not* just the resident missionary. First and foremost, she owed her duty to her husband.

The entire shape of her life and daily routine had altered; yet *someone* must continue teaching the Hawaiians, nursing them, and rooting out the evils of their culture—and if that someone wasn't her . . .

"I must get word to Uncle George to return immediately," she lectured her reflection in the small round mirror above the washstand. "I knew we should have delayed the wedding until his return."

But as she vigorously scrubbed, she realized they had done the right thing; her desire for Gerrick was so strong that if they hadn't married immediately, something shameful would have happened. Gerrick would have found other opportunities to seek her out alone, and she would not have been able to resist him much longer. The night—and especially the morning—had taught her what a fool she had been ever to think she could depend upon self-control to maintain her maidenly virtue. Where Gerrick was concerned, she *had* no control; her Celia was as ungovernable as his Mac.

Having completed her ablutions, she found a brush in the cupboard, and after several minutes of almost tearing the hair from her scalp, her long tresses were once again spilling down her back in a reasonable semblance of order. Rummaging through more of Gerrick's things, she discovered a large white shirt and quickly slipped into it. While she had lost much of her shyness before Gerrick, she still didn't think she could manage eating while in the nude. The food would stick in her throat.

Next, she turned her attention to the rumpled bed. The bloodstains embarrassed her, and reminded her of how sore she really was. But it was a soreness that had already begun to heal; even if it hadn't, *nothing* would keep her from surrendering to Gerrick's forceful ardor. She craved his skillful penetration of her body.

A third attack on the cupboards finally revealed the location of clean sheets, and with a speed that amazed even her, she soon had the bed and the messy room set to rights. When Gerrick finally came through the doorway carrying a heavily laden tray, Caitlin was calmly sitting at the table.

He glanced around his cabin, a smile lighting his handsome face. "I see you've been busy."

"I did everything except throw out the flowers that are

beginning to fade. I couldn't yet bear to part with them."
She returned his smile with one of her own and was
surprised when he suddenly frowned at her.

"What are you doing wearing my shirt? I thought I told
you not to bother dressing."

Wondering if he was still testing her commitment to her
wedding vows, she promptly reached for the shirt's
fastenings. "I had really rather leave this on, Gerrick, but
if you're *ordering* me to remove it . . ."

He set the tray down on the table, placed hands on hips,
and thoughtfully looked her over. "No, you can wear it—
for now anyway. Actually, it looks far better on you than it
ever did on me. After we eat, however, the shirt comes off.
I'd consider myself less than a man—and certainly not a
great lover—if I allowed my new bride to go about *clothed*
on   the   first   full   day   of   our   marriage."

"Husband, you truly are outrageous, do you know
that?" Caitlin giggled, her spirits soaring at Gerrick's
compliments. "What did you bring? I'll have no strength
left if we don't soon eat."

They dined on fresh fruits, hot tea laced with sugar, and
a chunk of cheese from which Gerrick had carefully
scraped away the mold on the skin. Clearly, he had
planned ahead on what they would eat today, and Caitlin
found the meal delicious, a wonderful change from her
usual spartan diet.

"This fruit is delicious," she exclaimed, biting into a
juicy mango.

Gerrick raised one eyebrow. "You act as though you've
never eaten one of those before."

"I haven't," Caitlin admitted, swallowing the delicious
morsel. "My father only approved of eating foods native to
New England."

Gerrick blinked. "How have you kept from starving?"

"We receive food periodically from the mainland. Of
course, sometimes it's spoiled, but we've never scorned
even the worst of our donated provisions. If the biscuits
have weavils, I just pick them out."

"What? Are you crazy? I never heard of such a thing!"

Caitlin put down the mango. "As I believe I've mentioned once before, my life has been very different from yours in almost all respects, Gerrick. I would thank you not to criticize unduly. As you can see, I've suffered no ill effects from eating boiled meats and what fresh vegetables we've been fortunate enough to grow. From now on, however, I will eat what you eat—for a wife should never complain of the food her husband provides, nor should she insist on doing everything *her* way, rather than his."

"You can't know how pleased I am to hear you say that."

Gerrick's obvious relief made Caitlin wonder if he had been worrying that she meant to make startling changes in his life. She *did* intend to change things—but not overnight. She wouldn't make the same mistake with him that she had sometimes made with the Hawaiians: expecting immediate results. Instead, she would acquiesce on *almost* everything, and hope he would reciprocate by not denying her the things that were most important to her.

"I'm sorry I've missed such a pleasure as this," she murmured, juice running down her chin as she took another bite of the mango. "I do hope you have a fondness for mangoes."

Gerrick shouted his laughter. "We'll eat them at every meal! And now, sweet Cait, if you've finished stuffing yourself . . ."

From the look in his eye, Caitlin knew exactly what he wanted—but first, she wanted something from him. Daintily, she wiped her mouth and fingers with the linen napkins he had thoughtfully provided. "Gerrick, could I discuss something with you that has me very worried?"

A furrow appeared in his brow. "Certainly. I would hope that you'd always discuss your worries with me. What is it?"

"It . . . it's the Hawaiians."

"I allowed no hula dancing last night," he reminded her, though she couldn't even remember protesting the dancing of the hula.

"I—I thank you for that, Gerrick, but dancing isn't my only worry. . . . You see, now that I'm your wife, there will be no one to . . . to look after the islanders while I'm busy looking after you."

"That's true," Gerrick responded patiently. "I intend to begin searching for . . . for my brother, Hadley, in the very near future, and I am expecting you to accompany me. The Hawaiians will just have to see to their own needs until your uncle finally returns."

"But that might not be for a very long time. And I shudder to think of his returning and not finding me while we are somewhere in the wilderness. If there was another ship in port, stopping over on its way to Maui, I could simply send him a message begging him to return immediately. But as it is . . ."

"You want me to go and fetch him. Is that it?"

This idea was far better than any she'd had in mind; if he had agreed to send John with a message, she would have been more than satisfied.

"Oh, would you?" she breathed ecstatically. "I feel so guilty for having married without even seeking his blessing."

Gerrick looked momentarily uncomfortable, and she guessed he was worrying about his brother. How thoughtless of her not to have taken his feelings into consideration! "I'm sorry . . ." she murmured. "No, of course you can't go. Hadley must be found at once. You've already delayed your search far too long."

"That wasn't what was stopping me from saying yes," Gerrick corrected. "I'm not as worried about Hadley as . . . as the rest of my family. He's a true Scott—which means he can and always has taken care of himself most admirably. He just forgets to write and tell us when he decides to spend years, instead of months, involved in his precious research."

Caitlin reached across the table and covered his hand with hers. "You don't have to hide your concern from me, my dear. If you wish to leave immediately, we'll leave."

"Damn it, Cait, stop pressuring me!"

Startled, Caitlin jerked back. She couldn't think what she had said to so offend him. "Gerrick, I—I . . . Just tell me what you want me to do, and I'll gladly do it."

Her answer seemed to please him, for Gerrick suddenly leaned across the table and entwined his fingers in hers. "You really *do* believe in wifely obedience, don't you?"

His question bothered her; why was obedience so crucially important to him? "Yes, I do. . . . But if you doubt it, you can test me."

A light blazed in Gerrick's eyes. "Caitlin . . . my dear sweet girl!"

He seemed on the verge of making some monumental request. Hoping she could willingly grant it, Caitlin leaned forward tightly gripping his hand. "Yes, Gerrick?"

"I . . . I can't *bear* to embark on a search for my brother without *first* having a honeymoon with you!"

A honeymoon? Was that all he wanted? Just what were they having now?

"Why, Gerrick . . . we could honeymoon and search for your brother at the same time! The wilderness areas of the island are so beautiful; no wonder Hadley has secluded himself for so long. Sometimes, my father used to take me with him to visit remote villages, and when he did, I *never* wished to return. You'll see; it will be perfect."

"You misunderstand my reluctance." Gerrick frowned. "John will be accompanying us—and probably an islander or two to help carry provisions. We'd have no privacy. However, if we first went in search of your uncle and brought him back, at least, we'd have a sea journey in which to get to know each other . . ."

"But your crew would be aboard," Caitlin reminded him, still not seeing the problem. "And mightn't John not also accompany us?"

Having noticed the way John and Pikake looked at each other, Caitlin had no intentions of leaving the two of them alone unattended.

"Yes, but we'd have this cabin all to ourselves . . . and when we finally did begin our search for . . . Hadley, at

165

least your uncle would be here to look after his little flock. You wouldn't need to feel so guilty about leaving."

"Oh, Gerrick! You *do* understand my feelings!" Overwhelmed with happiness, Caitlin sprang to her feet. Gerrick probably didn't realize it, but her uncle would also keep Gerrick's crew from debauching the island women while she and Gerrick were gone. Or perhaps he *did* realize it and didn't mind. Hurrying around the table, she flung herself into his arms.

"It's settled then?" Gerrick grinned lecherously. "We'll honeymoon enroute to Maui to find your uncle—and when we return, we'll go after my brother."

"Yes, Gerrick, it's settled!" Gerrick Scott was truly the best and most considerate of husbands, Caitlin thought, tearing at the fastenings of her shirt.

When she was once again naked, she pressed herself into his arms. Rising, he neatly swept her off her feet and began carrying her to his big bed. Eagerly, she clung to him, all the while thinking that never, *ever*, did she want the honeymoon to end. No matter where they went or what they did, she'd find some way to be alone with Gerrick. He was her beloved husband, now and forever, and with every breath she took, she would love him all the more.

Chapter Thirteen

"I thought we'd be leaving immediately to search for sandalwood." John frowned his displeasure at Gerrick's announcement that first they'd be going to Maui.

"Lower your voice!" Gerrick steered his friend away from the open hatch leading to the captain's companionway. Down in his cabin, Caitlin was still preparing to meet the new day, and the last thing he wanted was for her to overhear his conversation with John. "Cait wants to bring her uncle back to the island first," he explained when they had passed out of earshot. "She's worried about the survival of the natives without a missionary to oversee their every thought and breath."

"And has 'Cait' agreed to help us once her beloved natives are safely under her uncle's thumb?"

"She would feel more comfortable about it," Gerrick stated smoothly, not admitting any more than he absolutely must.

"Then, she doesn't mind about the sandalwood."

"She doesn't yet *know* about the sandalwood—and I'm not going to tell her if I don't have to."

"If you don't have to! You mean we're going to run all over this whole damn island looking for the stuff, while Caitlin believes we're only looking for your brother?"

"That's exactly what I mean."

Ignoring John's incredulous, angry expression, Gerrick leaned upon the gleaming, mahogany railing. It was a fine, sunny morning, following a splendid night, and he wasn't going to allow John to ruin it for him. His entire body hummed with contentment; yesterday and last night had been as near perfect as any twenty-four hours Gerrick had ever lived. If he wasn't yet ready to quench the passion and adoration in Caitlin's eyes by telling her what a scoundrel and liar he really was, that was *his* business, not John's.

"You've had your fling," John growled beside him. "Don't you think it's time you finally told her the truth? At least, *part* of the truth?"

Gerrick inhaled deeply of the humid, flower-scented air. The day would be hot; perhaps he and Caitlin could while away the afternoon swimming in their secret pool and plucking orchids. An arousing image sprang to mind: Caitlin standing naked and laughing beneath the waterfall, this time not at all minding that he saw and admired her loveliness.

"Well?" John asked. "Have you gone deaf as well as dumb?"

"I'll be the judge of when the time for honesty has come," Gerrick drawled. "I see no reason to make Cait miserable right away; the sandalwood isn't going anywhere. If we can't find it on our own, then I'll demand she tell us its location. But until that moment, we'll have her eager cooperation as interpreter. And if—when—we do stumble upon the treasure, she'll think it was accidental, instead of planned."

"Isn't it a bit late to start protecting sweet Cait?" John snorted derisively. "You must have had some wedding night. I can't *wait* to hear how you explain away your lost brother."

Instead of taking offense—a useless reaction when his feelings were so calm and happy—Gerrick gave John his most charming grin. "You know what, John? You brood too much. And your cynicism is becoming alarming. What you need is a woman to take your mind off your worries . . . which reminds me, how did you get along with little Pikake? From your mood, I'd say not well."

"Not well, indeed! Your dear 'Cait' has filled her head with all sorts of absurd, nonsensical notions. I *know* she wanted to lie with me, but just as things were getting interesting, she suddenly sat bolt upright and started weeping."

"Whatever for? She certainly seemed perfectly normal to me that night when I . . ."

John's head came up sharply, and his nostrils flared like a possessive stallion's. "When you what? I thought you only kissed her the night Caitlin interrupted to give you both a sermon."

"I did only kiss her. But you saw the way she shed her clothes like a snake sheds its skin. She was as eager as I to finish what we started."

"Apparently, she's only eager to a point," John said gloomily. "She said she loved me too much to risk my going to hell. For herself, it didn't matter—she'd willingly suffer eternal damnation. But she couldn't allow *me* to suffer."

"God's teeth!" Gerrick swore. "What utter foolishness! I'll speak to Caitlin about this right away."

John laid a restraining hand on Gerrick's arm. "I'd rather you didn't. Pikake would be mortified were Caitlin to learn how close her prized pupil has come to sinning. I won't have the little one shamed and scolded."

"So what did you do?"

"I held her and dried her tears and thanked her for her tender concern. She's the first female I've met who gave a damn about my future—other than whether or not I'd retain my health and wealth so I could keep *her* happy."

"Then, you're just going to let her go?" This was a side of John that Gerrick had never seen; usually, the more a woman resisted, the more his friend persisted. It was only *after* he'd had her that John lost interest in the chase.

"She'll . . . just take more time," John hedged. "I'll have to handle her more carefully. Of course, if we're going to go chasing off to Maui, I won't see her, and then we'll be leaving to search for the sandalwood. . . . Perhaps, I ought to pass on this one. She's little more than a baby anyway."

"Is this really John Reynolds talking—the man who breezily loves 'em and leaves 'em, without ever once giving his heart?"

"You are hardly one to talk!" John snapped. "Why, you're every bit as bad as I am!"

"I have an idea. Why not invite Pikake to come with us? She'd be company for Cait while I'm occupied with the ship. And what the two of you find to do while Cait is occupied with me is entirely up to you."

"Why don't you just leave me here to start hunting for the sandalwood without you—or is that what you're trying to avoid?" John glowered suspiciously.

"John, you may certainly stay if you wish—with or without Pikake. But aren't you also anxious to visit Maui and see if it's as beautiful as Kauai? If I'm going to leave anyone behind, it should be Erasmus. The less Caitlin sees of him, the better, and the old seadog just might find something. I'd have to swear him to secrecy first, of course, and—"

"How will Erasmus know what he's looking for?"

"Oh, he's acquainted with sandalwood. He's sailed everywhere, remember? And what he hasn't seen isn't worth seeing. He was an old hand when I first met him."

"I suppose that's as good a plan as any," John grudgingly agreed. "That is, if you're sure you can trust him."

"Today, John, I could trust the devil. You're looking at the old Gerrick Scott reborn."

John gazed at him in amazement. "Damn my soul if you *don't* look reborn, Gerrick. And damn if I don't envy you!"

"Take my advice," Gerrick advised with a wink. "If you want little Pikake, go after her. Don't let her get away. If she's anything like Caitlin, behind her prim defenses lies a treasure defying description."

"I thought we came here for sandalwood—not the treasure you have in mind."

"We did. But there's no harm in harvesting both kinds, is there?"

170

In answer, John only rolled his eyes and shook his head.

Caitlin stood at the rail in the twilight and watched Kauai slip away on the rosy horizon. Soon there was nothing but a purple hump against the darkening sky. Glancing upward, she saw stars appearing—each one a brilliant jewel set against deep blue velvet.

She knew now why Gerrick had suggested they wait until evening to set sail for Maui. The wind had freshened, and if it continued, they might even make their destination by midmorning of the following day, though Gerrick had said it would probably be afternoon or early evening. They had the dangerous channel to cross, and then must sail past Oahu and Molokai. But while the wind was strong, it was also steady, and the long, rolling swells of the Pacific gave no hint of an approaching storm.

Caitlin felt perfectly at ease and happy—except for one thing: Pikake's presence in the bow of the ship. Turning from the stern railing, Caitlin watched her little friend giggling and chattering with John Reynolds. John was leaning over her—a huge whale courting a tiny, irridescent sunfish, and Caitlin wondered what two such dissimilar personalities from two such different worlds could possibly have to say to each other.

She hadn't wanted Pikake to come, nor John to stay on the island with her, but Gerrick had put his foot down. Rather, he had kissed her senseless beside the tinkling waterfall and made her forget what they had even been arguing about. Now, while he was busy charting their course and doing whatever it was captains did when they first set sail on a sea voyage, she had time to consider it all—what she had said, what he had said, and what little good her protests had done.

"Caitlin, they are two grown people. It's up to them to make up their own minds about what they feel for each other."

"But John will completely cut himself off from decent society if he takes up with Pikake—especially so if he marries her."

"Then perhaps he should just dally with her."

"Gerrick! That's not funny. You are suggesting that they live in sin."

"I'm suggesting only that you leave them alone to discover what it is *they* want to do."

"But none of the missionaries will even speak to John, much less help him attain his goals, if they see him with Pikake."

"Should I tell Pikake to cover her head with a burlap bag when we get to Lahaina—and to deny she even knows him?"

"Well, what about Pikake? Her feelings will be dreadfully hurt if the missionaries treat her badly."

Exasperated, Gerrick had finally shouted, "Who are these damn missionaries anyway, that they should be so cruel and judgmental?"

"One is Reverend William Richards and the other is Ephraim Spaulding. They are both nice people, with nice wives and families—but they do frown upon commingling of the races."

"We're not talking horses or cattle here, Caitlin, but human beings. We needn't worry about purity of bloodlines."

"I have seen how those two look at each other, Gerrick, and I assure you that a mixed-race infant is a distinct possibility. Do you know what the Hawaiians sometimes do with half-breed children? Shortly after they are born, they are drowned in the sea—particularly females. That appalling custom is well documented."

"I can't picture little Pikake drowning anyone."

"No, she probably wouldn't; but she'd live all her life with a certain stigma, and so would her child. Attitudes are, of course, changing, but not fast enough to spare any offspring of John and Pikake. Just what *are* John's intentions toward my friend?"

"How in hell should I know, Caitlin? Maybe John doesn't even know. But whatever his intentions are, they aren't my business, nor I might add, are they yours. John invited her, Pikake accepted, and there's really nothing more to discuss."

"But, Gerrick . . ."

At that point, he had seized her and started kissing her, and the next time she remembered the subject, it was too late to do anything about it. Pikake, kapa cloth bundle in hand, was waiting on shore to board the schooner. "Oh, Tutu Caitlin!" the girl had exclaimed. "Pikake so happy come with you to Maui. I never sail on ship before."

Filled with a renewed determination to keep John and Pikake apart, Caitlin started across the deck toward them. But before she had taken two steps, a tall figure intercepted her.

"And where do you think you're going?"

"Oh, Gerrick, you startled me! It's so dark out here I didn't see you."

Gerrick's hands slid around her waist as he drew her nearer. "Soon, the light from the moon and stars will make this deck as bright as day."

"I'm glad to hear that," Caitlin said, thinking of John and Pikake.

"I'm not glad," Gerrick responded. "While it's still dark, let's take advantage of it."

"Gerrick, we mustn't . . ." Her protest was lost as his lips covered hers.

He tasted of the sea's salt tang and smelled of the wind's fresh breath. His arms held her tightly against him, and she could feel every hard plane of muscle, protrusion of bone, and . . . Mac. Flicking his tongue across her tongue, Gerrick deepened the long, searing kiss, and when he finally broke away, he was breathing hard, his heart thumping beneath her splayed fingertips.

"Shall we go below? Or would you prefer lying naked beneath the stars? I think I'd like the latter."

"Gerrick! You yourself said that soon it will be light as—"

"Relax, my prim little missionary. I'll just give orders for everyone to close their eyes."

"Below, please," Caitlin pleaded hoarsely, and only

173

after she'd descended the captain's companionway did she remember that John and Pikake were still alone together. Well, not quite alone—but tomorrow she'd find other tasks to occupy her little friend. And maybe she'd even have a heart-to-heart talk with John.

"I can't believe we're here already," Caitlin exclaimed, watching the approaching shoreline. "Even though it took two days longer than you said it would, the time flew past."

"Happy?" Gerrick queried softly, pressing her fingers to his lips.

"Oh, yes, Gerrick! I've never *been* so happy! Even when we became becalmed, the voyage was wonderful. . . . I—I never expected married life to . . . to be so agreeable."

"You *look* happy, sweet Cait, and lovelier than when I first saw you. Please continue to wear your hair down like that. . . . Your hair and your eyes are all the adornment you'll ever need."

Caitlin's free hand flew to her hair. The breeze was playing with the long silver-gold strands—blowing them this way and that. Later, there would be snarls, but she didn't mind as long as Gerrick liked it loose. A trill of laughter carried to her ears, and her eyes sought John and Pikake. They were standing close to each other beside the railing, hands entwined, enjoying the breeze and the sights as she and Gerrick were doing.

Vibrating with excitement, Pikake's voice rang as clear as a bell. "La-*high*-na, Maui this place is called, John, not La-*hay*-na. The island is named after the God, Maui, who lassoed the sun and made it go slower across the sky so his mother could have more hours of daylight in which to make *kapa* cloth. The word Lahaina means 'broiling sun,' though why it is called that I do not know for I have never been here."

Pikake's English had much improved over the past few days, and Caitlin felt guilty on two counts: *She* had never spent so much time correcting her little friend's grammar.

And neither had she spoken to Pikake *or* John about the dangers of their relationship. Gerrick had kept her so occupied that she hadn't exchanged more than ten words with Pikake since they came aboard. Where Pikake was sleeping she had no idea—and was afraid to ask.

"Stop worrying," Gerrick chided.

"How did you know I was worrying?" Caitlin's glance flew back to her husband, her tall, handsome husband whose teasing grin immediately erased every other emotion from her heart save love.

"Sweet Cait, you cannot hide anything. Your heart is always in your eyes. I only hope I never see hatred there; I don't think I could bear it."

Stroking his clean-shaven jaw with one finger, she murmured, "That you'll *never* see, Gerrick, for I love you with all my heart."

With a stab of dismay, she witnessed the dark flicker in his eyes that always appeared whenever she spoke of love. He seemed unable—or unwilling—to voice the feelings that his big body so eloquently expressed every time he took her in his arms. Rather than dwelling on her disappointment in this matter, she had come to feel even more tender and protective toward him. Sometime in the past, he'd been hurt; her sense of this was stronger now than ever. And she was determined to overcome this last reservation between them with great tact and patience.

"Oh, look! What is that?" She leaned over the railing and pointed to a tall geyser of water shooting skyward. A moment later, a huge, shiny black shape emerged from the blue, and she knew the answer to her own question. "A whale! It's a humpback whale!"

"Not whale—*whales*. And I hope they swim away fast, or every whaler in Lahaina will soon be in hot pursuit."

Caitlin shaded her eyes from the brilliant, late afternoon sunlight. Behind them, playing in their wake, a school of the huge, bumpy-skinned beasts were alternately surfacing and blowing, completely oblivious to any impending danger. Caitlin looked off to the side and spotted one swimming quite close to the ship. It had a thick, stubby body, fully fifty feet long, to which were attached huge side flippers about fifteen feet long.

Its dorsal fin was the humplike projection from which it took its name, and as it swam nearer, Caitlin could see its tiny, intelligent eye, and the barnacles hanging from its chin and throat. The animal's curiosity was evident; the whale seemed to be looking them over as closely and excitedly as everyone aboard was examining it. Suddenly, the great beast leaped clear out of the water, and as it came down in a nose dive, it momentarily stood on its head, its entire body in view.

As water splashed down all around, soaking both Caitlin and Gerrick, John and Pikake came rushing over. "Did you see that?" John demanded. "It lobtailed right beside us."

"We know, John," Gerrick drawled, wiping water from his eyes. "We're standing here watching."

"*Palaoa,* we call the whale, John," Pikake instructed. "Though we also have names for each kind of whale." Turning to Caitlin, she laughed and cried, "Tutu Caitlin! You are all wet!"

"I'm tempted to jump in and splash water on *him,*" Caitlin admitted, wringing water from the skirt of her dress. "I think he did that just for the fun of it. Look at him now. Why, I think he's enjoying a good laugh with his friends." She angled her head to watch the humpback whale returning to his frisky playmates.

"He might as well play now," Gerrick observed soberly. "This close to Lahaina, his days are numbered."

"Looks like a whaler or two might've already caught sight o' them, Cap'n," a sailor called out from the rigging. "I see men runnin' for their ships."

"Oh, no!" Caitlin wailed, dashing to the bow to see for herself.

But it was true. Ahead of them, the harbor that only moments before had appeared so drowsy in the sunlight had come alive. Men were sprinting down the beach toward their longboats, and upon reaching them, were shoving off the sand and into the sea, and then rowing toward the ships anchored farther out.

Gerrick was suddenly beside her, wrapping one arm around her waist and whispering in her wet hair. "I'm sorry, Caitlin, but there's nothing you or I can do to stop them—except pray that the whales escape."

"They'll kill every single one!" she cried. "The brutes! Oh, I'll never light another whale oil lamp again."

"Don't make promises you can't keep, darling."

"Maybe the wind is blowing in the wrong direction, and they'll not be able to sail."

"Ah, but I'm afraid they will, love. That's the beauty of Lahaina's harbor. Unlike most, it can be left or entered at will. There are no shoals to surprise the unwary, and the configuration of the island itself, with three other islands sheltering it, makes it possible for ships to come and go almost as they please."

"I hate whalers—*and* traders!" Caitlin cried without thinking. "Why does something so beautiful and free as the whales have to die—just so people can become rich?"

Beside her, Gerrick stiffened, and Caitlin turned to him in alarm. Gone was the gentleness and concern from his eyes; now they were hard and cold, glittering like emeralds but without the inner fire of the gem. "You must remember that *I* am a trader, Caitlin—and I'd be a whaler, too, if I thought it would make me wealthy."

"But I didn't mean you, Gerrick. You could never be a whaler; why, you enjoyed the beasts as much as I did. And by traders, I meant only those who came here years ago and stripped away the sandalwood trees."

"And did you care as much for the trees as you do for the whales?" An odd note had crept into Gerrick's voice—a note that made her shiver.

"I *wept* to see them destroyed, Gerrick. But what has that to do with us?"

Without answering, he suddenly strode away from her, shouting orders for trimming sail. Caitlin stared after him in confusion; she ought never to have criticized his livelihood. But after she had explained, why was he still so angry? Didn't he understand? She didn't hate *all* traders,

177

just the ones involved with sandalwood. And except for those determined few still hoping that some wood remained, the sandalwood traders had all but disappeared from the islands.

A stunning thought occurred: Had Gerrick's family once made money in the trade? Was that why he was so sensitive about it?

They still had not discussed their respective pasts; they'd been too preoccupied with the splendor of the present. And Caitlin resolved then and there to rectify this shocking oversight. If Gerrick's famliy *had* made their fortune in sandalwood, behaving like all the other, greedy, immoral traders, she would find it difficult to forgive, but certainly, she'd try—so long as Gerrick himself wasn't planning to emulate his forebears.

What *was* Gerrick planning, she wondered. After he found his brother, did he intend to sail for home? They must discuss and settle these things. Caitlin choked back sudden tears. She so desperately wanted this marriage to work, but how could it if they didn't start confiding in each other?

"Tutu Caitlin! Where are you going?" Pikake cried, as Caitlin rushed for the companionway. "Don't you want to watch our arrival?"

"I've got to change," Caitlin murmured distractedly. "My uncle mustn't see me dressed in wet clothing, with my hair hanging in tangles down my back."

As she clambered down the narrow ladder in the hatch opening, she gave scarcely another thought to the fate of the poor humpback whales; at the moment, the question of her own fate took precedence—hers and Gerrick's. Not even the prospect of seeing her uncle again gave her any comfort. Her uncle, too, would have questions; and how could she answer his when she couldn't even answer her own?

Chapter Fourteen

Lahaina, Maui

Slowly, taking his time, Gerrick traversed the bustling waterfront of Lahaina. He was in no hurry whatever to reach the house of Reverend William Richards, where Caitlin had gone ahead to find her uncle and break the news of their precipitous wedding. Indeed, while registering with the harbor master, a jovial Hawaiian who spoke broken English and wanted to hear all the news from abroad, Gerrick had delayed as long as possible, until even that garrulous official had run out of conversation. Now, having taken care of all his business, Gerrick knew he must finally face Caitlin's guardian and perpetuate the lie of their marriage.

That's the trouble with lying, Gerrick thought: One lie leads to another—and another and another, until there's no end to it. Had he been able to foresee his current feelings of guilt and shame, he never would have entered into this bogus marriage with Caitlin. But then neither would he have experienced the perfect bliss of the last few days.

He wished he could have stretched out the voyage even longer, but Caitlin surely would have grown suspicious when the wind rose and they didn't progress. He'd had a difficult enough time as it was backing off his sails and making it appear as though they were becalmed—which they had been for several hours, but not for a full day as he had allowed Caitlin to believe. Luckily, Caitlin knew nothing about seamanship—or even about the trade-winds, which never slackened for long.

And luckily, John had been too preoccupied with Pikake to voice any strong complaint. Where was John now? Gerrick wondered, glancing about the crowded little town. Caitlin had taken Pikake with her, while John had set out with an armful of presents to gift the local authorities. Fortunately, the young king, Kamehameha III, was absent from his island quarters, or the cost of this visit would have been quite high; the gifts were in addition to the ten dollars demanded by the fat, smiling harbor master.

In these delicate diplomatic matters, Caitlin was proving her worth beyond all of Gerrick's expectations; she knew precisely what protocol to follow, and on that score, at least, he had no regrets. Only when he thought about how he had obtained her wholehearted trust and cooperation—and how he intended to use her to gain the sandalwood—did he experience a deep regret, coupled with a burning desire to make things right between them. But he knew he could never do that without making a full confession and sacrificing his dreams of wealth and revenge against Amos. Even then, Caitlin might never forgive him.

Better to leave things as they are, he counseled himself, determinedly turning his attention to locating Caitlin and her uncle. Lahaina was, even more than he had anticipated, a busy, fascinating place. Hundreds of neat, grass houses and upwards of forty wood or stone structures crowded the harborfront, while scores of people, both natives and whites, strolled the hot, dusty streets.

Commissary establishments lined many of the streets, and Gerrick suspected there were also grog shops, though Caitlin had told him that spirits had finally been outlawed owing to pressure from the missionaries. Everywhere Gerrick looked, he saw sailors—and where there were sailors, there was always liquor, as well as women. The harbor itself was jammed with double-masted schooners, and the landing heaped high with barrels and boxes either enroute to the whaling ships or coming from them.

Behind the town, as on Kauai, the mountains rose lush and green, and the sea at its feet was the same beautiful blue with the same lovely crystalline beaches—but here, the similarities ended. Whereas Kauai still remained unspoiled, Lahaina was overrun with foreigners, their presence everywhere apparent. Gerrick studied the newly completed fort, built of coral rock and outfitted with several guns. From the water, the fort had been glaringly conspicuous, but it was even more so up close. He guessed the area within the quandrangular structure to be about an acre—though it was difficult to tell when the longest side of the imposing structure faced the sea and the walls all around stood twenty feet high.

Nearby was an inland canal, and on either side of it stretched the busy marketplace, most of the stalls roofed over with straw. Wanting to avoid the press of people there, Gerrick headed for a less congested area where he saw taro patches, fish ponds, and plenty of coconut, hala, and kou trees. In the midst of these stood a two-story brick house, exactly the sort of staid, solid edifice reminiscent of Massachusetts or Rhode Island where missionaries would choose to live.

"Excuse me, lad . . ." He gestured to a passing sailor. "What is that building there?"

The sailor stopped and looked where Gerrick was pointing. "Oh, that's the old king's palace, where th' first Kamehameha used to live. But it's only used as a warehouse now, I b'lieve."

The sailor's New England accent was slightly slurred, as if he'd been drinking, and he was unshaven and unkempt. By the dissipated look of him, he'd had a long leave from his ship and might, perhaps, be a deserter. Gerrick suspected that desertion was a major problem in the islands; nevertheless, he sought to learn all he could from the bandy-legged, middle-aged man. "You mean there's another palace now, a newer one?"

181

"Well, Cap'n . . . there's one bein' built down the beach farther, but the young king an' other members of the royal fam'ly don't stay there either. When they're in town, they live on a little island in the middle of a pond *behind* the new palace. They like their grass houses better than our stone ones, and they even bury their dead out there—an' when the missionaries ain't lookin', I heard the royal fam'ly still worships some old lizard god who lives in the bottom of the pond."

Gerrick was intrigued. He would have liked to go and have a look at the king's island, but he'd dallied long enough. By now, Caitlin would be getting worried.

"Can you tell me where to find William Richards's house?"

The sailor hawked loudly and spat on the ground, then glanced at him sidelong. "Y' mean William Richards, the missionary?"

Gerrick nodded.

"I can tell ya'—but I don't know why you'd want t' go there. Less'n you've a hankerin' t' sit in the new Masters' and Mates' Readin' Room and read edifyin', upliftin' stuff no self-respectin' seaman would ever want t' read even if he *could* read it."

Gerrick grinned at the sailor's obvious distaste for both Reverend Richards and the reading matter supplied to the sailors. "Is it far?"

"Naw, this here is the King's Road. Stay on it an' soon you'll be there. A big taro patch is growin' on the *makai* or sea side of the road, and the missionary compound is on the *mauka* or mountain side. When ya' get there, just look for the holes in the yard where the *John Palmer,* a British whaler, shot cannonballs at the preacher's house a few years back . . ."

"You certainly know a good deal of the town's history," Gerrick observed.

"I been livin' here for some time now." Grinning toothlessly, the sailor winked. "An' I ain't on shore leave; this is my new home. First time I saw this place, I thought it was a reg'lar paradise—an' it still would be if it weren't for them damn missionaries. I only wish the *John Palmer* had had itself a better gunner. The women and the liquor used to be as plentiful as palm trees; but now ya' have t' know the right people or you'll get nary a taste of either one. . . . F'r a dollar or two, I'd be happy t' show you around, Cap'n—and what I'd show you would be a heap more interestin' than anything t' be found in the Masters' and Mates' Readin' Room."

Gerrick plunged his hand in his pocket, withdrew a coin, and flipped it in the sailor's direction. "Sorry, lad, I can't spare the time just now. But thanks anyway. Next time I'm in port, perhaps I'll look you up."

"Ya' do that, Cap'n. Name's Nate. Nate Hampstead. Ask anyone down on the landin', an' they'll know who I am. I make it my business t' know every schooner in port— where she's come from an' where she's headed. Ain't you off that new one that just come in this afternoon—'bout the same time them whales was spotted?"

Surprised at the man's astuteness, despite his apparent drunkenness, Gerrick looked him over more carefully. "That's right. My ship is the *Naughty Lady*."

"And what's your business here?" the sailor asked bluntly.

"Whatever presents itself, Nate. Right now, I'm a trader looking for profitable cargo."

The sailor studied the coin he'd just caught in his palm. Glancing back at Gerrick, he again displayed his empty gums. "Well, I'll sure keep my eyes an' ears open for ya', Cap'n—especially if ya' got more where this come from."

"There's always more, lad; the challenge is to earn it."

"Right you are, Cap'n!"

Accepting the sailor's jaunty salute with a nod, Gerrick headed on his way, satisfied that he'd made a worthwhile contact out of a mere chance acquaintance. One never knew when a Nate Hampstead might come in handy. Maybe he never would—then again, he just might. Gerrick had learned long ago to look for hidden advantages in the unlikeliest places. If he could make a friend of a man, he never made an enemy; this was his secret weapon and the heart of all he'd ever learned about survival and success. A charming smile and a handshake always went farther than a scowl and a threat.

More at ease now with what lay ahead, he began whistling to himself as he headed down King's Road toward the Richards' house and his confrontation with Caitlin's uncle.

"I'm certain it's all a misunderstanding, dear Caitlin. Are you sure your uncle said he was coming to Lahaina?" Plain, kindly Clarissa Richards leaned across the table between them and patted Caitlin's hand. "You mustn't allow your imagination to run away with you, dear. He's probably safe and sound on one of the other islands and remembering you daily in his prayers."

Caitlin exchanged worried glances with Pikake, who also sat at the table in the main room of the Richards's two-story coral stone house. The windows were opened onto one of the two long verandas that graced the front of the house, and through them came the noise of hammering from next door where a house for the Ephriam Spaulding family was under construction.

"My uncle told me he had been summoned to an urgent meeting of the Missionary Board. I just naturally assumed it would be in Lahaina. Where else would such a meeting take place? The last two were held here."

"But my dear, *I* know nothing of such a meeting. Don't you think my William would have been invited—and Ephriam also?" Clarissa smiled at the thin, sallow-faced woman sitting next to Pikake. "Did Ephriam breathe a word of this to *you*, Emma, dear?"

"Not a word," Emma Spaulding answered in a high, thin voice. Her colorless lips pursed in disapproval. "And my Ephriam goes nowhere I don't go."

"I see . . ." said Caitlin. "Then I must have been mistaken. Perhaps Oahu or even the Big Island *was* his destination—only he *did* say he was coming here sometime. I *know* he mentioned Maui."

184

"Well, it couldn't have been a meeting of the board, dear, or else we would have been invited, too. Most likely it was a private meeting with Brother Bingham in Honolulu. And perhaps later he intends to visit us here on Maui. Of course, if he *were* on the island right now, visiting someone else, we wouldn't have any way of knowing. We are quite isolated in Lahaina, you know. Or rather, I should say that *other* parts of the island are isolated. One doesn't reach them by land—only by sea."

"I'm just so worried!" Caitlin blurted. "Anything could have happened to him—a sudden storm or a leak in his outrigger."

"We are all in God's hands," Mrs. Spaulding primly reminded her. "So long as we do not stray from the path of righteousness, we needn't fear the wrath of the Almighty."

The woman's tone suggested that she thought Caitlin already guilty of straying from the path; both women had been most surprised to hear of her recent marriage—and even more surprised to hear that she'd wed one of the enemy: a trader whose morals were likely no better than a whaler's. They especially had not liked the idea of her marrying in the absence of her uncle. Even kindly Clarissa had registered dismay—if not downright disapproval.

"Think, my dear," Clarissa entreated. "Has your uncle ever mentioned having other friends or acquaintances on Maui? Before you rush off to Oahu, it would be wise to consider all possiblities here."

Caitlin wracked her brain. "No, he never . . . Wait a minute! He did once say he knew a gentleman here that he'd known on the mainland. And he hoped to look him up one day!"

Clarissa's hazel eyes brightened. "There! I knew it! Sometimes an answer can be right under our noses, but we just can't see it!"

"Yes, but . . ." Caitlin's elation died abruptly as she grappled with this new idea. "Oh, I doubt Uncle George would come visiting *before* his mysterious meeting. Whatever it was about, my uncle was most anxious to leave at once."

"Perhaps we should begin a prayer vigil for him," Mrs. Spaulding suggested. "Though if his outrigger is already sunk, I don't know what good it will do."

"Why, Emma, prayers always do good!" Clarissa looked shocked.

"Not if the grim reaper already has you in his clutches, Clarissa. Of course, I'm not saying that Caitlin's uncle has met an untimely end—*or* that he's gone down to the devil—but the possibility does exist. We are—all of us—in a constantly hazardous position; one misstep is all it takes for our immortal souls to be condemned to hell fire for all eternity."

Again, it seemed that Mrs. Spaulding was directing her dire warnings specifically toward Caitlin.

"Do . . . do you mean if we commit *one* sin, we cannot be saved?" Pikake quavered. The little Hawaiian had been silent all this time, apparently intimidated by the missionary wives in their grand stone house, and now her eyes were wide and frightened.

"If you willingly succumb to evil—if you do not resist hard enough, with your very life, if necessary—yes, you will suffer eternal damnation," Mrs. Spaulding intoned in a preachy voice. "Hasn't Miss Price—excuse me, *Mrs.* Scott—taught you this simple truth, girl?"

"Of c—course!" Pikake stammered. "B—but I thought one had only to beg forgiveness for her wrongdoings, and she would be saved."

"*Saved?* You cannot be saved if you knowingly do wrong with the idea of repenting on your deathbed!" Emma Spaulding's pale watery eyes almost bulged from her head. "What heresy have you and your uncle been preaching, Caitlin Scott?"

Caitlin was so taken aback by the woman's ridiculous accusation that for a moment she was speechless. When she did finally find her tongue, she could only protest feebly: "We preach no heresy, Mrs. Spaulding. We—that is, *I*—have only told the islanders the truth. Our God is a merciful, forgiving God, not a—"

"Lies! Lies and heresy!" Mrs. Spaulding jumped to her

feet. "But what can be expected from a bold young woman who would marry without her guardian's consent—nay, without even his presence? No wonder you fear for his life! It would only serve you right if the Lord exacted a painful punishment for your rashness. Confess, girl! Did you marry so quickly because you *had* to?"

Caitlin also rose, her indignation making her reckless, not caring *what* she said. "How *dare* you speak to me so rudely? I'm old enough to make my *own* decisions, Mrs. Spaulding, and I married Gerrick Scott because I *love* him though I had *not*—I am pleased to inform you— already gone to bed with him. That pleasure we reserved until *after* we were married!"

"Caitlin!" Clarissa gasped, rising and coming around the table toward her. "Please, my dear . . . mind your manners and your conversation, especially in front of . . . one of the infidels. I'm sure Mrs. Spaulding meant nothing by her unfortunate remark. It's only that she's worried about conditions here with little Nahiehaena."

"Nahiehaena?" Caitlin repeated dumbly, wondering what the young Hawaiian princess had to do with anything.

"Oh, my dear . . ." Clarissa wrung her plump white hands together. "You just cannot know what trials and tribulations we've had here in Lahaina, trying to keep the princess and her brother, the young king, apart."

Slowly, it dawned on Caitlin what Clarissa was saying. Ancient Hawaiian tradition demanded that the royal mana be preserved and perpetuated by having brother marry sister, thereby keeping the blood of the royal family pure. Until the arrival of the missionaries, the Hawaiians hadn't known that incest was wrong—and the first thing the missionaries had done was to inform them of the eternal punishment for the heinous crime. So fervently had the missionaries preached against the custom, that Caitlin had believed it long since dead.

"You can't mean that Nahiehaena and Kamehameha plan to marry . . ." She trailed off uncertainly, so shocked by the notion that her own problems paled by comparison.

"Incest has already been committed—or so we hear," Mrs. Spaulding said. "Every time the king is in Lahaina, Nahiehaena allows him—nay, *invites* him—to stay at her house, and they have often been seen sporting together on the beaches."

"But what has that to do with—"

"Nahiehaena *dares* to do this—fully aware it is wrong—because she believes all can be mended before she dies." Mrs. Spaulding eyed Caitlin and Pikake knowingly, as if accusing them of a similar misbelief. "In the manner of the two queens who preceded her, her mother and her aunt, she plans to beg forgiveness for her sins on her deathbed. That way she can please us, the missionaries, and also please those among the unconverted heathen who are pressing her to preserve the old traditions and marry her brother."

"He is the last prince, and she the last princess of their line," Clarissa explained sadly. "Last year, when the prince became king, the pressures on both of them mounted. But while it's true that they have been drinking and carousing far into the night, Nahiehaena *does* still come to church, and Governor Hoapili has joined us in trying to keep the two apart. Often, in the past, before the prince reached his majority, Hoapili would *order* him to Honolulu, while we kept his sister here in Lahaina. And then came that awful time when the young king sought to kill himself, and everyone said it was because he couldn't *live* without his sister's affections."

"It's up to Nahiehaena, of course," Mrs. Spaulding cut in unsympathetically. "If she does not resist him and send him away, *her* sin will be the greatest, as it always is with the female in matters of the flesh."

"What a terrible burden that poor young woman is carrying!" Caitlin burst out, thinking only of the attractive, once-carefree youngster she had many times seen surfing and playing on the beach.

"From the earliest days of her youth, the princess was taught right from wrong. We did not mince words with her—nor will we with you, young lady," Mrs. Spaulding glared at Pikake. "If you have a thought in your head of sinning, don't think you can avoid the consequences. Evil is evil—and—"

"But what if evil is done *to* you, and not by your . . . your desire?" Pikake asked timidly. "Nahiehaena is not wicked for loving Kamehameha; royal brothers and sisters have *always* married each other."

"No evil is done *to* you, child!" Emma Spaulding shrieked. "Unless, of course, you invite it! Even a woman who is raped must examine her conduct to see how she deserved it. Neither the princess nor any other girl can claim innocence by right of circumstance or tradition. A woman *knows* when she's enticing a man to sin! She—"

"Now, Emma," Clarissa demurred, with a worried glance in Caitlin's direction. "Don't you think you're being a bit harsh?"

Caitlin's hands were clenched at her sides, and a flush had risen to her cheeks. The heat of anger coursed through her veins; Emma Spaulding was even worse than Uncle George at shaming the Hawaiians and making them feel guilty about their heritage. Of course, one could not condone incest, but one needn't destroy a person's self-respect in order to teach her Christianity. Pikake did not deserve a tongue-lashing for defending her sovereign, nor did Caitlin herself deserve Emma's sly insinuations regarding the reasons for her marriage.

If Caitlin *had* sinned in lusting after Gerrick before their marriage, she had rectified her error by marrying him— and in any case, it was none of Emma's business *what* Caitlin had or hadn't done.

"*Really*, Mrs. Spaulding . . ." she began, but just then a knock sounded at the door.

"Oh, that must be your husband, Caitlin!" Clarissa cried. Rushing to the door, she flung it open, and her sigh of relief was loud in the tense atmosphere of the room. "Why, it's *two* fine gentlemen. . . . Come in, please, sirs, come in!"

"After you, John . . ." Gerrick's voice boomed. "What a coincidence we arrived here at the same time."

"Good afternoon, ladies!" Grinning, John entered the house, his eyes immediately seeking Pikake, who, when she saw him, returned his grin with a smile that lit her entire face.

"Oh, John!" Pikake cried, running lightly to the big man's side. "I'm so happy you finally come. I have been missing you so much!"

The little Hawaiian's spontaneous clasping of John's large hand did not go unnoticed by Emma Spaulding or Clarissa Richards. But Caitlin was still too angry with Emma to care what the women were thinking. She, too, was overwhelmingly glad to see Gerrick. Hurrying toward him, she held out her arms—and he responded by sweeping her off her feet and planting a joyous kiss on her open mouth. The kiss was jolting in its intensity; they'd been parted for only hours, but it felt like weeks.

Drawing her nearer in his possessive embrace, Gerrick growled in her ear, "Well, now . . . lonesome for me already, sweet Cait? Where is your uncle? I can't wait to meet him."

Behind her, Caitlin could hear Emma Spaulding gasping in outrage—but whether it was because of John and Pikake's warm greeting or her own with Gerrick, she didn't know. Leaning back from Gerrick, she blurted out her bad news: "Gerrick, he isn't here! And no one knows where he is!"

Sudden tears blurred her vision, but with them came a lessening of anxiety; she wasn't facing this problem all alone. Gerrick was here now—her strong, capable husband. *He* would know what to do.

Chapter Fifteen

His mind whirring with the implications of the scene before him, Gerrick thought it best to breathe deeply and collect his thoughts before saying anything. Besides being happy to see him, Caitlin looked flushed, angry, and upset—as if she'd been arguing with the two missionary wives standing near the table in the center of the room. Noticing how Pikake clung to John's hand as if he had just saved her life, Gerrick studied the two missionaries for clues as to what had been going on before he and John knocked at the door.

One of the women was plump and kindly-looking, with rosy cheeks, hazel eyes, and light brown hair parted in the middle and fastened into a bun on top of her head. She seemed as distressed as Caitlin; her plump hands nervously smoothed the white apron she wore over her simple brown dress and her eyes radiated dismay as they darted from John to Caitlin and then to him.

The other woman was thin and stringy, with graying hair, disapproving eyes, a pinched nose, and a grim slash where her mouth ought to be. Her pale blue orbs regarded him suspiciously, as if he were a rat invading the sanctity of her home, and as her scathing glance swept John and Pikake, her mouth tightened even more.

"I'm sorry," Caitlin said breathlessly. "Let me introduce you first. This is Clarissa Richards and Emma Spaulding, the wives of William Richards and Ephriam

Spaulding, the resident missionaries here at Lahaina. Their husbands are away just now, visiting a sick parishioner, but they are expected back momentarily."

"Ladies . . ." Gerrick responded, stepping around Caitlin and taking each by the hand. "I had no idea Lahaina was graced by such beautiful representatives of New England womanhood."

Clarissa Richards smiled at the compliment, but Emma Spaulding only scowled the harder. "So you are the one who married Miss Price without her guardian's consent," she accused waspishly.

Having discovered at least one reason for the woman's hostility, Gerrick bent to kiss her hand, which she wrenched away from him before he could do so. "I am indeed the thief in the night, Mrs. Spaulding. Fortunately, I did not meet you first, or I might have ignored Caitlin and sought to woo you away from your husband instead."

"Likely you would have, sir! It's the sort of thing a man of your ilk might attempt."

Gerrick grinned at her response, watching as he did so for any telltale softening in the woman's stern countenance. Her eyes flashed her contempt, but as he only continued grinning and didn't respond in kind, Emma Spaulding tossed her head, and her mouth relaxed just the tiniest bit.

"You have me pegged precisely, Mrs. Spaulding," he purred, enjoying the challenge before she succumbed to his charm completely. "I can only beg you to tender a few prayers for me when next you consult with the Almighty. I'd be forever indebted were you to put in a good word on my behalf."

"And why should I do that, sir?" Emma Spaulding demanded, appearing mollified, despite herself. "You'd do better to get down on your knees yourself."

"Alas, I'm too great a sinner. I need someone to intercede for me. Would you do that, Mrs. Spaulding? The Lord could never resist the prayers of someone like yourself."

"I'll think about it—though all the prayers in the world

won't avail if your heart remains hardened by sin and greed."

"My dear Caitlin has been softening my greedy heart, Mrs. Spaulding—and drawing me closer each day to eternal salvation. She is an angel of the Lord, and each day that passes makes me value her even more." Pulling Caitlin forward, Gerrick almost laughed aloud at her expression of sheer amazement. "Now, what were you saying about your uncle, sweetheart?"

"He . . . he isn't here, Gerrick. Uncle George never arrived in Lahaina, and no one knows anything about the important meeting he was supposed to attend."

"Well, then, it's obvious we have come to the wrong place—an error we can quickly remedy." Though he himself was relieved at the news, Gerrick disliked seeing Caitlin so upset. The worry in her beautiful blue-gray eyes tore at his insides; she looked as frightened and helpless as a wounded animal, and taking her in his arms again, he smiled reassuringly. "Would you like to set sail immediately? There's no point in staying here if he's not on the island."

"I don't know what to do, Gerrick! He *could* be here somewhere—not in Lahaina, perhaps, but in one of the other villages. I just wish I knew which one!"

"We could spend a few days sailing the coastline and inquiring if anyone has seen him," Gerrick offered, willing to do anything to make her smile again. And the more he thought about it, the more appealing became the idea of prolonging their idyllic "honeymoon."

"Gerrick," John interrupted. "What about your *brother?*"

Gerrick frowned at the reminder. "I've waited this long to find him, John. Another few days won't matter. Besides, wouldn't you, ah, *welcome* the opportunity to become better acquainted with Maui?" As he mentioned the island's name, Gerrick glanced meaningfully at Pikake, still clinging tightly to John's hand and gazing at the big man adoringly.

"Well, I suppose . . ." John acquiesced, hooking an arm

193

about Pikake's slender waist and returning her tender glance with a warm one of his own.

"Gentlemen!" Emma Spaulding hissed. "Before you make your final plans, I have a suggestion."

"Of course, dear lady." Gerrick responded graciously, though he doubted that *any* suggestion from the sourfaced woman would be acceptable.

"Leave her with *us* while you search for Brother Price."

Gerrick was both startled and confused. "Leave *who* with you—my *wife?*"

The appellation rolled off his tongue with surprising ease, and Gerrick realized that he had never yet referred to Caitlin as his wife—much less actually begun to *think* of her as such. Now, suddenly, it had become difficult to think of her otherwise.

"No, not your wife—*that* one." Emma Spaulding jerked her head in Pikake's direction. "Your wife's little friend appears sadly lacking in Christian guidance and direction, but a few days with us would straighten out her thinking."

"*Mrs. Spaulding!*" Caitlin's eyes shot sparks, but before she could say anything, John moved protectively in front of Pikake.

"Pikake is coming with us," he growled in a tone of voice that Gerrick knew from experience would brook no arguments, not even those of Emma Spaulding.

"Just what is your interest in this girl?" Emma demanded, rounding on John accusingly.

"That is none of your business, madam. Neither she nor I are in any way accountable to you."

"I disagree, sir. My business is saving souls, which I've been mandated to do by the highest authority on heaven or earth, the Almighty God. And in order to carry out my duties, I must and *shall* root out evil in whatever guise I find it."

"Are you accusing me of evil?" John whispered hoarsely. "Are you accusing this . . . this beautiful, innocent child?"

Astounded, Gerrick watched as Emma Spaulding thrust

194

out her pointed chin and cast a condemning glance upon cowering little Pikake. "I am well acquainted with the loose morals of Hawaiian women, sir. And as for you . . ." Her lip curled when she looked at John. "I have seen enough of unbridled lust in this so-called paradise to know when a man desires a woman impurely. You, sir, have lustful designs on this girl. You are wicked and unprincipled, and if she is too weak to resist you, I must step in and safeguard her virtue."

"What if I intended to *marry* her?" John shot back.

"Then your sin would be even worse! You are not of the same race, the same culture. Therefore—"

"Stop it!" Caitlin shouted. "You have no right to speak this way to John. Why, his character is above reproach. He *came* to the islands to build a *church* . . ."

"Caitlin . . . Caitlin . . ." Gerrick intervened, knowing he must seize control of the situation before it deteriorated any further. "I'm sorry, dearest," he apologized when she turned stricken, questioning eyes upon him. "I didn't mean to interrupt, but we had best leave immediately if we intend to sail tonight or first thing in the morning. The day grows late, and I'd prefer to be aboard ship before nightfall."

There was a long tense moment, and then Caitlin said meekly, "Yes, of course, Gerrick. Thank you for reminding me. I, too, fear we've remained here far too long."

Clarissa Richards came to life with a flurry of movement in Caitlin and Gerrick's direction. "Oh, but I was so hopeful you'd spend the night with us. William will be most distressed if you leave before he's had a chance to say hello to you. Our home is always open to visitors, and we . . . we . . ."

She placed a beseeching hand on Gerrick's arm and lowered her voice to an embarrassed whisper: "Please, Captain Scott! Don't mind poor Emma. Sometimes, she gets carried away, but her heart is in the right place. Truly, it is!"

Turning, Clarissa held out her arms to John and Pikake. "I bid you all welcome to my home. I have sleeping room for all of you—separate quarters, of course," she added, blushing.

Over Clarissa's head, Gerrick shot Caitlin a questioning glance, leaving the final decision to her. But Caitlin silently shook her head no. Pleased that she had sided with him, Gerrick said kindly but firmly, "Forgive us for rushing off, madam, but we must return to my ship tonight. Perhaps next time we can remain longer. I understand you have a new Masters' and Mates' Reading Room; on our next visit, I *insist* upon seeing it."

"Of *course,* Captain! We would be delighted to show it to you. Wouldn't we, Emma?"

"Of course," Emma echoed grudgingly.

Behind the backs of the two women, Caitlin beamed her relief at Gerrick, and as he turned to leave, she entwined her fingers through his. Gerrick squeezed them tightly. It struck him that they had not needed words to communicate—a phenomenon he had never before experienced with any women save his mother and sister—and he felt an odd tugging sensation in the region of his heart; what was Caitlin *doing* to him?

As they passed out of the door to the Richards's house, Caitlin flashed him a sweet intimate smile that reverberated all the way to his toes. In the warm flush that enveloped him, he found it easy to continue his sorely tried gallantry. "Until we meet again, ladies . . ." He bowed to each of them, lingering over Emma Spaulding's small, bony hand—a hand as dry and withered as her soul. "Don't forget to pray for me, Mrs. Spaulding," he cajoled. "Do pray for *all* of us."

"You may be sure of my prayers, sir, though even a fool could see that you are quite *beyond* prayers."

"Then pray for yourself, madam, that you may continue to set such a shining example of Christian charity."

Later that night as Gerrick held Caitlin in his arms, he had time to reflect on their visit with the missionaries. His body was replete with satisfaction following an interlude

196

of such passionate lovemaking that it had left him breathless and in awe of the strength of Caitlin's love for him. Yet even as he basked in its glow, he was still afraid to think about that love, and so deliberately turned his thoughts to Emma Spaulding and Clarissa Richards.

"What were you and those missionary women talking about before we arrived at their house this afternoon?" he whispered in Caitlin's ear. "Did they take you to task for daring to marry a sinner such as myself?"

"Not in so many words—but yes, they did," Caitlin answered, her voice muffled against the pillow. "Don't forget that I was expected to marry a missionary and spend my life as they do—making the Hawaiians feel ashamed."

Gerrick chuckled as he nuzzled her sweet-smelling hair. "I'll bet they envy you every bit as much as they disapprove."

Caitlin turned to face him, but it was so dark he could not see her face—only the glints of her silver-gold hair and shining eyes. "Perhaps they do, but I doubt it. There's a great deal of comfort and security in . . . in knowing your future. And in believing in what you are doing. If anything, they probably pity me."

"You sound as if you have regrets," Gerrick teased, unable to imagine that Caitlin—or any woman for that matter—would want to trade places with Emma Spaulding.

"No, I have no regrets, my love. But I have been asking myself what I will do now. Rather, what will *we* do."

Gerrick's breath caught in his throat, but Caitlin only snuggled closer, unaware she'd touched a sore spot. "Gerrick, have you thought of our future together? Or do you only . . . think of *this?*"

By "this," he knew she meant the lovemaking they had just enjoyed, and he was dismayed that she was already thinking past it to things he would rather not face just yet. "Isn't *this* enough for you? Must women always want something more?"

His tone of voice betrayed his testiness, and Caitlin's surprise was evident in *her* tone. "What we share . . . why,

197

it's wonderful, Gerrick! Truly, it is. But I . . . I have a right to know your plans for our future. After we find your brother, what then? Will we be returning to New England?"

Gerrick rolled over and sat up. Her questions were not unreasonable, but that only made him feel worse, not better. He *couldn't* allow her to probe any further. "Probably," he hedged. "I haven't yet decided."

Undeterred, she pressed onward. "What exactly do you *do* in New England? Tell me about yourself, Gerrick. Tell me about your family and your business."

"Isn't it a bit late to start quizzing me about my finances? Since you seem so concerned about how I'll take care of you, I'm surprised you didn't ask sooner—*before* the wedding. What if I should tell you I'm penniless? Would you be sorry that you married me?"

"Oh, no, Gerrick!" Sounding stricken, Caitlin grabbed his arm. "Oh, how could you think I meant . . . I'm not in the *least* worried about our finances! Why, this cabin is *far* more luxurious than anything to which I'm accustomed. I could *gladly* live here forever—or in a hut on the beach, if necessary, so long as I'm with you."

Gerrick turned sideways and gathered her into his arms, his guilt almost more than he could bear. "Forgive me, Caitlin." He kissed her forehead and her hair. "You see, I once loved a woman who spurned my offer of marriage because I wasn't rich enough. She feared I couldn't supply the security—the freedom from want—that she craved. She married someone else, and I was devastated, almost destroyed. . . . I know you meant no harm by your questions, but it would please me so much if you would only trust me—and let the future take care of itself. Rather, *I* shall take care of it. You're not to spend a single minute worrying."

He could feel her reluctance and frustration, but then she melted against him. "Of course, my darling. I'm so sorry for having upset you. I had guessed that you had been hurt, but I had no idea . . ."

Her arms tightened sympathetically around his neck,

and he hated himself for deceiving her and making *her* feel guilty. Caitlin, of all people, had no interest in wealth or money. She *would* be happy living in a ship's cabin—or even in a cave. She wore dresses Madeline would have scorned as rags and viewed the humblest of meals as a banquet. Pushing her down against the pillows, he pressed his lips to the pulse point in her neck and tenderly kissed it. Before he could stop it, a regretful sigh escaped him. "Can't we just be happy living one day at a time?"

"Oh, my love, of course we can! Each day with you is a miracle—a precious, perfect gift. You're right; we must cease worrying about the future and savor every moment together. I *know* that whatever you decide will please me; I only hope I can please you half so well."

"You *do* please me, Caitlin. . . . Don't worry; when the time comes, we'll talk about what's to be done. If you hate my decisions, I won't force them upon you. All I ask is that you don't nag or badger me beforehand."

"I promise you I won't. Besides, if they're *your* decisions, I *couldn't* hate them—not so long as I know that *eventually* you'll tell me how I'm to spend my days as your wife."

"It isn't your days I care about, sweet Cait, it's your nights. With your days, you can do as you please. However, as soon as the sun goes down . . ." Gerrick began nibbling a path down the slender column of her throat, and Caitlin moaned softly as he approached the deep, fragrant valley between her full breasts. "All your nights belong to me, Caitlin," he growled possessively. "And so does your exceedingly delicious body."

Bending his head, he flicked his tongue across a succulent nipple, and Caitlin writhed beneath him. Delighted by her ready response, he then laved her other nipple until it stood upright and swollen. Tiny whimpering sounds issued from her throat, madly exciting him, yet he held himself in check and moved with careful, teasing motions to fuel her rising passions. Wherever he touched her, her flesh felt slick and dewey with perspiration. He probed between her thighs and discovered her already wet

199

and warm in anticipation of their joining, and he marveled anew that she had not—despite her upbringing—turned out like Emma Spaulding: as rigid, dry, and incapable of sexual pleasure as an old leather boot.

"My beautiful, sensual Caitlin," he murmured, overcome by his need for her.

Rising up on his elbows, he quickly positioned himself and, groaning his desire, plunged into her tight velvet sheath. The fact that he had just possessed her made no difference to his straining body; he could never get enough of her, and the urge to drive deeply, to sheath himself completely in her warmth and softness, was akin to a gigantic wave crashing over his head.

As he rose and plunged, Caitlin locked her arms and legs around him—lifting her hips and responding with a rocking motion that drove him to a frenzy. Almost brutally, he rode her, focusing all his strength and effort on reaching the very core of her, on possessing and being possessed so totally that *nothing*—not even his lies—could ever separate them.

Only dimly did he hear himself crying her name. The explosion of his passion splintered his senses into a thousand shimmering pieces—his pleasure more intense than any he had ever before experienced. Caitlin so absorbed him, so matched him thrust for thrust, that he could no longer tell where he left off and she began; they were one in mind and body, and he felt himself dying in her arms and entering a long-sought paradise. Together they floated on a diamond-sparkled plane of consciousness, while wave after wave of exquisite sensation washed over them. And Gerrick realized in the deepest, darkest corner of his soul that he would never again be the same.

This was how lovemaking was meant to be—not a crude release of body fluids accompanied by a jolt of momentary pleasure, but a perfect blending of flesh and spirit that forever joined a man and woman more completely than they had ever been or could ever be with anyone else. No matter if a distance of a million miles should separate them, they would belong only to each other—mated for life and as surely bonded as if they'd been forged in fire.

I love you, Caitlin, his heart acknowledged, and by the way she sighed and touched her fingertips to his lips, he knew she understood—or perhaps he had spoken the words aloud without realizing it. He drifted asleep entwined in her arms, and his sleep was deep and satisfying, as it had not been since before he lost his family and his fortune. And when he dreamed, he dreamed of Caitlin—her lips, her eyes, her hair, her body.

He would never leave her, never give her up—no, not for all the sandalwood on Kauai, or for that matter, in the world. She was the only treasure he truly wanted; in comparison to her, nothing else mattered, not now, not ever. Caitlin was his precious jewel for which he'd been searching all his life.

Chapter Sixteen

"What if we *never* find him?" Caitlin was so filled with worry and disappointment that she couldn't hide it any longer—not even to spare Gerrick. Dear Gerrick! Rather than complaining about the delay in searching for his brother, he still seemed more than willing to explore every nook and cranny on the island of Maui for her uncle.

This was the eighth—or was it the ninth?—place they had stopped and gone ashore to make inquiries, and everywhere it had been the same: No one had seen or heard of him. Despite her nagging certainty that he must be here somewhere, Uncle George could *not* have come to Maui, or they would have found him by now.

"You mustn't lose heart, Cait. Sooner or later, we'll discover his whereabouts." Gerrick slipped his arms around her waist and pulled her toward him. Tilting her face to his, he smiled down at her, and the love she saw in his eyes immediately gladdened her spirits.

No matter if they eventually learned that her uncle had drowned at sea, she would always remember these days with Gerrick as the happiest of her life. She needed no words from him to confirm what he felt for her; whenever he looked at her, his green eyes glowed, and when he made love to her, his ardent caresses swept her away to a world of joy and ecstasy that rivaled anything she'd heard about heaven.

Though they'd been searching diligently for Uncle

George, Caitlin had lost track of the sunlit days and lived breathlessly awaiting the starry nights. Her body craved the hours between dark and dawn, when Gerrick's lean hard torso joined with hers, and they entered a beautiful, exotic land where no one existed but themselves—man and woman, naked and alive, touching, caressing, and communicating in a language so special and private that it seemed to belong only to them.

Now, as she gazed up into his handsome, beloved face, the knowledge of the night shimmered between them, darkening his eyes with desire. Her own heart hammered. Moisture welled in the secret crevices between her thighs, and she knew if she moved closer to him she would be able to feel his arousal pressing against her. It would be wonderful to make love outside in the daylight, as they had done that afternoon at the hidden pool, but she mustn't think about such things now—not when she was so worried about Uncle George.

Despite her happiness in her marriage, she *was* growing anxious over their failure to find her uncle. The time had come to set sail for Oahu, the only other place he might likely be. Though she would hate to leave Maui's sparkling waters, at least she could take comfort in her memories; in the cabin aboard Gerrick's ship, she had learned more about herself than she had known previously in all her life. Gerrick had opened her eyes to delights she had never imagined existed, teaching her to revel in her female self rather than to suppress and feel ashamed of her body's wants and needs.

When and if they *did* find Uncle George, he would be seeing a new Caitlin—a poised, confident *woman*, not the prim, uncertain child he had left behind. Would he approve? Or would he, like Emma Spaulding, attempt to make her regret what she had become?

"Gerrick, we must admit the truth," Caitlin finally said, hating to disrupt the intimacy between them but knowing that she must. "My uncle isn't here. We've asked at every possible landing place. I don't know where else an outrigger could put ashore that we haven't already been."

203

"That doesn't mean he isn't here somewhere. It just means we haven't talked to the natives who might have seen him."

"The natives *couldn't* have seen him if he never arrived here. We should set sail at once for Oahu. If he isn't with Brother Bingham in Honolulu, then he's . . . he's probably dead."

"If he's dead, then we can't do anything for him," Gerrick responded matter-of-factly. "Therefore, there's no rush to leave, and we might as well enjoy what's left of the afternoon."

"Oh, Gerrick . . . that sounds so . . . so *unfeeling*. Uncle George is my only living relative. I can't relax and enjoy myself while his fate remains a mystery."

"You can't?" Gerrick's hands slid down to her hips and pulled her tight against him. "Now you know that's a lie, Cait. I can make you forget everything—even your precious uncle."

"Gerrick! John is standing right over there with Pikake."

"Then let's give them some privacy."

"Privacy is the last thing we should give them! They spend too much time alone together as it is."

Gerrick's green eyes sought John and Pikake, who were examining seashells washed ashore on the beach. Then they came back to her. "They'll be all right together for a few minutes, Caitlin. I've told you before, and now I'll tell you again: You can't chaperone them every minute, and even if you could, you shouldn't. Neither you nor Emma Spaulding has a right to interfere. Their relationship is their *own* business."

Stung that he had compared her to Emma, Caitlin snapped, "Pikake is my dearest friend! I care what happens to her."

"And John is mine. And frankly what's happening to *him* has me delighted. I've never seen him act so protective, so gentle and polite toward a woman. I assure you he means her no harm; he may indeed be considering marriage. You'll recall he mentioned it in Lahaina."

"Surely, you can't be serious! I had hoped he was only joking—or taunting Mrs. Spaulding."

"And I hope *you* are only joking. I thought you were more tolerant than that prejudiced old witch."

"Perhaps Emma Spaulding has reasons for her prejudice!"

Hearing herself actually defend Emma, Caitlin bit down on her tongue. She didn't want to *fight* with Gerrick. Why, only moments before she had wanted to make love to him! As if he had read her mind, Gerrick flashed her a crooked, endearing grin.

"While you were talking to the islanders about your uncle, I went exploring and found the most beautiful, secluded spot. . . . If I can't show it to you before we leave, I'll be deeply hurt and disappointed."

"I'd be honored if you would show it to me," she whispered, sliding her hand into his.

"Come on then. We'll have to walk fast if we want to make it there and back before sunset. If we hurry, we can still sail with the evening breeze and reach Oahu sometime tomorrow."

Glad that their spat had not erupted into a full-blown argument, Caitlin hurried to match her shorter strides with his long ones. Tomorrow would be time enough to worry about John and Pikake—and also about Uncle George.

"Oh, Gerrick, it's the most enchanting spot in the world!"

They were standing near the edge of a crystal clear pool cut out of black lava rock. Below the pool was a second one, into which pure cold water was cascading in a silver stream. And below that was still another. There were seven pools in all—each of them linked by a waterfall. The lowest basin spilled into the turquoise sea, and flowering trees and shrubs, as well as the usual palms, pandanus, and ironwoods, closely fringed the entire area, creating a secret, magical place where the only sound was the gurgle and splash of water tumbling onto mossy rock.

Caitlin guessed that the picturesque gulch had probably once been considered sacred—or else had been reserved for royalty. This was true of many of Kauai's loveliest, secluded spots and probably also true on Maui.

"How about a swim?" Gerrick asked, tugging at his clothing.

Caitlin scanned the jungle greenery; it was so dense the sunlight barely penetrated. The contrast of dark and light made the sun-splashed pools and waterfalls stand out in startling, brilliant clarity.

"It *does* look safe from prying eyes," she conceded. "But are you sure no one followed us here from the beach?"

Gerrick's grin was wicked. "Of course I'm sure. I left strict orders we were to be undisturbed for several hours."

"Gerrick, you are incorrigible!"

"Not me, my love—Mac. No sooner had I discovered this place when he was assessing the romantic possibilities."

"And I presume he found them to his liking."

"If Adam and Eve had it any better, I'd be surprised. Maui is a lovers' paradise. I only wish we had time to explore more of it—especially the mountain they call Haleakala."

"Haleakala's not a mountain; it's a volcano."

"Whatever it is, it's awesome—so seductive and mysterious poking up through the clouds. I want to go there with you someday. I want to make love to you on its peak, with the whole island spread out at our feet."

"It's sure to be icy cold up there! We might freeze."

"Not a chance," Gerrick said huskily. "Mac and I will keep you warm."

Tossing his clothing onto the rocks rimming the pool, he came toward her—so lithe and well proportioned that she sucked in her breath, overcome by admiration of his handsomeness. It still seemed incredible that a man such as Gerrick Scott was her husband, that he belonged to her, and that she was free to enjoy his nakedness anytime she wanted.

"What are you staring at, wife? Get out of those clothes at once or I'll rip them apart!"

"You wouldn't!" Caitlin backed away from him, then burst into giggles as Gerrick seized her and began wrestling off her dress.

"Damn ugly rags!" he swore. "You're the most beautiful female in all God's kingdom. Why must you dress like a beggar? In the absence of silk, the least you could do is wear one of those printed skirts and flowers in your hair, like the native women."

"Well, I'm *not* a native woman! I'm a missionary—or at least, I *was* one before I met you."

"Wait here a minute," he commanded. "And finish undressing. I'll be right back."

Hurriedly, remembering that Gerrick was fully capable of ruining her dress if she did not take it off soon enough to please him, Caitlin did as she was bid. In minutes, Gerrick was back with handfuls of delicate, deep pink *lehua* blossoms he had snatched from an *ohia lehua* tree.

"Here. I wish these were rare gems. If I knew how to do it, I'd make a necklace of them."

"You mean a *lei* . . ." Smiling, Caitlin accepted the feathery, short-stemmed blossoms though she had no idea of what he meant for her to do with them. The flowers were as airy and delicate as cloud wisps.

Gerrick plucked several from her fingers and tucked them into her long, flowing hair. Then he bent to entwine one in the curly hair at the juncture of her thighs. Laughing and protesting, she backed away.

"Hold still!" Gerrick cried. "Celia deserves a flower, too."

But Caitlin whirled and ran toward the pool. She waded in water to her knees, turned, and splashed sparkling droplets at a grinning Gerrick in hot pursuit. Large, round pebbles on the bottom made footing uncertain, and both were soon stumbling and falling as they chased each other around the pool.

The chase ended in a long, searing kiss, and Gerrick scooped Caitlin into his arms and carried her back to shore in search of a soft bower beneath the twisting trees. He laid her on the ground and knelt over her, and she pulled his head down to her breasts.

"Gerrick, my dearest . . . my darling husband, I love you so!" She sighed, surrendering to the rapture she knew awaited her.

Poised above her, Gerrick raked her body with a scorching gaze, his eyes the color of the afternoon sunlight illuminating the darkest depths of the sea. "No matter what happens, Cait, I want you to know this and never forget it: I love you, too."

It was the first time she had heard him admit it, and Caitlin's heart felt full to bursting. "What could possibly happen?" she queried lightly. "Do you mean hearing about my uncle's death?"

"That . . . or *worse*."

A dark shadow slanted across his face, and Caitlin suddenly felt threatened and afraid. Despite the day's warmth, she shivered. Noticing the shiver, Gerrick frowned his concern and moved to cover her more completely with his warm, strong body. "I'm sorry," he murmured. "I shouldn't have said that. Especially when I feel so certain we'll find your uncle before too much longer."

His words were reassuring—until she realized that it wasn't her uncle's death she feared more than anything; it was losing Gerrick. If her uncle died, she would grieve for him, but in time she'd get over it. However, if she somehow lost Gerrick . . . the consequences were too horrible to contemplate. Without Gerrick, her life would be meaningless.

"Love me, please, Gerrick. . . . Oh, please love me!" she begged.

"With pleasure, sweetling, with *great* pleasure."

"Well, Cait, this must be it." Gerrick nodded toward the complex of mission houses—a two-story frame structure that must have come straight from Boston, a larger new coral stone building, and a coral stone printing house—located on King Street in dusty Honolulu. "Shall I go in with you or would you prefer I wait here?"

Flashing him a nervous smile and clutching her shawl more tightly around her shoulders, Caitlin turned and scanned the houses while Gerrick studied her and patiently awaited her answer. He noticed she had worn her most severe dress this morning and arranged her hair in its old, plain style. This return to her old image bothered him; somehow, it made him feel threatened, and he wanted nothing more than to take her away from this hot, unattractive spot.

Honolulu's harbor had been spectacular from the deck of the schooner, but the town itself was built upon a muddy, stinking beach dotted with shallow swamps that far surpassed Lahaina for overcrowding, the presence of unsavory characters, and the grim, unmistakable influence of the missionaries. All the islanders they had thus far encountered went about with a curiously restrained manner, as though they were afraid to smile, and all the women were dressed decorously in high-necked *holukus*, instead of their usual lighthearted, half-naked state.

Gerrick sensed a shamed submissiveness in the Hawaiians, as if they'd been so brow-beaten they'd lost all pride in themselves, and this could only come from having been repeatedly told what great sinners they were.

"Wait here, please, Gerrick—at least until I find out if the Binghams or the Chamberlains are home."

Gerrick wondered if Caitlin dreaded introducing him as her husband. Considering the reaction of the Lahaina missionaries, she probably did. "Cait, if he *isn't* here, don't put yourself through any more misery than you must. There's really no reason to tell them about me."

She smiled at that, her blue-gray eyes shining in the afternoon sunlight. "Why shouldn't I tell them about you? I'm *proud* to be your wife. I only suggested you wait here until I inform them of my arrival. As soon as they recover from the shock of this surprise visit from *me*, I'll spring *you* upon them."

"And John and Pikake? Will you spring them as well?"

Caitlin's smile dissolved into a frown. "I . . . I haven't decided. If we remain here very long, I suppose I'll have to. Or else I'll have to warn John and Pikake to stay away, because I already know how the Binghams will feel about their relationship."

"And will you then tell John and Pikake how *you* feel about their relationship?"

Caitlin's long lashes dipped downward, but the gesture did little to hide her chagrin. She has reason to be chagrined, Gerrick thought irritably, remembering what had passed between them yesterday. Their rapturous lovemaking at the seven pools had nearly been spoiled by Caitlin's ire when, upon returning to the beach, they had discovered the ship's crew sporting with the local women and John and Pikake nowhere in sight. It had been dark by the time their two friends reappeared, holding hands and wearing telltale dreamy expressions that left little doubt as to where they had been and what they had been doing.

Caitlin had managed to hold her temper until after they had eaten a light supper and gone aboard ship, but then, in the privacy of the cabin, she had exploded.

"Gerrick, you *must* speak to John *and* to your crew members. What happened this afternoon must *never* be repeated."

"No, I will not, Caitlin," he had informed her. "Nor will you speak to Pikake. If you start ranting and raving about hellfire and damnation, I swear I'll toss you overboard and drown your self-righteousness in the ocean."

"I'm not being self-righteous; what they are doing is *wrong!*"

"Oh? Have you and Emma Spaulding *both* been divinely appointed to judge your fellow man?"

Caitlin had fallen silent at that, but she had looked so hurt and unhappy that he had taken her in his arms and apologized. He had also promised to restrain his men when next they came to port, but he had *not* agreed to lecture John. That prickly issue still lay between them, and in order to get John and Pikake out of the way of the missionaries, Gerrick had sent them to greet the harbormaster. John had orders to refuse paying any tribute, and Pikake was to translate his arguments against it—a task sure to occupy them until late tonight and even perhaps through tomorrow.

"I wish I knew how I do feel, Gerrick," Caitlin said with a sigh. "I've grown so confused. On the one hand, if John and Pikake truly love each other, perhaps a marriage between them could work. On the other hand, such a marriage goes against everything I've ever been taught. They are *worlds* apart in everything—race, culture, language, religious beliefs."

"So are we, my sweet," Gerrick gently reminded her. "Except for race—and I fail to see how the color of one's skin has anything to do with why two people should or shouldn't love each other."

"Perhaps you are right. Race *shouldn't* make any difference." Caitlin's sparkling eyes caressed his face. "I myself would love you no matter if you were colored green with purple spots."

"Ah, now that is true love, indeed," Gerrick quipped, though a vise suddenly squeezed his heart, causing a pain that was fast becoming wrenchingly familiar. "Go see if anyone is home, now, Cait—and I'll wait here like a good little boy until you give me permission to present my humble self to your friends for inspection."

"Boor!" Caitlin wrinkled her nose at him. "How shall I ever prepare the Binghams for your sharp wit and sense of humor? We missionaries aren't known for our ability to laugh and take things lightly."

"I know," Gerrick said dryly. "I was sure I could charm poor Emma, but I never even got her to smile."

"All that matters is that you make *me* smile." Blowing him a kiss, Caitlin started toward the missionary homes, and Gerrick watched her go with a sinking sensation in the pit of his stomach.

As long as they were alone together, he could forget that

he and Caitlin weren't really married and that he had deceived her and would go on deceiving her for as long as possible. Alone with her, he could forget everything, even his reasons for coming to Hawaii in the first place. The past seemed to fade away and the future was inconsequential. Only the present—only the moments in Caitlin's arms, loving her and being loved—counted.

But each time they came into contact with some reminder of Caitlin's past, he found it difficult to breathe because his chest felt so constricted with guilt. Lately, he'd caught himself wondering if there wasn't some other way besides the sandalwood to gain a fortune. Without even exploring bustling, sprawling Honolulu, he knew he could make money here—and certainly, he could do so in Lahaina. But he couldn't make it fast enough or respectably enough to keep Caitlin from learning about his deceptions. He *was* almost penniless; all he had was his ship and enough ready cash to keep going until he found the sandalwood, transported it, and sold it in Canton.

Anything else, any trade deals he could put together, would likely be as unacceptable in Caitlin's eyes as the sandalwood itself. And the profit margin would be far slimmer. Without cash to purchase a cargo, he would either have to steal one or somehow take advantage of someone else's trading misfortune to gain one. And he could easily guess how she would feel about those two unsavory choices.

Nor could he simply sail for home. He had even fewer prospects there. Not only had everything of value his family owned been sold to cover the debts of Amos Taylor, but there were debts remaining to be paid out of any future monies earned by the Scotts. John didn't even know it, but if Gerrick reappeared in Rhode Island without the means to pay off these debts, he would likely be jailed. His only hope of avoiding debtor's prison was to amass a speedy fortune—which he had hoped to do with the sandalwood.

The sandalwood meant survival as well as revenge. Until meeting Caitlin, Gerrick had been focusing only on revenge, but now he realized he must focus on survival—

and he could think of no way to survive that would retain Caitlin's approval and respect. In Caitlin's innocence and naïveté, she would surely condemn what he found quite acceptable. Being honorable did not preclude being flexible, and a little subterfuge in business dealings had never bothered him or his father overmuch; they had always done what they must to succeed.

No matter what I do, I risk losing her, Gerrick thought dismally. But his best bet still remained the sandalwood. As soon as they found her uncle, he must get back to Kauai and start his search. . . . With any luck, he'd simply find the wood "by accident." And then maybe if he *did* actually finance the building of a church . . .

"There's no one home at the Chamberlains," Caitlin called out to him. "I'm going to try the Binghams now."

Gerrick waved to her as she walked around the corner of the coral stone house and headed for the front door of the little frame structure. For her sake, he hoped her uncle himself opened the door. For his own sake, he still dreaded meeting her uncle but was now anxious to get it over with so they could leave. He pondered what he should say to Caitlin's guardian; what if her uncle should quiz him concerning his ability to provide for her?

He would have to lie again, and he was getting thoroughly sick of lying. In fact, he was getting thoroughly sick of himself. Why did Caitlin have to be so damn *good*, so wholesome and fine? By comparison, he really was a devil, not fit to enjoy her company. For the first time in his life, he cared for a woman's good opinion of his character—cared desperately, in fact. He wanted to shield and protect her, as much from his own wickedness as from harm caused by anyone else. And he didn't need to be hit on the head to realize how deeply Caitlin would be hurt if she knew the truth about him.

Following Caitlin with his eyes, he felt a spurt of annoyance at her uncle. The man must be an insensitive lout to go off as he had done, without telling Caitlin exactly where he had gone and how he could be reached. Caitlin's lovely face was shadowed with worry as she

213

banged on the closed door of the little frame house. It, too, looked deserted; then, suddenly, the door opened, and a short, fat Hawaiian woman peeped out.

Caitlin and the woman conversed for several moments, and then the Hawaiian shook her head no and gestured helplessly with her hands. Caitlin turned and pointed to Gerrick, and he nodded and smiled. The woman smiled back but could offer no encouragement to Caitlin, for again, she shook her head no. Caitlin did not persist much longer. Though the precise meaning of the Hawaiian words eluded him, Gerrick could hear the disappointment in Caitlin's voice, as she took her leave with a *mahalo*, or thank you, and an *aloha*, the only two words he recognized.

"Well, what did she say?" he asked, as Caitlin approached him with a downcast expression. "Obviously, your uncle isn't here. Does she know where he is?"

"No," Caitlin said with a quiver in her voice. "The Binghams and the Chamberlains left early this morning to go to Waikiki to visit the king. Kamehameha is surfing there with friends and relatives, and Brother Bingham has gone to chastise him for setting a bad example for his people."

"I take it your uncle never arrived here."

"He has not been here and is not expected." Caitlin suddenly covered her eyes with her hands and burst into tears. "There's no meeting either. There's been none recently and none are planned in the near future."

She broke into despairing sobs, and Gerrick wrapped his arms around her and held her while she wept. "Sweetheart, if there never *was* a meeting and isn't going to *be* one, then your uncle wasn't being truthful with you."

"But why would he lie to me? He *wouldn't* lie, Gerrick! Lying is a sin!"

Gerrick's stomach knotted as he wondered how to explain the unexplainable. "Cait, sometimes people *have* to lie in order to protect someone from knowledge that would hurt them if they knew about it."

"There's no excuse for a lie!" Caitlin vehemently insisted. "If Uncle George uttered a falsehood in order to protect me or to keep me from accompanying him, he committed a grave sin. He should have just told me the truth."

"Maybe he *feared* to tell you the truth. Maybe he knew you wouldn't approve of where he was going. Maybe . . . maybe he had a perfectly good reason for lying," Gerrick finished lamely, all too shamefully aware that he was defending his own actions as well as her uncle's.

Caitlin appeared to ponder this, and he saw a light come into her eyes. "Yes," she said softly. "Maybe he *was* afraid. I never considered that possibility before, but . . ."

"But what?" Gerrick urged, curious as to what she was thinking.

"Oh, nothing. . . . It's just . . . just useless speculation anyway."

"*What* is?" Gerrick pressed.

"Oh, I . . . I shouldn't mention anything about this, Gerrick. It probably has no connection."

"Damn it, Cait! *What* has no connection?"

She wavered a moment, glancing at him in pained indecision. "Well . . . I was just wondering if . . . if my uncle's disappearance has—or had—anything to do with . . . with the men who have come to Kauai asking about sandalwood."

"*What* men?" Gerrick demanded, the hairs prickling on the back of his neck.

Caitlin's eyes shifted uneasily away from him, and he held her tightly until she looked back at him, her mouth trembling in distress. "Over the past few years—ever since my father died, we've had visitors now and then, searching for sandalwood rumored to still be on the island."

Again, she hesitated, as if not wanting to tell him more, and Gerrick had to shake her to prompt additional revelations. "*Rumored* to be? You mean it *isn't* there?"

"I . . . I . . . don't know *where* these men got the idea there might still be some undiscovered sandalwood. But I've always suspected that . . . that . . ."

215

"Spit it out, Cait! What have you suspected?"

"I've always suspected that my father's death was in some way related to this rumor. And now to have my uncle suddenly go off so mysteriously—God knows where!—well, I'm just worried, that's all."

In his rising excitement, Gerrick could hardly catch his breath. Now was the time to coax from her everything she knew and was afraid to disclose; but dare he pressure her? Did she trust him enough now? "Are you saying that your father was threatened and killed because he knew about the existence of a previously undiscovered stand of sandalwood? How in God's name did your father die?"

Caitlin's eyes clouded with sorrow. "He . . . he was found with his head split open at the bottom of a deep gorge."

"So he fell and dashed his head against a rock. That could have been an accident. Why do you think it might not have been?"

"I . . . I don't know, except . . ." Anguish filled her eyes, and her voice shook. "My father was very surefooted, even over the worst terrain. He traveled constantly into the remote areas of the island. And his body was found where he had no reason to be. No reason, that is, except . . . except if someone forced him to go there."

"And who might that someone be?"

"There was a man—*men*—who came several times to speak with my father. They thought he knew but wasn't telling where some sandalwood might still exist. A few weeks before my father's death, I was coming home in the early evening, and as I approached the house, I heard someone shouting at my father, calling him a liar and threatening to harm him if he didn't tell what he knew. I was afraid and ran and got Inamoo, Pikake's brother. But by the time we returned, the men were gone . . ."

"And you never saw them again?"

"No, never. But after them, there were others—traders, whalers, deserters from off the ships. After my father's death, my uncle always handled their inquiries. He sent them away disappointed but never violent. At least, I've

216

never seen any violence. However, when it comes to sandalwood . . . In the past, men have foolishly spilled blood over it, and doubtless more would be spilled if any wood remained to be fought over."

An angry gleam came into her eyes. "That's why I hate traders, Gerrick. They care for nothing except exploiting others for their own personal gain. Traders *may* have killed my father and dumped his body in a gully because he refused to tell them what they wanted to hear. And if they did, their crime will go unpunished because no one witnessed it. I'll *never* know how or why he died."

"But your father *did* know something."

Caitlin stared at him, a flush rising in her cheeks. "I never said that."

"You never said otherwise. Come on, Caitlin. I'm your husband; you can trust me. If I can prevent it, I'll do nothing to hurt you or your precious island."

Immediately, the gleam of wariness disappeared, and her eyes softened, though her smile was still tentative. "I . . . I do trust you, Gerrick. Only please don't ask me to tell you more. My uncle's mysterious meeting probably had nothing to do with the continuing search for sandalwood on Kauai. I don't know why I thought of it, except that I have the same feelings of anxiety now that I had then. My father was missing, his whereabouts unknown, for quite some time before his body was found. Like Uncle George, he said he was going one place, and then turned up in another—dead. I only hope this isn't the same thing happening again."

"I hope so, too, Cait. Our only recourse now is to return to Kauai—and perhaps you better show me exactly where your father's body was found."

"Oh, no! I don't think . . ."

"Oh, yes, you do, Cait," Gerrick disputed. "You're thinking just what I'm thinking: Your uncle may have suffered an 'accident' similar to your father's—and for the very same reason. Someone—*not* Brother Bingham— lured him away from Hanalei. The question is: Does your uncle know where to find the wood? If he does, he might

217

still be alive. Or he might already be dead, having divulged what he knows."

"My uncle knows *nothing*, Gerrick! He didn't even come to Hawaii until *after* my father's death. If anything, *I* am the one who . . . who . . ." She stopped, aware she had said too much, and clamped her jaws together.

"You know where the sandalwood is, don't you, Cait? And you know, don't you, that you're going to have to tell me—if only to save your uncle."

Stubbornly, despite the tears spilling down her cheeks, Caitlin shook her head. "I'll show you where my father's body was found, but that's all. If my uncle's body isn't there, I . . . I'll just wait at home for him to come home while you go looking for your brother. I can't take you to the sandalwood, Gerrick . . . I won't even confirm or deny your suspicions. Please don't ask me any more questions, because I . . . I just *can't* answer them, that's all!"

"Hush, Cait, don't cry . . ." Gerrick enfolded her in his arms, and she pressed against him, sobbing on his shoulder. He soothed and patted her back until her misery at last abated. Unfortunately, his misery had only increased. What was he going to do now?

Only one thing seemed abundantly clear to him: The honeymoon was over. Reality had finally crashed down upon him and Cait, bursting the bubble of their lovely, fragile world. It was only a matter of time before Caitlin learned why he'd come to the islands, and then she would learn to hate him. Now that he knew the treasure actually existed, he couldn't turn his back on it and walk away; that much of a change in his greedy nature was too much to expect. If Caitlin really loved him, she'd have to love him for what he was—a sinner, not a saint.

Chapter Seventeen

"All right, you two, what do you think?" Gerrick raised his booted foot, placed it on the bow of the little longboat, and leaned on his knee as he eyed his best friend and his first mate with a detached calmness he didn't feel.

The *Naughty Lady* had just arrived back in Hanalei Bay, and he, Caitlin, John, and Pikake had rowed ashore in the ship's gig, and found Erasmus back from Waimea and eagerly awaiting them. Now, while Caitlin and Pikake were checking among the villagers for news of Uncle George, he was informing John and Erasmus of his suspicions.

"Someone else is after that sandalwood. Caitlin's father's disappearance and subsequent death coupled with her uncle's disappearance are too suspicious to be mere coincidence. Don't you see it that way, too, gentlemen?"

Erasmus Mockensturm scratched under his beard and plucked at the wisps of bushy gray hair around his prominent ears. The old man looked even more fierce and disreputable than Gerrick remembered him, and he hoped Caitlin would simply excuse Erasmus's rough appearance on the grounds that the first mate had been combing the island ceaselessly for the mythical Hadley Scott since their departure.

"'Twould seem you're right, lad," Erasmus conceded. "Whilst I was goin' about the island, askin' after yer supposed brother, Hiram . . ."

"Hadley," Gerrick corrected.

"Hadley . . . I received more'n my share of suspicious looks. Like I wasn't the first or only *haole* to come pokin' around an' botherin' folks. 'Course, without someone t' translate f'r me, I had a devil of a time makin' meself understood. I kept tryin' t' tell the islanders I was lookin' f'r a another white man, and they kept askin' me was I lookin' f'r sandalwood, 'cause if I was, it was all gone."

"You understood that much of the language?" John queried incredulously. "I'm amazed. I've been studying daily, and I doubt I could do as well."

"Been practicin' with that little island gal, have ye?" Erasmus chuckled. "No wonder y'ain't learned much. I seed the way you two was eyein' each other when ye got off this here gig. 'Pears t' me you got more on y'r mind than learnin' t' speak Hawaiian."

Looking offended, John flexed his powerful biceps. "That little island gal, as you call her, has a name; it's Pikake, and I'll thank you to show more respect when you speak of her."

"Oh me, oh my! Don't tell me I've got *two* lovesick donkeys on my hands. With you an' the cap'n both brayin' after your she-asses, I don't see how we'll ever latch on to that sandalwood. Especially if some other fellah's already got the jump on us."

"I don't *know* that, I'm only guessing." Straightening, Gerrick put down his foot. "But if I'm right, it means we're fast running out of time. Just how much of the island have you searched, Erasmus?"

Erasmus stretched and rubbed the small of his back. "Damn near all the easy places; what's left is the hard. I've been over them Na Pali cliffs a good ways, but they're near impossible to explore thoroughly. And the day I tried t' climb Mt. Waialeale, I almost drowned. That mountain's gotta be the wettest place on earth—don't know if sandalwood trees could even grow up there it's so wet."

"So what do you suggest?"

"Well, goin' inland from Waimea is a big deep canyon we could explore. And I also think we should keep on tryin' to search more of the Na Pali coast. There's a few beaches we could bring a gig into, and then hike up into the mountains. I heard tell about a hidden valley thereabouts that sounds as good a place as any f'r sandalwood t' grow undiscovered."

"What's it called—this valley?" Gerrick's instincts were suddenly humming.

"The Kalalau Valley, a real wild place where the cliffs're so steep, only goats can climb 'em. If we assume others have been lookin' f'r the wood and not findin' it, then we have t' assume they've already looked every place we have. But this valley is real isolated. In Waimea, they told me that islanders who'd run afoul of the old kings used t' hide out there 'cause nobody could *ever* find 'em."

"Then that sounds like a possibility. What do you think, John?"

"I think if you really want to find the sandalwood, you ought to ask your so-called wife. That's why you married her, isn't it?"

Gerrick locked glances with his big, brown-eyed friend, but the challenge in John's voice did not extend to his expression. John was watching him with a mixture of sympathy and exasperation. "You've been putting it off too long, Gerrick. First, the voyage to Maui and then to Honolulu. If you've changed your mind about pressuring Caitlin, you owe it to us to tell us. I want to know what comes first with you: Cait or the sandalwood."

"Maybe Pikake knows something," Gerrick suggested irritably. "Have you thought about asking *her?*"

"I've thought about it," John said evenly. "But like you, I'm afraid to broach the subject. Pikake's father died of a lung ailment he contracted while bringing sandalwood down from the mountains during the boom days. Her mother sickened from a combination of grief and lack of food because she had no male to provide for her, and soon followed her father to the grave. That's how Pikake and Inamoo became orphans, looked after by Caitlin's father. Amazingly, Pikake feels no bitterness—but I do. The Hawaiians have grievously suffered because of the white man's lust for their treasures."

"Does that mean you want us to abandon the search?" Gerrick half hoped John did; then he himself wouldn't feel so pressured to hold to their original plan.

"Of course not. If we don't find the sandalwood, someone else will. At least, if we do find it, we can make certain no one suffers because of it. I intend to use part of my share to do something *good* for the islanders."

"You mean you're really going to build them a church?"

"Probably not, but I might consider a school. Pikake is as bright and clever as any white woman I've known. Of course, she's been taught by Caitlin, but there must be plenty of smart Hawaiian children who could benefit from a similar education."

"You care very much for her, don't you, John?" Gerrick probed.

John flashed him a self-deprecating grin. "I confess I don't know what I feel. I'm old enough to be her father, and sometimes, I feel almost paternal toward her. Other times though, I can hardly keep my hands to myself. I'm still as randy and lustful as I ever was."

Gerrick envied John his ability to admit his confusion and ambiguity. For himself, especially where Caitlin was concerned, Gerrick felt tongue-tied when it came to discussing his emotions. "If I have to, I *will* pressure Caitlin," he stated. "I guess I'm still hoping I don't have to. Cait is imbued with the bitterness Pikake should feel. I think I've found a way to convince her to lead us to the sandalwood, but I'll have to go very slowly . . . easing her into acceptance rather than compelling her to bend to my will."

"Sounds like you're treading upon nails, my friend." John sighed and studied his boots. "Erasmus, did you ever think you'd see the day when Gerrick and I would allow our hearts to rule our heads, thereby possibly depriving ourselves of a fortune?"

Erasmus snorted and spat in the sand. "Naw, I never did. But I'll tell you this: You can't make a woman happy by guessin' what she wants. Neither of you is bein' honest with them two females, and if'n they ever discover it, it'll be worse than if you'd told the truth in the first place."

Gerrick and John exchanged glances of surprise; where had Erasmus come by this bit of wisdom? Erasmus grinned and hitched up his pants. "Jus' 'cause I'm wedded t' the sea don't mean I've no experience with the gentler sex. I know neither of ye is fool enough t' sacrifice the sandalwood f'r a lady's affections—so my advice is t' make a clean breast of it, swear t' mend your wicked ways, and then beg f'r help. Never did know a female who could resist a man's promisin' t' reform. Jus' make sure she knows you'll do your reformin' *after* this one last sin."

Now, Gerrick and John burst into spontaneous laughter. "Cait would *never* agree to that!" Gerrick howled. "Neither would Pikake! All she ever worries about is whether or not John will go to hell. Isn't that true, John?"

"Regrettably, that's true," John confirmed.

Their tension-easing hilarity ended abruptly, destroyed by Caitlin's frantic call. "Gerrick! Gerrick, come quickly!"

Whirling around, his heart in his mouth, Gerrick saw her running down the beach toward him, her silver-gold hair streaming behind her like a flag. He sprinted toward her, but even before she ran breathlessly into his arms, he knew that her excitement was caused by good news, rather than bad. Her face was radiant, her luminous eyes dancing, and his heart plummeted into his boots as he realized what her news must be.

"Gerrick, he's here! Uncle George isn't dead, after all! He returned to the island two days ago."

"Then where is he?" Gerrick looked past her, trying to keep his lack of excitement and happiness from showing.

"Inamoo told me he went inland to visit Chief Laanui but is expected back tonight. That means he could be here any moment. *Finally* you can meet him, and we can ask his blessing on our marriage and—"

"Wait a minute, Caitlin. Slow down. . . . Do you mean he wasn't worried enough about *you* to be tearing the island apart looking for you? And where in hell has he been? Did he say anything about his mystery meeting?"

"Oh, Inamoo told him I was wed in his absence and that we set out to look for him on Maui. And he then told Inamoo I had misunderstood; he wasn't going to Maui but to Waimea. He's been on Kauai all this time! I don't know what happened about his meeting, but—"

"Caitlin . . ." Gerrick gripped her arms to stop her babbling and to give himself time to think. "Don't you think you should ask yourself what in thunder is going on here? Why would your uncle have told you he was going to Maui for a meeting of the missionaries, if he was actually only going round the other side of the island?"

"Gerrick, I have no idea! And at this point, I really don't care! I'm simply relieved to know he's alive and well. Why, I'd been conjuring all sorts of horrible fates for him. Tonight, we can ask him to explain. I'm planning a late supper at our house for just the three of us . . ."

"Our house?"

"I mean my uncle's house, now. *My* home is wherever you are."

"Well, I'm pleased to hear that, Cait, but why didn't you invite your uncle to have dinner aboard the schooner?" Aside from his other worries, Gerrick was suddenly beset with visions of eating salt beef and drinking water when he *could* be dining on fresh pork and quaffing wine.

"Oh, Gerrick, please let me do this! Just this once, I . . . I want to act like a real wife, the mistress of the house, preparing the evening meal and serving a guest." Her blue-gray eyes pleaded, and her winsome smile melted his heart like the sun melting butter.

Feeling guilty again, he realized that Caitlin needed a home of her own—not just a ship's cabin—and he wondered anew how he could ever provide one for her without the sandalwood. "All right, if it will make you happy, Cait . . . but I can't come to your uncle's house right away. I've got too many things to do here. Now that your uncle is back, we can set out to look for my brother immediately."

"Yes, we must, Gerrick. Tomorrow we'll go—or to-

FREE

BOOK CERTIFICATE

ZEBRA HOME SUBSCRIPTION SERVICE, INC.

YES! Please start my subscription to Zebra Historical Romances and send me my free Zebra Novel along with my first month's Romances. I understand that I may preview these four new Zebra Historical Romances Free for 10 days. If I'm not satisfied with them I may return the four books within 10 days and owe nothing. Otherwise I will pay just $3.50 each; a total of $14.00 (a $15.80 value—I save $1.80). Then each month I will receive the 4 newest titles as soon as they come off the press for the same 10 day Free preview and low price. I may return any shipment and I may cancel this arrangement at any time. There is no minimum number of books to buy and there are no shipping, handling or postage charges. Regardless of what I do, the **FREE** book is mine to keep.

Name _____
　　　　　　　　　　(Please Print)

Address _____

City _____ State _____ Apt. # _____

Telephone (_____) _____ Zip _____

Signature _____
　　　(if under 18, parent or guardian must sign)

Terms and offer subject to change without notice.

morrow night, when the wind rises. And I don't want you to come right now anyway. I need time to clean house and prepare a meal. When all is ready and my uncle has returned, I'll send Pikake to show you the way."

"Sounds wonderful," Gerrick enthused, but it required great effort to put a smile on his face.

With Uncle George's return, he no longer had a reason for asking Caitlin to show the location of the sandalwood. Obviously, her uncle's trip—for whatever reason it had been made—had nothing to do with the sandalwood. So what could he possibly say now to get her to lead him to the treasure? All he had left was the truth—that he wanted the wood for himself.

"I'll see you later, my wonderful husband." Caitlin lightly patted his jaw. "How good it is to have nothing to worry about except whether or not Uncle George will like you. And I'm certain he will once he gets to know you. Whether or not you'll like *him* is another question. He's a . . . a typical, self-righteous missionary, Gerrick, but he *is* my uncle, so try and be civil to him for my sake, won't you?"

"I'll try," Gerrick promised, wondering how he could keep such a promise. From what he'd so far learned of George Price, the man had little to recommend him.

It was after dark by the time Pikake finally came for Gerrick. He was sitting on a supply barrel beneath a torch on the beach and savoring a solitary cup of wine before he had to make do with tea or water.

"Tutu Caitlin has everything ready," the little Hawaiian said shyly to Gerrick while her eyes unabashedly searched the deserted beach for John.

"Did her uncle make it back from the interior?" Gerrick asked, carefully setting down the goblet.

"Oh, yes, he come before sunset. And Tutu Caitlin is making a game of not telling him her new name until after he meets you. She wants you to sign your names in her family Bible after her uncle bless you . . ."

"Blesses you," John corrected, coming toward them out of the darkness. "And you should have said 'came' before sunset, not 'come.'"

He added a crate of mangoes to the growing heap of fresh foodstuffs on the beach, then straightened and smiled at Pikake.

"'Blesses you' . . . 'came,'" Pikake repeated, her brown eyes shining in the torchlight as she smiled back at John. "When will we have lessons again, John Reynolds? There is still much I do not know about speaking English, and plenty much you don't know about speaking *my* language."

"Either much or plenty, but not plenty much." Tenderly, John gazed down at the girl. "And I'll give you a lesson right now, if you'd like."

Pikake's long black hair swirled as she shook her head, disappointment erasing her smile. "I am sorry, but I must show Captain Scott the way to Tutu Caitlin's house."

"Just point me in the right direction, Pikake, and I'll be able to find it," Gerrick assured her.

It was obvious the two longed to be alone with each other, and Gerrick saw no reason why they shouldn't be. Caitlin's house couldn't be that far; he could probably find it just by watching for the lamplight shining through her windows.

"You do not mind if I don't accompany you?" Pikake's eagerness to remain with John made Gerrick smile.

"No, sweetheart. And I'm sure John would be glad if you stayed. Wouldn't you, John?"

John glowered at Gerrick. He was already angry that Gerrick had not confronted Caitlin about the sandalwood, and Gerrick's teasing tone did nothing to mollify him. "You *know* I would. And as for finding Caitlin's house, there's nothing to it. Just follow the path leading away from the beach. That's all I did that day I went to ask her advice on dealing with Chief Laanui."

"Oh, yes," Gerrick grumbled, fighting jealousy. "Now I remember; while I myself have never even seen it, you've already been there."

226

"You haven't missed all that much. It's only a thatched-roof house, though as I recall, it had a pleasant veranda all along the front."

"Veranda?" Pikake questioned. "What is veranda?"

"A porch," John explained.

"Oh, you mean a *lanai!* Yes, the house has one in front and also a small one in back."

John threw up his hands. "There, you see? It's easy to find. If you're not sure you have the right place, just walk around back and check."

"Is not necessary for Captain Scott to walk so much." Pikake giggled. "Tutu Caitlin's house is only one at the end of path." She turned and pointed to a gap between the palm trees lining the beach. "There is path. You can see it from here."

"Take the torch if you need it," John invited. "We certainly have no use for it."

Pikake giggled again, and Gerrick stood and stretched his leg muscles. "No, I'll leave the torch here. Caitlin will feel much better if your lessons are well lit."

At this reminder to observe good behavior, Pikake sobered instantly, and Gerrick shot John a wry grin as he sauntered past him in the direction of the path. "Have fun, kids!"

"Thanks a heap, old friend," John growled. "Have fun yourself with Caitlin's uncle."

Minutes later, Gerrick was climbing the steep path leading up through overgrown palms and pandanus trees toward Caitlin's house. Several times, he tripped over exposed roots made invisible by the darkness and cursed at his clumsiness. At least he'd been right about one thing: The light from Caitlin's windows proved an easy beacon to follow. However, as he drew closer, he saw that it wasn't just the light from her windows illuminating the night; a whale oil lamp had been lit and placed on a table on the veranda, and both Caitlin and her uncle were seated there awaiting him.

Caitlin's hair shone like diamond fire in the lamplight, and Gerrick wondered if her uncle possessed the same distinctive silver-blond coloring. He paused a moment to study the man who might possibly prove to be his adversary; what would Caitlin do if her uncle refused to bless their marriage? In his initial perusal, Gerrick saw a balding head fringed with pewter-colored hair that must have been dark once, not light.

Palm fronds obscured his view, and Gerrick moved closer and held the branches aside. The large head set upon broad shoulders seemed somehow familiar, but he could not see more because the porch railing still remained in his way. Gerrick wished the man would stand up, and no sooner had he formulated the wish than Caitlin's uncle suddenly rose and faced him.

Recognizing the man, Gerrick started, his heart slamming against his ribs. He blinked several times to clear his vision, but his eyes had not deceived him; the man with the barrel chest and heavy jowls was none other than his worst enemy: Amos Taylor.

Several moments slipped past, while Gerrick grappled with shock and the urge to dash up the steps to the porch and throttle Amos with his bare hands. He could scarcely believe what he was seeing; had Amos accompanied Caitlin's uncle back from the interior? Was he one of the sandalwood hunters Caitlin had mentioned who had arrived on Kauai recently? Gerrick scanned the veranda, but there was no one else present except Caitlin and Amos—and the table between them was set with three places.

There were three plates patterned in blue against a white background, three sets of cutlery, three linen napkins, and three cups and saucers. In the middle of the three place settings stood the whale oil lamp, and off to one side was a vase with flowers.

Caitlin looked nervous, her fingers plucking at the white linen tablecloth and her eyes glued to Amos Taylor's back. Quite distinctly, Gerrick heard her say, "Do sit down again, Uncle George. I'm sure my husband will be here soon."

The man she had addressed as "Uncle George," but

whom Gerrick knew as his father's traitorous, murdering business partner, turned and frowned at her. "This is not a very auspicious beginning, niece. If your new husband is as devoted as you say, he should be here by now. Can you not at least tell me the man's name before I meet him? Obviously, you already know I will disapprove of his character, or you wouldn't be so closed-mouthed about him."

"Now, Uncle," Caitlin said placatingly. "I haven't revealed his name or occupation, because I didn't want you to meet him with your mind already made up. I doubt you'd recognize his name if you heard it, but it's possible you might. His family is well known in New England, or so I understand."

"And decidedly *not* a devout, religious family such as your father or I would have chosen."

"He is not a missionary, if that's what you mean . . . but he's not unscrupulous either. I believe him to be a man of honor; he *insisted* we marry before we sailed out to look for you because he didn't wish to risk my reputation."

"More likely he didn't wish to risk my anger; I'd have taken a rod to him had he done less—and I still may beat him senseless."

Caitlin looked down at her plate. "Such violence is against the Lord's teachings, Uncle. Besides, he is my husband, and nothing you say or do will change that. I love him with all my heart, and if you will not bless us and wish us well, then I will leave you and never look back. You'll not hear from me ever again."

"You are a foolish, obstinate young woman, Niece! It's lucky your father and mother cannot hear you speak thusly. You shame them with your arrogance; they would have wanted you to marry a man that *I* or Brother Bingham had chosen."

"You told me you were going to *visit* Brother Bingham. Why did you lie? I'm still waiting for some explanation as to why you went to Waimea instead of Maui or Honolulu."

"I did *not* lie!" Amos shouted, and Gerrick almost flew

out of his hiding place to defend Caitlin from this vile imposter. Only the realization that he had the advantage of knowing Amos was here, while Amos did not yet know he was here, kept him immobile, waiting to see what more he could learn of Amos's intentions before he himself decided on what should be done.

"You simply misunderstood," Amos continued. "And I am not the one who owes explanations for irresponsible actions. You are."

"If it pleases you to think so, I will not argue." Caitlin sighed. "We are both adults who are entitled to keep our own counsel. If you refuse to confide in me, then I shall not confide in you. I only ask that when Gerrick comes, you treat him civilly, and—"

"*Gerrick?* Your husband's name is Gerrick?"

Gerrick froze, for it was obvious from Amos's alarmed expression that he was wondering if Caitlin's new husband could possibly be the son of the man he'd ruined.

"Yes," Caitlin said. "His first name is Gerrick, but having revealed that much, I will not say more until he comes."

"Now I cannot *wait* until he comes," Amos said, but Caitlin did not appear to notice the hint of menace in Amos's tone. "Excuse me a moment, Caitlin," Amos added. "Before your husband arrives, I wish to get something from my belongings."

Caitlin only nodded as Amos entered the house, and Gerrick had little doubt as to what Amos had gone to get: a pistol or other weapon—in case Gerrick's last name was Scott. Moving as silently as he could, Gerrick retreated back down the path. He needed a few minutes to think—and reinforcements wouldn't hurt either. Caitlin was alone with a madman fully capable of killing them both before Gerrick could do a thing about it; his own pistol and cutlass were in his cabin aboard the schooner.

But I'll be back, Amos, he swore to himself. You're almost as good as dead.

Chapter Eighteen

"Gerrick, be sensible! You can't just dash back to Caitlin's house and kill the fellow she believes is her uncle." Hands on hips, John regarded Gerrick as if he'd suddenly sprouted two horns and a tail.

"Yes, I can," Gerrick disputed calmly. "Watch me. Don't we have a weapon ashore here somewhere?"

Gerrick continued rummaging through the small heap of supplies piled on the beach awaiting transport to the ship. Mostly, there were fruits and vegetables, but Erasmus had also procured dried fish and a good quantity of tapa cloth. Not finding what he wanted in the crates and bundles, Gerrick broke open the barrel he had earlier been sitting upon, but it contained only fresh water that quickly flowed out onto the sand.

"What fools we are to leave all our weapons on the schooner," he muttered in disgust. "From now on, every member of the crew, including you and me, is to be armed with something—even if it's no more than a dagger."

"Don't be ridiculous, Gerrick. If the men carry weapons, they are only going to use them—possibly on each other. I strongly advise against reversing your previous orders and allowing them to once again sport pistols, daggers, and cutlasses. This is the most peaceful, tranquil spot in the Pacific Ocean; let's keep it that way."

"It won't be tranquil for long, John. If I have to, I'll row out to the ship and get a weapon. Are you sure you don't have one hidden somewhere?"

"No, I don't. But if I did, I wouldn't give it to you." Grabbing Gerrick's shoulder in his iron grip, John finally forced him to stop and listen. "Gerrick, you *can't* kill Amos Taylor. Think of how Caitlin would react if you did."

Gerrick regarded his friend coldly. "Caitlin hasn't made such a spineless coward of me that I will not avenge the wrongs done to my family."

"Does that mean you don't care if *she* gets killed when the pistol balls start flying?"

"Of course, I care." Gerrick glanced past John's scowling face to where Pikake was standing behind him, her brown eyes terrified. "I won't allow Caitlin to get hurt," he assured her as well as John.

"How will you prevent it? As soon as Amos sees you, the fight will begin—unless you kill him *before* he sees you, and I doubt your sense of honor will permit you to shoot him in the back."

"You're right," Gerrick conceded. "I want Amos Taylor to *know* who's killing him and why. I want to see his face go gray with fear; he deserves to suffer before he dies."

"I beg you, Gerrick. Don't do this. The risk of harming Caitlin or yourself is too great. There are other ways to deal with Amos besides killing him on sight."

"What ways, John? We're too far from home to place any faith in New England-style justice. Even if I could be sure of capturing Amos, securing him in chains, and transporting him back to Rhode Island, I wouldn't do it. I don't want my ship fouled by his stink for so many long months. Besides, there's the . . . the . . ." Gerrick hesitated to mention the sandalwood in front of Pikake, but then decided what-the-hell. She'd find out about it soon enough anyway.

"There's the sandalwood," he continued. "The best market for it is in Canton so it may be years before we return to New England."

"Isn't the most important thing to rescue Caitlin?" John asked. "And *then* to go after the sandalwood? Amos may or may not have found it yet. Indeed, it's mere speculation that he's here on the island because of it.''

"Come now, John. Why else would he be here, posing as Caitlin's uncle? It's plain as day that he came for the same reason we did—to get rich quick. He probably went through my father's money faster than a sailor on shore leave can squander a month's pay on women and liquor. What I don't understand is how Caitlin fell for his act. You'd think she would have recognized he's no relation to her; Amos doesn't even have blond hair.''

"John? Captain Scott?" Pikake stepped closer to the smoking torch, beneath which Gerrick and John were arguing. "Tutu Caitlin did not know she even have uncle until he arrive here. I do not understand all you are saying—especially about sandalwood—but if *Makuakane* George is wicked man, if he is not Tutu Caitlin's uncle, then she should be told.''

"I'm going to tell her, Pikake," Gerrick growled. "Just before I kill the bastard.''

John groaned and rubbed his forehead as if it pained him. "Why not get Caitlin away from him first, Gerrick? And why not beat him to the sandalwood before he learns we're here looking for it? I doubt he himself has found it yet, or he'd be halfway to Canton by now.''

"And just how do you propose I rescue Caitlin without revealing my presence? As you've already pointed out, I'm not invisible—which leaves us exactly where we started this discussion; as soon as Amos sees me, all hell will break loose.''

"Well . . . let's think a few moments. If we try hard enough, we should be able to come up with something.''

"I could go get Tutu Caitlin and bring her to you," Pikake suggested. "I could say you are ill and cannot come to dinner.''

"Too simple . . ." Gerrick scoffed. "Amos would see right through such a flimsy excuse. He's grown suspicious as it is. Caitlin told him my first name is Gerrick.''

"Hmmmmm . . ." John murmured, mulling the problem. "How about if we send Pikake to Caitlin on the

233

pretext that she is needed to translate something important for you? We could say we have another thorny problem with Chief Laanui."

"No, too risky. Amos supposedly met with Laanui earlier today; he'd wonder why Laanui never mentioned any problems." Gerrick stared down the darkened beach, frustration eating at his insides. "But I'll bet he wasn't meeting with Laanui. I'll bet wherever he's been lately has something to do with the sandalwood."

"How about . . . Hadley?" John suggested. "Pikake could say that a messenger has just arrived with news of your lost brother, and you need Caitlin to come at once to translate and ask questions."

At the moment, nothing sounded good to Gerrick. Nevertheless, he considered the suggestion carefully. "That's an idea," he finally responded. "Amos knows I have no brothers—only a sister, and she's dead. Such misinformation may throw him off guard and lead him to believe I'm some other Gerrick."

"If we set sail at once, taking Caitlin with us, she'd be safe, and Amos would never learn you were here, until it was too late."

"Too late?"

"Until after we locate the sandalwood and steal it right from under his nose." John grinned. "Lord, wouldn't he hate to learn it was you who got there first."

"Yes . . ." As he thought of how furious Amos would be to discover that a Scott had bested him, a slow grin spread across Gerrick's face. "Yes, I like that. . . . First, I'll steal what he wants most, and then I'll kill him. It's what I had planned all along: to make him suffer before he dies."

"Then it's settled?" John looked relieved. "While we wait here, Pikake will go and get Caitlin."

"You're not afraid for Pikake?" Gerrick queried. "Amos is a brutal fiend. What if he harms her?"

"He hasn't any reason to harm her." John drew the little Hawaiian into his arms and tilted her worried, puzzled face toward his. "Sweetheart, I know you don't understand what's happening, and there isn't time for me to explain. I can only tell you this: The man Caitlin believes to be her uncle is really a killer who came here in search of sandalwood. His true name is Amos Taylor. He's Captain Scott's worst enemy and will kill Gerrick and Caitlin should he learn that Gerrick is Caitlin's new husband. We want you to go and explain to Amos that Gerrick needs her for a few moments but that both will return for dinner shortly. He is to wait there for her. . . . Do you think you can do that?"

Pikake nodded, her dark eyes brimming with love and confidence. "If you ask it of me, John, I can do anything."

"That's my dear sweet girl." John kissed the tip of Pikake's nose. "Just keep Amos at the house until we get safely away. Tell him . . . whatever lies you can think of in order to gain us time."

"But where will you go, John Reynolds? And when will you return?"

"I . . . I can't tell you, Pikake, because I don't know. I can only promise you: I *will* return. And when I do . . ." He bent and kissed her lips. "You'll be here waiting for me, won't you?"

"Oh, yes, John!" Pikake clung to the big man, until John gently set her away from him.

"Go quickly, sweetheart, before Amos and Caitlin get too impatient and come looking for Gerrick."

"I go, John Reynolds." Pikake blew him a kiss and fled into the darkness on swift, silent feet.

"He just better not harm her," John muttered. "Or I myself will kill him with my bare hands."

Understanding his friend's fears, Gerrick said nothing. He himself was worried about Pikake. A great deal—including her safety—depended upon her ability to fool Amos and keep him occupied until the *Naughty Lady* had sailed away. After that, she was still in danger. Amos would wonder why they had sailed so precipitously, and Gerrick dared not leave one of his crew members behind to explain that they had to leave at once to rescue his brother, Hadley—the story he was planning on telling Caitlin. Amos might recognize one of his men, or else the crew

235

member might inadvertently mention something to arouse Amos's suspicions.

As for telling another lie to Caitlin, Gerrick felt he had no choice; he could hardly tell her the truth about her uncle without revealing everything else. Even if he confessed all, and Caitlin magnanimously forgave him, he doubted she would condone his eventual return to Kauai to kill Amos. And on that subject, his mind was made up. Amos must *die* for his crimes—and he must die groveling on the ground and begging for Gerrick to spare him.

"You're still not going to admit to Caitlin why we came here, are you?" John asked suddenly.

Gerrick eyed his friend across the barrels and foodstuffs heaped between them. "No, I'm not."

"Then I suggest that you at least have Caitlin send her uncle a message telling him where she's gone. I presume you're going to claim that your brother is desperately ill or some other such nonsense, and waiting for us to come to his aid. Whatever you decide, I'll play along. However, I don't want Pikake endangered trying to hold Amos in that house forever."

"I'm sorry, John, but I dare not dispatch a crew member bearing messages; Amos might recognize him. I don't suppose you have a sheet of foolscap in your pocket, and a pen and ink . . ."

"Hardly," John snorted. "I'm not in the habit of carrying writing materials on my person."

"Well, then . . ." Gerrick said, thinking hard. "How about leaving a message in the sand? Sooner or later, Amos and Pikake will come down to the beach to see what happened to us. If we write the message above the waterline . . ."

"And it doesn't rain tonight. . . . Oh, damn it all, Gerrick! I don't mind telling you I *hate* leaving Pikake here with Amos."

"She'll be all right," Gerrick soothed, hoping it was true. "You yourself said she's very clever."

"She is. But she's also naive and trusting. The more I think about it, the more afraid I am that she'll forget and say something stupid—something to alert Amos to what's going on."

"Quit worrying. Our only other choice is for both of us to go storming up there to rescue them. We could, you know . . ."

But before Gerrick could continue speculating on possible alternatives, he heard a distant, anxious cry: Caitlin calling his name. He and John exchanged troubled glances; Caitlin was already on her way down to the beach, and just in case Amos had decided to follow her, they simultaneously stepped back into the darkness.

"Go hide under the trees," Gerrick hissed, stooping and picking up a heavy piece of driftwood. "And don't come out until you're sure it's safe. If Amos is trailing her, I'll have to kill him here and now. Though God only knows how I'll explain the deed to Caitlin."

"You might try telling her the truth," John spat, melting into the night.

Caitlin well knew that the path down to the beach was hazardous and crisscrossed with protruding roots. Nevertheless, she raced down it, overcome by her need to see Gerrick and feel his strong, loving arms about her once more. Thus far, her evening had been most trying; she'd forgotten what a mean-spirited person her uncle could be. How had she ever lived with him these many long months since his arrival on Kauai?

By comparison to Gerrick, her uncle was an ill-tempered, judgmental, old curmudgeon bent on making everyone as miserable and unhappy as he was. Before, she had always made excuses for him and overlooked his nasty nature because he was her uncle; but now that she was Gerrick's wife, she felt much less forgiving. Two people did not need to live in constant tension and irritability. Gentleness, tenderness, and respect between them was possible even when they differed from each other in almost everything. Living with such a direct opposite as Gerrick had taught her this amazing truth.

Uncle George had not even shown the least interest in learning why Gerrick had been delayed. When Pikake had announced the arrival of a messenger bearing news concerning Gerrick's brother, her uncle had only said, "A brother? You say the chap has a brother?"

And upon hearing that he did, Uncle George had seemed to lose all interest in Caitlin's husband. "Don't you want to come with me and find out what's happening?" she had asked him, to which he had replied, "No, I'd much prefer to stay here and eat my supper before it gets cold."

If it hadn't been for Pikake offering to serve dinner to the old so-and-so, Caitlin would probably have had to serve it before she left. How could Uncle George be so self-centered as to care more for his dinner than he did for meeting his niece's husband?

Holding her skirts high above her ankles, Caitlin darted from beneath the trees and ran toward the flaming torch. Not seeing Gerrick, she called his name again. "Gerrick, where are you? I came as fast as I could."

"Here, Cait. Did you come alone?"

"Yes, Pikake and Uncle George are still at the house."

Caitlin whirled about, looking for him, and suddenly Gerrick was there, taking her in his arms and embracing her before he even said one word about his brother. "Gerrick!" she cried, laughing. "Stop! Where's the messenger Pikake said has come? Is it true you've received word of your brother? Is he alive and well?"

Gerrick took her face in his hands and gave her a long, tender look before he answered. "Yes, my love. Hadley is alive—but he's *not* well, from what I've heard."

"What did you hear, Gerrick? Where is this messenger? I thought I was to translate for you."

"He, ah, had additional messages for Chief Laanui and couldn't stay long enough for you to get here. Anyway, I had no trouble understanding him. My Hawaiian is improving, just like John's . . . and besides, the man spoke a bit of English."

"Well, what did he *say*, Gerrick? Is Hadley ill?"

"Yes, I'm afraid so. Extremely ill. I must go to him at once."

"I'm so sorry, Gerrick. But where is he? Is it far?"

"He . . . he's somewhere in the Kalaulau Valley. I don't know exactly where—that's why I need you to come with me, Cait. That's why I sent Pikake to get you. Have you ever been to the Kalaulau Valley?"

"Only as a young girl, Gerrick. And I . . . I don't remember much about that journey." Caitlin shivered a little as she fibbed. Actually, she remembered every detail; that was when she and Pikake had trailed after her father unbeknownst to him, and had discovered sandalwood growing on one of the valley's high, steep slopes.

"But you've been there at least," Gerrick said. "And you can convince anyone we meet to help us look for my brother."

"Didn't the messenger tell you where in the valley to look?" Caitlin wrinkled her brow in alarm. The valley was large, rugged, and wild; it could take weeks and weeks to conduct a thorough search of it. Without knowing where to begin, they'd waste precious time; Hadley Scott could die long before they found him.

A startling thought suddenly occurred to Caitlin: What had Gerrick's brother been doing so long in that wilderness? Instead of studying plants, could he possibly have been searching for sandalwood? And if so, had he found it? If he had, she must persuade them all to abandon any thoughts of claiming it.

"Certainly, I'll come with you, Gerrick. But first, do you mind if I return to the house and tell my uncle I'm leaving? Why don't you come, too, and meet him before we depart?"

"No, Cait, I'd rather meet your uncle when I have more time to make his acquaintance. Actually, I must insist that we leave immediately. The wind has been shifting back and forth all evening, and has only just now been blowing steady enough for us to make our departure. If we *don't*

239

leave now, we may be delayed indefinitely."

"But you haven't even loaded these supplies into the longboat!"

"That can't be helped; they'll have to remain. The only person I'm waiting for now is John . . . and here he is. John, grab that crate of mangoes, and let's be on our way."

"John, aren't you even going to say good-bye to Pikake?" Upset by the abruptness of their leave-taking, Caitlin was willing to try anything to forestall their departure.

"You heard what Gerrick said. There's no time, Caitlin. I did, however, trace a message in the sand back there." John nodded toward a stretch of level beach behind the supplies. "Maybe someone will find it tomorrow morning and fetch your uncle to read it. However, if they don't, you needn't worry; Pikake understands the seriousness of the situation and will guess that we left immediately in search of Hadley."

"But this is all so sudden!" Seeing Gerrick pick up a crate of fruit and head for the longboat, Caitlin quickly grabbed a tapa-wrapped bundle and hurried after him. "For heaven's sake, Gerrick, wait! Or do you intend to leave me behind?"

"Not unless you insist upon it," Gerrick said teasingly, pausing to allow her to catch up. "Do you?"

"No! I said I'd come, and I will!"

Despite his easy grin, Gerrick's relief was evident. "Good. Because if you'd given me any arguments, I would have been forced to hog-tie you and toss you in the bottom of the longboat. It's high time I asserted my authority over you, Cait. Wherever I go, you go."

"Honestly, Gerrick." Caitlin sighed, pleased by his possessiveness but exasperated as well. "I guess I'm just sorry to have my lovely dinner go to waste."

"What were we having for dinner?" Gerrick set his burden down in the longboat and began shoving the craft into the surf. "No, don't tell me. I think I can guess—and frankly, I'd rather eat mangoes."

"Gerrick! Is your brother as terrible as you? I can't wait

to meet him."

"Let's just hurry. Or it may be too late for you to meet him."

On that somber note, Caitlin scrambled into the boat and sat down, balancing her bundle on her knees. John and Gerrick soon joined her, and after wrestling the boat past the curling surf, they settled down to rowing steadily for the ship.

Chapter Nineteen

"Is this the only entrance into the valley?" Gerrick asked Caitlin, and she averted her face so he wouldn't see that she was lying again—she, the missionary who condemned all lies and liars.

"Yes, I think so," she said quietly, declining to mention that first time she and Pikake had sneaked into the valley. They had followed her father as he entered it from a direction entirely different from the one they were facing now. Then they had come overland, laboriously making their way along the ancient Na Pali Coast Trail that bypassed a crumbling old hula temple, and scaling cliffs frequented only by seabirds.

Now, on this her second visit, she was approaching the valley from the sea, where a small, crescent beach offered limited access to a shoreline dominated by steep, forbidding cliffs, breathtaking in their bleak, awesome solitude. The Kalaulau Valley lay nestled between sheer black cliffs, and as the longboat bearing herself, John, Gerrick, and Erasmus Mockensturm drew nearer the beach, seabirds screamed at them over the surf's roar, and Caitlin felt a twinge of grim foreboding, fed by her guilt from lying to Gerrick.

The valley was a place of shrouded mystery, where rain clouds often dipped low to form a swirling mist. Here, for centuries unknown, had lived the island's outcasts, men and women who had broken the *kapus* of the ancient kings, and been forced to flee for their lives. Here, her father had come to deliver the good news that the *kapus* had been abolished and a new religion instituted. And here, though he'd found no wrongdoers still skulking in terror, her father had discovered the sandalwood that was to cause him so much anguish—even, perhaps, the loss of his own life.

"My God, it's spectacular!" John exclaimed, pausing in his expert maneuvering of the oars to admire the incredible setting.

Caitlin looked up at the towering cliffs and screaming birds; among the swooping terns and boobies, a frigate-bird with a seven-foot wingspan wheeled through the mist, as if standing guard at the entrance to the valley. Their unexpected approach caused him to veer inland, and the magnificent creature was soon lost to view in the low-hanging clouds.

"Hang on, Cait, while we bring her in!" Gerrick cried, and the next few moments were a wild, wet scramble as the heaving green sea lifted the longboat and flung it shoreward.

With each manning an oar, Gerrick and John joined in a frantic effort to keep the boat headed for the beach and away from the towering walls of solid, black rock on either side. Spray repeatedly dashed Caitlin's face, making it impossible for her to see. By the time she cleared her eyes of the stinging salt, the longboat was scudding across wet sand, and the men were jumping out to haul it ashore before the ocean could drag it back again.

"Are you all right, Cait?" Gerrick offered her his hand, and she took it as she climbed out of the boat.

"'Twas a dandy ride, wasn't it, Miz Scott?" Erasmus Mockensturm winked. "Enough t' put the most unrepentant of sinners in a prayerful mood."

Caitlin only nodded, still ill at ease with the man who served both as chaplain and first mate aboard the *Naughty Lady*. She walked a short distance across the sand and stood studying the dense, steeply rising forest at the beach's edge. Behind her, she could hear Gerrick giving orders for John and Erasmus to unload their canvas-wrapped supplies. His boots, as he came after her, squeaked on the sand.

"Where do you suggest we start, Cait? This valley looks huge."

"It is huge," she answered. "And what paths there might once have been are now overgrown and choked with ferns and young trees. I don't know how your brother has survived all alone here for this long."

Dense jungle growth marched determinedly up the sides of the steep cliffs, ending only when it came to solid, serrated rock. The sun, having to fight its way through constantly shifting clouds, streaked the rock face with astonishing deep-hued colors: dark reds, oranges, and purples, soft mauves and pinks. Caitlin remembered how difficult it was to climb these rugged cliffs soaring thousands of feet into the air, and she could not imagine living on such inhospitable terrain. The cliffs and the valley itself were frequently rain-lashed, and even now, a fierce wind was whistling down the valley. No wonder Hadley Scott was ill. To live in this mournful, isolated place, so far from human companionship and comforts, would try the hardiest of souls.

"Hadley is a rare fellow," Gerrick replied. "He, uh, doesn't care much for people. His tastes run to exotic plants. I mean he eats them as well as studies them. The messenger who told me he was here met some other islanders who had come to the valley hunting goats. They described Hadley perfectly, right down to his, uh, hermit ways."

"And his illness? Did they say what was wrong with him?"

"He's got a—a fever of some sort."

"Why didn't they take him back to civilization? There are large communities at Waimea and Wailua. The islanders would gladly have cared for him."

"The fool wouldn't go with them. Always was a stubborn cuss."

Caitlin was suddenly darkly suspicious of Hadley's

motives for remaining—especially if he were ill. Turning to Gerrick, she took his arm. "What if he won't come with *us*, Gerrick? Perhaps your brother has no desire to be rescued. Perhaps he's found something here that's worth the risks he's taking . . ."

Gerrick's green eyes perused her face, but he didn't ask what that something might be. "He'll come, Cait. When I get through blistering his ears with tales of the family's wrath, he'll be begging me to take him home. I just hope he's still got enough strength to make it back to this beach. His illness may be quite serious."

For the first time, Caitlin doubted the truth of what Gerrick was saying. That he didn't mention the possibility of Hadley having found sandalwood struck her as odd. In light of their previous conversation regarding her father's death and her uncle's disappearance, she was surprised Gerrick *hadn't* resurrected the topic. He'd been most anxious to discuss it then; why not now? She chided herself for not trusting her husband, at the same time wishing that the story of Hadley Scott did not sound so . . . so incredible and made up.

"We must fashion a canvas sling or stretcher," she said matter-of-factly. "So if your brother is weak and cannot walk to the beach, we can carry him here."

"An excellent idea," Gerrick concurred. "After we set up camp, we can do that this evening."

"Gerrick, it's none of my business, of course, but why doesn't your crew come ashore and help us?"

When Gerrick didn't answer immediately, Caitlin felt a flicker of cold dread. Raking her fingers through her windblown hair, she lifted her eyes to his and stared intently into their sea-green depths. How beautiful his eyes were! Like the lush, mist-shrouded valley, they were shadowed, mysterious, and full of secrets. Tell me your secrets, Gerrick, she pleaded silently—but she was also deathly afraid to hear them.

"I doubt that my crew members could do any better than the four of us, Cait. But more than that, I don't want my men discovering things they shouldn't see."

"You mean things like sandalwood."

"Precisely. If sandalwood *does* still grow here, I hope you and I are the only ones who find it."

"What will you do if we f—find it?" Caitlin could hardly keep her voice steady; her heart was thudding in her ears.

Gerrick gave her a long assessing look. "A better question would be: What will *you* do, Cait?"

Now Caitlin found breathing difficult. Gerrick knew how she felt about the sandalwood, and she knew how he felt. One of them would have to sacrifice their life-long beliefs to please the other. Could she stand by and silently watch while the islands were once again overrun by fortune-seekers? And the islanders were forced to toil in the rainy mountains while their families died of starvation?

Gerrick might be able to secure trade rights from Kamehameha and thus protect his claim from others; but neither he nor the king could prevent the unscrupulous from swarming to the islands in frantic search for riches they might claim for their own. The mere thought of it made her feel ill; she had seen how her own father had suffered from the impulse to exploit his discovery of the sandalwood. At least, her father would have been harvesting and selling the wood for the church's gain, not his own. But thank God he had *not* succumbed to temptation; like her, he had realized just in time what would happen. . . .

"We won't find any sandalwood," she asserted calmly. "Because there's none to find."

Gerrick did not dispute her, but his eyes condemned her for the lie. He knew how she felt about lying, and her cheeks flamed with shame. "We'd better help John and Erasmus unload the longboat," she muttered, hurrying away from Gerrick and his all-seeing eyes.

Pikake stood on the beach beside Caitlin's uncle—or the man who *claimed* to be Caitlin's uncle. Fearfully, she watched as the hard-eyed, stern-faced man in the black frock coat read the message scrawled in the sand: *Pikake: Gerrick's brother ill. Gone with Gerrick and Caitlin to rescue him. Love, John.*

She had found the message shortly after dawn and guessed that John had written it in order to furnish *Makuakane* George with an excuse for their sudden departure. What she did not understand was why John had publicly declared his love for her; now, *Makuakane* George was angry and full of questions.

"You know what this says, don't you?" The paunchy, heavyset man was frightening in his livid anger. His tiny gray eyes gleamed like polished pearl shells, reminding her of the eyes of the ancient *aumakua*, or wooden idols once worshiped by her people.

Trembling, Pikake nodded. "Tutu Caitlin teach me to read long time ago."

"You and this John are guilty of sinning together, aren't you? Don't deny it. I can see by your face that you are."

"Yes," Pikake whispered. "I love John Reynolds."

Makuakane George looked up and down the beach. In the early morning light, it was deserted and lying silent. The only sounds were the murmur of the surf and the hammering of her heart as she wondered what he would do next. That he *would* do something—something bad and wicked—seemed as certain as the sunrise; she had never liked or trusted this man. From the day he had arrived on the island, she had known he was evil.

Apparently satisfied that they were alone, *Makuakane* George suddenly seized her arm and twisted it behind her back. Unable to stop herself, Pikake screamed and dropped to her knees. The pain was excruciating; with the tiniest bit more pressure, her arm would break.

"Do not hurt me, please," she whimpered, but *Makuakane* George was unmoved by her tears.

"Where have they gone?" he thundered. "Caitlin and her husband and this John?"

"Pikake not know! That is why I come and get you when I find message in sand. I think maybe *you* know where they go."

"Don't lie to me, you godless heathen! Have you no fear for your immortal soul?" He jerked her arm a little higher, and sparks danced before Pikake's eyes. "Answer me: I demand to know where they've gone! Who is this lost brother of whom they speak? How long has he been here, and what is his name?"

"I . . . I think his name Hadley. Captain Scott say he come here to—"

"*Scott*? Did you say Captain Scott?"

Too late, Pikake realized her error. "N—no, not Scott! I no say Scott!"

"Yes, you did! His name is *Gerrick* Scott, isn't it? But he has no brother named Hadley that *I* know of."

In his excitement, *Makuakane* George let go of her arm. Appalled that she had let slip Gerrick's name, Pikake hunched over in the sand.

"Of course," *Makuakane* George muttered, pacing up and down in front of her. "I should have realized when you said John Reynolds. John is that old boyhood chum of his; I'd forgotten him, but now I remember. The two were always getting into trouble and then begging their rich papas to bail them out. But Gerrick's papa never would—on *my* advice, of course. Well, well . . . so this is where Gerrick's wound up: chasing after the same rainbow I am—that damn sandalwood Caitlin's father supposedly found."

At the mention of sandalwood, Pikake looked up. So it was true. *Makuakane* George had somehow found out about the sandalwood in the Kalaulau Valley. And he had come here to steal it. Thank all the gods—including the god of the missionaries—that Tutu Caitlin had never told him of its existence, much less its location.

Makuakane George suddenly looked down at her, and a new light blazed in his eyes. "You know where it is, don't you?"

Cowering at his feet, she denied it. "Pikake not know what you are talking about!"

"Yes, you do! Your eyes tell me everything! Damn, why

248

didn't I question you before? And if you know, then Caitlin knows, too. I thought she might, and that eventually she'd trust me enough to tell me. But the damn stubborn wench kept play-acting, pretending she knew nothing . . ."

Once again, he seized Pikake's arm in a bone-crushing grip. *"Tell me where the sandalwood is or I'll snap your arm in two like a piece of kindling."*

Screaming, Pikake fought to get free. Almost before she felt it, she heard a crunching sound, and the world exploded in splinters of agony.

"I tell you! I tell you!" she shrieked, cradling her injured arm and pitching face-first into the sand.

"Wrong. You'll *show* me, little bitch. You'll take me there this very day, or else I'll break every bone in your skinny little body."

"Face it, Gerrick," John advised. "At this rate, we're never going to find the sandalwood. It's been five long, back-breaking days, and—"

"Be quiet, or she'll hear you." Gerrick nodded toward Caitlin, whose back was to them as she sat slumped upon a rock, her head nodding in fatigue, her clothing torn and dirty, and her hair hanging in a single, disheveled braid down her sweat-soaked back.

"Gerrick, she's too damned exhausted to pay us the slightest heed no matter what we say. Look at her. How can you do this to her? It would have been far kinder to have told her the truth from the very beginning."

"Shut up, John. I don't need you lecturing me when I've got eyes to see for myself how tired she is."

"Well, what are you going to do? We can't stay here forever climbing up one godforsaken cliff and down another. If you won't look at her, look out there!" John pointed to the valley, spread out below them like a Turkish carpet of multihued greens, ambers, and purples. "It might be years before we find the damn sandalwood— if we live that long. We've tried our best, and we simply can't find it. Either you demand that Caitlin help us—after she rests, of course—or I'm going back to the beach to join Erasmus. The two of us can hail the ship and await you there."

Gerrick's gaze traveled down the length of the long valley to where the beach appeared as a tiny ribbon of gleaming white sand. Beyond it, the turquoise sea was placid and diamond-sparkled, the surf's roar lost in the distance, replaced by the constant soughing of the wind.

"Caitlin *is* helping us," he reminded John. "Not once has she complained. Indeed, as soon as we stop to rest, she urges us onward."

"That's because she thinks we're looking for a sick man, not a bunch of aromatic trees! For pity's sake, Gerrick, tell her the truth. If she refuses to lead us to the wood—or if she doesn't know where it is—I'm giving up. And if you don't tell her the truth, I'm through. We've tried it your way; now try it mine. Or you can forget you ever knew me, because I'm sure as hell going to do my damnedest to forget I ever knew you."

Gerrick rubbed his hand across his eyes; his head was throbbing, his mouth dry as dust. He felt as if he'd been pummeled in a fist fight. John was right; it was time to tell Cait the truth. He had hoped to spare her the pain he knew awaited them both, but luck had deserted him. The sandalwood and all it represented seemed less obtainable now than it had seemed those many years ago when Captain Moses Nottingham had first told his father about it.

"Wait here," he said to John. "Give me a few moments alone with her."

John nodded, and Gerrick walked toward Caitlin, dreading each step he took. Her head bowed, she appeared half-dozing as she sat slumped upon the rock. Placing his hands on her shoulders, he began kneading the muscles of her lower neck. She tilted back her head and smiled up at him, her blue-gray eyes lighting with pleasure at the sight of him.

"I'm sorry, Gerrick. I sat down to enjoy the breathtaking

view, and I'm afraid I fell asleep—or almost asleep. Is it time to resume our search? Shouldn't we fire the pistol first?"

At Caitlin's suggestion, they had been firing Gerrick's pistol every time they stopped or made camp, hoping to alert Hadley to their presence, and also advising Erasmus of their whereabouts. Caitlin was certain the signal would work; if it didn't bring Hadley running, it would at least signal any Hawaiians in the vicinity who might know of his location. But thus far, despite evidence of other humans—a few weed-choked taro patches and, once, a grass hut—the shot had brought no one, leading Gerrick to believe that the valley was uninhabited.

"Cait, I have to talk to you." Gerrick moved around in front of her, took her hands in his, and knelt down on one knee. In the position of a supplicant, he felt more confident—for that was exactly what he was.

"Sweetheart," he continued. "There's no easy way to tell you this except to blurt it out—and to assure you beforehand, that I truly love you, more than I've ever loved anyone. You've come to mean everything to me, Cait."

"Why, what is it, Gerrick?" Releasing one hand, she smoothed back a lock of his hair with her fingers. "Stop frowning so. You haven't given up hope, have you? Because if you have, you should be ashamed. God hasn't brought us this far in order to disappoint us in the end. You must have faith. We'll find your brother; I know we will. And Hadley will be all right. I've been praying for him every night."

"Caitlin . . . oh, my sweet Cait, you're wrong. We'll never find him because he doesn't exist."

Caitlin's face went blank, and then gradually filled with suspicion. "Doesn't exist? What do you mean?"

"Cait, I made him up. I never had a brother named Hadley—only a sister named Abby. I only told you that ridiculous tale about my plant-loving brother, because I needed an excuse to mask the *real* reason I came to the islands . . ."

As his words finally sank in, Caitlin's blue-gray eyes

251

dilated, and he could feel her withdrawing to some far distant place where he'd never be able to reach her. Her mouth was suddenly trembling, and her hands felt cold as ice. "And what is the real reason?" she whispered, her voice gone hoarse and raspy.

"I—I came to find the sandalwood your father discovered."

"How exactly did you learn of it?"

"From a sea captain who once worked for my father. Perhaps you remember how it came about. Your father was ill, and you asked Captain Moses Nottingham to take you both to Lahaina where there was a missionary doctor at the time. Your father was delirious with fever, and during a storm at sea, he—"

"I remember!" Caitlin said sharply. "His condition became worse, and he talked incessantly about the wood. But afterward, he denied knowing anything about it! I remember his exact words: *'There is no sandalwood.'*"

"I know what he said, Cait, but do you also deny knowing about the sandalwood? Can you look me in the eye and swear you know nothing?"

"Why should I swear anything?" She jerked her hands away, her eyes darkening to the hue of thunderclouds on the open sea. "That's why you married me, isn't it? To get your hands on the wood."

Caitlin jumped to her feet, almost knocking him over. "You thought if you married the poor ugly daughter of a missionary too stupid to exploit the discovery to his own advantage, she would trustingly tell you where it was. She'd be so happy to finally land a husband she'd do anything you asked. But first you had to drag her away to the wilderness where there's no place to escape—no place to run and hide. You had to lie to her—lie about everything! Even loving her—so that she would want to tell you about the sandalwood just to make you happy . . ."

Gerrick rose and again tried to take her hands. "No, Cait. I didn't lie about loving you. That's the one truth in this whole damn mess. I fell in love with you the first time I saw you. . . . I love your goodness, your beauty, your—"

"Liar! You lie like the devil! Damn your honeyed words and sweet declarations! Every word you say is a lie. Oh, you are wicked, evil. . . . You're nothing but a whited sepulcher, all gleaming paint without, and containing only sin, death, and corruption within!"

"Cait, please . . . please listen to me." Gerrick reached for her, but she shoved against him so hard that he lost his footing and stumbled backward.

"Get away from me!" she cried. "Don't touch me ever again! I hate you, Gerrick Scott! I hate you so much I could die from it!"

Before he could stop her, she darted past him and went running down the steep side of the cliff overlooking the valley.

"Cait, stop! You'll fall and hurt yourself!" Gerrick vaulted after her, but she was running blindly, heedlessly, not even picking up her skirts so she wouldn't trip. "Cait, watch out! You're coming to the edge!"

Before Gerrick's shocked eyes, the scene unfolded like some hideous nightmare, with himself as the tortured dreamer trying to prevent something from happening that was going to happen anyway. He pounded after Caitlin, knowing he couldn't catch her in time but determined to try. Her braid came undone and her bright hair streamed out on the wind. Her skirt billowed out from her flying feet. She arrived at the cliff's edge, realized the danger, and tried to stop herself—but the momentum of her headlong flight was too great. She teetered a moment and then plunged forward, dropping like a stone over the edge.

Gerrick heard her body hit, followed by the sound of rock and gravel sliding down the incline. "Oh, my God!" he groaned, dashing to the edge and peering down— down—down to a rocky shelf where Caitlin lay sprawled in a heap, a crumpled porcelain doll whose beautiful silver-gold hair was now streaked bright red.

"Oh, my God," he repeated, praying fervently for the first time in his entire life. "Dear God, don't let her be dead."

Chapter Twenty

John helped Gerrick load Caitlin into the canvas sling they had fashioned at her insistence for his brother, and they carried her back up the mountainside to an indentation in the cliffs where she would be sheltered from the wind.

"At least, she's still breathing," John informed Gerrick, after examining her while Gerrick looked for the water skin. "And I don't think she's broken any bones."

Too worried to bother answering, Gerrick ripped off his shirt, liberally splashed it with water, and applied it to the gash in Caitlin's forehead. For so small a cut, it had produced an amazing quantity of blood, but what concerned Gerrick even more than the prodigious bleeding was the size of the abnormal, purple swelling just above it, and the fact that Caitlin was still unconscious and showed no signs of awakening.

"Cait, can you hear me?" he pleaded. "Cait, wake up."

Gerrick patted her cheeks, rubbed her hands, and even pinched her arm, but Caitlin did not stir. "We've got to get her back to the schooner," he muttered distractedly. "Did we bring any brandy?"

"I think so," John responded. "I wrapped a bottle in an extra shirt so Cait wouldn't find it and toss it away—though I suppose I could have convinced her we might need it for medicinal purposes. Wait here, and I'll get it."

As his friend hurried back to where they'd dropped their

canvas bundles and supplies, Gerrick gave vent to the emotions swamping him in a chilling wave. "Oh, Cait . . . Cait, I'm so sorry. If you die, I swear I'll throw myself off the same cliff and die, too."

Gathering Caitlin into his arms, Gerrick carried her to a narrow ledge of rock and sat down, cradling her as he would a baby. "Cait, I love you. . . . I'm everything you said I was—wicked, evil, a whited sepulcher. . . . You're the only good thing that's ever happened to me. You're the *best* thing, and all I did was hurt you, maybe even kill you. Forgive me, Cait."

Swept with an awful certainty that Caitlin would *never* awaken, Gerrick buried his face in her silver-gold hair and wept. He wept as he could not remember weeping for his mother, sister, or father. Or for Madeline. This time he couldn't turn his grief into hate. He couldn't blame everything on Amos Taylor. This time the blame was his and no one else's. Caitlin had given him wholehearted love, passion, tenderness, and loyalty. And he had repaid her in the false coin of deceit and treachery—the same coin Amos Taylor had used to repay his father for all his years of trust and friendship.

I'm a worst bastard than he is, Gerrick accused himself. For I *know* better, and still I sinned.

"Here's the brandy," John said, waving a bottle under Gerrick's nose. "But I think *you* should drink it, instead of Caitlin. You'll be no good at all to her if you fall apart now."

"I'm not falling apart," Gerrick growled, freeing one hand and reaching for the brandy. "I'm just realizing what a despicable wretch I am. I wish you'd take a sword and skewer me with it. I can't stand myself any longer."

"Drink," John snorted. "If you get any more maudlin, I *will* run you through."

Gerrick unstoppered the bottle, took a long swig, and then attempted to pour some of the brandy between Caitlin's pale lips. The amber liquid trickled onto the ground, and it was obvious she'd drown before she swallowed. Swearing in vexation, Gerrick drew back his

255

arm to heave the bottle against the rock wall, but John grabbed it before he could do so.

"Easy, lad, easy. I'll take this for now. Later, she might drink some. Why don't you just sit here and hold her while I set up camp for the night. We can't start back down these cliffs until morning, so we might as well get a fire going and make her as comfortable as possible."

"Do what you like. She'll probably die before morning anyhow. Look at the sky, it's going to storm soon; a fire is out of the question."

"Like hell it is." Prowling the areas like an angry, determined bear, John began picking up brush and sticks, anything that might be burnable.

Meanwhile, Gerrick rocked Caitlin in his arms, crooning to her in hopes she'd hear him and awaken. Not until thunder rumbled, and he looked up and saw low-hanging, iron-gray clouds directly overhead, did he think to get the canvas sling and wrap it around Caitlin to protect her from the oncoming rain.

"Gerrick, bring Caitlin over here!" John shouted, and Gerrick rose, grabbed the sling, and headed toward his friend's voice.

John had found an overhang, not deep enough to form a cave but adequate enough to provide shelter from the rain already beginning to pelt the rocky ground. Gerrick quickly carried Caitlin beneath it. John unrolled the blankets they had brought for sleeping and made a kind of pallet for her to lie on. Gerrick hated to release Caitlin from his arms, but John pointed out that he needed help getting the fire lit, so reluctantly, Gerrick laid her down and covered her with canvas.

The two men labored for a quarter of an hour trying to light the fire, but there wasn't enough wood or tinder. What they had gathered soon became damp from the heavy humidity. The rain fell in a solid wall of water, obscuring visibility and rendering speech impossible because of the drumming noise. Giving up on the futile chore, Gerrick went back to Caitlin and shielded her as best he could from the blowing, splashing water.

John, however, refused to admit that he was beaten and continued his attempts to make a flame leap up from the small pile of brush and tinder. By the time the rain lessened to a gentle pitter-patter, he had a tiny, wavering fire going in the corner where two walls of rock came together.

Grinning, John sat down, crossed his legs native-style, and announced his triumph. "Gerrick, move Caitlin closer so she can feel the warmth from this."

"What warmth?" Gerrick asked skeptically. Nevertheless, he did as John bade him.

Caitlin was deathly pale, her lips as colorless as her cheeks, and after setting her down as close as he dared to the fire, Gerrick massaged her hands, then moved to take off her footgear—a pair of sturdy, leather boots he had loaned her to replace her impractical slippers. Her feet slipped out easily from the boots that were far too large, and he swore under his breath as he saw the blisters caused by the chafing leather. In several places on each foot, the skin was rubbed raw and bleeding, yet Cait had never mentioned any discomfort.

Moved by a tenderness too poignant and painful for words, Gerrick wiped each foot with his shirt sleeve, then kissed each toe and each reddened sore spot. This visible proof of her love for him shamed him more than anything she had said or done up until now. For his sake, she had endured so much, plodding bravely on when each step must have been agony.

Across the narrow space separating them, John met his gaze and growled, "I curse the day you ever mentioned sandalwood to me, Gerrick Scott. We two are the biggest fools who ever lived. We came in search of riches—and yet both of us are guilty of rejecting the greatest treasure a man can ever know: the love of a sweet, gentle woman who wants nothing more than to be loved in return."

"That surely applies to me," Gerrick agreed. "But how does it apply to you? You haven't hurt Pikake the way I've hurt Caitlin."

"Yes, I have. I told her I couldn't marry her because one

day I might have to go home, and she could not accompany me. In *my* world, in my *old* life, she would never fit in."

"You were only telling her the truth; what's so cruel about that?"

"Any woman I'd said that to back home would have slapped my face and bid me be gone. Pikake—that dear, precious child—only threw her arms around me and told me it didn't matter. She would love me now anyway, and be happy the rest of her life just remembering how it had been with us. . . . Mind you, she said this believing she's already going to hell for my sake. Once I convinced her that hell is my ultimate destination whether she makes love to me or not, she readily agreed to make love. Hell will be just fine with her, so long as I am there."

Gerrick shook his head in disbelief. Sitting down beside Caitlin, he carefully covered her feet and then, not knowing what else to do, simply sat, holding her hand. "I can't believe these two women, John. Their selflessness is enough to make a convert of me—except that I know I could never live up to their high moral standards. Even hating myself as I do, I still covet that damn sandalwood. Now, more than ever. I can't allow Amos Taylor to have it. And no matter that I know it's wrong, I still intend to kill him."

"Did you tell Caitlin about Amos?" John rummaged through a canvas sack, withdrew a stale ship's biscuit, and held it out to Gerrick. "Here, you'd better eat this while you can. Later, when this damn rain lets up, we'll see about boiling water to make tea. I'll wager Caitlin will be ready to drink some when she finally wakes up."

"*If* she wakes up." Too sick at heart to eat, Gerrick waved away the biscuit. "I never had a chance to mention Amos to Cait. All she heard was my admission that Hadley doesn't exist, and she ran away. Couldn't stand my horrible presence a minute longer."

"Can't say that I blame her," John said, gnawing at the hard biscuit. "She must have been shocked as hell."

"Not so shocked as furious. She accused me of marrying

258

her just to get the sandalwood."

"Then you haven't yet explained you're not really married."

"No," Gerrick said. "And that's one thing I intend never to tell her. As long as she thinks we're still married, I've still got a chance with her—or at least, I did have a chance, before this happened. . . . How do I get myself into these messes, John? Why does tragedy and disaster stalk me at every turn?"

John left off chewing and gazed at him thoughtfully. "Damned if I know, Gerrick. . . . I can only suppose that since the first half of your life was charmed, it's only fair that the second half be tortured. Life is full of unanswerable questions. Why should a big man like me fall in love with a little bit of a girl like Pikake? It makes no sense, but still it's happened. And even hating myself for what I'm doing to her—and knowing that I'm a fool, to boot—I can't and won't marry her."

"Maybe marriage to Pikake wouldn't be as bad as you anticipate, John. Before you decide the situation is hopeless, think about it again. Maybe it could work after all."

"I *do* think about it. Day and night. I think about taking her home with me, back to Boston, and having people laugh at her quaint lack of manners and odd way of speaking. I think of dressing her in whalebone corsets and those ridiculously wide sleeves so in fashion just now, and piling her hair in silly ringlets on top of her head. . . . Why, she wouldn't be the same person anymore. Then, I think of my family wondering if I've gone mad. . . . But mostly I think of the half-breed children we'd have, children who'd no more be accepted by genteel Boston society than their misfit mother."

"You've got a point," Gerrick conceded, remembering Caitlin's fears. "Even if you stayed here and made a new life for yourself, it wouldn't be easy. The missionaries would condemn you . . ."

"And I'm a man who's learned to enjoy the respect of all and sundry. Oh, yes, Gerrick. . . . Over the past few years,

259

I've changed and mellowed. In my own way, I've become a first-class citizen. Even my affairs are more discreet than they once were. Before you whisked me away to these islands, I was thinking of marrying into a sedate, long-established family. The girl is a blue-blooded Bostonian, proper as any missionary . . . and her family has excellent connections which would further my own family's shipbuilding interests."

"You never told me that."

"You never asked. You just presumed upon my friendship, doubtless thinking I had nothing better to do than trail after you like an amiable puppy. Actually, I came because the promise of gaining a fortune was too good to pass up; Elizabeth, or Liddy, as we call her, has expensive tastes."

"She wouldn't be happy just to curl up in your brawny arms and giggle while you nibble on her earlobe."

"No, she wouldn't be. And she damned well wouldn't understand or forgive my attraction to a little brown Hawaiian who loves me with such childlike enthusiasm that even I am sometimes embarrassed. . . . So you see, Gerrick, the reason I'm so tolerant of *your* sins is that I've got a bucketful of my own. As I said at the start of this discussion, we two are the biggest fools in all of God's creation."

John fell silent after that, and Gerrick had nothing more to say either. After a short time, seeing John lean back against the wall and close his eyes, Gerrick stretched out beside Caitlin, but kept his hand in hers so he would know if she stirred or awakened. The coming night promised to be long, dark, and uncomfortable, not to mention threatening. He couldn't shake the premonition that Cait was going to die here on the cliff face. She simply wouldn't awaken.

He tried to pray, but the words that had before come so easily now refused to surface. God was Caitlin's friend, not his, and he saw no way of closing the yawning gap between himself and his Creator. Finally, he allowed his own eyes to close, though his ears remained attuned to the gentle patter of the rain, through which he strained to hear Caitlin's slightest breath or sigh. And at long last, without knowing that he did so, he slept.

It was morning when Gerrick awoke. Chilled to the bone, he came awake with a violent start. How could he have slept so long in complete disregard for Caitlin's precarious welfare?

Scrambling to his feet, he bent over her, fearing to find she was cold and dead. Instead, to his intense relief, he discovered she was sleeping peacefully, her color normal, and her breathing calm and restful. Tears of relief sprang to his eyes, and he uttered a heartfelt "thank-you" to whatever celestial being had stood guard over her during the night.

Then, he stretched his cramped, aching muscles and surveyed the morning. It was just after dawn, the sky streaked with rose and purple as the sun's warming rays probed the cliffs. Gerrick rubbed his bare arms and chest, wondering what had happened to his shirt. Then he remembered using it to clean Caitlin's injuries and made a mental note to put it back on before the sun rose high enough to burn his skin.

John, he noticed, was still snoring, his head lolled to one side. Gerrick nudged him with one foot and bade him awaken. "A fine pair we are," he informed his groggy friend.

"Cait?" John mumbled, as appalled as Gerrick.

"Sleeping like a baby. Let's get moving. Before we start back to the beach, I want to get something hot into her."

By the time the sun had risen high enough to dry the cliffs, Gerrick and John had eaten, and Caitlin was sitting up sipping tea from a tin mug. She had straightened her clothing, brushed her hair, and otherwise taken care of her own physical needs despite Gerrick's clumsy efforts to perform even the most intimate tasks for her.

The one thing she *hadn't* done was speak to him. Though obviously stiff, bruised, and sore, she said not a single word of complaint, not even when Gerrick helped her back into her boots.

"Now, we're just putting these on to protect your feet. You're not going to walk. John and I will carry you in the sling."

He indicated the long pole to which he and John had affixed all their belongings, half at each end. In the center part of the pole was the canvas sling where Caitlin could either sit or lie down. Carrying her down the steep terrain would be difficult, but neither Gerrick nor John believed Caitlin capable of walking, though earlier she had taken several steps with only a slight limping hesitancy.

Gerrick held out his hand to help her to rise, but Caitlin pushed it aside and rose to her feet under her own power. He attempted to support her by the elbow, but she jerked her arm away.

"Damn it, Cait! I'm trying to assist you over to the sling."

Her response to that was to fling the remaining contents of her tin cup into his face. Gasping as the still-warm tea streamed down his cheeks and onto his chest, Gerrick stared at her in amazement.

"Cait, I know you're angry and upset, but childish displays of temper won't help either of us. We're going back to the ship now. Do you understand me?"

Wild-eyed, she stared back at him, daring him to lay a hand on her. He couldn't tell if she understood what he was saying or not. The look in her eyes was eerie; had her brain been injured in the fall?

"Cait," he said gently, reaching out to her.

This time, she flung the cup itself at his head. Ducking, he narrowly avoided being struck with it.

"Leave her to me, Gerrick," John suggested. "Here, you steady the pole and I'll try to get her into the sling."

Placing the pole on the ground, John walked confidently toward Caitlin. "Come along, sweetheart. It's a long way back to the beach. I doubt we'll make it before evening of the day after tomorrow. And if you don't cooperate, we may not get there at all."

All the fight suddenly went out of Caitlin. Just as John reached her, she slumped and would have fallen had John not caught her. Gritting his teeth in helpless frustration, Gerrick watched as John picked up Caitlin and carried her to the sling. Minutes later, they were negotiating the steep trail leading downward from the cliffs.

The day proved long and wearying. Twice, rain showers forced them to seek shelter, and the rain, coupled with sucking mud and tiny streams eddying down to the sea, made the going extremely slow. Complicating matters further, Caitlin refused to remain long in the sling, so they had to stop frequently to allow her to get up and walk around. Each time she did, they had to watch her carefully, for her unsteady legs would inevitably give out, and she would suddenly collapse.

Nor would she permit anyone but John to help her. Whenever Gerrick came near, she reacted violently; once she raked his cheek with her nails, and another time, attempted to kick him in the groin. Such behavior shocked and worried both men—especially since Caitlin remained utterly silent. Reluctant to say anything in front of her, they nonetheless exchanged anxious glances: What mental damage had been done by Caitlin's fall? Would she ever speak again?

Evening found them not even a quarter of the way. Leaving John to look after Caitlin, Gerrick searched the area around their chosen campsite for dead wood. Despite the lush vegetation, finding something to fuel their campfire was a real problem. Everything was either too green or too damp. Knowing his best bet was dried leaves and palm fronds, Gerrick had to scavenge far before he found enough to build even a small blaze.

Returning to camp, he was startled to hear Caitlin's voice. "I want to go home," she said petulantly, and after a moment, came John's careful response.

"Well, Cait, I think that's where Gerrick is taking you— back home to the ship."

"No," Caitlin said. "I mean I want to go home to my uncle. Back to Hanalei."

"That's something you'll have to discuss with Gerrick. He'll be here soon. He's gone to get firewood."

"Why can't you take me, John? Gerrick will never let me go—at least not until he finds that sandalwood."

"I couldn't do that, Cait. The only way we can leave is the way we came—on Gerrick's ship."

"I know another way out of the valley. I can lead us back to Hanalei," Caitlin persisted. "We could leave now, before Gerrick returns."

"No, Cait. What you're asking is impossible. I wouldn't do that to Gerrick."

"But I want to go home, John! Home to my uncle! Please, take me home, John. Don't make me stay with Gerrick. Please!"

Gerrick had heard enough. Striding into the forest clearing, he dumped his firewood at John's feet, and then took Caitlin by the arm and marched her a short distance away.

"So you haven't lost the power of speech, have you? And you're well enough to contemplate running off with my best friend. Well, Cait, I won't let you do it . . . at least not before I finish explaining what I set out to explain yesterday, before you dashed off that damn cliff. Not only is my brother, Hadley, a fraud, but so is your precious uncle . . ."

"What are you saying? My uncle is *not* a fraud. He's real—he's flesh and blood."

Caitlin's voice spiraled upward, but Gerrick got a good grip on her shoulders and held her still, determined to explain everything now that she was well enough to understand. "Yes, he's real, but only in the sense that he actually exists. However, he most definitely is *not* your uncle, Cait. I knew him by the name of Amos Taylor back home in New England. He was my father's best friend and business partner, and he heard about the sandalwood the same time I did, and from the very same source: Moses Nottingham."

"I don't believe you! You're just trying to confuse me!"

"No, Cait. I'm trying to *un*confuse you. Amos Taylor told you he was your uncle hoping to win your trust and confidence . . ."

"Just as you told me you had a brother . . ."

"Yes. And we both lied to you. You no more have an uncle named George than I have a brother named Hadley. We both hoped to use you, only *I'm* admitting it and begging your forgiveness, while Amos will probably try and kill you when he finds out you know his true identity."

"Why should he do that? I doubt if he's any worse than you are, Gerrick."

"Trust me just this one more time, Cait. He is far, far more dangerous than I. At least, I've never murdered anyone—not yet, anyway. Amos *has*. He caused the deaths of my mother and my sister, then made a helpless cripple out of my father. It's a long ugly story . . ."

"Spare me the heartbreaking details! I can't trust a word you say, Gerrick. You've lied about everything else; how do I know you're not lying about my uncle?"

Gerrick steered her toward John. "You trust John, don't you? Go on, John, *tell* her. There is no George Price. There's only Amos Taylor—a thief as well as a murderer."

John gave Gerrick a black look. "I wish you wouldn't bring me into this argument."

"Sorry, John, but Cait won't take my word for it. So tell her the truth about her so-called uncle."

John sighed before he answered. "It's true, Cait. And I deeply regret my part in deceiving you. If I had it to do over—"

"Then you *both* lied! Does that mean you also came to the islands in search of sandalwood—and not to build the islanders a church as you claimed?"

A dark flush crept up John's neck. "I do intend to do *something* for the islanders before I leave."

"What, pray tell? Get Pikake with child? Leave a half-breed bastard behind to bear the shame of being fatherless and unwanted, either by the whites or by the Hawaiians? What a fine upstanding gentleman you are, John Reynolds! The two of you sicken and disgust me."

Caitlin began to weep uncontrollably, but when Gerrick tried to put his arms around her, she screamed,

"Leave me alone! I told you never to touch me again."

"All right, Cait, I won't touch you—so long as you promise not to go running off again."

She wiped the tears from her eyes and glared at him. "Why, Gerrick, where shall I run? To the beach? To the ship? Your plan has worked out so beautifully. I'm here, alone, with no one I can turn to—no one to aid me. Why don't you just torture me and be done with it? I'm sure you could devise terrible agonies to force me into telling you what you so desperately want to know. We've already established the valley as uninhabited; who would possibly hear my screams? Why don't we just get it over with?"

"Stop it, damn you, Cait!" Did she really believe he could torture her? Her goading cut Gerrick like a knife. "You know damn well I could never hurt you. Every hair on your head is precious to me. I—"

"Lies, and more lies! Don't say another word, Gerrick. I can't bear your heartless lies. Indeed, don't speak to me ever again. For I tell you this now, I intend never to speak to you."

"For God's sake, Caitlin . . ."

Again, Gerrick would have gone to her and taken her in his arms, but the hatred in her eyes stopped him cold. Their color had turned wintry gray, with no longer even a hint of summer blue. With a swish of her skirts, she whirled and faced the encroaching forest as if the very sight of him was unendurable.

In his misery, Gerrick kicked at the pile of kindling wood and sent it flying. With a long sigh, John stooped and began picking it up. "Leave it alone, I'll see to it," Gerrick snapped.

"Suit yourself."

John's brown eyes radiated sympathy, as well as shared guilt and shame. Then John, too, turned away, and Gerrick was left utterly alone. No not quite alone, he realized, for he still had to face himself. And if he could have turned away from himself, he would have—so great was his self-disgust.

Chapter Twenty-One

After another long, uncomfortable night, Gerrick awoke to find Caitlin missing. A third of the food and water was also missing, and Gerrick could not find his pistol.

"Damn my soul for being the biggest jackass there ever was!" Cursing and mumbling, he tossed the remainder of their belongings left and right, as though Caitlin might somehow reappear in the midst of them.

"What in God's name are you doing?" John grumbled, rubbing the sleep from his eyes as he sat up and fixed Gerrick with a baleful glare.

"She's gone," Gerrick coldly informed his friend. "I was too stupid to think of restraining her while we slept, but why didn't you think of it?"

John groaned and clapped his palm to his forehead. "Because I'm as big a jackass as you are."

"Well, now that we have that established, let's get moving."

Quickly, the men gathered together what was left and made ready to break camp. As Gerrick kicked dirt over the remnants of the fire, he paused to consider which direction to take. By now, Caitlin could be anywhere—even dead at the bottom of a cliff. Not wanting to waste time running in circles, he had to think carefully.

"There's always the possibility she's on her way back to the schooner." John's doubtfulness showed in the grim set of his lips. "If she is, we'll know it when she signals the ship to come in for her."

Gerrick had left word for the *Naughty Lady* to stand out in deep water and sail in close to shore only on the signal of three pistol shots in close succession. "She could do that, I suppose," he conceded. "But if she did, I'd be greatly surprised. How would she explain to Erasmus why she was returning to the beach without us?"

"She wouldn't want to discuss any of this with Erasmus," John agreed. "My bet is she's going to try and make it back to Hanalei on foot. She said she knew another way out of the valley besides the beach."

"Stubborn little fool. You tell me how she's going to make it overland in her present weak, unstable condition."

"I didn't say she'd make it; I said she was going to try."

"So what do we do?" Sick with worry and frustration, Gerrick wanted to sit down and cry, but settled instead on running his fingers through his hair. "She hasn't a chance in hell of leaving this valley alive. Regardless of where she's headed, she'll soon collapse, and by the time we find her, she could be in worse shape than I care to think about."

"Look, why don't you attempt tracking her, while I keep going toward the beach?" John pointed to the damp, spongy earth. "This ground is so wet, she'll have to leave footprints somewhere. You stay and look for them, and I'll go get help. If I find her on the beach, I'll signal you with three shots."

"And if I catch up to her, I'll signal you. At least, she wasn't fool enough to flee without a weapon. Of course, if she somehow loses the pistol—or if I don't find her—you won't know where I am. . . . I know. I'll build a campfire. Keep a close lookout for smoke. If I can manage it between rain showers, I'll light a fire each evening before it gets dark. You can track my progress through the valley by watching for it."

"Sounds good," John concurred.

Neither of them mentioned the risk they'd be taking by

allowing Gerrick's crew members to scour the valley for Caitlin; somehow, the possibility of someone else discovering the sandalwood—and claiming it for their own or demanding the lion's share of it—had faded to unimportance. The only thing that mattered now was finding Caitlin before she came to any more harm.

Shouldering half the supplies, John set out in the direction of the sea, while Gerrick divided up the area around the campsite into small sections that could be searched one at a time. Watching for the imprint of Caitlin's oversize boots in the damp, steamy ground, he determinedly began his quest. Barely twenty minutes later, a single strand of silver-gold hair snagged on a low-growing, thorny tree caught his eager attention.

Seizing the treasure, he held it up to catch the first rays of sun penetrating the lush, jungle growth. The long strand glinted golden, and Gerrick remembered that Caitlin's hair had been tumbling down her back when she rolled in her light linen blanket and lay down to sleep last night. As anxious as she had been to escape from him, she probably had not taken time to confine her hair in a braid when she had slipped away this morning.

He began watching for more strands, and as the land slanted upward toward the awesome Na Pali cliffs—on the other side of the valley from where they had been yesterday—he found another. Then he discovered footprints and trampled ferns. Following Caitlin was not going to be as difficult as he had feared, at least not until she reached rocky ground.

Dropping everything but a waterskin and a canvas sack of the ever-present ship's biscuits, Gerrick broke into a run. He would just have to catch Caitlin before she reached the cliffs, and once he did find her, he swore to himself, he would never *ever* let her out of his sight again.

Caitlin was gasping for breath, her head and her heart pounding, before she permitted herself to stop and rest. Even then, she took a few moments to hide herself in a grove of pandanus trees whose huge, twisting roots reminded her of gigantic snakes erupting and undulating along the ground.

Collapsing amid the fantastic roots, she dropped her gunny sack of supplies and wrapped her arms around her middle to still the thumping of her heart and the cramping of her stomach. She knew she must eat or she'd never make it, but the thought of ingesting anything—especially the dried foods and stale biscuits brought from the ship—made her feel nauseated.

When she had first awakened that morning, she had felt entirely recovered from her bad fall. But perhaps it was only her desire to flee Gerrick that had convinced her she was better. Now her legs were again shaky, and the same hateful, dreaded weakness was creeping over her; she wondered how she'd ever make it across the dangerous Na Pali Coast Trail and back to Hanalei.

She wasn't sure she could make it as far as the grove of sandalwood through which she must pass in order to get to the trail's beginning, high on the highest of the cliffs. Each step had become a challenge, and scaling the steep mountain incline separating her from her goal seemed impossible.

"I must rest a few minutes. That's all I need," she muttered aloud, reassured by the sound of her own voice.

Fortunately, she needn't worry overmuch about Gerrick's finding her. Gerrick and John had been soundly sleeping in the chill, predawn hours when she had stolen away from camp. She had no idea how far she had come, but it had to be far enough now for her to be safe. A jungle wilderness lay between her and Gerrick. First, the land had sloped downward, but for more than an hour now, it had been uphill. She intended to go as high as she could. At some point, the vegetation would thin, she would reach the sandalwood grove, and from there, mount the last difficult incline leading to the Na Pali Trail that traversed the treeless, wind-and-rain-lashed cliffs.

She was so tired—too tired to eat, though she knew she must. Surely, it wouldn't hurt to close her eyes a moment.

Giving in to the irresistible urge, she was dismayed to discover that Gerrick's image seemed to be imprinted on the insides of her eyelids. There was his mocking grin and the teasing glint in his seagreen eyes. Why did he have to be so damnably handsome? Why did his auburn curls have to tumble across his brow in just such a virile, artless fashion as to temper his handsomeness so he did not seem too pretty, but instead exuded strength and masculinity?

Gerrick Scott had the face and body of some rugged, charming archangel; but just as Lucifer had fallen from grace, so had Gerrick. Heart and soul, he belonged to the devil. Somehow, she had found the strength to run away before succumbing to his insidious charms and forgiving his unforgivable lies. That she might die here in the wilderness seemed less a threat than that she might shamelessly embrace him and confess her need for him despite the terrible person she knew him to be.

That she was still his wife did not concern her. She would honor her marriage vows by never so much as glancing at another man, but she would never live with Gerrick, never lie in his arms again, and never permit herself to remember the physical pleasure—nay, the ecstasy—she had experienced in his bed. Pray God she wasn't pregnant with his child! Because a child would make her return to the severe, self-sacrificing life of a missionary just that much more difficult.

If she *was* pregnant, she'd mold and fashion their offspring into a God-fearing individual who would never dare stray from the path of righteousness. She would allow none of Gerrick's immorality to surface in the child's behavior; from its earliest years, it would be taught right from wrong, and any transgressions would be severely punished.

As for herself, if necessary she'd fashion a knotted whip and flagellate herself in order to subdue her errant desires. No matter if it was the hardest thing she had ever attempted, she would teach herself to cease wanting that devil of a man who had tutored her body in the delights of the flesh. Marrying Gerrick had been rash and foolhardy;

271

loving him, knowing what he was, was surely sinful. For these and all of her many sins, she would atone by offering years of lonely labor and servitude, never once complaining, not even if and when Emma Spaulding said, "I told you so."

Sniffing back tears of self-pity, Caitlin drew up her knees, leaned her head on them, and momentarily allowed sleep to overtake her. But her short rest was troubled and unrefreshing; all too soon, she was startled awake by some inner alarm and, lurching to her feet, pressed onward.

All day long, Gerrick followed Caitlin's trail, sometimes losing it, and then rediscovering it again, after long, careful searching. He was amazed she had made it so far from their campsite. He came upon her discarded gunny sack in a grove of twisted pandanus trees, and his stomach cramped in fear. Now Caitlin had no food or water and, in several hours, would be engulfed in darkness. Unlike New England, the island had no lingering twilight; instead, night fell swiftly, like a smothering blanket. Nor was it the right time of month for a full moon. Caitlin would be alone in a black, treacherous wilderness, and the mere thought of it made Gerrick's blood run cold.

Near evening, he stopped to rest in a grove of tall trees growing near the top of the mountainside. Gasping for breath, he set down his supplies, leaned against a tree, and became eerily aware of the stillness and quiet. A rich, aromatic scent flooded his senses. His nostrils twitching in pleasure, he inhaled deeply, noticing that another tree nearby had been split in two, possibly by lightning, revealing a heartwood that was yellowish-brown in color. Suddenly, he realized what he was smelling—sandalwood!

His weariness evaporated in an instant. Straightening, he glanced around. There were more trees than he could count: a veritable forest of precious trees.

"Cait! Cait, where are you?" Gerrick cried, suddenly brimming with certainty that she was somewhere nearby.

Knowing he would follow her, she had led him to this

very place; the discovery could not be mere coincidence. Did this mean she had relented and forgiven him?

"Cait! Sweetheart, come out. I don't give a damn about the sandalwood—it's you I want!"

Gerrick ran from tree to tree searching for her. Gradually, it began to dawn on him that perhaps Caitlin had *not* forgiven him. Perhaps she had given him what she thought he wanted, but was still determined to punish him by withholding herself.

"I swear to you, Caitlin. Nothing is more important to me than you are. I crave the sandalwood, yes—but not if it means losing you. Why must you force me to choose? If you'd only let me explain why I wanted the wood in the first place . . ."

Watching and listening, and hoping with all his heart that Caitlin would come to him, Gerrick stood in the midst of the grove. The waning rays of the sun gilded the leafy canopy overhead, making him feel as if he were standing in some grand cathedral, awaiting a sign of God's mercy and forgiveness.

"I beg you, Cait, show yourself. I know you can hear me, but I don't know what more I can say to convince you that I truly love you."

Behind him, Gerrick heard a sound—the barest suggestion of a footfall. He twisted around just as a sharp click shattered the silence, halting him in his tracks.

"So it *is* you, Gerrick," Amos Taylor said, ponderously stepping from behind a tree. "I thought I recognized your voice."

Gerrick's shock at seeing his old enemy was greatly multiplied as he realized that Amos was pointing a pistol at him.

"What a pity you found this place," Amos continued. "Because now I've no choice but to kill you."

"Was murdering my mother and sister your only choice also?" Gerrick inquired coldly, stalling for time as he looked for a possible weapon to use in defense.

"No, that was an accident." Amos frowned, his heavy eyebrows beetling downward. "I loved your mother—

loved her for as long as I can remember. When I set the warehouse afire, I had no idea she and your sister, Abigail, were inside."

"If you loved her, then why did you steal from her? Why did you plot to bring her husband—your best friend—to ruin?"

"Because he stole her from *me!*" Amos shouted, his jowls quivering in livid rage. "Had she not met him, had I not introduced the two, Maggie would have married me."

"No, she wouldn't have," Gerrick disputed, edging toward a fallen tree limb. "My mother could never have loved such a liar and a cheat. Did you think if you ruined my father, she'd turn to the likes of you for comfort and support?"

"Yes! And I would have been able to offer her a brand new life—a life of luxury and travel to exciting places . . ."

"Provided by my father's money, which you were able to embezzle from him only because he trusted you."

"She never would have discovered that. That's why I had to burn down the warehouse—to destroy the evidence in my office records. You may recall I kept excellent records—so precisely detailed that your father disliked taking time to examine them and never did so on a regular basis."

"So what happened to all my father's money, Amos? Why were there debts piled upon debts?"

Gerrick already knew that Amos had made poor investments—thus losing even more money—but he hoped to keep Amos distracted long enough to give himself time to grab the fallen tree limb and launch an attack. "Is my father's money gone, now? Were you unable to hang on to it without my father there to guide you?"

"Cease goading me, for your ploy will not work . . . Pikake!" Amos suddenly shouted. "Come remove this tree limb before Captain Scott gets hold of it."

Employing his free hand to smooth his black frock coat down over his paunchy stomach, Amos took careful aim at Gerrick. "Don't take another step, Gerrick. I am not the fool you think I am."

"I so sorry, Captain Scott," Pikake quavered, emerging from the woods behind Amos. *"Makuakane* George force me bring him here."

As Gerrick scanned the girl's bedraggled appearance, a murderous rage welled in him. Pikake's face was pale and streaked with dirt, her flower-printed *holoku* torn and filthy, her hair tangled and unkempt. Even worse was the sight of her arm, held gingerly in a makeshift sling. Gerrick did not need to be told that the arm was broken and hadn't been set; the suffering in Pikake's brown eyes, and the rim of white around her pale lips, told him that. She seemed on the verge of collapsing.

"Remove that tree limb!" Amos shouted, and Pikake jumped and hurried to do his bidding.

"You bastard," Gerrick snarled. "What have you done to her?"

"Don't worry about Pikake. Eventually, her injury will receive proper care. I have great plans for Caitlin's little friend. It's your own fate which should concern you now; I suggest you make amends for your sins. You are about to join your sister and mother—for I cannot permit you to leave this valley alive."

"Shoot me, if you must, but don't harm Pikake. She's an innocent bystander in all of this, Amos. You've nothing to fear from her."

"How noble of you to put a little heathen ahead of your own welfare. Since you're so concerned, I'll tell you what I intend for her. There's a certain sea captain in Honolulu who does a brisk business in the buying and selling of island girls. Having loved your elegant mother, I've never found native women in the least appealing, but some, especially men in foreign ports, will pay exceedingly high sums for such exotic fare. As soon as I've no further use for her, I'll clean her up and take her to Honolulu. If there was a market for arrogant men, I'd do the same with you. Unfortunately, there isn't. And you'd be too much trouble anyway."

"You'll never get away with murdering me, Amos. My crew members are close on my heels. They'll hear the shot

275

and come running. You won't escape this valley alive either."

Amos scowled. "I don't believe you. If it's true your men are nearby, then where is your friend John Reynolds? Apparently, you didn't trust him enough to allow him to accompany you while you searched the valley for sandalwood. A wise decision, I might add, since this grove of trees is worth a fortune. Whoever gets to Honolulu first, and stakes his claim with the king, will likely be granted exclusive trade rights—you see, I've learned from my past mistakes. This time I went to the trouble of finding out how things are done here. Contrary to your opinion, I never needed your father to do my thinking for me."

Gerrick hid his surprise. He himself had not been aware of how to handle his claim to the wood once he found it. Now that he thought about it, what Amos said made sense; only Kamehameha could protect the trade rights—in exchange for his rightful share. Had he chanced discussing this with Caitlin, she probably would have told him the same thing.

"Aren't you forgetting something?" Gerrick asked. "Even if my men don't hear the shot, you won't get away with this. There's one problem you haven't considered."

"What problem? Once I kill you and get rid of Pikake, there will be no one to stand in my way. Your men may eventually find your body and the wood, but they won't know who killed you—and by then, I'll already have staked my claim with Kamehameha."

"You're forgetting Caitlin. She knows who you really are and why you came here. In fact, she knows everything, because I told her."

Amos's scowl grew deeper, and Gerrick earnestly prayed that Caitlin wouldn't suddenly appear on the scene. If she did, she, too, would die.

"Where *is* Caitlin?" Amos asked suspiciously, and Pikake lifted her head and stared at Gerrick with sudden interest. The only other time she'd taken notice of their conversation was when Gerrick had mentioned John's name; but soon afterward, she'd resumed the dull lethargy of one browbeaten into submission by pain and fear.

"She's . . . somewhere safe. Somewhere you'll never find her."

"Tell me!" Amos cried, advancing menacingly toward Gerrick.

Now was the moment Gerrick had been awaiting; heedless of Amos's firearm, he flung himself at the older man, his arms outstretched to grapple with him. But even as he soared through the air, he realized Amos was still too far away. Something flashed in Amos's hand; at the same moment, Gerrick heard a loud report.

Fire seared his left temple, and he felt himself flying to one side and crashing into a tree. A brilliant white light blossomed and exploded into fragments inside his head. Then a wall of darkness bore down upon him. Desperately, he sought to hold on to consciousness, but the effort proved impossible. The last thing he heard was a woman screaming, "You killed him, *Makuakane* George! You killed him!"

Chapter Twenty-Two

Caitlin sat up with a start and rubbed her eyes. She hadn't meant to doze off, but upon her arrival at the grove of sandalwood trees, she had almost collapsed from fatigue. Some loud noise had awakened her, but she had no idea what it could have been. Perhaps the noise had occurred in her dreams, not in reality. Rising shakily to her feet, she clung to a tree for support, and with great effort, tried to clear her sleep-fogged brain. Had Gerrick been calling her name—or had she dreamed that as well? Her eardrums were vibrating, and she was thirsty, weak, and dizzy; where had she left the gunny sack containing her food and water?

Suddenly, she heard a familiar voice crying, "You killed him, *Makuakane* George! You killed him!"

Frozen with dread, she listened disbelievingly as another familiar voice growled, "If he's dead, then get away from him. Before nightfall, I want to leave this place and start back to Hanalei."

The sound of copious weeping nearly drowned out the muttering and cursing of a man's familiar voice. "Come along now! Get up and follow me! Get up, I say!"

A woman screamed—a high-pitched scream of terror and pain. Jolted into action, Caitlin staggered several steps forward, felt herself falling, and grabbed on to another tree. Beyond her, not a quarter league distant, Uncle George was dragging Pikake along the ground. The arm by which he had hold of her was supported in a dirty,

278

torn sling, and whimpering like a half-crazed creature, Pikake finally lurched to her feet and began stumbling after Uncle George. Oblivious to her gasps of pain, Uncle George turned, seized her, and started shaking her.

"Cease your mewling! Weeping over a Scott is a waste of tears. Maggie was the only one worth grieving over. The rest were all insufferably proud and arrogant, and I'm glad they're all dead—or almost dead."

Letting Pikake go, Uncle George stared off into space a moment, his eyes glazed with a mad angry light. "Yes, the Scott family deserves to be wiped out. I wonder how my old friend will feel when he hears there's no one left to carry on the Scott name. Perhaps I'll go home to New England and tell him how his precious son, Gerrick, met his untimely end. That should finish him completely, and the world will then be rid of *all* the damnably arrogant Scotts."

Dumbfounded, Caitlin attempted to make sense of the strange, nightmarish scene. What did her uncle mean— Gerrick had met an untimely end? She mouthed her uncle's name, but her lips and throat were so dry no sound came out. She forced her unwilling legs into action, but Uncle George was departing so rapidly she could never dare hope to catch him.

Where was he going in such a hurry? And why was he being so mean to Pikake, who was obviously suffering and in need of care? As she mulled these perplexing problems, her last argument with Gerrick suddenly sprang into mind with stunning force: Gerrick had said her uncle's real name was Amos Taylor, and that he wasn't her uncle after all.

I hope he *isn't*, she thought vehemently. Whatever the man's identity, he's far too cruel to be related to my gentle father.

From the corner of her eye, she caught a movement on the ground. A dark premonition took hold of her and propelled her forward. When she recognized the man sprawled on his back, every nerve ending in her overtired body suddenly vibrated with new life.

"Gerrick! Oh, my God! What's happened to you?"

She hurried to his side as fast as her shaky legs could carry her. Dropping to her knees beside him, she frantically searched his prostrate body for signs of life. His hand flopped once, and she seized it, feeling for a pulse. The beat was strong and steady, though more rapid than it should have been. Blood was spattered across his shirt-front, and when he suddenly moaned and turned his head, Caitlin saw the wound that had caused the bleeding: a deep black crease along his left temple that was slowly oozing crimson liquid.

Gerrick had been shot, she realized, but the wound appeared more like a burn than a penetration.

"Please wake up, Gerrick! Besides your head, where else are you hurt? You must tell me, so I can help you."

She was terrified that he had sustained some other, far more serious injury. Pikake had believed him dead; was he going to die? Not if she could help it. With a newfound strength that amazed her, she rose to her feet and looked around for her gunny sack of food and water. Several moments passed before she remembered she'd lost it some time ago; all she had with her was Gerrick's pistol, tucked into her waistband—and she didn't even know how to fire the weapon. Why she had even brought it, she could not remember; oh yes, she didn't want John and Gerrick to be able to signal the schooner to come for them, and thus be able to beat her back to Hanalei and be waiting there when she herself arrived.

What a miserable tangle it all was! But sorting through this morass of problems seemed beyond her at the moment; until she got help for Gerrick, nothing else mattered. Feeling more anxious with each passing moment, Caitlin searched her surroundings for anything that might possibly be of use to Gerrick. She herself needed water and suspected that Gerrick also needed it. Without water, she couldn't even properly clean his wound. Why wasn't it raining now, when she really needed it?

She wracked her brain to think of the kinds of tropical plants that stored moisture in their root systems. If one knew the identity of such plants and how to recognize them, one could always find a source of water even on the arid side of the island where rain did not frequently fall. Caitlin remembered Inamoo showing her how to take a long knife and whack open a particular plant in order to get to the water trapped inside.

She scanned the grove of trees for any low-growing plants, but the tall sandalwoods had overpowered any lesser growth. Then, some distance away, she spied a canvas sack, quite similar to her own, lying upon the spongy ground. Hurrying toward it, she recognized it as one of those used to transport their supplies. Gerrick must have dropped it.

Tears sprang to Caitlin's eyes as she opened it; the sack contained both food and water, and she drank deeply from the water skin before carrying it back to Gerrick. If she was ever going to be successful at getting herself and Gerrick back to the beach and ship, she must first regain her strength.

Returning to Gerrick, she sat down beside him and cradled his wounded head against her bosom. "You've *got* to be all right. You've got to!" she murmured, putting the neck of the leather container to his pale lips.

Gerrick choked and gasped as the water ran into his mouth. His eyes flew open and glared at her accusingly. "Are you trying to drown me?" he barked.

"No, my love, no! But you've been shot—and you're losing blood. I was trying to help you."

Recognition dawned in Gerrick's green eyes, and his look of annoyance became one of wonder. "Cait?" He touched her face with trembling fingers.

Grasping his hand, she pressed it to her lips, and sudden tears trickled down her cheeks. "I thought I'd lost you for good, Gerrick. I thought Uncle George—I mean, Amos Taylor—had killed you. Pikake thought so, too. That's how I found you; I heard the pistol shot."

Gerrick struggled to rise, his eyes glinting alarm. "Where are Amos and Pikake?"

"No, lie still!" Caitlin pleaded. "They've gone. I don't know where—back to Hanalei, I suppose. Yes, that's what Amos Taylor said. He wanted to start back on the Na Pali Coast Trail before nightfall."

Gerrick leaned back with a troubled sigh. "Then at least we're safe for the moment. But I won't be much good at defending you if he changes his mind and returns. I don't even have a weapon."

"Yes, you do. I've got your pistol." Caitlin patted the butt of the weapon poking out from her waistband. "Oh, Gerrick, I'm so sorry I ran off like a fool! I'm sorry I didn't believe you when you told me about my uncle . . ."

"Hush," Gerrick said, sliding one arm about her neck and shoulders and pulling her closer. "I'm the one who should be sorry, Cait—and I am. Sorrier than you'll ever know. I despise myself for what I've done to you. I don't blame you for running away—either the first time or the second."

"But you were almost killed because of me! If you hadn't come after me, you'd never have been shot, and . . ."

"And you were almost killed because of me. If I hadn't lied to you and been scheming all along to get the sandalwood . . ."

There was a short awkward pause, and then Caitlin straightened and said stiffly, "Well, you've got the wood now, Gerrick. Look around. There are hundreds of trees. You'll be rich . . ." More tears spilled over as she realized that nothing much had really changed between them.

"Cait . . . Cait . . ." Gerrick held her face still, his thumbs wiping away her tears. "Cait, listen to me. I love you. I never planned to fall in love with you, but I did. And now I've found that my love is far, far greater than my greed. You've made a new man of me, Cait—a man who's discovered what real riches are. . . . Tell me to forget the sandalwood, and I will. Amos Taylor can have it; that's where he's headed after Hanalei—to Honolulu to file his claim with the king."

"What?" Caitlin stared at Gerrick, aghast, still struggling to make sense of everything that had happened.

"Let me explain . . ." Gerrick then went on to tell her the entire story of Amos Taylor and his family. As she listened, Caitlin was horrified. Coupled with what she herself had seen and overheard, she finally understood why Gerrick had been so anxious to regain his fortune and take his revenge upon Amos.

"Oh, Gerrick, he's a terrible man! Of course, we can't let him have the sandalwood. We must get to Honolulu ahead of him and explain all this to the king. And Pikake! We *must* rescue her before he has a chance to sell her. Did you see her poor arm? He was actually dragging her along the ground, and she was screaming . . ."

At the memory of that awful sight, Caitlin fell silent. The pistol had been right in her waistband; had she thought of it, she could have used it to stop him. She herself could have rescued Pikake.

"Cait, don't blame yourself. You're in no condition to have done anything. Indeed, you're scarcely in condition to hike back down to the beach, let alone take on Amos Taylor. Stopping Amos is *my* job."

"*I'm* in no condition! What about you? You've been shot!"

Wincing as he did so, Gerrick touched his head wound. "It's nothing but a powder burn. In a minute, I'll get up and find us a place to pass the night. We both need food and rest. Tomorrow, we can start down the mountainside . . ."

"You'll do nothing but lie perfectly still, Gerrick Scott! Just tell me what needs to be done and I'll do it. Regardless of what you might think, right now, of the two of us, I'm the stronger." Caitlin scrambled away from Gerrick and stood, hands on hips, glaring down at him. Her knees still felt wobbly but somehow she managed to remain upright, without swaying even the slightest.

"All right," Gerrick responded, grinning lazily as he leaned back against a tree. "Here's what I want you to do."

Nightfall found them cozy and safe inside a small shelter made of ferns and palm fronds heaped over a frame of lashed-together saplings. Caitlin's main job had been foraging for the foliage and hanging vines, while Gerrick busied himself creating a kind of roof suspended between several trees.

A roof, he had informed Caitlin, was necessary to keep off the frequent rain showers, as neither of them could afford to spend the night drenched and shivering.

His foresight stood them in good stead, for shortly after they lay down to sleep, a nasty storm blew up, and rain pelted the tiny shelter inside which they huddled in each other's arms. The closely growing trees protected the hut from the wind, and what might have been a disastrous situation turned out to be only mildly inconvenient. A fine mist penetrated their hideaway, sifting over them like fog, but they counted themselves extremely fortunate that the shelter did not collapse or blow away.

Earlier, there had been no time to build a fire or to eat, but now they gorged themselves on stale biscuits, dried beef, and some tiny wild bananas Caitlin had found while searching for palm fronds. Reflecting upon the day's revelations, Caitlin wondered how they could stop Amos Taylor from carrying out his evil plans, if he arrived in Honolulu before they did.

She had no doubt they could stop him from selling Pikake; Kamehameha would never approve of such wickedness and cruelty. However, when it came to the wood, she suspected the young king would gladly approve granting exclusive trade rights to any man who agreed to share the profits accrued from the sale of the wood on the Chinese market.

Kamehameha had debts reaching as far back as the first Kamehameha—and he himself had a great appetite for foreign luxuries. When everything was explained to him, would he be willing to rescind the rights from Amos and grant them to Gerrick instead? Would he demand a greater share for doing so? And if Gerrick did obtain the rights, what would Amos do? Amos was a cold-blooded killer who wouldn't easily step aside. And Caitlin was beset with frightening visions of Amos stalking Gerrick through the valley and making certain, next time he shot Gerrick, that Gerrick was actually dead.

"What's the matter?" Gerrick whispered, wrapping his arms around her waist. "Are you cold? You're shivering and shaking."

The storm had lessened in intensity, but the trees were still creaking in the wind, and rain was still pattering on their makeshift roof. Caitlin wasn't cold—just terrified, but she knew Gerrick would never understand her fears.

"I'm t—trying to figure out a way to make sure that Amos T—Taylor doesn't get the sandalwood."

"He won't get it," Gerrick said confidently, and when she didn't respond, he nuzzled her ear and drew her downward until they were lying spoon-fashion upon their bed of palm fronds. The inky darkness pressed on every side, but her fears began to evaporate as she felt his heart beating against her back. "I promise you he won't get it, Cait. Now that you've told me you don't mind if *I* get it, I'll do everything I can to stop him."

"But Gerrick, how can you stop him? He's a dangerous man. Amos Taylor tried to kill you once; he's sure to try again.

"Not if I kill him first."

"Gerrick, no! You can't . . ."

"Hush, Cait, hush. . . . I'm afraid I'll have to kill him, sweetheart. There's no way in hell that Amos Taylor and I can go on inhabiting the same planet together, much less the same island."

"But killing is the worst of sins!"

"Then how can you allow Amos to get away with it? I've already told you what he's done to my family—and you saw for yourself what he tried to do to me. The man has to be punished, Cait."

"Then let the king punish him! Or else take him back to New England and let him stand trial."

"Cait, a man can't always depend upon others to do his dirty work for him. Amos is my responsibility, my problem. . . . I'm the one who should punish him; I'm the one who's been wronged."

"The Gospels say we should turn the other cheek," Caitlin countered, knowing as she said it that Gerrick would not agree.

"Oh? Then maybe I should just say a few prayers and smile when next he aims a pistol at me. Should I also allow him to do what he pleases with Pikake? And should I allow him to shoot John when John hears about all this and goes after him?"

Caitlin had no answer to such piercing questions; she

only knew that as close as she and Gerrick had come to each other today, as much as they had gained in finding a common ground on which to rebuild their battered, crumbling marriage, they still seemed leagues apart. Were they doomed to spend the rest of their lives discovering new areas of conflict? She had agreed that he could have the sandalwood; for what purposes the wealth should be used they had yet to discuss. And now they already had another serious argument brewing between them—one she couldn't simply ignore or walk away from.

"Gerrick, I'm begging you—for my sake if not for the sake of your immortal soul—please do not kill Amos Taylor. Let us try and reach Honolulu before Amos and convince Kamehameha to give *you* the rights to the sandalwood. Let us then try and rescue Pikake before Amos can sell her to some wicked sea captain. But when we finally catch up with him, please do not lay a hand on him. I could not bear to have you make love to me with . . . with hands that are tainted with another man's blood."

"Christ Almighty!" Gerrick swore, jerking away from her and sitting up. "Woman, I am no damn coward or sniveling weakling! I am no damn missionary. I will grant any request you make except that one: Amos Taylor must die—and he must die by *my* hand. Long before I ever met you, I swore an oath to that effect."

Caitlin also sat up and hugged her knees. "Then I take it you no longer wish to . . . to be intimate."

With another muttered oath, Gerrick suddenly seized her from behind, bent her backward over his arm, and crushed her to him. His mouth ground down upon hers, robbing her of breath, and he began devouring her lips and tongue until she was no longer able to think rationally, until all her senses were centered upon his physical assault and the way her body was responding to it. With his free hand, he assaulted her breast, cupping it possessively and teasing her nipple with his thumb, and the darkness shrouding them came alive and pulsated with erotic possibilities, in which the need to be intimate overrode all other needs and possibilities.

286

Then Gerrick's mouth came free of hers, and he growled against her throat: "Don't think to win my compliance by threatening to deny me my husbandly rights. It won't work, Cait. I'll simply take them. And don't think you can remain cold and distant while I do. Before I ravish you, I'll tease you so thoroughly that you'll be begging me to take you. The one thing between us that's right is our passion—we *crave* each other. I don't know how it happened between such a saint and such a sinner, but it did. You and I are fated to spend the rest of our lives in helpless thrall to our mutual passion. . . . Now, lie down and go to sleep before I forget completely that neither of us is in any shape for lovemaking tonight."

Too shaken to resist or argue further, Caitlin did as she was told. Was there no way she could keep him from killing Amos Taylor? No, she realized, there wasn't. Gerrick would do whatever he wanted—no matter how much she disagreed. And all he had to do afterward was kiss or fondle her, and she would helplessly melt in his arms. He was absolutely right; she craved him with all her being, and if he asked her, she'd risk hell itself just to be with him.

The realization was at once humbling, exhilarating, and frightening. What more in addition to the sandal-wood would he eventually demand from her? What more besides standing back and wringing her hands while he sought revenge? He had wrought so many changes in so short a time that she hardly knew herself anymore. It terrified her to think she was so vulnerable, so uncertain in defending beliefs and values she had cherished all her life. Love should make one stronger—not weaker! Yet hadn't she become weak and ambivalent? What was right and what was wrong? She no longer knew the difference!

She lay sleepless for what seemed like hours. But then, sometime before morning, Gerrick's arms slid snuggly around her, and for the first time that night, she felt safe enough and protected enough to close her eyes and fall asleep. My love for him is right, she thought, and so is his love for me. Everything else is . . . is just a problem we somehow have to work out.

Chapter Twenty-Three

"I'll kill him!" John vowed, nostrils flaring, as he stomped up and down the beach like some huge, enraged bull. "I swear to you both; I'll kill him!"

Gerrick cast a worried glance at Caitlin, who was silently standing nearby, still paler than usual but otherwise unharmed by their long trek down the mountainside and through the valley. Then he raised a hand to calm his irate friend. "Get in line behind me, John. I have first chance at killing Amos; my reasons go back a lot longer and farther than yours."

"He actually threatened to sell Pikake—*my* Pikake—to some whoremongering sea captain?" John was all but frothing at the mouth, and Gerrick knew he'd have a difficult time restraining his friend if and when they did catch up to Amos.

"Yes, he did, John, but getting all upset about it now won't help. First, we've got to get to Honolulu and stake our claim for the sandalwood, and then—"

"No, *first* we've got to rescue Pikake and kill the bastard! *Then* we'll stake our claim."

"All right, if that's what you prefer—but consider this: Amos spoke of caring for Pikake's injury and cleaning her up so she'll bring a better price. He may already be on his way to Honolulu, in which case we could miss him altogether in Hanalei and arrive too late at Oahu to plead our case before Kamehameha."

"I don't care! I can't sail to Honolulu until I'm certain she's already left Kauai."

"John's right," Caitlin agreed. "We have the advantage of the ship. Amos and Pikake can't have arrived at Hanalei much faster than we arrived here. The trail across the cliffs is every bit as slow-going and dangerous as our trip back to this very beach. If we sail immediately, we can be in Hanalei by tonight."

"Good lord, I forgot something!" John howled, clapping one hand to the side of his head.

"What, for God's sake?" Gerrick exploded, grabbing his friend's arm. From the expression in John's face, whatever he'd forgotten must be terrible. "Tell us, man, before I lose patience altogether and sail for Honolulu without you."

"You're not sailing anywhere—with or without me. Do you remember that storm the night before last?"

"Of course," Gerrick replied, recalling how he and Caitlin had spent it huddling and arguing in their little shelter. "It wasn't that bad. Surely, it didn't damage the ship. If it did, then she wasn't being handled properly."

"Erasmus and I handled her perfectly!" John retorted in a wounded tone. "But we were struck by lightning, and—"

"Lightning!" Gerrick felt as if a bolt of it had just struck him. "Was anybody hurt?"

"No, fortunately, but our topgallants were sheared off and the upper half of the mainmast split down the center. The crew has begun repairs, but it will be four or five days before we're ready to sail again."

Gerrick groaned in frustration and stared out to sea where his ship was anchored. Now that he took time to notice, he could spot the damages she had sustained. "Where's the crew now? I don't see any action aboard her decks."

"I sent a party of half a dozen men inland to find a tree tall enough for the mainmast. And two other parties are out fishing in the longboats. Since we left those supplies on the beach in Hanalei, we need fresh food—and we can't sail without a mainmast. There was nothing else I could do, Gerrick. I know you don't want anyone poking around

289

in the valley, but—"

"It's all right, John. You did the right thing," Gerrick conceded wearily. "Besides, Cait and I could use several days rest before we have to face Amos again—and Kamehameha."

"We'll work not only days but nights as well, every night, until repairs are completed. You and Cait can just eat and sleep—I'll handle everything."

Gerrick knew John was as good as his word, but the speed with which the big man completed repairs on the *Naughty Lady* was astonishing. Three days later—not the projected four or five—found them sailing into Hanalei Bay. It was a breezy, sunlit afternoon, with a long rolling surf, and the islanders had flocked to the beach to engage in the forbidden sport of surfing.

Gerrick and Caitlin stood together at the rail, anxiously studying the beach for any sign of Amos or Pikake. Not that they expected to see the pair riding one of the long, slender boards across the waves—but they did hope to discover Inamoo or one of the other islanders hurrying to greet them and share the latest news concerning Amos's arrival back in Hanalei and his present whereabouts.

"Look, there's Chief Laanui." Shading her eyes against the sun with one slender hand, Caitlin pointed with the other.

Gerrick scanned the bay and finally found the chief's flower-draped, double-hulled canoe bearing down upon them. In the bow sat Laanui himself in his feathered cape and strange-looking centurion's helmet. Moments later, the canoe was within hailing distance, and Gerrick shouted a greeting and gave orders for his men to stand by for the chief's arrival aboard ship.

After a ponderous climb up a rope ladder that nearly gave way beneath his great weight, Laanui stepped down upon the deck. All smiles and alohas, he held out his arms to Caitlin and enfolded her in a bear hug that Gerrick feared would crack her ribs. He then rubbed noses with her and, grinning hugely, turned to embrace Gerrick.

"Tell him we are honored by his visit," Gerrick

instructed Caitlin behind the big Hawaiian's back. "Then ask him about Amos Taylor."

But the Chief of Hanalei soon made it clear that he would not be hurried into divulging information, no matter how politely it was sought. Conversing smilingly with Caitlin, he moved about the deck, running his pudgy hand along the railings, pushing against the big capstan amidships, and pretending he was steering the ship's wheel. His tiny alert eyes took in everything, even the clothing worn by members of Gerrick's crew, and when his eyes fastened with pleasure upon a silver chain worn about the neck of one of Gerrick's men, Gerrick demanded that the man remove it and give it to the chief.

"I'll make it worth your while, Samson," Gerrick promised the startled crew member. "After the chief leaves, I'll pay you enough in either coin or trade goods to purchase two silver chains."

At first, Samson frowned his displeasure, but then, as Gerrick upped the ante to three chains, he grinned and shrugged his shoulders. "Whatever you say, Cap'n Scott."

The seaman handed over the chain, and Chief Laanui lowered it over his own head with a grunt of delight. *"Mahalo . . . mahalo . . .* thank you," he exclaimed.

Gerrick bowed and smiled. "You're welcome . . . and now perhaps you'd like some refreshments while we exchange news of what's been happening. Cait, let's take our guest below and make him comfortable in our cabin."

He shot Caitlin a meaningful glance, but it was John who eagerly stepped forward to escort the chief down the captain's companionway. "Come along, your excellency, and I'll show you the way."

An hour later, the chief still hadn't answered any of Gerrick's or Caitlin's questions, as with a grin and a shake of his head, he deftly changed the subject every time *Makuakane* George's name was mentioned. "Cait," Gerrick whispered while the chief was consuming a huge hunk of cheese with great relish. "For pity sake, can't you speed things along? Why is he refusing to say whether or not he's seen Pikake and Amos Taylor?"

"Because you're too anxious!" she shot back. "Now, he won't tell us anything unless we bargain for it."

"Well, offer him whatever you think he wants. We can't spare any more time. If they aren't here, I want to leave for Honolulu within the hour."

"He still wants the ship. Shall I offer him that?" Caitlin's blue-gray eyes sparkled with annoyance—directed at him as much as at Chief Laanui.

Gerrick hesitated only a moment. "Yes. But only if he agrees to guard the sandalwood until we return from Honolulu with the king's permission to cut and ship it to Canton."

"What?" Seeing that he was serious, Caitlin's eyes sought John's, and the two of them stared at Gerrick as if he'd suggested something utterly crazy.

"Just tell him what I said. I want his personal guarantee that no one—particularly Amos—will be permitted to enter the Kalaulau Valley until our return. Tell him he must post guards along the Na Pali Coast Trail and also at the beach. He may have to obtain the governor's consent in order to do that, but how he gets it is *his* problem. If we prove successful in obtaining the trade rights, then as soon as I return from selling the wood in Canton, I will give him the *Naughty Lady*."

"Not a bad idea . . ." John murmured.

"But what if we don't obtain the trade rights?" Worry puckered Caitlin's brow. "What if Kamehameha gives them to Amos instead?"

"If Laanui wants this ship badly enough, he won't allow Amos Taylor to have the wood no matter what Kamehameha does or doesn't do."

"Gerrick, you're stirring up civil war! You're fomenting rebellion against the king!"

"No . . ." Gerrick shook his head. "All I'm doing is buying time, Cait—time to get back here and settle things once and for all with Amos."

Gerrick waited patiently for Caitlin to accept his logic, but she only bit her lip and stared at him with huge, disapproving eyes. The only sound in the cabin was

Laanui's grunts of satisfaction as he chewed and swallowed the last morsel of cheese, his attention riveted to the sea biscuits and fruit still remaining before him.

"All right, I'll make the offer," Caitlin finally said. "But I don't approve. You shouldn't be bringing the Hawaiians into this . . ."

"They're already in it. Kamehameha controls the sandalwood—but Laanui controls its location. In order to get what we want, we have to consider what *he* wants— and give it to him if at all possible."

"I don't like it," Caitlin insisted with a haughty lift of her chin.

"Neither do I, Cait. But I can't think of anything else to do—can you? If you can, tell me what. And tell me *now*."

Gerrick's offer was immediately accepted. And so pleased was Laanui by the possibility of gaining the ship that he wasted no more time pretending he knew nothing about Amos and Pikake. "They go Honoruru," he explained in his fractured English. "Come beeg ship and take them see Kamehameha."

Caitlin asked the chief several more questions, but Laanui knew nothing more than that *Makuakane* George had returned to Hanalei and set sail the same day for Honolulu aboard a passing merchant ship stopping by for fresh fruit and water.

Caitlin asked the chief about Pikake's arm, but Laanui denied any knowledge of the injury; he hadn't seen the two personally, but only heard about them from one of his retainers—his "eyes and ears everywhere" as he called the unknown informant.

Gerrick felt worse for John's sake than he did for his own; John had been most insistent upon returning to Hanalei before sailing for Oahu. Now, there could be no doubt that Amos would arrive in Honolulu ahead of them. Aware of the necessity for speed, Gerrick hurried Laanui to the rope ladder and from there to his canoe, before the surprised official had even finished eating. As lines linking the canoe to the *Naughty Lady* were cast off, Caitlin leaned over the railing and soothed the chief's wounded dignity with many compliments and flowery phrases. Gerrick understood only a smattering of what was said, but afterward, as the ship's sails caught and filled with wind, he went to Caitlin and hugged her.

"Thank you," he said softly. "Without you, we'd still be stuffing Laanui with food—trying to gain his cooperation but uncertain how to go about it."

Caitlin lifted tear-bright eyes, her voice oddly hushed and subdued as she said, "You're quite welcome, Gerrick. I only wish I could feel as happy about all this as you do. I knew the discovery of the sandalwood would cause trouble—and already it has . . . No, don't deny it."

With her hand, she covered his mouth to forestall him from disagreeing. "You have engaged Laanui to protect the wood—against the wishes of his king and perhaps even his governor, Kaikioewa, who as yet knows nothing of this. You yourself have sworn to murder Amos and take the wood for yourself. John cares only for freeing Pikake before she's sold and he loses her forever. And I . . . I care only for keeping your love, despite how much I hate what we're doing, knowing how wrong it is. . . . Who among us cares for the island and the islanders, Gerrick? Who among us is capable of putting *their* needs ahead of his own? I'm afraid for them . . . afraid of what will happen as more and more people hear about the sandalwood."

Gerrick pulled her close to him and held her, stroking her silver-gold hair. "Nothing so bad is going to happen, Cait. You worry too much. I have a feeling everything will work out fine."

"I don't," Caitlin sobbed against his shoulder. "I have a feeling things are going to get far worse before they get better—if they ever do get better. I have a feeling disaster lies ahead for all of us."

"Don't weep," Gerrick begged, rocking her in his arms. "I can't stand it when you weep. Think about Honolulu. . . . We'll be there soon. And maybe Kamehameha will solve all our problems. After we explain about Amos, maybe the king will order him drowned in the sea."

"Oh, Gerrick . . . must you always think of violent solutions? Is violence your answer to everything?"

"I'm sorry, Cait," Gerrick apologized, angry with himself for once again saying the wrong thing. "And after this is over, I swear to you—I'll honestly try and mend my ways."

"I hope so, Gerrick. I hope so. And I pray the Lord forgives us all."

This time when they arrived in Honolulu, they learned that the young king, Kamehameha III, was in residence at Haleuluhe, or House of the Uluhe Ferns. As Caitlin explained enroute, Haleuluhe stood inside a high, walled compound of several acres containing numerous thatched-roof houses set amid palm trees near the inner curve of the bay. The Palace, as Westerners referred to the entire complex, was aswarm with the king's many relatives and retainers and amply guarded, but Caitlin easily won herself, Gerrick, and John an interview with Kamehameha by using her missionary connections.

At first, they were told that Kamehameha was in conference with Reverend Hiram Bingham, and could not be disturbed, but when she informed the portly, uniformed guard that she was a personal friend of Reverend Bingham's, he hastened to grant them entrance to the compound.

Gerrick was greatly impressed and told Caitlin so. She flashed him one of her breathtaking smiles and asked him whether he was sure she was dressed appropriately. For this interview with the king, she had worn the gown in which she'd married him, and though it had not improved with age and frequent usage, he assured her she was beautiful.

"You are lovely no matter what you wear," he whispered seductively. "And even lovelier when you wear nothing at all."

"Gerrick!" she exclaimed softly, reddening and

glancing at John, whose back was to them as he walked ahead, following the guard through the forest of palm trees lining the path.

"I mean it," Gerrick insisted. "You charm everyone we meet."

"Well, I just hope I can charm the king!" Caitlin retorted, picking up her skirts and hurrying after John.

Haleuluhe's size and design greatly surprised Gerrick; the imposing, single-room structure was more than one hundred feet long, fifty or sixty feet wide, and at least forty feet high. The exterior boasted an exquisite ornamentation of dark brown uluhe fern fronds, beautifully set off by bands and patterns of sennit cordage that had been bleached white. The roof was made of perfectly thatched pili grass, and at each end of the structure were folding glass doors hung with crimson damask draperies.

Upon entering, Gerrick immediately noticed the floor, a pavement of stone and mortar closely resembling marble, overspread with mats. Caitlin saw him gazing with wonder at the workmanship of the mats, and she leaned over and whispered, "Those are *Makaloa* mats, island-made, though they seem to go very well with the king's foreign furnishings."

Looking up, Gerrick saw what she meant: The huge, long room was furnished with elaborately carved tables, chairs, mirrors, glass chandeliers, and even oil portraits in ornate gilt frames, all of which must have come from Europe or other distant shores. Yet somehow, everything combined to form a gracious blend of native and new that was most astonishing.

Nor were Kamehameha and Hiram Bingham at all what Gerrick had expected. As he, Caitlin, and John passed uniformed sentries waving feathered *kahili*, or symbols of royalty, two men rose from a table where they had apparently been looking over some documents. Both were dressed in formal Western or European-style clothing, and both had sun-darkened skin; Gerrick could only ascertain which was which after a moment of careful study.

The twenty-one-year-old Kamehameha had dark eyes,

dark wavy hair, and a neatly trimmed mustache, while the other man, thinner, shorter, and in his forties, had lighter hair and eyes and was clean-shaven. The two undoubtedly would have caught Gerrick's attention in a crowd; despite his youth, the king had a most commanding, authoritative presence—though if one looked closely, one could already see signs of dissipation on his full-lipped, handsome face.

The formidable Hiram Bingham was most notable for his intensity. His eyes glowed with purpose and enthusiasm; here was a true zealot, Gerrick guessed, a man who would leave his mark on the islands. When Bingham recognized Caitlin, he crossed the finely woven mats with outstretched hands. "Sister Caitlin! Why, my dear, this is such a delightful surprise!"

Gerrick noticed how carefully Caitlin first curtsied to the king before she said one word to Reverend Bingham. Afterward, she greeted the king in Hawaiian, and then smiled pleasantly at the eager minister. "I'm so pleased to find you here, Reverend Bingham. Please allow me to introduce the gentlemen accompanying me, and then I will explain why I have come."

As Caitlin introduced him, Gerrick bowed to Kamehameha, and John did likewise. The king solemnly extended his hand. Hiding his surprise, Gerrick shook it. After Laanui, this tall, cultured gentleman in morning coat, brocaded silk vest, nankeen pantaloons, and snowy white shirt was something of a shock. Yet behind him, draped across an armchair, was something that reminded Gerrick of the king's island heritage: a magnificent yellow-feather cloak, far grander than Laanui's, but made of bird feathers just the same.

The king smiled and said in near-perfect English: "Welcome to Oahu, the Gathering Place, Captain Scott . . . Mr. Reynolds. Do join us at table. We are discussing the new church to be built at Kawaiaha'o."

"It will be magnificent!" Reverend Bingham enthused. "One hundred and forty-four feet long, and seventy-eight feet wide. . . . The king has graciously agreed to contribute three thousand dollars to the building fund. Perhaps you gentlemen would like to match his offer?"

Gerrick smiled and shook his head. "I'm afraid I couldn't begin to match the king's generosity—at least, not at present."

He allowed a moment for them to ponder what he meant by "not at present," and then nodded to Caitlin to begin her explanations. Nervously, she moved to one of the intricately carved chairs drawn up to the table, and after the king and the minister sat down, Caitlin, Gerrick, and John did likewise.

Caitlin smiled and cleared her throat. "Gentlemen, I have a most incredible and distressing story to tell you . . ."

Both the king and Hiram Bingham listened attentively as she related how she had first met her "uncle" and then went on to tell everything that had happened after that. "So you see," she said breathlessly, nearing the end of her lengthy discourse. "It would be quite unfortunate if you have already granted Amos Taylor trading rights to the sandalwood. The man is a thief, a liar, and a murderer."

"I am stunned," Hiram Bingham confessed. "Worse than that, I am ashamed."

"Why is that?" Gerrick queried. "You had no way of knowing the man was lying when he claimed to be a minister like Caitlin's father."

"Yes, I did. I could have written the board in New England and had his credentials carefully examined. Instead, I . . . I took the easy way out—welcomed him among us because his arrival meant I no longer had to worry about Caitlin living on Kauai alone, with no family to see to her welfare." Reverend Bingham gazed sorrowfully at Caitlin. "Can you ever forgive me, my dear? I've failed in my responsibility both to you and to your very dear father."

"Nothing so terrible has happened to me, Brother Bingham," Caitlin denied. "I'm now happily married to Captain Scott, and therefore no longer a burden upon either you or the church."

"You were never a burden!" Hiram Bingham protested.

"But I did worry about you—with reason, it appears. To think of you in the clutches of a scoundrel such as that! Why, it makes me shudder. And Sybil will be horrified."

"Sybil is Brother Bingham's wife," Caitlin explained to John and Gerrick. "But really, you must not concern yourself with *my* safety. What matters now is that Pikake be rescued—and the sandalwood rights returned to my husband, Gerrick, who, after my father and myself, was first to discover the wood's existence."

An awkward silence ensued, as everyone awaited the king's reaction to Caitlin's story. Finally, the king sighed and passed his hand over his face. When he had finished doing this, he looked ten years older, as if the weight of bad news had suddenly aged him.

"I fear you have come too late," he said to Caitlin in elegant English. "I have already given the rights to *Makuakane* George—or this Amos Taylor, as you call him. We have sealed our bargain in the *haole* manner, with a handshake, and all that you now tell me cannot undo what I have done."

"Why not?" Gerrick demanded. "Isn't Amos still here in Honolulu? If he is, you have only to order—"

"Do not tell me what I must do!" the young king suddenly shouted. His lower lip thrust out petulantly. "Always I am being given advice, pushed this way and that—first, by Hoapili and my other chiefs and governors, then by the *haole* traders and whalers, and always and most forcefully by the Longnecks . . ."

"The Longnecks?" John repeated, speaking for the first time.

"The name by which the missionaries were first called by the islanders," Caitlin explained. "Because their high collars made their necks seem so long."

Hiram Bingham started to say something, but Kamehameha held up his hand, his handsome, dark face flushing with annoyance. "No, Binamu, do not offer the excuse of my tender years as the reason for the unwanted advice. I am weary of hearing how young I am to be ruler of Hawaii."

Binamu? Gerrick realized the king was addressing Hiram Bingham but did not know if the word meant something in particular or was merely a quaint way of saying the minister's name.

"Your majesty," Bingham said placatingly. "Why did you not inform me of the discovery of sandalwood? Why didn't you tell me George Price—rather, Amos Taylor— was in Honolulu?"

"This was not a matter for the interfering Longnecks," Kamehameha said haughtily. "The man came to me with a business offer I found greatly to my advantage. He sought me out openly; he did not go behind my back to steal the wood. Instead, he agreed to share his profits. I knew nothing about the Kauaian girl . . ."

"Where is Amos Taylor now, your majesty?" Gerrick felt they were wasting precious time. The terms of Amos's offer had obviously been generous enough to win the king's wholehearted support. What happened next would be up to himself and John.

"As one who has gained my favor, he is residing in a special house within the royal compound," Kamehameha answered. "I gave him the house so he may pass the time comfortably until I myself can journey to Kauai and order my people into the Kalaulau Valley to cut the wood. . . . I also ordered him not to leave the compound without my permission; I am no foolish, trusting child, gentlemen. I did not want him to suddenly disappear, and with him, this fine opportunity."

Gerrick saw Caitlin's head come up, her delicate features contorted in startlement and anguish. "Your majesty!" she burst out before he could stop her. "If you send your people into the mountains again to cut wood, they will die! They will sicken and starve to death just as they did during the time of Kamehameha the First and Second. Not only that—but the *haole* traders—and yes, even the whalers—will tear the island apart trying to find more of the treasure. There will be outbursts of disease and fever. With so many falling ill, famine will stalk the land, and—"

"Silence!" The young king's eyes bulged in their sockets. "Will it be any different if I grant the trade rights to your husband instead?"

Caitlin shot Gerrick a stricken glance, and Gerrick groaned inwardly. Caitlin's emotions had run away with her, and she had spoken what was in her heart—but the king could only see her pleadings as the jealous mewlings of one who had been deprived of a share in the fortune the sandalwood would bring.

"Your majesty," he cut in, sparing Caitlin from having to answer. "One thing you must understand: My wife never approved of *my* having the wood, much less someone like Amos Taylor. In her eyes, I am only the lesser of two evils. She is hoping that if I am granted the rights, we can and shall do this differently than in the past. Perhaps, with your permission I could take a small number of men, return to the valley, and cut the wood in secret. Then, the problems she mentioned would not occur. . . . If you wish, you yourself could accompany us."

Kamehameha pursed his lips, looking suspicious rather than won over. "I will need to think on this. It may or may *not* be to my advantage for others to join in searching for more sandalwood. If wood still remains on Kauai, it might well remain on other islands, too—and new wealth would *benefit* my subjects, not harm them. As my brother and my father did before me, I could order my male subjects to each bring me a half or a full picule of wood. And in order to keep the wood from being stolen by the *haoles* before I've received my rightful share, I could also order the harbormaster to stop any *haole* ships from sailing."

Caitlin's eyes betrayed her horror at the young king's greedy speculations, but it was John who spoke.

"Well, while you are debating all this, can't something be done to rescue little Pikake? Surely, your majesty does not condone the selling of female flesh—no matter how high the profit."

"Of course, he does not!" Having been silent all this time, Hiram Bingham's voice was now quivering in agitation. "Please, my son . . ." he begged the king. "Send

301

someone at once to bring the girl here. This Amos Taylor must not have a chance to sell her. That is a wickedness and an abomination no God-fearing man could tolerate."

"If you insist, Binamu . . ." The young king sighed. "But if I find out the girl journeyed from Kauai of her own free will, I will be very angry. This Amos Taylor came to me as my friend. How do I know these others are not lying out of jealousy and spite? If I give the trade rights to Amos, he has promised me twenty place settings of the finest Chinese porcelain—so that I may entertain as befits a great monarch. What do these others promise?"

"More churches and schools!" Caitlin cried. "So that your loyal subjects may all learn the *palapala*, or alphabet, and become as educated as you, your majesty."

Again, Gerrick groaned inwardly. By the time Cait and Kamehameha finished spending the profits from the sandalwood, he'd be left with not a penny for his own uses, even if he did get the trade rights.

"Now, that is something to think about," Kamehameha conceded, a thoughtful frown puckering his dark eyebrows. "Enough of this discussion. Let us send for this Amos Taylor and have him bring along the girl."

Chapter Twenty-Four

As everyone awaited the return of the guard sent to fetch Amos and Pikake, silence filled the thatched-roof house. Caitlin used the time to think about the promises she had so rashly made. She hadn't meant to anger Gerrick by suggesting a course of action they had not yet discussed; indeed, she hadn't meant to say half the things that had popped out of her mouth during this disastrous interview with Kamehameha.

But perhaps it was better to have everything out in the open at last. The king was young, greedy for riches, and as she already knew from Emma Spaulding's accusations regarding him and his sister, morally weak. Yet somehow Caitlin also believed him to have an honest concern for the welfare of his people. Like his predecessors, he stood in awe of education and the ability to decipher meanings from written symbols. From the day the missionaries had first set foot in Hawaii, members of Hawaiian royalty had taken the *palapala* to heart.

Eagerly, they had pored over the little blue spellers the missionaries gave them, and then singlemindedly had applied themselves to learning how to scrawl the strange symbols spelling out their names. Their ultimate goal had been reading the Bible, Jehovah's Holy Book, but the enticement of being able to impress foreign dignitaries with their ability to read and write as well as any white man had been equally powerful.

303

After he'd had time to think about it, Kamehameha would surely prefer books and lessons to porcelain dinnerware. The question was: What would Gerrick prefer—and permit?

Caitlin darted him a furtive glance from beneath her lashes; his unabashedly intense gaze communicated disappointment and anger that she had brazenly made plans without him. She longed to explain that she had simply blurted the suggestion without really having carefully considered it, and that part of the blame for her impetuosity could be laid upon him; he had either deliberately or unconsciously avoided discussing the matter with her. She had no idea how he intended to use his share of the fortune—other than that he needed funds to cover his expenses in wreaking revenge on Amos Taylor.

Caitlin's eyes strayed to the doorway; soon Amos Taylor would be walking through it, and when he did, what would happen? As she saw Gerrick surreptitiously finger the pistol in his belt, her stomach heaved alarmingly. Did Gerrick intend to shoot Amos as soon as he walked into the house?

John, too, was preparing himself—flexing his powerful neck and shoulder muscles as if readying himself to do battle. The tension in the room was mounting to unbearable proportions; even Kamehameha seemed suddenly nervous as he straightened his carefully tied stock. Hiram Bingham smiled encouragingly at her, but she did not feel in the least encouraged and almost leapt out of her skin as voices sounded outside the house.

A moment later, a tall guard burst inside and hurried to the king. He barely had time to bow respectfully before Kamehameha demanded angrily, "Where is he? Why have you not brought him as I ordered?"

"Forgive me, your majesty. . . . I did exactly as you said. I went to his house to fetch him, but he wasn't there."

"Then search the royal compound! He would not dare leave here without telling me!"

"Your majesty, I have already given orders for the palace

grounds to be searched."

"He must be found!" Kamehameha cried, pushing past him and shouting orders that created a commotion among the guards outside.

Gerrick moved to Caitlin's side and whispered in her ear. "If I can trust my faltering Hawaiian, they're saying he's gone, aren't they?"

"Yes," she answered, uncertain whether to feel disappointed or relieved.

"Then I'm going after him. Would Brother Bingham mind if you went home with him?"

Caitlin whirled round to face him. "But where will you go? Where will you look?"

"Everywhere." He regarded her levelly, his green eyes cool. "John and I will search Honolulu until we find him."

John had come up beside him, his eyes glittering in unspoken agreement. "I'm ready when you are, Gerrick. Now, while the king is busy elsewhere, would be a good time to make our departure."

Caitlin stared at both of them, her mind spinning with protests she already knew would fall upon deaf ears. Instead of voicing them, she hastened to apologize. "Gerrick, I'm sorry I said what I did. I never—"

"Save it for another time, Cait. Right now, I don't even care about the sandalwood. I just want to find that bastard and settle my debts with him—and do it *before* he gets rid of Pikake."

"Let's go!" John urged impatiently. "My guess is he spotted our ship in the harbor and realized where we were headed. He's probably down at the waterfront, booking passage on the next schooner out of here."

"My assessment exactly," Gerrick concurred. "Though I don't know how he would have recognized the *Naughty Lady*. She wasn't one of my father's leased ships."

"I . . . I believe I might have mentioned her name to him," Caitlin stammered, embarrassed that *she* was probably to blame. "That night when we returned to Hanalei and discovered him there ahead of us, I was

305

teasing him about who you were and—"

"I remember," Gerrick interrupted.

"You do? But you weren't even there."

"Unbeknownst to either of you, I overheard part of the conversation. Never mind how or where—we'll untangle it all later. Just go home with Brother Bingham and wait for me. I'll come for you there."

"But, Gerrick . . ."

He kissed her quickly on the forehead and, before she could say another word, followed John down the length of the hall toward the folding glass doors.

"Why, where is your husband off to in such a great hurry, my dear?" Frowning, Brother Bingham came toward her around the table. "Shouldn't he at least stay long enough to bid farewell to the king?"

Caitlin glanced toward the entranceway where Kamehameha had departed. The young king's voice could still be heard outside, shouting and issuing commands. "He should, but he won't, Brother Bingham. You'll have to help me explain so that the king will not be angry. Gerrick is instigating his own search for Amos Taylor and my friend, Pikake."

"Do you think that it is wise of him to take matters into his own hands? I doubt it's even possible that he can find him on his own."

"I'm afraid I don't know what wisdom *is* anymore," Caitlin admitted. "Just . . . pray, Brother Bingham. All you and I can do now is pray."

"Now, Sister Caitlin, you're sure you can find your way from here?" Brother Bingham pointed down the crowded, dusty street. "It isn't far . . . and Sybil will be overjoyed to see you."

"I'm sure I can find your house, Brother Bingham. I was here not long ago and led Gerrick straight to it. That's when I still thought Amos Taylor was my uncle, and we were searching for him, but he, apparently, was off searching for sandalwood. . . . Anyway, I'll have no trouble. You go right ahead and meet with the workmen who will soon be building the new church. Now that you have the king's blessing on the project—and even a promise of funding to get started—you must be anxious to begin."

"Oh, I am, Sister Caitlin!" Brother Bingham's eyes were alight with excitement—an emotion Caitlin shared and envied, despite being distracted by her own worries.

"It's a dream come true for me," he continued. "Of course, the actual construction won't be completed for years. We may not be alive to see it. But at least, we'll witness the church started . . . a monument to bring light into the darkness long after we have gone to our eternal rewards."

Caitlin smiled at his typical missionary optimism. "I'll tell Sybil you'll be along soon . . . I mean, I'll tell her you'll be along *some*time."

Brother Bingham smiled back. "'Twould seem that *you*, no less than my wife, know me far too well."

"I do!" Caitlin laughed. "You forget; I had a father just like you!"

Waving good-bye, Caitlin then began weaving her way through the throngs of islanders, seamen, shopkeepers, and children traversing the same dusty thoroughfare. The afternoon light had grown long and golden, and the voices around her were soft and mellow, brimming with news of the day, relaxed and happy, as people strolled homeward and left unfinished what could wait until another day.

Anyone who lived long in the islands soon succumbed to the Hawaiian penchant for enjoying life rather than working at it. Even the missionaries had not been able to change that. Caitlin remembered how Gerrick had thought the natives of Oahu more subdued than those of Kauai or Maui. Perhaps they were—but no amount of sermonizing could alter or destroy the basic Hawaiian spirit of gentleness and friendliness. Almost everyone Caitlin passed smiled at her and said, "Aloha."

Responding in kind, Caitlin forgot to watch where she was going. Suddenly, she realized she had angled toward

307

the waterfront and harbor, instead of staying on the road to Brother Bingham's. Uncertain where she was, she stopped walking and glanced around. The missionary complex was nowhere near the marketplace, but somehow, she was heading straight for it; should she turn back and retrace her steps to where she'd parted from Brother Bingham?

As she pondered the idea, she felt something cold and hard pressing into her side, and then behind her, a male voice snarled, "Keep walking, dear niece. Or I'll shoot you right here and now."

Caitlin did not have to turn around to know who had spoken. Her blood leapt in her veins, but her voice remained surprisingly steady. "It will do you no good to shoot me, Uncle George. The king already knows who you are. Everyone, including Gerrick and John, is searching for you."

Amos Taylor's arm came around her waist and propelled her forward, while the cold, hard muzzle of his pistol remained pressed into her side. "I am distressingly aware of that fact, dear Caitlin. With my own eyes, I watched you and your husband row ashore. Your hair reflects the sunlight like pure gold, my dear; it attracted my eye like a beacon."

"You could see us all the way from the palace?" Desperately resisting each step forward, Caitlin sought to distract Amos with conversation.

"No, I was already on the waterfront making arrangements for a quick escape should the necessity somehow arise. Seeing you and Gerrick—very much alive after I thought I'd killed him—was quite a shock. It spoiled all my plans, my dear. But now, you've appeared just in time to give me a brand new idea."

"What idea?"

The muzzle of Amos's pistol pressed harder between her ribs. "Time enough for explanations later, niece. Wouldn't you enjoy seeing your little Hawaiian friend again? Give me no trouble, and I'll take you to her. But try and escape, and I'll not only shoot you, I'll also kill her."

"You wouldn't . . . you couldn't be so cruel and heartless."

"Could I not? I've already broken her arm, Caitlin. Killing her would be an even greater pleasure. Shall I break *your* arm to prove my heartlessness?"

As he spoke, he twisted her arm sharply behind her back. Caitlin stumbled and uttered a short cry. Whether anyone noticed, she couldn't tell, for sparks were dancing before her eyes. Amos's voice droned on pleasantly beside her. "Poor girl! What a shame you're so ill. Come along now, and I'll take you out to Captain Cutter's schooner where someone with medical skills will have a look at you and soon fix what's wrong."

She stumbled along beside Amos for quite some distance, only vaguely aware that they had entered the rough waterfront area where rude seamen were far more plentiful than kind, gentle Hawaiians.

"Smile, my dear, we're almost there. . . . Ah, here we are." Caitlin looked down from a high wooden pier and saw a small gig, its oars already fitted into the oarlocks, bobbing in the water. "All you have to do is climb down the rope and get in, Caitlin, and soon you can see Pikake."

"No!" Caitlin cried, her lethargy vanishing as quickly as it had come. "No, I won't go anywhere with you."

The brass-trimmed pistol flashed in the waning sunlight as Amos raised it high above her—and then the butt of it came crashing down. Lightning crackled inside her head, and then . . . nothing. Caitlin neither saw nor heard another thing.

Caitlin awoke to a darkness as black as pitch. Her head ached abominably, and her limbs felt weighted with iron. When she tried to move them, she discovered she could not. Stout ropes bound her hands and feet, and she could do little more than wiggle helplessly. Finally, she lay still listening, trying to guess where she might be.

A dank musty odor tickled her nostrils, and when she turned her head, she could feel something rough and scratchy beneath her cheek. She was lying upon a rolled-up square of . . . canvas! It was ship's canvas, and then she remembered what Amos Taylor had said: *I'll take you out to Captain Cutter's schooner . . .*

Caitlin gritted her teeth against the awful realization that she was aboard a strange ship in Honolulu's crowded harbor, where Gerrick would probably never be able to find her.

As yet, she could ascertain no pitch or sway, as when a ship put out to sea, but to be confined in a dark, smelly hold was every bit as bad. Unless someone had seen Amos striking her on the head with the pistol butt and then lowering her unconscious body into the gig, she hadn't a single hope of rescue. What did Amos intend to do with her? Who was this mysterious Captain Cutter? And where was Pikake?

Nausea clogged her throat, and Caitlin concentrated on wiggling her fingers and toes to restore her circulation and give herself something else to think about. Faint scurrying noises reached her ears, and she froze in horror. Other living creatures shared her cramped accommodations. She strained her eyes to penetrate the thick, cloying darkness, but nothing revealed itself. However, the sounds continued. Then Caitlin felt something run across her foot.

Screaming, she sat up. In the silence that followed her outburst, the scurrying noises could be heard receding. Caitlin breathed a sigh of relief. But then a new noise distracted her: Something or someone much larger than a rat was breathing and moving about only a short distance away.

A female voice suddenly spoke out of the darkness: "Who is there? Who was it that screamed? Do not be afraid. It is only I—Pikake."

Pikake launched into a Hawaiian translation, but Caitlin didn't give her a chance to finish. *"Pikake?* Is it really you? It's me, Caitlin. . . . I'm over here, wherever here is."

"Tutu Caitlin?" There was a rustle of chains, and Pikake's voice sounded closer, but still too far away for

Caitlin to reach out and touch the girl. "Oh, Tutu Caitlin!" Pikake cried. "I cannot come to you for I am chained to a fat post."

"Chained? You mean chained like a dog? How dare they!" Caitlin tried to scoot closer and promptly became tangled in her own skirt and fell over to her side.

"Where are you?" Pikake called fearfully. "Are you all right?"

"I'm fine. I just . . ." Caitlin struggled to regain a sitting position. "I'm bound hand and foot. But if you keep talking so I know where you are, I think I can wiggle over to you. Tell me how you got here and exactly where we are."

"Yes, Tutu Caitlin . . . of course! This ship is called the *Pegasus*, after a strange kind of horse with wings such as I have never seen before. Her captain is a man named Captain Jack Cutter. He is a very bad man, Tutu . . . like *Makuakane* George."

"You mean Amos Taylor." Caitlin grunted as she inched forward and rolled off the edge of the folded canvas on which she'd been lying.

"Yes, Amos Taylor. He and Captain Cutter both very wicked men. *Makuakane* George break my arm when I don't want to do what he say."

"Dear God, I almost forgot! How *is* your poor arm?"

"Better now. Captain Cutter find *kahuna* to fix it. He wrap sticks around it and tie it so it cannot move."

"Then you aren't bound with ropes?" Heedless of the obstacles separating them, Caitlin slowly and painfully squirmed toward Pikake.

"No. Captain Cutter put heavy collar around my neck. It has a big padlock that opens only with key. A long chain holds me fast to the post."

"How awful!" Caitlin exclaimed. "How long have you been here—chained to that post?"

"I don't know. I think maybe three, four days have passed. *Makuakane* George give me to Captain Cutter as soon as we arrive in Honolulu. . . . Are you thirsty? I have water, but no food. I also have . . . bucket . . . if you need to . . . to . . ."

"At the moment, I'm helpless to do anything, Pikake. I'll be lucky if I can get to you."

Grunting and groaning with her exertions, Caitlin tried to stand upright, only to discover that standing was impossible; there wasn't headroom. Bruising herself frequently on unseen boxes and barrels, she finally made it to Pikake's post, and Pikake flung her arm about Caitlin, sobbing her happiness at their reunion and her dismay that Caitlin, too, was now a prisoner.

"Oh, Tutu Caitlin, I never think I see you again! How did you get here? Now, you must tell me everything."

"I will, my dear friend . . . but while I do so, will you see if you can undo the knots in these ropes?"

While Pikake worked at unfastening the knots—a slow chore with her broken arm still held in a sling—Caitlin related all that had happened since last she saw Pikake in Hanalei. As the ropes fell from her wrists and ankles, she gratefully massaged them and then turned her attention to the iron collar encircling Pikake's slender neck.

"I think I could break this padlock," she told Pikake. "If I only had a tool of some kind. It's old and rusty."

"Lock has been used many times before," Pikake sadly informed her. "Captain Cutter say he many times kidnap island girls to sell to rich merchants in China."

"China! Is that where this ship is bound? Why, this is outrageous!" Caitlin fumed. "And I intend to tell him so just as soon as we get out of here."

"He no listen, Tutu Caitlin . . ."

"Yes, he will. I'll deliver such a sermon about hellfire and damnation that his knees will buckle in fear. I'm not my father's daughter for nothing, Pikake! Then I will simply demand that we be returned ashore."

Pikake suddenly burst into tears, and Caitlin stopped fumbling with the rusty padlock and enfolded her friend in her arms. "Hush, Pikake. Don't be afraid; I'm not," she lied. "Soon I'll have you out of this iron collar and musty hold. Soon you'll see the sea and sky again."

"Captain Cutter *never* let us go. He already tell me what

going to happen as soon as ship sail . . ." Pikake sobbed. "He say he bring me up on deck and make me dance hula for his crew. Then he . . . he and his men, they . . . they . . ."

"They *what*, Pikake? Tell me all of it. I'd rather know the worst now than be surprised later."

"They teach me whore tricks. They teach me how to please rich Chinese merchants so I bring a better price in Canton."

"You mean they'll . . . they'll *use* you during the journey?"

Pikake's slender shoulders were shaking as she sobbed, "Yes . . . and he say if I don't please him and his crew, and do all he asks willingly, then they feed me to sharks in little pieces. First, my little finger . . . and then my toes, one by one . . ."

An icy chill raced up Caitlin's back. She had never heard of anything so horrible. Pikake had been thoroughly terrified and then chained in the darkness, with only her lurid imaginings to keep her company. Doubtless, Captain Cutter knew exactly what he was doing; by the time he brought Pikake on deck, she'd be an eager partner to any sexual demands he made upon her.

"Tutu, I will *try* and resist them! I swear I will! But I'm so afraid. . . . If I cannot resist, will I go to hell? Will the Evil One come for me when I die? What will happen to me, Tutu Caitlin? Oh, I'm so afraid . . . I'm so afraid . . ."

Pikake was fast becoming hysterical, so Caitlin slapped her—hard, across the face. "Stop it, Pikake! You must not lose control. Of course, you won't go to hell."

"But Emma Spaulding say—"

"*Forget* Emma Spaulding. What she told you about Princess Nahienaena and her temptations has nothing whatever to do with this situation. No matter what Captain Cutter makes you do, you will not go to hell. Is that understood? Your heart is pure, Pikake—at least, it was before you fell in love with John. If you want to worry about sinning, worry about that . . ."

Caitlin bit down on her tongue; she was saying all the

wrong things. Poor Pikake was terrified enough without being scolded for her sins—whatever they were.

"I . . . I *love* John Reynolds, Tutu Caitlin. And I do not believe loving him is wrong." Pikake sniffled. "If it is, then I no understand it. Our love harms no one—and one day, I think maybe John marry me."

"John has asked you to marry him?" Caitlin questioned, surprised to hear it.

"N—no . . . he say he *can't* marry me, but I know he will one day. My English is all the time improving. I work very hard—so John not be ashamed to take me home to his *haole* family . . ."

"Oh, Pikake . . . you shame no one. *We* are the ones who should be ashamed."

"You think maybe John and Captain Scott come for us soon?" Hope filled Pikake's voice—a hope Caitlin feared was sadly misplaced.

"I think we must do all we can to save ourselves, Pikake. If I can somehow get you free, and if we can somehow escape this hold before the ship sails, then we can leap overboard and swim back to shore. I'm going to feel around on the floor and see if I can find a tool or something to pry off that padlock. Maybe even a nail would do it."

"Oh, I hope so, Tutu Caitlin! Now that you are here, I am not so afraid. I am not so alone."

"No, you're not alone anymore, Pikake," Caitlin agreed, falling to her knees. "Whatever happens to you will probably also happen to me."

Chapter Twenty-Five

It was past midnight by the time Gerrick sought out Hiram Bingham's darkened house and banged on the door. John was still combing the waterfront, visiting the secret taverns and grog shops where unrepentent seamen could drown their pangs of conscience in whiskey and rum. As yet, they'd learned nothing, and Gerrick wanted to let Caitlin know that he'd be gone the entire night and for as long as it took to find Amos. He also wanted to make certain she was being cared for in his absence.

Brother Binghim himself opened the door, and in the light from the whale oil lamp he held in his hand, the minister looked surprised. "Captain Scott! What are you doing here?"

Uncertain what to make of the question, Gerrick responded, "May I come in? If my wife is still awake, I'd like to speak with her."

Bingham stepped back, his eyes widening in alarm. "Of course, you may—but, sir, your wife isn't here!"

"Then where is she?" Entering the house, Gerrick peered into the shadowy corners, half expecting a thoroughly annoyed Caitlin to be tapping her foot in one. "Didn't she come home with you?"

"When I left her on the street, Sister Caitlin said she was coming here, but when I reached home sometime later, Sybil told me she never arrived. Nor did she send a message saying where she'd gone instead."

"Damn!" Gerrick swore, causing the minister's eyebrows to shoot skyward. "Pardon my language, but Caitlin is the most unpredictable female I've ever known. She is constantly surprising me—and not always pleasantly. Are you certain she never mentioned stopping somewhere else?"

"I'm positive, Captain Scott. And if she got lost, she could easily have found her way. Everyone in Honolulu knows where I live. I concluded she'd changed her mind and decided not to stay here after all. It did seem rude of her not to have sent word . . . but with the strain she's been under lately, I resolved not to judge her too harshly for such a minor breach of courtesy."

"Brother Bingham, neither Amos Taylor nor Pikake have yet been found, and Amos Taylor is a dangerous, scheming scoundrel. Maybe something has happened to Caitlin. Didn't that thought ever occur to you?"

Brother Bingham's mouth twitched worriedly. "Forgive me, but I never once considered the possibility. I suppose I should have, but Sister Caitlin is such a sweet, innocent young woman. . . . I cannot imagine anyone wishing her harm."

Gerrick started for the door, then paused just short of it. "If you wish to help, Brother Bingham, you might consider hurrying to the palace and informing the king that Caitlin is missing. Ask him to issue an order restraining all ships from leaving Honolulu's harbor; the harbormaster can then stop and search any schooner attempting to sail out tonight under cover of darkness."

"I'll go at once," Brother Bingham promised.

"Good. As soon as I'm able, I'll check back with you."

"But where will you be if I need to reach you?"

"I'm going back to the waterfront. I can't let Amos slip past me—especially if he's got my wife!" And having said that, Gerrick bolted into the night.

Gerrick spent the better portion of the night skulking in the shadows of the waterfront, watching for Amos Taylor.

If Amos was ever going to make his move, it had to be now, while darkness cloaked the harbor. Herding two reluctant women into a longboat and rowing them out to one of the scores of schooners anchored in Mamala Bay would not be easy without getting caught; yet Gerrick was certain that's what Amos intended on doing.

The more he thought about it, the more positive he became; Caitlin must have been waylaid by Amos. Had she simply changed her mind about staying with the Binghams, she would have informed them, for she was courteous to a fault.

Perhaps Amos hoped to use Caitlin as a pawn in his effort to control the sandalwood rights. If this was the case, Kamehameha would soon hear from him. An island girl wouldn't be considered valuable enough to hold as hostage—but a white woman, especially a missionary, clearly would.

As he prowled the waterfront, Gerrick wracked his brain to think the way Amos would think. The man was no fool; kidnapping Caitlin would be a masterstroke in gaining the advantage in this little war. Just picturing Caitlin in Amos's clutches made Gerrick's heart pound furiously in his rib cage; his fears and worries greatly increased as he noticed the heavy black thunderclouds stealing across the sky and obscuring the new moon.

A severe storm would likely hit before morning, hampering the full-scale search effort Gerrick intended to mount with or without the king's help and permission. If he and John did not find Amos before first light, Gerrick intended to seek the aid of every sea captain in the harbor and every member of Hiram Bingham's church. Someone, somewhere must know the identity of a ship's captain trafficking in island girls . . . and suddenly Gerrick remembered Nate Hampstead, the sailor in Lahaina who had claimed to know every ship in port, where it had come from and where it was headed.

What he needed was another Nate Hampstead, someone in Honolulu as savvy and unscrupulous. But where was he to find such a man?

Struck with a wildly crazy idea, Gerrick headed for the nearest grog shop. Upon entering it, instead of acting stone-cold sober, angry, and upset, he staggered drunkenly into the thatched-roof dwelling. After ordering a bottle of rum and taking a long swig of it, he stared at the other dim figures in the hut and demanded belligerently, "Anybody in this stinkin' hellhole know where I can buy me a sweet l'il island gal? I don't mean for no one-night stand; I mean one I can take aboard ship to warm my bed all the way t' the Marquesas."

"Hell," someone growled. "Ya' used t' be able t' git 'em free. Now, ya' can't buy one at any price. Them damn missionaries have taught all the island gals that warmin' a man's bed puts 'em on the sure road t' perdition."

Undeterred, Gerrick reached into his pocket, withdrew a handful of coins, and scattered them across the dirty pandanus mats underfoot. "This is for any man who can answer my question. And if I find just what I'm lookin' for, I've a case of rum aboard my schooner I'll deliver anywhere he wants."

A moment later, a short squat man whose rank smell preceded him sidled up to Gerrick and motioned him over to a table. "Come join me, Cap'n," he invited in a low whisper. "I think I know just what inf'rmation y'r be needin'. There's a certain ship in port that never sails without a lass or two aboard—f'r sale to whoever can pay cold cash an' keep their mouths shut."

"Well, that's me. Tell me the ship's name an' the rum is yours," Gerrick promised.

The rolling and pitching of the *Pegasus* awoke Caitlin from a restless, nightmare-ridden sleep. Grasping Pikake's post for support, she struggled to her feet and mumbled, "Pikake, wake up. I think the ship has set sail."

Moaning softly, Pikake stirred. "Yes, Tutu, it does feel like we're moving, doesn't it? Maybe now they will feed us. I'm so hungry my belly hurts."

No food had yet been brought to them, and Caitlin was

hungry, too. But the mere thought of eating while the ship creaked and swayed made her stomach cramp with nausea. At the moment, she would have given anything for a breath of fresh ocean air.

"We'd better keep looking for a chisel to pry open your padlock, Pikake. Or in the absence of that, something with which to defend ourselves."

"It is of no use, Tutu Caitlin. We going to China now. John is . . . is lost to me."

Pikake sniffed loudly, and fearing another outburst of tears, Caitlin snapped, "I don't care where we're going! I refuse to just sit here and give up. Get on your knees and feel around the floor, Pikake—or if you can't do that, then pray. Pray that at least I can find us a weapon."

Caitlin could hear her friend scrambling in the darkness, as she herself was scrambling. The wooden planks beneath her hands were rough and full of splinters, and her fingers were already scraped raw and bleeding from her previous exertions. She herself wanted nothing more than to sit staring into the blackness and succumb to weeping. Gerrick hadn't found them; maybe he didn't even know she was missing. Would she ever see his flashing green eyes and mocking smile again? A fierce longing for him rolled over her, as powerful as one of the big waves now rocking the ship.

Blinking back the hot tears stinging her eyes, Caitlin reminded herself that self-pity would accomplish nothing. Determinedly, she focused on the pitching and yawing of the schooner. The waters of Mamala Bay had grown turbulent—or else they were already past the channel and out on the open sea.

It must be going to storm, she thought irrationally. Maybe the ship will break apart and sink.

"Tutu Caitlin!" Pikake called. "Where are you? I . . . I hurt my arm just now, when the ship rocked."

"Stay where you are, and hold on to the post. I'm coming," Caitlin said.

She was halfway to Pikake, crawling on her hands and knees, when the hatch was thrown open, and a blinding

319

light illuminated the hold.

"*Ahah!* What's this? I *knew* it was time t' check on you."

Caitlin peered past the glow of a lantern outlining the hatch opening. The man who had spoken was nothing but a blur—a big blur—and the hand that reached down and hauled her to her feet was also big, and as strong as Gerrick's or John's.

"Weasled outa your ropes, eh?" a gravelly voice boomed. "I should've insisted Amos chain you like the other one . . . aaah! You *are* a beauty like he promised, ain't you?"

Caitlin struggled against the hand that held her so effortlessly, but her strength was no match for that of the huge, black-bearded man squinting at her in the lantern light. "Gus!" the man thundered. "Free the other one and bring her up on deck where I can see them better. Now that we've outrun the harbormaster—and who tipped him off I'd give my eye teeth to know—I want to find out if our catch was worth all this trouble."

"Yes, sir, Captain Jack! Right away, sir." A short, gray-whiskered fellow elbowed past Caitlin and entered the hold, while Caitlin herself was hauled out into a narrow corridor.

"Go on . . . git up that ladder!"

Caitlin could barely keep her footing as the ship rose and plunged beneath her feet. Nor did Captain Jack have any sympathy to spare for her plight.

"Git a move on, gal! Why, this pitchin' ain't hardly nothin'. Just a little hurricane whistlin' down our throats. 'Twill git much worse afore it gits better. Hah! Nothin' like a storm t' cover our tracks. Maybe the harbormaster'll be swamped afore he gits back t' Honolulu."

Captain Jack's huge hand suddenly cupped Caitlin's buttocks, and the shocking intimacy made her bolt up the ladder. Emerging through the square opening, she found herself in another narrow corridor, propelled toward another ladder, this one leading to the main deck. The wind almost knocked her over as she climbed out of the companionway and clutched at the rigging with one hand and her billowing skirts with the other. The sky was a muddy green, except along the eastern horizon where a smear of crimson was spreading like a bloody stain.

"Sunrise!" Captain Jack announced, as if he himself had produced the phenomena. "Sunrise b'fore a storm at sea!"

Caitlin gazed toward the stern, where the mountainous coastline of Oahu was fast disappearing. The ship's canvas strained taut in the wind, and a salty spray was kicking back over the ship's bow.

"Ahoy, mates! Look whut ole Captain Jack has got this time—a yellow-haired missionary! Won't some rich, slanty-eyed mandarin pay a pretty price f'r this one!"

Heads turned in her direction, and Caitlin shrank against the rigging.

"Does she dance the hula, Cap'n Jack?" A seaman wearing a black patch over one eye peered at her from his position high on a yardarm.

"Don't know yet, laddie! That's whut I brung her up here for—t' find out!"

"Me, I druther watch an island girl dance," another crewman called. "They kin move their hips faster than any white gal."

"Hell, I got one o' them, too!" Captain Jack roared, reaching down and lifting Pikake through the hatch opening.

Caitlin thought she might be sick; from every corner of the ship, scarred and grinning faces avidly watched her and Pikake. Fighting to keep from retching, Caitlin boldly returned their lewd stares and, in the process, noticed the men's ragged, dirty clothing, and their assorted weapons—pistols, knives, and cutlasses—tucked into waistbands or fastened to belts. Gerrick's crew members had been a rough lot, but these men far surpassed them.

Though the ship itself seemed swift, sturdy, and in reasonably good repair, the crew reminded her of a pack of wild, mangy dogs, and she wondered how Captain Jack was able to maintain authority over them. A moment later, she found out.

"All right, trim those jibs afore they rip away! Any man who wants his chip in the lottery t' see who gits t' tame one o' these fillies t'night, better step fancy. We outran the harbormaster; now we gotta outrun this gale."

"Captain Cutter!"

Caitlin whirled to see Amos Taylor leaning against the wind and slowly making his way across the tilting deck. Clutching at the same rigging to which she was still clinging, Amos ignored Caitlin and again shouted the captain's name. "Captain Cutter! We must turn back at once! Before this storm overtakes us and sinks us all."

"What storm? Y' mean this wee little blow? I'd sooner rot in hell, lad! We can't r'turn to Honolulu after defyin' the harbormaster. Fact is, I'm crossin' Honolulu off me list o' safe ports. Some blasted missionary has probably told the king whut we've been up to—else why would the harbormaster be a-chasin' us?"

"Captain, we'll never make Canton! The sky, sir, look at the sky!"

Amos's knuckles were bone white where his hand clutched the rigging beside Caitlin's; his fear ignited a corresponding terror in her. The clouds overtaking the ship did indeed appear ominous and ghostly—unlike any clouds she had heretofore seen. Lightning forked the sea, and a tremendous boom of thunder rocked the ship from bow to stern.

"Go back, Captain! Turn round! If we don't, we'll perish," Amos pleaded.

He was probably right, Caitlin thought. Nonetheless, she felt prompted to goad him; after all, *he* was responsible for their present precarious predicament. "I hope we do perish, Amos Taylor," she shouted over the rising wind. "For I cannot wait to see you groveling on your knees before the Lord Almighty. What explanations will you make for why you kidnapped and brought us aboard this ship? How will you explain what you did to the Scotts?"

Amos stared at her, his pale eyes wild and unblinking.

The hair fringing his bald spot stood on end in unruly tufts; his lips were blue and compressed, and his jowls actually quivered. So great and irrational was his fear, he seemed on the verge of madness. Caitlin had a sudden flash of insight; even on a calm day, Amos mistrusted the sea. On a stormy one, he was petrified, half driven out of his wits.

"I ain't turnin' back, lad!" Captain Jack bellowed. "'Twas your decision t' come along. Now, you're stuck, an' so am I. 'Twill be a long time b'fore I dare sail the *Pegasus* into Honolulu again."

Letting go the rigging, Amos gripped the lapels of the captain's blue serge coat. "I had no choice but to accompany you! If I thought I still had a chance at the sandalwood, I would have remained behind—but Gerrick Scott would have killed me, and the king would not have honored our bargain in any case, not after Brother Bingham learned the truth and condemned me. It was pure luck I ran into Caitlin. . . . But when I did, I knew she was still the key to making us both rich."

"I'd 'ave paid you a fair price for her, lad. Sight unseen, 'cause she was white and the Chinese fancy white gals over natives, I'd 'ave paid you handsome. Oh no, you said, I'll come along and auction her off meself, you said . . . so I said, fine. And here you be . . . and here you'll stay. So quit your whinin', lad. Go below if you've no belly for a wee small hurricane. As f'r me an' me hearty buckos, we'll feast our eyes on these two lasses dancin' the hula, an' shake our fists at the storm at the same time."

"Dear God, we'll perish! We'll never see land again!" Amos cried as Captain Jack forcibly removed his hands. Again catching hold of the rigging, Amos stared in horrified fascination at the churning green clouds.

Caitlin put an arm around Pikake and drew her closer. The two of them should stay as close as possible, she reasoned; in case one lost her balance and fell, the other could keep her from being swept overboard by the waves crashing across the bow.

"Hah! Are ye as scared as that snivelin' coward?"

Captain Jack demanded. "Here now, dance the hula f'r us, an' you'll 'ave no time t' be thinkin' o' dyin'."

The big, bearded man seized Pikake by the waist and dragged her away from Caitlin. The little Hawaiian's brown eyes clung to Caitlin, even after Captain Jack succeeded in tearing them apart. "Dance!" he commanded. "Dance t' please the rain god, so he keeps our ship safe from harm."

At that moment, a huge wave flooded the deck and drenched them all with warm, salty-tasting water. "She'll be washed overboard!" Caitlin screamed as Captain Jack shoved Pikake ahead of him toward a cleared area of the deck.

Spying a rope lying coiled at her feet, Caitlin let go of the rigging long enough to grab it. She was struggling to tie one end around the mast and pass the other around her waist, when Captain Jack suddenly grabbed her.

"She ain't gonna be too good at dancin' with one arm held in a sling. How 'bout *you* doin' the dancin', little silver-haired missionary?"

"Let go of me! Even if I had the slightest idea how to dance the hula, I'd *never* dance it for you."

"Yes, you will, gal! You'll dance it for all of us! But first, you gotta git rid of this damn, ugly dress!"

As she fought to be free, Caitlin felt Captain Jack's huge hand fumbling at her neckline. She twisted and kicked at him, breaking loose just as a startled cry came from the masthead. "Sail, ho!"

The ship plunged into a deep trough of water, and Caitlin lost her footing and went down in a heap. It was Pikake who grasped her hand and held tight to it as the sea cascaded over the bow. Choking and coughing, Caitlin stumbled to her feet and snatched the rope before it was washed away. Only after she'd managed to tie both herself and Pikake to the mast did she take time to notice what had happened to Captain Jack.

Shouting for a spyglass, he had rushed to the stern and was now leaning over the low railing and training his glass on their pursuer. "Whoever she is, she's comin' up

324

fast," he announced. "Must be crazier than we are!"

"It's him! It's Gerrick Scott!" Amos Taylor cried, staggering to the stern. "Who else could it be?"

Who else, indeed? Caitlin thought, grinning at Pikake. The girl hugged Caitlin with her one good arm. "I knew John would come for me," she said. "And Captain Scott would come for you."

"More sail!" Captain Jack shouted. "Let's show that landlubber who's got the better ship."

Caitlin and Pikake were forgotten as the crew of the *Pegasus* scrambled to outrun the *Naughty Lady*. Clinging to Pikake, Caitlin closed her eyes and prayed, *Please let him catch us, Lord. Oh, please let him catch us, and I'll not ask you for another thing.*

In answer to her prayer, lightning crackled along the yardarm, and thunder vibrated the deck. Then, the first shockingly cold wet droplets began pelting them from the turbulent sky. Whether or not Gerrick could catch them suddenly seemed inconsequential; the storm had them in its clutches, sheeting the horizon with rain against an eerie backdrop of greenish gray.

"Tutu Caitlin, the clouds hang so low I think maybe they swallow us."

"Don't worry," Caitlin said. "Gerrick and John will not turn back. We must have faith they'll eventually find us, even if they lose us for a time in this storm."

Opening her eyes and glancing upward, Caitlin saw that what Pikake said was true; clouds were enveloping them in a damp gray mist that threatened to obscure even their own sails. And she then began to pray for survival instead of rescue. What good would it do to be rescued if none of them survived?

Chapter Twenty-Six

The storm battered the ship with wind and rain, causing huge waves to nearly swamp it. As Gerrick pursued them with expert seamanship and sails drawn taut, Caitlin tried to keep track of the *Naughty Lady*'s progress, but found it difficult to watch the fog-shrouded schooner and still hang on to Pikake and the mast. From Captain Jack's curses and cries of outrage, she knew Gerrick was gaining on them, but even if he caught up to them, he'd be unable to stop them or board the *Pegasus* until the storm abated.

If it ever did abate. Caitlin watched helplessly as boxes, barrels, and crates full of squealing pigs and chickens went careening over the side and into the sea. Everything that wasn't lashed down risked being washed overboard as the ship rose and plunged in the enormous waves. Amos Taylor was now clinging to the capstan, his eyes squeezed tightly shut, his face a frozen mask of terror.

Caitlin almost felt sorry for him—except that if they all died, it would be his fault. Only Captain Jack Cutter seemed oblivious to the storm. Straddling the deck like a determined rider on a runaway horse, he bellowed orders to his beleaguered crew. For the most part, the crew obeyed. One man was knocked unconscious by a flying rope that suddenly snapped free of the rigging and lashed him in the face. Another was struck in the chest by a loose barrel and momentarily pinned against the railing. When the barrel finally rolled away, he clutched his sides as if his ribs had been broken and staggered toward one of the hatches to go below.

The scene had all the elements of a nightmare unfolding its horror bit by bit. Caitlin was numb with cold and fear, while at the same time, she could scarcely convince herself that this was real and actually happening. She felt she ought to do something to help, but didn't know exactly what. When Amos Taylor lost his balance and fell, his fingers frantically clutching at the heaving deck, she never hesitated; in his blind terror, Amos could not get up again without assistance.

Motioning to Pikake to hold tight to the mast, Caitlin let go of it and inched toward him, stretching out her hand for him to grasp. With the rope around her waist acting as a tether, she discovered it was possible to remain upright on the slippery, tilting deck. The discovery made her more confident, and she leaned against the rope to balance herself.

"Uncle George, take my hand!" she shouted, remembering only after she'd said his name that he wasn't now nor ever had been her uncle.

Amos Taylor's eyes sought hers. They no longer had human awareness, but rather resembled those of a crazed and terror-stricken animal. He got on his knees and tried crawling to her, but his limbs were so stiffened with fear he couldn't control them.

"Hurry! Take my hand! Before another wave crashes over the bow." Reaching the end of her rope, Caitlin could go no farther. Unless Amos crawled several feet toward her and grasped her hand, she couldn't save him. Anxiously, she looked for Captain Jack; the burly sea captain possessed enough strength to lift Amos and get him to a companionway to go below, but Captain Jack was now at the ship's wheel, assisting the helmsman.

Teeth bared in a laughing grimace, Captain Jack wrestled the wheel to keep the vessel facing into the wind. Caitlin knew she could expect no assistance from him and, glancing about, saw that many of the ship's crew were abandoning the deck and racing for the hatch openings.

Most of those who remained were doing as she had done, looping ropes around their bodies and fastening themselves to immovable objects.

"Please help me!" she cried to anyone who would listen, but the sound of her voice was lost to her own ears in the shrieking of the wind through the sails and rigging.

The only illumination now came from the lightning, which flashed so frequently as to be an almost constant source of light. Rain slashed her face and clothing, and Caitlin could feel Pikake tugging on the rope to pull her back to the mast and safety. But she could not simply abandon Amos Taylor.

Dropping to her knees, she again reached out her hand to him. "Take my hand! You can do it! Just come a little closer."

Amos Taylor got to his knees. Balancing shakily, he lifted one hand.

"That's it!" Caitlin encouraged, knowing he couldn't hear, but hoping he might read her lips.

Suddenly, the deck slanted sharply, and Caitlin was flung forward, banging her nose as she landed on her face. When she looked up, Amos was rolling toward the railing. Then a great wall of water crashed over her head, and she herself was rolling, the rope around her waist her only anchor. She tasted salt and gagged, felt her body slamming into things, and instinctively brought up her hands to protect her face.

As the ship rolled on her beam, the water receded, rushing back into the sea. Strained timbers groaned and creaked. It seemed the ship would split apart, but slowly, it righted itself—leaving Caitlin on her back, flopping and gasping like a beached fish. Turning onto her side, she grasped the rope and used it to help herself rise. Then she wiped her eyes, squinting to see where she'd landed. The deck was washed clean of everything—men and objects— that hadn't been tied down or holding tightly to something.

One arm still around the mast, Pikake was choking and coughing up sea water. Crewmen were similarly lurching to their feet and clearing their lungs. Both the helmsman and Amos Taylor were gone, but Captain Jack still stood upright at the wheel—only now he was no longer smiling.

"You yellow-haired vixen! You God-cursed missionary!" he roared, shaking his fist in the air. "This is all your fault!"

"No!" Caitlin screamed back. "It's *your* fault. God is punishing you for your wickedness. You will be *next* over the side."

To her astonishment, instead of growing angry, the remaining sailors cringed away from her. One of them hurriedly crossed his forehead, chest, and shoulders in a gesture he'd obviously learned in childhood but used little since. Even Captain Jack looked stunned and fearful.

"All right!" he cried his big shoulders shrugging in defeat. "I'll not make you dance the hula. I'll not make you spread your thighs f'r me and my men."

"Nor will you make Pikake either!" Caitlin retorted.

"No, not the little island girl either, if you insist. But you gotta ask your God t' make the storm pass. Another wave like that last one, and we're goners. The *Pegasus*'ll split open like a coconut."

"I will ask Him. But don't be surprised if He refuses. I doubt He'll hear the prayers of anyone aboard this evil ship."

Caitlin stumbled to the mast, where she and Pikake immediately knelt down. She prayed for the souls of Amos Taylor and the helmsman. She prayed for herself and Pikake. But most of all, she prayed for Gerrick and John, that they, too, would survive the storm. The wind and high waves continued battering them. The rain fell in gusty torrents. But there came no other rogue wave such as the one that had swept Amos Taylor and others into the sea. Finally, the storm abated.

A murky gray dawn heralded the morning after the tempest. Caitlin and Pikake, still tied to the mast, awoke and wearily hugged each other, and then Caitlin examined

329

Pikake's arm. The girl had many bruises, but somehow, the arm looked and felt no worse than it had the day before. Caitlin smoothed back Pikake's long tangled hair, then raked her fingers through her own wild snarls.

She was stiff and sore, hungry and thirsty, and chilled to the bone. How they had managed to sleep, curled on deck with only each other's body heat to warm them, Caitlin did not know. But sometime during the night, exhaustion had overtaken them, and they had lain down without a moment's thought and sought refreshment in sleep.

On the uncluttered deck, Caitlin saw no one else, and hurriedly, she fumbled with the knots in their rope. When she had untied them, she rushed to the railing. The ship was calmly bobbing at anchor on a placid sea, and no other ship was in sight. Only gray-green ocean stretched endlessly in every direction, with not even a sea bird or dolphin to give evidence of other life having survived the storm.

"Do you think John and Gerrick coming soon?" Pikake asked beside her.

"I don't know," Caitlin answered. "I hope so. We'll just have to wait and see."

She glanced down at the gentle swells and saw that the sea was littered with rubbish, clumps of seaweed, and patches of a frothy substance. The usually clear Pacific had been churned to a filthy mess. A short distance away, a splintered spar, still draped with canvas, floated on the water. Caitlin swallowed hard. The *Pegasus* had weathered the fierce gale, but the *Naughty Lady* might never be seen again.

Struggling to hold back tears, she tore her eyes from the broken spar. "We must find Captain Cutter and convince him to return at once to Honolulu. After that, we'll get something to eat."

"You think he keep the promises he make?"

"We'll soon find out, Pikake. But just in case he plans on ignoring them, we'll first look for a weapon before going below."

A thorough search of the deck revealed nothing but a

belaying pin wedged between a small cannon and the railing. Caitlin hefted it in her hand and judged it heavy enough to damage a man's head if it was brought down hard enough. Then she and Pikake descended the stern companionway and went looking for Captain Jack. They found him sprawled on a narrow bunk in a cabin and snoring loud enough to wake a dead man.

"Captain Cutter!" Caitlin shook his shoulder.

The huge man never moved, but his snoring faltered, and thus encouraged, Caitlin prodded his ribs with the belaying pin.

"What? Who?" Captain Jack mumbled, rubbing his eyes and rising on his elbows.

"Captain Cutter, it's me . . . Caitlin Scott." She stood over him with the pin at the ready in case he should rear up like an enraged animal and attempt to harm her or Pikake.

Captain Jack gazed at her with some annoyance, his beard in as much disarray as her hair, and his clothing stiff with salt. Then he calmly reached up and grabbed her arm, taking away the belaying pin as easily as if she'd given it to him. Having vastly underestimated his strength and self-possession, she backed into Pikake, stepping on her friend's bare toes before finding the courage to stand still and face him.

"What do you want, lass? Why've you come in here interruptin' a man's badly needed sleep?"

Stiffening her spine, Caitlin glared at him. "Captain Cutter, the storm is over, and the ship is safe. God heard our prayers and spared us. Now, you must keep your part of the bargain and return us immediately to Honolulu."

As if questioning her sanity, Captain Cutter merely stared at her for several moments before growling, "I didn't never promise t' go back t' Honolulu."

"Yes, you did! You said you wouldn't make us dance the hula, or . . . or . . . be intimate with you or your men."

"Oh, that . . ." Yawning and scratching his belly with the belaying pin, Captain Cutter sat up. "I guess I did swear t' that."

"Well, then?" Caitlin prompted. "Surely, you wouldn't

go back on your word and risk another bad storm."

"No, I s'pose I wouldn't." The captain lurched to his feet. "But that don't mean we're goin' back t' the islands . . ."

The captain towered over her, his breath fouling the air between them. Caitlin studied him with growing alarm. "We *must* go back. If Gerrick's alive, that's where he'll go, looking for me . . ."

"Ahah! That's exactly why I won't r'turn there. I've other plans for you, wench."

"But you said . . . you promised . . ."

"I said I wouldn't make you spread your thighs f'r me or dance the hula . . . an' I won't. But I wasn't *never* fool enough t' promise not t' sell you in Canton. You an' y'r little friend are goin' on the auction block as planned. Soon's we make repairs, we're sailin' on across the Pacific. Only reason why I'd stop now would be t' take on more cargo—more l'il island gals. Though I expect I'll git more from you alone than I'd git from a whole passel of hip-wigglin' natives. An' t' pick up more of them, I'd have t' go south, which is out of me way."

"You . . . still plan on selling us in China?" Stunned nearly speechless, Caitlin was also furious. "I'll throw myself overboard before I'll allow you to auction me off like a . . . a . . ."

"A slave on the mainland? A pig or a cow? Hah! How you gonna stop me? I'll just chain you in the hold 'til we get there. I've auctioned off pretty females plenty of times b'fore. Only I ain't never had a silver-haired white woman t' offer the rich mandarins. You oughta be glad I'm still goin' through with it. A lass like you'll spend the rest of her days dressed in silk and wearin' jade ear bobs."

"I don't want to wear silk and jade. I want to go back to Honolulu. I *demand* that we go back."

"Tutu Caitlin . . ." Pikake whispered behind her. "It do no good to make him angry."

"There now," Captain Jack snorted. "You oughta listen t' your little friend. We're sailin' t' Canton, an' there ain't nothin' you can do about it. An' if you keep on arguin' and makin' threats, I jus' might f'rget that I promised not t' touch ya'."

"If you touch either of us, I swear I'll kill you," Caitlin gritted, then she shut her mouth abruptly, aghast at what she had said.

Captain Jack grinned. "You do that, and you'll join me in hell. I betcha you, me, an' Amos would have a fine ol' time jawin' with ole Lucifer . . . an' while we're on the subject of damnation, don't you missionaries frown upon drownin' yourselves? Seems t' me I heard once that takin' your own life means you're bound over t' the devil for all eternity."

Caitlin knew when she was defeated. It required every shred of dignity she possessed to keep from bursting into tears of frustration. "Come, Pikake," she said levelly. "While everyone's still asleep would be a good time for us to find the galley and see what still remains left to be eaten."

"A good idea." Captain Jack winked. "And while you're there, you can fetch my breakfast. One of the lads we lost durin' that storm was the cook, and the two of you can just take over. 'Twill keep you busy on our journey to Canton."

Gerrick crossed the littered deck, sidestepping smashed yardarms and torn canvas, and headed for the bow, where he leaned against the railing and intently perused the still, gray-green sea. The *Pegasus* was nowhere in sight. Had she been rolled over and torn apart by the killer, rogue wave?

Gerrick had seen it coming and been able to position the *Naughty Lady* to ride the great wave in relative safety. His schooner had sustained serious damages, but none more serious than what she'd already suffered during the storm off Kauai, when he and Caitlin had been searching the Kalaulau Valley. A few days' hard work, and she'd be seaworthy again.

The problem was that Gerrick had no idea whether to pursue the *Pegasus* to Canton or to assume that Caitlin was dead and sail back to Honolulu to secure the sandalwood rights. If only he had managed to overtake Cutter's ship before the storm broke. The *Naughty Lady* had only one cannon, a long-range piece set on a pivot amidships, but this was all the weaponry Gerrick had ever felt he needed. Had he caught the *Pegasus*, he could have peppered her into submission, while he himself remained just out of firing range of the shorter, more popular cannons employed by the schooners on the China run.

Was the *Pegasus* even bound for China? Several drunken sailors on the waterfront had sworn she was—and the harbormaster had Canton listed as her ultimate destination. But Gerrick trusted Captain Jack Cutter about as much as he'd trust a shark. Cutter had likely lied about his plans, just as he'd lied about his cargo. The listing for the cargo had read: tapa cloth, coconuts, ginger, and other Hawaiian plants used for medicine in the Orient.

The only thing the Chinese might covet would be the ginger, Gerrick suspected. Everything else was merely a front for the more lucrative trade of comely women such as Pikake—and now, Caitlin.

Gerrick couldn't bear the thought of Cait being put up for auction; yet his informant had told him that female slave auctions were not all that uncommon. In China, members of the feminine sex were counted as nearly worthless—unless one happened to be extremely pretty, in which case she might aspire to become a rich man's concubine, sold off by her own family. And Cait, an educated white woman with a rare, delicate beauty, would be worth almost as much as the sandalwood.

Yes, he decided, if the *Pegasus* had outsailed the storm, she'd be headed for Canton—and neither he nor John could return to Honolulu unless they knew for certain that Caitlin and Pikake were dead.

"Gerrick! . . . Oh, there you are," John cried, picking his way across the deck toward him. "I think we can patch up the ship without returning to land for more wood."

"Good," Gerrick responded. "Because I want to set sail for China as soon as possible."

Fatigue lines crisscrossed John's full face, and his eyes

held a desperate hope—one badly in need of reassurance. "You really think they survived the storm?"

"Logic says they shouldn't have," Gerrick conceded. "That wave came out of nowhere, and if I hadn't just happened to see it, we'd be food for the fishes right now. My heart, however, refuses to accept that I'll never see Caitlin again. . . . Damn! She isn't really my wife, yet I feel as if soul and body have suddenly been torn in two."

"I know," John said, laying a sympathetic hand on Gerrick's shoulder. "If Pikake is still alive, and if we find her, I'm marrying her just as soon as I can locate a real ship's chaplain."

"If they're still alive, we'll find them. The trick will be to get hold of them before they disappear forever into China's interior."

"What do you mean?" John growled. "Aren't we going to turn the country upside down looking for them?"

"I haven't sailed this part of the world as much as some others," Gerrick informed his friend. "But I do know this: Canton is the only port open to foreign ships—and in Canton itself, foreigners, or *Fanquis* as they are called, are confined within a stinking, crowded area of only four blocks. No one, on pain of death or imprisonment, is permitted to set foot outside that area."

"Then Caitlin and Pikake could be killed?"

"No, not if they become the property of a rich Chinese merchant who can do with them whatever he pleases. But *we* could be killed, simply for trespassing. We've got to rescue them before they're sold and spirited away. Because once that happens, we'll never find them."

"How in hell are we going to do that?" John's fist smashed down upon the railing. "I can't believe this! I just can't believe it. When I think of little Pikake in the hands of someone like Jack Cutter, I shudder . . . but when I think of her in a strange land, among a pack of foreign-tongued heathens, and brought there for evil, perverted purposes . . ."

Now it was Gerrick's turn to console his friend. "Don't think about it, or you'll go mad. My family had a business contact there, a member of the Cohong—the merchant's group. As I recall, his name is Ling Wei. He should not be too difficult to find, and he even speaks English. He knew my father well and often sent him shipments of fine silks, brocades, and of course, soochong tea, even after we were no longer so active in the China trade because we couldn't get hold of sandalwood. . . . I'm certain he'll help us now, especially when I tell him I can pay him in prime wood."

"How can you tell him that?" John scoffed. "Kamehameha still hasn't taken back the rights from Amos and given them to you."

Gerrick felt hatred welling up in him like a fountain. "If Amos is still alive—and we have every reason to believe he, too, went aboard Cutter's ship—then I'm going to make certain he never returns to Hawaii. If Kamehameha wants his share of the profits, he'll have to deal with me; I'm the only one besides Caitlin and Pikake who knows exactly where it is."

"God help us all." John sighed. "When this is all over, I may have to become one of Brother Bingham's most devoted converts."

"I'll settle for becoming one of Caitlin's." Gerrick rubbed his hand along the railing. "We just have to believe they're still alive, John, and go on believing it until we learn differently. Somewhere out there on the sea, they're watching and waiting for us to rescue them . . . and Cait is probably praying for us."

Emotion clogged his throat, and Gerrick could say no more. But he had a vision of Caitlin standing at the railing, as he was standing now, and searching the gentle ocean swells for a sign of his sails. Her silver-gold hair would be tangled and blowing in the breeze, her blue-gray eyes sad, her cheeks robbed of color . . . and her soft pink lips would be shaping his name.

He could almost hear her calling him.

I'll find you, my love, he promised silently. *If I have to journey to the ends of the earth, I'll find you . . . and then I'll wrap you in my arms and take you home to your beloved islands. . . .*

Chapter Twenty-Seven

Canton, China, 1835

Street noises wafting through the bamboo window screens awoke Caitlin from a troubled sleep. As usual, the city was astir quite early, with dogs barking, chickens cackling, cart wheels rumbling past, pots clanging, and high-pitched, singsong voices jabbering in a language that sounded unlike anything Caitlin could readily identify—except perhaps brightly colored birds quarreling in a treetop.

She turned her head to gaze toward the latticed opening through which light, air, and sound, but not visual detail, easily filtered. Beyond the bamboo screen lay an exotic, spice-scented world of which she'd seen almost nothing; immediately upon their arrival at Whampoa, a dozen miles downriver from chilly, aromatic Canton, Captain Jack had herded her and Pikake into curtained sampans for the journey up the Pearl River, and then into sedan chairs hung with heavy brocaded drapes. They'd been hoisted onto the shoulders of unseen coolies and carried through the narrow winding streets to a walled house located in the very heart of the restricted area where all *Fanquis* must remain while conducting business with the Cohong, the Chinese merchant princes.

Since their arrival a month ago, they hadn't seen much of Captain Jack either; his time was entirely occupied with

337

arranging and advertising the auction at which she and Pikake would be sold.

Bored and restless, Caitlin sat up and pushed back the heavy quilt that had kept her warm during the night. On the opposite pallet, Pikake was still asleep, and Caitlin saw no reason to awaken her. If this day was like every other, they had little to look forward to: water for bathing, clean cotton-padded tunics to be worn over loose-fitting trousers, and rice, tea, and vegetables would all be brought to them at the appropriate times. They were not permitted to do anything for themselves. Instead, a fat, bald, ever-smiling Chinese man in a short blue tunic and black nankeen trousers did it all—even bringing the towels they used to dry themselves after bathing.

Caitlin had protested this, but the man hadn't understood, and Captain Jack had later explained that old Fu Lin was a eunuch and as tractable as a kitten. They need not guard their modesty in front of him. Neither Caitlin nor Pikake had understood what a eunuch was—and both were shocked when Captain Jack explained. Caitlin felt deeply sorry for the strange, grinning fellow, but as the language barrier was insurmountable, Fu Lin understood neither her complaints, her questions, nor her expressions of sympathy.

Life in the screened house with its inner walled courtyard as the only source of late winter sunshine and view of the sky, was quiet and terribly frustrating. Aboard the *Pegasus*, they'd at least had work to occupy their time and thoughts. Most of their day had been spent toiling in the galley, but in good weather, they'd had the star-studded evenings on deck to look forward to. Nor had it been necessary to fear Captain Jack or his crew. Caitlin had only to bow her head and close her eyes in prayer, and even the boldest of the rough sailors retreated and left them alone.

Fear and superstition were powerful tools, Caitlin had discovered, but she was unable to use them here, because she couldn't communicate with anyone but Captain Jack and Pikake. The thought of her bleak future as a sexual plaything for a man with whom she couldn't even speak was so depressing as to make her shy away from thinking about it. And she no longer spent endless hours daydreaming of Gerrick rescuing her.

If Gerrick were still alive, he would have come for her by now. They had drifted at anchor for more than a week while the *Pegasus* had undergone repairs, and even after she was able to sail again, her progress had been unusually slow because they hadn't had enough canvas left to take full advantage of the prevailing southwest winds. Of course, Gerrick's ship might have been damaged, too, but surely during the month they'd been in Canton, the *Naughty Lady* could have caught up with them.

From what Captain Jack had said about the size of the area in which all foreigners were confined, Gerrick should have little trouble locating them. She had faith in Gerrick's ability to save them—but only if he was still alive.

Caitlin sighed and closed her eyes again, conjuring up his image. Even after all this time, she could still see him perfectly, still recall his rakish grin, and the way his eyes changed color with his moods. She remembered the exact feel of his big body pressed against hers, and his hands caressing her flesh, touching her breasts, roving feather-light down her stomach. . . .

Her body quivered with a painful longing to experience those same delicious sensations once more. Gerrick was her husband—her mate, friend, and lover. To go on living without him seemed an utter waste and an impossibility; she'd rather die than submit to Captain Jack's evil plans for them. But how could she and Pikake stop him—especially here in a foreign country where no one even knew their names?

Tears squeezed out from beneath her eyelids, and she felt powerless to rise and face another day. *I'll get up and brush my hair,* she thought, planning the act as if it were of great importance. After that, she'd straighten her pallet, drink the tea Fu Lin would soon bring, bathe, and change her plain, padded tunic for another just like it. And after that . . . what?

Her own torn, soiled clothing had been taken away, though if she'd had them, she couldn't have mended them, because she possessed no needle or thread. It would be late afternoon before they were permitted to walk in the courtyard; how was she to fill the empty hours until then?

Rising and shivering despite the glowing brass brazier in the corner, Caitlin found the hairbrush Captain Jack had given her and then began savagely yanking it through her long tresses. Her hair crackled with its own energy, and she wound it around her hand and examined it in the soft orange light cast by the brazier. Lately, since she'd had so little to do, she'd been brushing it more, and it was soft as silk and the color of sunlight shining on water. She walked to the oval mirror framed in bamboo and hanging on the wall, and idly studied herself.

Her cheeks looked fuller and were rosy and glowing with good health. But her skin had lost its golden cast and was white as milk, almost translucent now that she was no longer exposed to the tropic sun. The whiteness of her skin made her blue-gray eyes appear much larger than normal—but they were not happy eyes gazing back at her from beneath their thick golden lashes. And her mouth wasn't happy either.

"Caitlin," she whispered to her reflection. "You'll go mad if you're kept locked up in this house much longer."

Suddenly, she heard Fu Lin's heavy tread in the outer room. It was still early for her morning tea, and clutching her heavy tunic tightly across her breasts, she tiptoed past Pikake's sleeping mat and stepped around the bamboo screen separating the two chambers.

Fat, smiling Fu Lin bowed to her and handed her a folded square of foolscap. Caitlin took it, opened it, and read, "Auction today. Prepare yurselves."

Besides the misspelling, the ink was splotched, and there was no signature, but Caitlin didn't need one. She knew Captain Jack had either written it or gotten someone else to do it for him.

"Where's the man who gave this to you?" Caitlin

demanded, but Fu Lin only grinned more widely and shook his head.

Then he exited through the door to the courtyard, which was always kept locked until the single, daily afternoon visit they were permitted. Caitlin crinkled the message into a tight little ball and hurled it across the room. Today, the message had said. Today was the day they'd been dreading; she and Pikake would be sold at auction.

A moment later, Fu Lin returned bearing two wrapped packages. Bowing and grinning, as excited as she'd ever see him, he held them out to her. She took the top one, unwrapped the plain brown paper, letting string and paper drift to the matted floor, and shook out the contents. It was a tapa cloth *pa'u*, one of the short skirts island girls wore with flower *leis* as the only covering for the upper half of their bodies.

"Surely, Captain Jack doesn't expect *me* to wear this. Or Pikake either. Not only is the garment indecent, but the wearer will catch cold in it."

Fu Lin pointed toward the sleeping chamber behind her, and Caitlin realized the garment was intended for Pikake. Then he made motions with his hands, indicating that something more would soon be coming—something that was supposed to go around one's neck and in one's hair. Flowers, Caitlin guessed, though where he would get them this time of year she couldn't imagine.

Draping the scant, hip-hugging *pa'u* across the back of a chair, the only Western-style furniture she had thus far seen in the house or courtyard, Caitlin reached for the second package. It contained a beautiful blue silk robe embroidered lavishly with flowers and exotic butterflies.

Fu Lin grinned his approval, indicating that *this* was for her. Caitlin tossed the robe in his face. "You can tell Captain Jack I won't wear it," she informed the startled Chinaman.

He frowned, having no difficulty understanding her tone, if not her words. Arguing in high, shrill Chinese, he thrust the robe back into her hands. Again, she threw it in his face.

His rounded, flat features flushed bright red; even his ears turned crimson. But Caitlin didn't care. She would do nothing to help Captain Jack Cutter get a better price for her.

This time, however, Fu Lin did not attempt to make her take the lovely silk garment. Instead, he reverently laid it on the chair, then advanced toward her with an odd gleam in his slanted black eyes. Caitlin backed away, but Fu Lin was quicker. His fat pudgy hands suddenly darted out and caught the front of her cotton tunic. With a hard jerk, he ripped it down the center, exposing her full breasts to his triumphant, albeit disinterested, gaze.

Gasping in shock, Caitlin clutched the torn sides together, as Fu Lin calmly picked up the silk robe, bowed to her, and held it out, his round face now a mask of perfect politeness as he waited for her to take it.

"Are we to dress in these now?" Caitlin asked coldly, accepting the garment with trembling hands.

Fu Lin made no answer, and to her surprise, the door behind him suddenly opened, admitting a half-dozen Chinese women Caitlin had never seen before, carrying the tub she and Pikake used for bathing, along with numerous wooden buckets of hot, steaming water and several additional charcoal braziers. Apparently, she was supposed to bathe first, though why Fu Lin himself hadn't just brought the tub, water, braziers, and towels and left, as he usually did, she had no idea.

Fu Lin grinned, bowed, and departed, leaving Caitlin amid the smiling, jabbering women who wasted no time in letting her know that *they* intended to bathe her. "Pikake!" Caitlin cried in alarm, as small yellow hands plucked at her torn tunic.

A moment later, Pikake appeared from behind the screen masking the doorway to the sleeping room. "T—Tutu Caitlin, what is happening?" she asked through chattering teeth. Rubbing her eyes, Pikake glanced at the women in surprise.

By then, Caitlin was stark-naked and being shepherded

toward the low, steaming hip bath, now emitting the unmistakable fragrance of the fragile white gardenias the Hawaiians called *kiele*.

"Pikake, today we're being *sold*."

Pikake only stared at her with wide, wondering eyes, and Caitlin said no more as she stepped into the scented water. There was nothing more to say; tonight, she would be sleeping in the bed of a Chinese mandarin—and she and Pikake would probably never see each other again.

Gowned in the lavish blue-silk robe, her hair brushed and combed until her scalp ached, and her face stiff with rice powder, Caitlin stood dead center of the heated room leading to the courtyard. Beside her, Pikake was quietly weeping, her gentle sobs and reddened eyes the only blemish to her otherwise radiant, dusky loveliness. Chains of *kiele* encircled the girl's brow, wrists, and ankles, and more *kiele* lay across her bare, delicate breasts.

Her long black hair gleamed like ebony, and her oiled skin glowed a burnished bronze. With her arm now completely healed, and her body pampered by the extra warmth, Pikake was more beautiful than Caitlin had ever seen her—and also more miserable.

"I going to miss you so much, Tutu Caitlin . . . almost as much as John. I never, ever forget you."

"I won't forget you either, Pikake," Caitlin said softly, determined not to cry. "Let's just hope we're bought by the same mandarin."

Caitlin wondered when Captain Jack would come for them. When he did, she intended to make one last plea—to save Pikake, if not herself. The little Hawaiian would be lost in this strange land, pining as she was for John and for Kauai. This year, the winter had been exceptionally mild, or so Captain Jack had informed them. But what would happen next year? Caitlin wasn't sure how cold it could get in Canton, but she did know it was much colder than the islands. And despite their warm tunics and heated rooms, Pikake suffered from it even worse than she did.

A voice outside the locked door jolted her to anxious attentiveness; then the door swung open, revealing not Captain Jack or Fu Lin, but a tall, thin white man with a waxy mustache and black button eyes. Dressed in an elegant black satin robe embroidered in silver, he wore not only Chinese clothing but also a Chinese hairstyle. His black hair, oiled to make it lie flat, had been pulled into a queue hanging down his back. But the thing that most repulsed Caitlin were his extraordinarily long silver fingernails.

He saw her staring at them in astonishment, and his thin lips turned up in a sly smile. "You must forgive me," he said in a smooth, velvet tone of voice. "I've been in China so long that I forget what a shock my appearance can be to other whites."

"Who are you?" Caitlin demanded. "And where is Captain Cutter?"

"I am known as The Gardener, because I am the one who plucks the blossoms that grace the sleeping chambers of the Flowery Kingdom. I am also called Sir Charles. Neither names are my real one, of course, but in my business, it's best to be discreet."

"What exactly *is* your business?" Caitlin recalled that China itself was sometimes called the Flowery Kingdom; were women the blossoms to which Sir Charles referred?

"I conduct the auctions of beautiful women such as yourself. And may I say that of all the women I've auctioned off in the last five years, you are by far the loveliest. You took my breath away when first I saw you upon your arrival a month ago."

"I don't recall seeing you before." Caitlin frowned, unable to remember any moment when she and Pikake had been exposed to view. If anything, they'd been kept carefully hidden.

"No, you haven't seen me. But I've watched *you* almost every day. I've watched you both walk in the courtyard, nibble at your meals . . . even bathe in the hip bath. And so have many others."

Caitlin was stunned. "But how can that be? And why

would anyone want to spy on us anyway?"

"Ah, my dear, your naiveté is so refreshing!" Sir Charles laughed a low, mocking laugh. "There are peep holes everywhere in these two rooms. And in the courtyard, there are specially designed bamboo screens on the second level of the balcony, behind which a man—or men—may watch a lady without being detected. All of those who have come to bid on you today have seen you at least once, and some several times during the time you have been here."

Shock vibrated through Caitlin's entire body—even making her toes twitch. "Have we been . . . exposed to view . . . the entire time? Have we never had privacy?"

She was thinking of those times when she herself had used the chamber pot, stepped naked into her bath, or changed her tunic, while Pikake had discreetly waited in the adjoining room—as she had always done for Pikake. Shame suffused her from head to toe, making her feel alternately feverish, then chilled.

"Never. You've not had one single moment in this house when someone has not been observing you." The nasty mocking smile flashed again. "You see, I have discovered that when a girl learns what has been happening, she realizes that maidenly modesty at this point is ridiculous, and she then willingly cooperates and does everything I ask her to do during the auction."

Caitlin stepped protectively closer to Pikake. "Just what is it you are asking us to do?"

Now Sir Charles smiled benignly, as if their conversation was as innocuous as discussing the weather. "Your little Hawaiian friend will be required to dance the hula— in whatever fashion she pleases so long as she moves enchantingly and displays her special charms as an island maiden."

Pikake's distressed eyes sought Caitlin, but Caitlin had no comfort to offer, no way of preventing the inevitable. "And me?" she asked. "I know nothing about dancing the hula."

"You, my dear, will only be required to walk about the courtyard and stand a moment facing each direction, so that the gentlemen behind the screens may have another look at you before they bid for your favors."

"That's all?" Caitlin was relieved, but still suspicious.

"Well . . . not quite." Sir Charles moved closer and reached for the front of her robe. "You must open your garment and allow the bidders to see the heavenly charms that lie beneath it."

Before he could touch her, Caitlin jumped back. *"I will not!"*

"Oh, but you *will* . . . and that is not all. You will also wear this." Probing a slit in his robe with his long fingernails, Sir Charles produced a tiny brass object that Caitlin did not at first recognize. "This is a Burmese Bell," he explained, shaking it so it jingled. "Something to titillate the already jaded appetites of our bidders."

"You mean I'm to stand there ringing that little bell?"

Sir Charles's eyes crinkled like a cat's. "Oh, no, my dear . . . you *insert* this bell inside your Jade Chamber, as the Chinese so quaintly call a woman's private parts . . . so that every time you move there is a faint, elusive tinkle, tempting all who hear to search for it."

"You can't be serious!"

"If you refuse, your little Hawaiian friend will suffer a most unpleasant experience . . . one that will necessitate a lengthy period of healing before she can be transferred to the house of her new owner. And I also regret to add that the same will prove true for you if *she* refuses to cooperate."

Pikake's cry of horror echoed on the heels of Sir Charles's threat, but Caitlin wasn't about to accept anything with the meekness he expected. "Then you had better call off the auction and kill us here and now, Sir Charles. Neither Pikake nor I will consent to play your perverted little games . . ."

"I do it! I do it!" Pikake interrupted. "But please do not harm Tutu Caitlin! For myself I am not afraid, but—"

"Hush, Pikake! Let me handle this. We may be powerless to prevent the auction, but we will not be degraded any further. I *insist* upon speaking with Captain

Cutter; he will put an end to these ugly threats and shocking demands."

Sir Charles threw back his head and laughed—this time a high, thin sound that raised goose flesh along Caitlin's shoulder blades. "What a proud, arrogant beauty you are! And how very much you have to learn. If you strongly protest so harmless a thing as the Burmese Bell, I wonder how you will take to the Goat's Eyelid, the Happy Ring, and numerous other devices meant to enhance a man's pleasure and increase a woman's ability to satisfy him."

"Need you wonder?" Caitlin retorted. "Whatever those things are, I'll stuff them down your throat before I ever submit to their use."

Sir Charles's long silver nails suddenly collided with Caitlin's wrist, scoring a crimson line along her forearm. "Enough! Do not make promises you cannot keep. At least one of the gentlemen bidding on you this day is a man well known for his insatiable appetites. He greatly enjoys the judicious use of artificial stimuli. Any woman who resists or does not please him, no matter *how* beautiful, does not last long in his household."

"Good. Then if he buys me, I'll soon be gone from there."

"No, you'll soon be dead—but before you die, you'll suffer agonies conjured only in nightmares. You'll go mad from the torture, and *nothing* will be too distasteful for you then. Unfortunately, by then it will be too late; when Low Ping You becomes displeased, he never forgives. I have been supplying him with women for years; I know his habits well."

"If you know him so well, then tell him this: He ought not to waste his money bidding on me. For I will fight him with every breath I take."

Sir Charles stared at her, his button eyes gleaming with malice and displeasure. "What you do or don't do when you leave here concerns me not at all. But if you don't obey me this morning, it will be your little friend who suffers."

Before Caitlin could think of a suitable reply, the door to the courtyard opened, and Fu Lin rushed in. Jabbering

347

and gesticulating wildly, he exchanged heated words with Sir Charles. Finally, Sir Charles sighed and turned back to Caitlin and Pikake. Raising the Burmese Bell, he tinkled it under her nose.

"On this one issue, you win, my dear. It seems there isn't time now for us to bother with it—though I believe it was just what was needed to raise the buying fever to a pitch just short of delirium. The bidders have all arrived promptly and are anxious to begin. Low Ping You is threatening to depart and never return if we keep him waiting. . . . At times like this, I wish I were Captain Cutter; his work is finished, and now he has only to sit waiting patiently to learn how rich his last voyage has made him. *My* work, on the other hand, is just beginning."

"Surely you don't expect any sympathy from *me*."

"No, my dear. From you, I expect only obedience. Your little friend will go first. And then it will be your turn."

"Tutu Caitlin!" Pikake sobbed, reaching for Caitlin.

But Sir Charles, aided by Fu Lin, quickly seized Pikake and thrust her ahead of them out into the courtyard.

"Dance," Caitlin heard him hiss, and then the door closed again, and she was left to await her fate in loneliness and despair.

Chapter Twenty-Eight

"My God, it's her. It's Pikake." John rose from his velvet-upholstered, ornately carved chair, and Gerrick had to restrain him from going round the louvered screens that hid them from prying eyes while at the same time giving them an unobstructed view of the brazier-lit courtyard below.

"Of course, it's her—who else would it be? That's why we're here, remember? To buy her back. And Caitlin, too."

Gerrick was able to keep his voice light, steady, and matter-of-fact, but he, too, felt a thrill of recognition, mingled with anxiety and outrage. The memory of all they had gone through to get here burned like a fire in his brain. There had been the long, stormy voyage in the crippled schooner, and then their arrival at crowded, bewildering Whampoa, where the difference in language and culture had made it almost impossible to find out anything. Two nightmarish weeks had passed before Gerrick had even been able to make contact with his father's friend, and then it had been another horrible week of waiting for news—news that might tell them that Caitlin and Pikake had already been auctioned off and taken deep into the heart of China.

Without the help of someone like Ling Wei, bumbling, ignorant foreigners such as he and John were helpless to accomplish anything—and even with Ling Wei's help, things were still difficult and dangerous. But at least they were here now and, for the first time, could dare to believe that Caitlin and Pikake might actually be rescued. It had begun to seem as if rescue was impossible, and they would never again lay eyes on the women they loved.

"At least her arm has healed," Gerrick commented. "And she doesn't appear to have been mistreated."

John only grunted, his eyes glued to the slender figure in the courtyard. Gerrick fell silent, sharing his friend's intense emotions. He, too, hated to see Pikake looking so vulnerable and frightened . . . and also so seductive, half-naked as she was in her island costume. Like him, John would be thinking of all the other men in the courtyard ogling her behind the unique screens; and he would be consumed with fury that Pikake should have to be so humiliated as to be auctioned off like a piece of livestock.

"Your friend will not do anything rash and foolish, will he?" Worry lined Ling Wei's usually serene, pleasant features. "Please remind him that you are here as my guests. I should be deeply embarrassed if he were to become impatient and difficult during the bidding; as I warned you before, it is forbidden for the Fanquis to attend, much less participate in these proceedings. I have risked much by bringing you here; my family's honor and good name are at stake."

"Don't worry, Ling Wei. As I promised you, we'll do nothing to jeopardize your position in the Cohong . . . will we, John?" Gerrick shot John a warning glance. "We deeply appreciate your doing this for us; without you, we'd never have made it in here, and we'd certainly never see our wives again."

Gerrick winced a little when he repeated the lie that he and John were married to Caitlin and Pikake. But knowing the Chinese opinion of women, Gerrick hadn't dared to tell the truth; Ling Wei would never have agreed to attend the auction and bid on the women if he thought they were merely mistresses or concubines, as the Chinese called them. He would not have thought them worth the trouble—and might even have considered bidding upon them himself to add to his own household of concubines and female servants.

The members of the Cohong were fabulously wealthy, for they controlled all of China's imports and exports to and from the West. The elegant green satin robe Ling Wei was wearing must have cost a fortune; it was lined with white silk and had long, flowing sleeves encrusted with pearls. Chains of precious jade hung down his chest, and his white satin slippers, with their turned-up toes, boasted more jade in charming ornaments. A blue button topped his round silk cap, and Gerrick knew that it was both the symbol of his rank and the barometer of *Fanquis* behavior; if serious trouble occurred, he would be "unbuttoned" and in disgrace.

Nor were the Cohong merchants, each with their own tiny brazier and velvet footstool, the only rich men in attendance. A number of high-ranking mandarins or Chinese officials had been enticed into coming by the promise of Caitlin's rare blond beauty, though how they could have known without seeing her just how beautiful she was, Gerrick didn't understand. Ling Wei had only said that word had spread quickly through Canton, and that even certain officials from Macao, the off-shore oriental city jointly governed by the Chinese and the Portuguese, had journeyed to Canton especially for the auction.

Gerrick prayed that Caitlin's price wouldn't go so high that not even the sandalwood profits would cover it. Hoping to calm himself and maintain clear thinking for the ordeal that lay ahead, he inhaled deeply and only succeeded in bringing on a coughing fit. A pall of whitish smoke hung over the courtyard, and unaccustomed as he was to the sweetish odor of opium, Gerrick almost gagged. The chill air was very still, the sky dark, as if presaging a heavy rain or sleet; the spring monsoon season was fast approaching, and rain might well drive the auction indoors. If it did, Gerrick wondered how he would fare then, breathing the smoke from the unseen opium pipes in use on every side.

Wiping his streaming eyes he smiled apologetically at Ling Wei. Fortunately, the thin, ascetic man beside him did not indulge in opium smoking. A gong sounded, and

Ling Wei nodded toward the courtyard two floors below, where Pikake stood uncertainly, shyly glancing about, in the center of the charcoal braziers. Apparently, she was unable to see any of the onlookers hidden behind the screens.

"After she dances, the auction will begin," Ling Wei explained.

"She's going to dance?" John asked raggedly.

"It has been promised," Ling Wei informed them. "Half the appeal of these island girls is their ability to arouse a man's lust by performing the hula. A girl who can do it well brings a much higher price."

Gerrick sighed, and John scowled. As they both remembered, Pikake danced beautifully. Hoping to distract his friend, Gerrick inquired, "Tell us again how the bidding will be conducted."

"You see the abacus at the far end of the courtyard," Ling Wei said.

"Yes, I see it."

"On either side are screens behind which stand servants who will quickly adjust the abacus to reveal the amount bid. The bidding itself is completely silent. Each of us has a runner who informs Sir Charles—the man I told you about who is also called The Gardener—of the amount we wish to bid."

"You'll explain as we go along how high the bids are going?" Gerrick reminded him.

"Of course," Ling Wei assured him. "We bid in *taels*— one of which is equal to slightly less than two American dollars. The abacus will compute and keep track of everything. Ah, we must be silent now. . . . The drums are starting."

Gerrick was startled to hear the throbbing beat of drums, the mournful blow of a conch shell, and the haunting sound of a nose flute, such as he'd heard only in Hawaii. He craned his neck, but the musicians, too, were secreted behind a screen, and not even Pikake could see them. Her eyes darted anxiously about, but she nonetheless began to dance a slow, hesitant dance.

As the drums increased their tempo, Pikake finally

began responding to the familiar rhythms, and Gerrick clamped his hand upon John's shoulder to hold him in his seat. Closing her eyes to her surroundings, she used her hands, arms, hips, and body to communicate a sorrowful yearning so vivid and compelling that tears sprang to Gerrick's eyes. Pikake's dance was telling a story—a tale of lost love and distant homeland that needed no words to convey its meaning.

She indicated the swaying palms with the sway of her body, the wind rippling the waves of the sea with her expressive hands, and the feel of her lover's arms about her with her own arms hugging herself. Tears streaked her cheeks as she tilted back her head, her long black hair sweeping the ground, her arms uplifted, imploring her lover's return.

Pikake danced with all the love and longing consuming her slender, delicate body, and Gerrick knew why his friend was prepared to tear China apart to rescue her. He himself was wracked with intense emotions that shuddered his frame as they were shuddering John's.

"Relax, old friend . . . rest easy," Gerrick whispered, suddenly afraid that he would no more be able to bear Caitlin's disgrace than John could bear Pikake's.

Every muscle in John's large body was strained taut, and he appeared not to hear a word Gerrick was saying.

"You are a fortunate man, Mr. Reynolds," Ling Wei said quietly. "Your wife is a delight to the senses, but also a whip upon one's conscience. At this moment, although I, too, have purchased concubines at these auctions, I am ashamed of myself and my countrymen that this lovely child should be so mistreated. If she remains in China, she will only fade and die—as the blossoms of spring wither and die in the autumn. I shall buy her and return her to you without anticipation of repayment."

"That is very kind of you, Ling Wei," John answered gravely. "But I prefer to purchase Pikake's freedom on my own."

"As you wish." Ling Wei inclined his head, his nostrils flaring slightly, and Gerrick hoped he had not been offended.

Then John said sharply, "Ling Wei, please know that you enjoy my greatest respect and gratitude. Your generosity is exceeded only by your kindness; because of you, my memories of China will be far more pleasant than they might otherwise have been."

Ling Wei smiled. "For a barbarian, a *Fanquis*, you are very civilized, Mr. Reynolds. Thus it pleases me to know that you will not judge all Chinese by the actions of these few here today."

"There are white men involved in this, too," Gerrick reminded him. "And they are the ones who have made it possible."

Ling Wei put his finger to his lips, nodded toward the abacus, and Gerrick and John both fell silent. Pikake's dance had ended, and she stood pale and trembling in the center of the glowing braziers. A tall, thin white man in a black satin and silver-trimmed robe joined her there, bowed, and addressed the assemblage in Chinese.

"That is Sir Charles, The Gardener." Ling Wei frowned deeply. "It is considered very poor manners to extoll the virtues of a maiden we have just judged with our own eyes, but Sir Charles, being one barbarian whose impoliteness is exceeded only by his greed, either does not know this or does not care whom he offends. I shall complain of it to the Cohong, and it may be that we will refuse to patronize these auctions in the future."

"That would only be what he deserves," Gerrick encouraged, hoping that the abominable practice could be abolished, not just unpopularized.

Sir Charles then exited the courtyard, leaving Pikake behind. As the giant-sized abacus began clicking furiously, Gerrick could also hear the soft pad-pad of running feet carrying bids back and forth. Ling Wei smiled at John and held up his hand, indicating it wasn't yet time to make his offer. Gradually, the clicking slowed, and just before it came to a standstill, Ling Wei motioned to a moon-faced servant in the traditional loose trousers and cotton tunic.

"Are you ready to begin, Mr. Reynolds?" Ling Wei did not insult John by telling him how high the bidding had gone, but Gerrick was worriedly trying to figure out how many *taels* had been offered for Pikake, and what the sum converted to in American dollars.

"Whatever it takes, bid it," John said calmly.

Ling Wei issued instructions to his servant, and the man scurried away. A moment later, the abacus began clicking again in a steady monotone.

"How will your servant know how high to go?" Gerrick asked.

"I instructed him to bid one tael higher than the last bid offered." Wing Lei's eyes sparkled with the excitement of the bidding. "There is no sense wasting good taels; eventually, my opponent will tire of the game, and Pikake will be ours."

"Who is bidding against us, do you think?"

"I do not know, but I can find out." Ling Wei clicked his fingers, and from behind the chairs, a second servant obediently appeared and waited with downcast eyes for his master's orders.

Ling Wei issued them, and the servant disappeared, returning several moments later. He whispered something to Ling Wei that obviously displeased him, for their host's black eyes snapped. "I do not like this. Our main opponent is Low Ping You."

"Who is he?" John asked even before Gerrick had a chance.

"An extremely wealthy mandarin with a taste for cruelty when it comes to women and servants. Even his wife and daughters are not safe from him, and the Cohong thinks so little of his vices, which include dishonesty and cheating in trade, that they appealed to the emperor to have him removed from our ranks. He *was* removed and, since then, has curried the emperor's favor while bedeviling us in small ways as well as in large. The greater the interest I show in your wife, John, the greater *his* interest will be in obtaining her. And the crueler he will be to her should he win her."

"Then if he wins, I shall kill him." In his typical gesture when agitated, John flexed his powerful shoulder muscles. His face was set in stone.

"I'm afraid that would be quite impossible. Now that he

is no longer a member of the Cohong, he rarely comes to Canton, for he cannot abide the *Fanquis*. When he does come, he is heavily guarded and goes nowhere without his specially trained guards who are sworn to protect him with their very lives."

Understanding that John would be killed if he went after this Low Ping You, Gerrick reminded John that murder was not the solution to difficult problems. "As you have often counseled me, my friend, revenge solves nothing. I'm still itching to get my hands on Amos Taylor, but if we can merely rescue Caitlin and Pikake, I'll be more than willing to let Taylor, Captain Cutter, and even this Sir Charles fellow go."

"The abacus has stopped clicking," Ling Wei suddenly noticed, leaning forward. "Now, we shall see who has won."

Grinning hugely, Sir Charles crossed the courtyard to Pikake. In a pleased, ringing voice, he announced the winner. Ling Wei's eyes crinkled at the corners as he looked at John. "Your wife will be awaiting you below in a cloistered room. You see where Sir Charles is now taking her. Go quickly down the back steps with my servant, who will show you where to find another entrance to that room. Go and stay with her until I come for you."

It was as if the sun had suddenly broken through the storm clouds in John's brown eyes. His dark face glowed with happiness, and a blinding grin split it in two. "Ling Wei," he said huskily. "I'll repay every single *tael* she cost. Thank you. This day, you have given me back my life, my hope, and my happiness."

"It is good you will repay me," Ling Wei replied, his black eyes dancing. "Because your wife cost as much as twenty piculs of sandalwood—a high price indeed for an island girl."

As John eagerly followed Ling Wei's servant, Gerrick leaned back in his velvet upholstered chair. Caitlin had yet to appear, but already he felt exhausted. Ling Wei's hand brushed his arm. "Fear not, my friend. The auction will go as well for you as it did for your friend. While we wait, tell me about your father. Is he well? Does he still trade goods from around the world? I've heard nothing from him in years."

The mention of his father made Gerrick sit upright. "My father is a broken man, Ling Wei. His business partner ruined him financially, mentally, and physically. It was in the process of finding the sandalwood so I could then go after the man and exact my revenge, that I met Caitlin. At the time, my heart was filled with bitterness and despair, but Caitlin has changed all that. Now, I want nothing more than to return home and persuade my father to come with me to Hawaii so that he might spend his last days in the company of the grandchildren I one day hope to give him."

"Then you will no longer sail the seven seas and trade in the world's riches?"

Gerrick shook his head. "I'm not sure what I will do yet. But I do know I can survive anywhere. The islands are Cait's home; I doubt she'd be happy in New England, so I've been thinking of settling on Maui or Kauai."

"You must love this woman very much," Ling Wei observed. "To be willing to sacrifice so much for her."

"I'm sacrificing nothing. Wait until you see her. She is beautiful, but her beauty is only half her charm. She is also incredibly good, kind, and innocent. She even champions the cause of whales and dolphins, and where the islanders are concerned, she would do anything to help them."

"Another fortunate man." Ling Wei sighed. "I do not understand the Western concept of love, but I envy it. Apparently, there is more about a woman than her body to compel a man's fidelity and devotion. In my house are many beautiful females, but none has truly captured my heart—though at one time, I did feel something for my shy little wife."

"Perhaps that's your problem. Get rid of all the others *except* your wife, and maybe you can rediscover the special relationship that is only possible between one man and one woman."

"An intriguing idea. Have you always possessed such wisdom?" Ling Wei inquired wryly.

"No," Gerrick admitted. "I came to know these things

only after I met my wife. Caitlin opened my eyes to many things. She—"

"Ah, there she is . . ." Ling Wei interrupted, his eyes alighting. "And you are right; she is breathtakingly beautiful."

Gerrick swiveled in his chair to look where Ling Wei was gazing. As Caitlin walked slowly to the center, absolute silence reigned in the courtyard. And Gerrick sucked in his breath, unprepared for the sudden hammering of his heart and the sweating of his palms.

As he had known she would be, Caitlin was an incredible vision with her long, flowing, silver-gold hair. As she proudly lifted her chin and glared accusingly at the row of screens lining the double balconies, he saw that the blue silk garment she wore matched her eyes. And then he heard Sir Charles hiss, "Open your robe, so they can see you!"

Caitlin stubbornly stiffened her spine, and without realizing he did so, Gerrick stood in stunned outrage. Immediately, Ling Wei's servant urgently tugged at his sleeve, and Ling Wei himself leaned over and cautioned softly, "Patience, my friend. You must do nothing to upset the proceedings. Not only because it would harm me, but because it would also harm your wife. She'd be taken far from here into the interior where another auction would be held—and that one, you'd never attend. Nor would I. In disputes over women, the women are removed—and sometimes even given to the emperor as gifts."

"I will do nothing—*yet*," Gerrick promised through clenched teeth. He sat back down, but it required all his self-control to remain calmly seated while Caitlin's trembling hands sought the silk cord fastenings of her robe.

Slowly and reluctantly, she opened her robe, affording a dazzling display of creamy, white flesh, high, rounded breasts, and tight, golden curls at the juncture of her thighs. Gerrick bit down so hard his jaw ached. Quickly, she closed the robe, pivoted on her heel, and turned to face the opposite direction. Her normally graceful movements were wooden and forced, and Gerrick knew how humiliated she must feel. He wondered what threats had been made to force her compliance. Nothing short of death itself would have made his stubborn, headstrong Caitlin do something so utterly despicable and foreign to her nature. And he felt her shame as if it were his own, and vowed to rescue her or die trying.

After Caitlin had faced all four directions, each time opening her robe and displaying not only her body but also her embarrassment in the crimson blush that stained her high cheekbones, she stood silently in the center, and Sir Charles rushed to stand beside her. The man's face was shiny with triumph, and this time, he didn't even bother to extoll the virtues of his merchandise; his gleaming black eyes betrayed his belief that in this case, nothing more need be added.

The bidding began immediately, and so rapidly did the abacus clack, that Gerrick could not keep track. The sound was almost dizzying. "How high?" he demanded of Ling Wei, but Ling Wei only shook his head, his slanted eyes glued to the abacus in worried disbelief.

When the clacking finally slowed, Gerrick said, "Where is your servant? Did you give him the same command as last time?"

"Yes," Ling Wei responded in a hushed voice. "But for every *tael* I've gone up, someone—Low Ping You, I think—has gone ten higher. No one else would be so foolish or so vindictive."

"Low Ping You! Who is ahead now—you or him?"

"He is. My servant must be afraid to bid any higher. We are so high now, you cannot possibly pay the purchase price."

"Send another servant at once to continue the bidding. I'll pay it."

Ling Wei seemed in shock, his already pale yellow skin as pasty as milk curds. "It . . . it would require more than a hundred piculs of prime sandalwood to satisfy this debt."

"Then I shall produce it," Gerrick said recklessly. "Send your servant. What is this Low Ping You trying to do? We must not show that we are weakening."

"Low Ping You is trying to ruin me," Ling Wei

whispered. "He is angry that I won the last time and is determined I shall not win now. We cannot outbid him. No matter what we bid, he will bid higher . . . and in the end, he knows he can win."

"Bid!" Gerrick insisted. "Try at least one more time. Bid one hundred *taels* and see if that gives him pause."

"All right. Then you will see I am right. He will bid twice as much, if not more."

"*Two* hundred taels?" Gerrick didn't even want to figure it out. "If he does that, he's mad. I think he's only bluffing. Bid, Ling Wei. I promise you, I'll repay you somehow, some way."

Ling Wei sent his remaining servant with the message. The abacus clacked. Then there was a pause, and the abacus clacked again.

Ling Wei's shoulders drooped. "It is no use. I told you so. He has answered my bid with a bid of five hundred."

"*Five hundred taels over and above what's already on the abacus?*"

Ling Wei nodded. "I am sorry. I will bid no higher. If I do, it will become necessary for me to first sign notes showing where I will obtain such a huge sum. That I cannot do; the risk to my family's fortunes would be too great. For Low Ping You, it is no problem. At the moment, he enjoys the emperor's favor; it is even rumored he will soon be back in the Cohong. While I could not demand immediate payment, he could. And if I could not produce payment fast enough, he could demand I resign my position and give it to him."

For the second time in his life, Gerrick felt utterly, totally defeated. Caitlin was as good as sold to Low Ping You, and while his mind could comprehend this, his heart could not. *It can't be true,* he thought. *It can't be.*

A moment later, Sir Charles's voice could be heard announcing the outcome of the auction.

"I'm sorry," Ling Wei repeated. "She is lost to you. But perhaps, in time, you will find another woman you can love as much as this one."

Chapter Twenty-Nine

Following the auction, Sir Charles led Caitlin to a strange room which she'd never before entered. He thrust her inside, but before he could lock the door, she pleaded, "Wait! Where is Pikake? Who bought her?"

Sir Charles was in such high spirits that he didn't seem to mind her questions. "A man named Ling Wei paid an absurdly high price for such a frightened, worthless child. He must have been greatly moved by her dance, which I admit was well done, even if overly sentimental."

Caitlin's hopes soared; this Ling Wei might turn out to be far more compassionate than Sir Charles or Captain Cutter. "Was I purchased by the same buyer?"

The old evil gleam returned to Sir Charles's button eyes. "No, my dear. I am pleased to say you were not. Low Ping You has bought you, and I shall greatly enjoy imagining the uses to which he will put your lovely, golden body. When you depart this room, it will be in the company of his guards. I advise you to leave your pride and arrogance behind; they will not serve you well in the house of your new master."

His words chilled Caitlin to the bone. "May I at least say good-bye to my friend before we are parted?"

"It is forbidden for you to speak with anyone. Pikake is being held in another room. Only your masters may unlock the doors of your chambers and take you out. From this moment on, they hold the power of life and death

361

over you."

"But surely it wouldn't hurt if we were allowed to say good-bye . . ."

"Forget her!" Sir Charles said sternly. "You are now the property of Low Ping You. All that you have known is finished. You must turn your thoughts toward pleasing your lord, lest he be forced to teach you a lessson the very first night you spend in his house."

"I pity you," Caitlin said, swallowing the bitterness, outrage, and tears that threatened to engulf her. "One day, your sins will catch up with you, just as they finally caught up with Amos Taylor, the man who started all this."

Sir Charles only smiled his evil, mocking smile. "Ah, but while I live, I will live like the most pampered mandarin. You have made that possible, not only for me, but for Captain Cutter. Today marks the end of my role as The Gardener. Thanks to you, I now have enough taels to spend the rest of my days surrounded by luxury. I will invest most of my earnings . . . but there will still be enough money left to purchase some worthless females to serve me in bed. Perhaps, I will ask Low Ping You to sell you to me when he tires of you. By then, you'll be meek and submissive, *anxious* to serve, your youth and beauty so diminished by his rough handling that I should be able to afford you."

"God forgive you, Sir Charles, for I know I never shall."

"Farewell, my dear. Oh, wait . . . let me give you this. If you go to your master wearing it, perhaps he will *not* abuse you." Grinning, Sir Charles held out the Burmese Bell.

This final insult proved too much to bear. Caitlin slapped the odious object from his outstretched hand, badly scratching herself on his long, silver fingernails. The tiny brass bell rolled into the corner of the bare, windowless room. Still smiling, Sir Charles bowed to her and left. She heard a bolt slide into place, and then she was alone in the darkened chamber with only the bamboo floor mats upon the floor and a clay chamber pot to keep her company.

No one came to Caitlin's prison until long after nightfall. In the blackness, she had been listening by the door for the sound of footsteps and male voices. But the only sound she had heard was the distant rumble of thunder. Hunger and thirst cramped her stomach, and she felt dizzy and disoriented. She was numb with cold, for the chamber was unheated. At the first footfall outside her door, however, her senses sprang to life, and she waited with bated breath for the bolt to be released.

The door opened, and light momentarily blinded her. But she was not so blind that she couldn't count the six strong men marching into the small room, filling it with their menacing presence and making her cringe against the wall in fear.

Curved metal weapons struck sparks of light, and as she blinked and tried to focus her eyes, someone thrust a delicate porcelain cup filled with steaming green tea into her hands. Caitlin took it with trembling fingers, too fatigued and weakened by her day-long fast to refuse. Heedless of burning her tongue, she drained the cup, and a new strength flowed through her limbs.

"Which of you is my master?" she asked in a clear, calm voice.

None of the men replied, and she noticed that all were dressed exactly alike, in yellow tunics, black trousers, and crimson sashes. Their heads were bald, and even their eyebrows plucked. All had obviously been chosen for their strength and brawn, and would make an easy task of escorting her to her new home; they towered over most men she had thus far seen in China.

One of them approached her holding a hooded cloak. He held out his hand for the teacup, which she gave him, and then laid the cloak across her arm, indicating with his free hand that she should put it on. Remembering the thunder, she did so and was somewhat heartened to think that anyone in the service of Low Ping You should consider her comfort.

"Has it begun to rain yet?" she inquired, and her voice sounded strange and distant. "Shall I raise the hood to cover my hair?"

Startled by what seemed like an echo, she looked behind her, but could not discover the source of the odd sound. Her ears were ringing, and when she stepped forward to follow the men out of the room, she had the sensation that she was floating instead of walking. Suddenly, she had no fear, but only wished she might lie down on the bamboo mats and go to sleep.

The men gave her no opportunity. One on each side, they grasped her arms and half carried her out the door and through the darkened courtyard. Her slippered feet skimmed the stone pavement, and she found herself losing all interest in where they were taking her; it had become extremely difficult to hold open her eyes.

She was dimly aware of leaving the main entrance to the house. The six men who accompanied her joined many others standing in rows beneath paper lanterns. Four of the men shouldered a litter, hung with heavy, blue velvet drapes tied with shiny, gold tassels. The men lowered it so she could climb inside and lie down, and as soon as she had done so, the drapes were drawn closed, and thick darkness encased her.

She lay staring upward, feeling the litter lift and move forward. Thunder rumbled much closer now, prompting her befuddled mind to wonder if rain would ruin the lovely velvet hangings concealing her from view.

What does it matter? she thought. What does anything matter?

She tried to think of the name of the man who had bought her, but couldn't. Her brain simply refused to function. The sensation of movement became confusing and made her wonder if she was aboard a ship, bound for some distant port. Anything seemed possible, and nothing seemed real. She suspected she was dreaming with her eyes open. If she was going to dream, she wanted to dream of Gerrick, but no amount of effort conjured him out of the

364

dense fog inside her head.

Then that, too, ceased to matter, and sighing, she closed her eyes and slept.

"Lads, they're finally comin' this way," Erasmus whispered, and Gerrick quickly began dousing his shirt and jacket with rum.

"Are you sure you know what to do?" he asked his first mate for the fourth or fifth time.

"Of course, I know. Haven't ye always been able to count on me?" Erasmus inquired gruffly. "This sort of work is meat an' drink t' me, lad. It's playin' at bein' a preacher that near scares me out of my britches."

"But are you sure the men understand what *they*'re supposed to do?" Gerrick handed the bottle of rum to John, who silently poured some into his hand and patted the front of his clothing.

"Aye, aye, Cap'n, they understan'. Soon's you give the signal, they set off them Chinese rockets you got offen that slant-eyed friend of your father's."

"His name is Ling Wei," Gerrick said stiffly. "Either call him by name or don't mention him at all."

"Sorry t' rile your feathers, Cap'n. . . . Anyway, that's what they're t' do. An' if that don't scatter them yellow bastards, givin' you and John a chance t' git hold of Miz Caitlin, we'll have t' try an' take 'em fightin' hand t' hand."

"You did tell the crew that if we have to fight, we'll have to do it fast and dirty. Caitlin's guards are specially trained warriors. Once they realize what's happening and gain their wits about them, we won't stand a chance."

"I told 'em. At first, there was a few didn't want t' do it, but when I explained about the auction, they was madder than hornets and ready t' kill the first Chinese mandarin they saw."

"They're not *all* as bad as Low Ping You, Erasmus. Our goal is to get Caitlin. Once we've got her, the men are to scatter, make their way downriver, and get back to the ship as soon as possible. The sooner we set sail the better. Pikake, of course, is already safe on board a flower boat on the river. That's where we'll take Caitlin, but she won't really be safe until we're aboard the *Naughty Lady* and halfway back to the islands."

"Now don't ye worry, Cap'n. Me an' the lads won't let ye down. We'll create such a stir an' commotion, them guards will drop her sedan chair and take off like scairt rabbits."

"Not *these* guards," Gerrick predicted gloomily. "Well, let's get into position. It's too late now to think of a new plan; we'd better just make *certain* this one works."

Motioning John to follow him, Gerrick stepped into the alley between two high walls and crouched down. John set down the rum bottle and began flexing his muscles. "Will you stop that?" Gerrick hissed, his nerves drawn taut as an anchor cable. "You're annoying the hell out of me."

John only grinned, unabashedly happy that Pikake was safely ensconced among a bevy of lovely ladies who made their living pleasing sometimes difficult and unmanageable men. It was a place no one would think to search for a white woman, and though Caitlin would be horrified when she learned that the innocently named barge was actually a floating brothel, she must at least give him credit for being inventive. Both the captain of the flower boat and its leading lady had assured him that Pikake and Caitlin would come to no harm—and no one would question the movement of the barge down the river to Whampoa and Gerrick's waiting schooner. Many such gaily painted barges plied the Pearl River, attending to the needs of the *Fanquis* men—for *Fanquis* wives were not permitted in Canton, but had to remain year round in Macao.

The sound of approaching footsteps caused Gerrick to straighten and peer round the corner of the wall. Erasmus had retreated to the other side of the street and could not be seen. But their quarry was fast drawing nearer. Lanterns at the front and rear of the convoy marked the progress of Caitlin's litter down the street toward them.

Gerrick was surprised to see so many guards, and the size of the men gave him serious pause. He had been expecting tiny, but fierce Chinese to be guarding Caitlin, but these men were giants by comparison, and even more fierce-looking than he'd anticipated.

"Ready, John?" he growled over his shoulder.

"Ready when you are," came the relaxed reply.

"All right . . . *now!*" Singing a bawdy, waterfront saloon song at the top of his lungs, Gerrick stumbled into the path of the guards.

John staggered after him, and pretending not to see the caravan coming toward them, the two linked arms, joined voices, and danced a jig down the center of the narrow, twisting street. The guards at the front stopped walking and shouted in angry Chinese—apparently ordering them to step aside and clear for the litter.

Ignoring them, Gerrick sang, "Oh, I once knew a woman named Caitlin, and I loved her oh so true; but she came to China without me, and left me feeling blue. So now I'm here to rescue her and spirit her away, so we can be together again forever and a day . . ."

Gerrick fairly shouted the song in hopes Caitlin would hear him and not be frightened by what was going to happen next. Out of the corner of his eye, he studied the heavy velvet drapes of the litter, but they never so much as stirred.

Bleating like a wounded sheep, Gerrick continued the ditty, "Don't panic, Cait, when the noise begins; it's only me, my dear. My men are all about you, and John is also here."

A roll of thunder drowned out the last few words of his song, and Gerrick wondered if rain would help or hinder them. If it started raining before the fireworks, he'd have to think of some other way to distract the guards—or maybe the rain itself would distract them.

The caravan had stopped now, and some of the guards had started grinning, amused by the antics of the two drunken Fanquis. "Let 'er rip, boys, let 'er rip," Gerrick sang, leaning heavily upon John. "We'll put these monkeys to flight. And if they don't flee fast enough, we'll give 'em a rip-roarin' fight."

A moment later, the night sky exploded into pinwheels

of color, showers of stars, and the pop-pop-pop of firecrackers. Startled by the unexpected light and noise, the guards shrank together, angering Gerrick, who'd been hoping they would scatter and search for the instigators of the impromptu display.

"Damn!" he swore.

A second volley of fireworks went off, this one even grander, louder, and more colorful, and the guards looked increasingly alarmed as they gazed about in wonderment, uncertain if this was a late celebration of the New Year, a special show for someone's birthday, or a possible attack.

Lowering his head like a charging bull, John swung into one of the guards and knocked him down. As another turned to see what was happening, Gerrick tapped him on the shoulder, and when the man turned back, tripped him with his foot. Pandemonium broke out, with guards dropping lanterns and fumbling for their weapons. But before they could muster themselves to overpower John and Gerrick, a rocket whined overhead and exploded directly above the litter, showering sparks everywhere.

Then, dozens of rockets descended from the sky. Thoroughly distracted, the guards milled about in confusion, peering into the darkness for unseen enemies. Gerrick withdrew his pistol, partially concealing it inside his sleeve, and began firing, aiming for legs and ankles. John did the same, but the noise from the bursting rockets obliterated the sound.

One by one, the guards mysteriously dropped, screaming and clutching wounded extremities. The remaining guards ran in circles waving their swords and lances, but seeing no one except two drunken Fanquis still singing at the tops of their lungs. After calmly reloading his pistol, Gerrick took careful aim at one of the guards bearing the front end of the litter, and shot him in the knee. Then he himself grabbed the litter and kept it from falling. John followed suit at the back end, and at the exact moment when the remaining guards took note, Gerrick's crew members emerged from their hiding places and began clubbing them with belaying pins.

Not waiting to see the outcome of the fight, Gerrick held

tight to his end of the litter and ran down the alley where he and John had been hiding. After a series of dizzying turns and switchbacks, he came to a walled house with Chinese dragons adorning the lacquered red gate. This was the house Ling Wei had told him about—where he would find a peasant cart filled with vegetables awaiting him in the yard.

Gerrick pushed against the gate and was relieved when it swung open. There was no one in sight, but the cart stood ready and waiting, a lit lantern dangling from its back end, and two coolie hats and folded peasant tunics resting atop the winter cabbages. Quickly, he and John set down the litter, and Gerrick tore open the velvet drapes. He was amazed and then alarmed to find Caitlin curled peacefully on her side, completely oblivious to the preceding turmoil.

"Sweetheart, wake up. It's me, Gerrick." When she never so much as stirred, Gerrick shook her roughly. "Damn it, Cait, wake up!"

"Quite a tender reunion," John observed disapprovingly.

Gerrick gathered her into his arms, and as he lifted her, her head rolled back, and he realized she was unconscious, not sleeping. "Good lord, what have they done to her? She acts like she's drunk, but I don't smell whiskey on her breath."

"Maybe she's been drugged," John suggested.

"Well if she has, so much the better. We'll just hide her inside in the vegetable cart, and hope she doesn't awaken before we get to the flower boat. Uncover the box, will you?"

John was already tossing cabbages aside, revealing a long, low box punctured with air holes, inside which a person could be hidden. He opened it and held up the hinged cover while Gerrick deposited Caitlin inside.

"Hurry!" John urged, as footsteps raced past the gate. "Regardless of who wins the fight, it won't be long before Low Ping You has guards searching everywhere for his newest, most expensive purchase."

"I am hurrying," Gerrick complained, though it gave

him a wrench to lower the lid on Caitlin's still, motionless form. He uttered a silent prayer that she wouldn't awaken and panic, thinking she was inside a coffin. Despite the fact that it was slightly shorter and deeper, the box reminded him of a coffin.

Quickly, he piled the cabbages back on top and around the sides, so no one would think the cart any different from the hundreds of others passing day and night through the crowded city, bound for the waterfront marketplace or for one of the ships or barges anchored in the river. Then he and John donned the peasant tunics, and the triangular, round coolie hats that fit low over their faces, offering some concealment of their race and identities.

The cart was a two-wheeled affair that could be drawn by either one or two men. Gerrick opened the gate, and he and John each took a shaft and began pulling the clumsy wooden vehicle out of the yard and into the alley. The alley was deserted, but shouts and the sounds of fighting still came from the street two blocks over where they'd left the guards grappling with Gerrick's crew.

"I sure as hell hope you know which way to go," John growled. "All these streets and alleys look alike to me, especially in the dark."

"As I recall, the waterfront isn't far from here. But we do have to go past the Hothouse."

"The what?"

"Where the auction was held by that bastard, The Gardener—Sir Charles as he calls himself."

"Good. As we go by, I'll run in and break his neck. And Amos Taylor's and Captain Cutter's, too, if I can find them."

"Ling Wei said Cutter was there today, but no white man of Amos Taylor's description had anything to do with the auction. I don't know what happened to Taylor—and he's the one I'd still most like to get my hands on."

"We'd better shut up and get moving," John said nervously. "It sounds like the fighting is moving this way."

The men fell silent and concentrated on maneuvering

the clumsy cart through the tight passageways. Since he had never before pulled a cart, Gerrick found it awkward and uncomfortable. They were not pulling in unison, with the result that the cart lurched and swayed from side to side—toppling cabbages and probably creating a most uncomfortable ride for Caitlin.

As they turned down a street that looked familiar, Gerrick heard men shouting and running after them. In unspoken agreement, he and John pulled the cart to one side, then bowed subserviently. Gerrick held his breath as five men in yellow tunics thundered past, their lanterns temporarily illuminating the street. The guards paused now and then to bang on doors and gates. Shuttered windows swung open, startled exclamations were made, and questions asked. The guards responded with a readily apparent authority and confidence that chilled Gerrick even through his extra layer of clothing.

He began praying for rain—preferably a heavy downpour that would swamp the guards in midsearch. All day, rain had been threatening, but though the air was heavy with expectancy, the low-hanging clouds released nothing more than occasional rumbles.

"Come on," he whispered. "Let's go before we start arousing suspicion."

They set out again, skulking in the deep shadows at the front of the cart, but with Gerrick all too intensely aware of the light spilling from the lantern behind them. He worried that someone would notice their boots and breeches, thus realizing that they weren't what they seemed: simple peasants on their way to market. Anxiously, he cast about for some diversion they might create—something to engage the attention of the guards who'd escaped the melee with his men.

Looking up, he saw that they were passing a familiar house—The Hothouse—and a murderous rage fountained in his chest. Amos Taylor, Sir Charles, and Captain Cutter were probably inside, gloating over their good fortune. Tonight would be a night for them to celebrate— their first night as wealthy men, made rich by Caitlin's rare blond beauty and Pikake's stirring plea to return home to John and Kauai.

"John, wait a minute," Gerrick hissed.

John stopped walking, and Gerrick left his shaft and hurried around behind the cart. Removing the lantern from its hook, he studied the house where Caitlin and Pikake had so recently been held prisoner. Through the open gate, carelessly left ajar, he could see that although the house boasted the typical, high protective wall of sun-baked clay, it was itself constructed partly of wood with generous portions of bamboo trim. The roof was tiled, but inside the house, Gerrick recalled seeing all that bamboo screening and the flammable mats upon the floor.

"What are you going to do?" John demanded, coming around the side.

"Create a diversion—*and* settle a few scores. Do you think there's even *one* person inside that house whose life is worth sparing?"

John glanced at the lantern and then at the house, his face registering thoughtful speculation as he realized what Gerrick intended to do. "I haven't any idea. A better question would be, if you fire the house, won't the whole city go up in flames? Despite the clay walls and many tile roofs, there's still enough wood for the fire to spread quickly, and if it reaches the hongs on the waterfront . . ."

The hongs were the Fanquis factories, and the idea of starting a fire that could destroy so much and threaten so many lives almost decided Gerrick against the idea. But then two things happened almost simultaneously: A fat drop of water fell on his hand, and as he lifted the lantern, he felt another. It was starting to rain. Not only that, but the door to the house suddenly opened, and a plump, grining Chinese man exited in the company of a half-dozen chattering Chinese women. In the doorway stood Sir Charles, bowing them on their way. A great mood of celebration swept the group out of the house and down the front steps.

Gerrick and John ran to the cart and backed it out of view, just as the group came toward them and passed laughingly into the street.

"Well, there's a bunch whose lives have been spared,"

Gerrick mused aloud. "And as for burning down the city, I think the rain will prevent it."

"Then what are we waiting for? Give *me* the lantern," John instructed. "My aim is better than yours."

"Don't worry; I'm not going to miss," Gerrick answered, holding tight to the lantern and ducking inside the yard. "Wait here. I'll be right back."

He dashed toward the house. The front door had swung shut, but on either side of the door, bamboo-screened windows emitted a soft glow from the light inside. Gerrick stopped running, raised the lantern, and was about to heave it through the screen when a better thought occurred to him. He ran up the front steps, yanked open the door, and tossed the lantern inside.

It crashed to the floor, and flames leapt up and greedily licked at the mats. A startled Sir Charles stood in the foyer, staring at Gerrick as at a mad man.

"Whut's wrong, Charlie?" a man's voice said. "Them servant girls and that old eunuch of yours couldn't be back yet. They only just left. And it'll take 'em half the night t' go down t' the flower boats and bring back all the delicacies we asked f'r."

From out of an adjoining room stepped a huge, heavyset man dressed like a sea captain, with a bristling black beard and unkempt hair. He, too, looked startled as he saw the flames, and then noticed Gerrick standing in the doorway. Before either man could react, Gerrick took out his pistol and calmly shot them, each in one knee, first Sir Charles and then the bearded sea captain.

Howling and clutching their injuries, the two men fell, and Gerrick calmly turned and walked out of the house and back down the steps. John was running toward him, motioning him to hurry. "What did you do?" he asked breathlessly as again they picked up the shafts of the cart and started running through the rain toward the waterfront.

"Nothing much," Gerrick replied, panting. "But I don't think either man will ever bother Caitlin or Pikake again."

Chapter Thirty

A gong sounded in her dreams, but Caitlin refused to acknowledge it. Instead, she snuggled deeper into the incredible softness of the bed on which she was lying. The gong sounded again, echoing in her brain with insistent invitation; she must wake up *now*. She'd slept long enough. But she didn't want to leave her blue-misted, incense-scented dreams and continued resisting it. Then a bell tinkled beside her ear, and she was jolted to full awareness. It reminded her of the Burmese Bell, and abruptly she remembered where she was being taken when she'd lain down so sleepily in the litter.

Rigid with fear, she opened her eyes to a smiling, painted face whose owner was bending over her and ringing a small brass bell, far too big to be a Burmese Bell, in her ear. "Missy Caitlin awake now, yes? Is good. You sleep too muchee velly long."

"H—how is it you speak English?" Caitlin murmured in surprise.

"I learn from sailors. They teachee me speak velly good Ingleesh, and I teachee them speak velly bad Cantonese."

"Sailors . . . oh, yes." Caitlin struggled to digest this information, but try as she might, could not understand how a servant or slave in the house of Low Ping You might have come into contact with English-speaking sailors—unless the unscrupulous mandarin cultivated friendships with foreigners in an effort to win trade concessions.

374

That must be it, she thought. Perhaps he plies the sailors with liquor and hospitality in order to find out where to get the best prices for his tea and silks.

Beneath the girl's face powder, lip rouge, and elaborately painted eyes, she looked quite young but might have been old for all Caitlin could tell. Brightly colored lacquered combs adorned her glossy black hair, and she wore a robe similar to Caitlin's, except that it was a deep rose color that offset her powdered skin most strikingly. Her fine-boned, tiny hands fluttered about Caitlin's hair, and her slanted, black eyes crinkled as she smiled.

"Velly bee-u-ti-ful hair," she said admiringly. "No wonder you worth so many taels."

Before Caitlin could ask what taels were, the girl abruptly changed the subject. "You hungly? You want to eat now?"

"Yes," Caitlin answered, sitting up. "I'm famished . . . oooh, and also dizzy."

"You eat, dizziness pass," the girl said, pattering away. "Stay here. I leturn soon."

Caitlin closed her eyes a moment, and the spinning sensation soon stopped. When it did, she opened her eyes and examined her surroundings in more detail. Her bed was a large, raised pallet draped with flowing blue silk, on which enormous, cream and rose silk pillows with gold tassels lay scattered. The ceiling and walls of the room consisted of the same airy blue silk as the bed coverings, with the addition of glittering spangles, so that the effect was that of a hazy, star-bright sky.

Off to one side, a charcoal brazier glowed, providing light and warmth in the chamber, which was so small that it held no other furnishings except a tiny gilt stool and a carved table beside the bed. On the table was a brass bowl emitting a thin curl of heady, fragrant smoke that made Caitlin's nose twitch in astonishment, if not exactly appreciation.

The low murmur of men's voices reached her ears, and she trembled, swept with a numbing fear, and weakly slumped against the pillows. Beyond the silk curtains,

Low Ping You was doubtless taking his ease. She could ascertain the clink of cups and china bowls, the click of chopsticks, and what sounded like pebbles—or maybe it was dice—rattling in a container. Occasionally, the voices rose in excitement; they were Chinese voices, and now and then came the soft, subservient tones of women speaking to the men.

What would she do when Low Ping You finally parted the blue silk curtains and entered the gently rocking chamber? Struggling to emerge from her helpless, dull stupor, Caitlin realized that she was on a boat of some sort, probably enroute to whatever island or river city Low Ping You called home.

Tears welled in her eyes, but she determinedly shut them and refused to weep. The girl had said she would bring food; Caitlin would eat and grow strong again. Whatever happened to her in the next few hours, she would try to keep her dignity and self-respect intact. And when the opportunity finally presented itself, she would escape. Somehow, she would find a decent, god-fearing gentleman in this hellhole of heathen rascals, and beg him to protect her until she could arrange passage back to Honolulu.

For the moment, she could do nothing to save herself from Low Ping You; if all his guards had come aboard, fleeing from this boat would be impossible.

Lord, give me strength for the ordeal that lies ahead, she prayed, and so earnest and intent was her prayer that she never heard anyone enter the chamber and was unaware of another presence until the faint clatter of a tray with dishes being set down upon the table caught her attention. She ignored the sound, for her appetite had fled. But then a familiar voice said, "Cait, are you awake? Sweetheart, are you all right?"

Hardly daring to believe her ears, Caitlin opened her eyes. Gerrick's face was inches away, his expression worried and anxious, his sea green glance radiating love for her. Uttering a startled cry, she reached for him just as he reached for her. Wordlessly, they clung to each other, their hearts thumping out a triumphant melody of joy and overwhelming gratitude.

"I can't believe you're really here," Caitlin sobbed. "I was sure you'd perished in the storm, and I'd never see you again."

"And I was sure you'd spend the rest of your life in the arms of a cold, cruel despot who'd abuse the hell out of you, crush your pride, and make you rue the day you were born."

"I almost despaired, Gerrick. God forgive me, I lost faith in Him *and* in you. I thought I was forever lost and forsaken. But . . . how did you find me? How did you get here? What happened to Low Ping You's guards?"

"Hush . . . hush . . ." Gerrick drew back and placed a finger on her lips to forestall her questions. "I'll tell you the whole story from beginning to end, but first you must eat. John thinks you were drugged, and it would be wise to counteract the drug with something hot and filling."

"John! Is *he* here?"

"Yes, he's on deck playing dice with the head oarsman. Pikake is aboard the *Naughty Lady* waiting anxiously for you both."

Caitlin was dumbfounded by these revelations. "But . . . how did you rescue Pikake? By now, I thought she'd have been locked up in the house of her new owner."

"We didn't have to rescue her. John bought her at the auction—or rather, a friend of my father's bought her for him. We tried to buy you, too, but your price went way too high. When Low Ping You outbid us, we were forced to adopt a more daring plan, one that *appears* to have worked."

Caitlin's hands clutched at the sleeves of the peasant tunic Gerrick was wearing. "Are we still in danger? Will Low Ping You come after us?"

Gerrick took her fingers, pried them from his sleeves, and kissed them. "For the moment, at least, I think we're safe. We managed to get aboard this barge without being seen; it belongs to a friend of that friend of my father's. We just have to take our time and not look too anxious to get

377

to Whampoa and the ship, and we should be all right. My only worry is if Amos Taylor should again discover the presence of the *Naughty Lady* in the anchorage at Whampoa."

"Amos Taylor! Taylor is *dead*, Gerrick. He was swept overboard by a huge wave during that storm that separated us at sea."

Gerrick jerked at the news, his mouth hardening in anger. "Thank God. . . . I thought he had once more escaped with his pockets overflowing with cash—silver taels, this time."

"He did not die a happy death, Gerrick. Remember him with pity, not malice, for his life and his death were sad and mean-spirited."

A slow, loving smile spread across Gerrick's face. "My precious Caitlin," he whispered huskily. "Forgiving even when forgiveness isn't merited."

"None of us merits forgiveness, Gerrick. We have all said, done, or thought things of which we should be ashamed—especially since we've spared so little time in mending our faults and shortcomings."

"Enough sermonizing, my beautiful Cait. No more talk until you've eaten every last bite of food on this tray."

Gerrick took a bowl of rice and two chopsticks and thrust them at her. Recalling that she was faint from hunger and the lingering effects of whatever drug had been in the tea she had drunk, she took the bowl and began eating, managing the chopsticks easily after her month's experience with them. Gerrick, meanwhile, lounged on the bed watching her, his eyes avidly consuming her every movement, so that she felt awkward shoveling food into her mouth.

"Aren't you hungry?" She waved a chopstick under his nose. "There's plenty to share."

"Yes, I'm hungry," he admitted with a sly grin. "But not for food."

"Oh . . ." A warm flush crept up her cheeks as one appetite flagged and another sharpened. "How, um, long will it take for us to get to the ship?"

"Long enough . . ." Gerrick growled suggestively. "And unless there's trouble on the journey, no one will disturb us. John said he'd keep everyone out."

Caitlin blushed more deeply at the thought of John standing guard to assure them privacy. But then she realized how foolish it was to cling to maidenly shyness after all that had happened. Leaning over, she set down the rice bowl on the table and then calmly slipped out of her robe and held out her arms to Gerrick. He needed no other invitation. With a low moan, he rolled toward her and buried his face between her breasts.

"Cait . . . Cait, I love you so. I've missed you so. When I think of how many times I've almost lost you, and how, this time, I was sure I'd lost you, first to a storm at sea, and then to a sadistic Chinese mandarin . . ."

"It's over now, my love. It's finished." Caitlin stroked his silky chestnut curls. "And there's no reason why we should ever have to be parted from each other again."

Tenderly, he kissed her breasts, first one, then the other. "Cait, swear to me we'll never allow anything or anyone to come between us again."

Overcome with a sudden giddiness, Caitlin slid down on the bed until she was face to face with Gerrick. "What about Mac? Isn't Mac allowed to come between us?"

Wriggling her hips, she moved closer to Gerrick, as close as she could get. "Come inside me, Gerrick," she whispered urgently, need and desire burgeoning within her until her entire body was throbbing with it. "Fill me with your beautiful strength and make me forget all my terror and grief. I'm your woman, Gerrick, your wife . . . and I need you so terribly. I'll never need anyone as I need you. Please, Gerrick, come inside me!"

"Hush, sweetheart, hush . . . there's plenty of time."

Gerrick stilled her pleas and protests by kissing her long and thoroughly, making of the kiss a tender, loving hello and an invitation to relax and allow him to love her unhurriedly. He leaned back slightly, gazing into her eyes, and took a plait of her hair in each of his strong hands. Wrapping the silver-gold tresses around his neck and shoulders, he smiled down at her. "I should have done this long ago . . . bound us together with shining gold cords. You are all the woman I'll ever want or need, Cait, the only woman I'll love through all eternity. Your lips are the only lips from which I'll ever drink or draw sustenance, your breasts are my only nourishment . . . and Celia is my only home. I adore you, Cait, I worship you . . ."

His lips nibbled her cheek, her hair, her nose, and in the hollow between her neck and shoulder. Slowly, imprinting kisses that seared to the bone, his lips moved down her body. Though she writhed helplessly beneath him, he would not cease kissing her and finally give her what she wanted. From head to foot, he teased her with his kisses, and she felt as if she were floating on mist-blue clouds, then careening crazily high above the earth and arcing toward the stars in the firmament.

Her hands touched his chest, divesting him of his shirt, and somehow—she knew not how or when—he was suddenly naked. Her fingertips had long ago memorized the texture of his skin and the feel of his body hair—where he was smooth and where he was not. But now they delighted in rediscovering the familiar, beloved terrain. When she closed her fingers around Mac, Gerrick's reaction thrilled and excited her, and eagerly she guided Mac home.

"Cait! My darling Cait!" Gerrick gasped, thrusting deeply.

Wrapping her legs around Gerrick's hips, Caitlin locked him in place. "I won't let you go," she murmured. "I'll never let you go."

As they rocked in their impassioned embrace, the blue-vaulted chamber ceased to exist, and the gold spangles paled to pinpoints. They spiraled into another world, a dazzling, shimmering paradise where nothing mattered but the straining of their bodies to reach cataclysmic union. Spasmodic shudders wracked Caitlin's body, each one greater and more satisfying than the one before. As the last one shook her, robbing her of breath and very nearly of consciousness, she felt Gerrick go rigid above her, clasping her so tightly that nothing—not even a wisp of air—could separate them.

Golden light flooded her being, a light so pure and liquid it seemed poured from the sun, and she and Gerrick blissfully floated in it, loath to disturb the perfect communions of their beings. Many long moments passed before the light trickled slowly away, leaving a faint, rosy afterglow that warmed and illuminated her soul, even as the charcoal brazier warmed and illuminated their bedchamber.

Gerrick lifted his head, his eyes conveying a wonderment she needed no words to understand and share. Drawing his head down to her breast again, she held him as she would an infant, a child of her own body. In this moment, with passion sated and exhaustion held at bay, they were as close as they could ever come to complete immersion in each other. They were as happy as any man or woman could ever hope to be on earth. They were *home* again, and safe at last.

"Cait . . . Cait, love, wake up. It's time to dress and board the *Naughty Lady*." Gerrick lifted the heavy masses of Caitlin's hair and planted a kiss on the back of her neck.

Without opening her eyes, Caitlin stirred and smiled, burrowing more deeply into the silken bed coverings, and Gerrick had all he could do to keep from crawling back into bed with her. He wanted to spend the rest of his life in bed beside Caitlin—but first, he had to get her safely away from China.

"Come on, Cait. I know you're awake. I'll send Ling Ling to help you dress, and then we must get into a gig and row over to the schooner."

"Ling Ling?"

"The little Chinese girl who speaks English."

"Oh, yes," Caitlin said, rolling over and affording him an entrancing view of creamy white flesh. Reaching for the sheet and smiling at him, she covered herself and cocked her head. "Gerrick, what sort of boat is this? I think

381

it's remarkable that Ling Ling knows English, and when I asked her how she learned it, she said sailors taught her."

"Well, ah, I already told you: This boat belongs to a friend of a friend of my father's. He, ah, lodges here when he comes to Canton on business. The rest of the time it's a . . . a place where sailors on shore leave can come and get a good Chinese meal and . . . and conversation."

"Why, what a grand idea! A floating boarding house. Please thank your father's friend for me. The food was delicious, and I'll always count the hours we spent here as some of the happiest in my life."

Gerrick saw an opportunity to change the subject and took it. "You mean you've been happier here than on Maui or Kauai or even aboard my ship?"

He handed her the blue silk robe that had been lying carelessly tossed across the foot of the pallet.

"In some ways, yes," Caitlin said, doffing the sheet and slipping into the robe. "Then, I was always worried about my uncle, and I felt guilty about being so happy. Now, there's nothing to worry or bother me any longer—except how you decide to go about harvesting the sandalwood and spending the profits. And after all that almost happened here, those are minor worries I'm sure we can work out once we get back to the islands and meet again with Kamehameha."

"Yes," Gerrick agreed with more enthusiasm than he felt. "Yes, I'm sure we can work it all out."

Caitlin's smile was so dazzling and radiantly happy that Gerrick had to look away; once again he had lied to her, and his fib about the barge wasn't the only falsehood still lying between them like some ugly, threatening creature. Now was the time to tell her they weren't really married and must do something about that as soon as they could locate a proper minister—which probably wouldn't be until they reached Hawaii.

"Cait . . ." he started out, and she ceased fastening her robe and gave him her wholehearted, trusting attention. "We'd better hurry," he finished lamely, as unable to say the damning words as he had been to admit the truth about the barge.

"I *am* hurrying!" she assured him. "I can't wait to see John and Pikake again—but most of all, I can't wait to go home. I mean I'm already home as long as I'm with you, but I do so miss the islands, Gerrick. They're a part of me, and they always will be, I guess . . . just as you will always be a part of me."

She rose from the bed and came toward him, her arms outstretched for a last embrace before they left the flower boat's silken bower. "I know where I belong, Gerrick, and to whom I belong. Do you love the islands, too? If you plan on our returning to New England one day, I'll understand . . . but the islands will always travel with me in my heart."

Gerrick held her a moment, his thoughts in a guilty turmoil. "I can't even imagine you in New England, Cait. . . . All the while I was searching for you, I had but one unshakable conviction: I must find you and take you home to your beloved islands. Let's go home, Cait. And let's not even think about the future until we get there."

"Yes, let's go home," she whispered. "Hurry . . ."

And hand in hand, they went out to find John.

Chapter Thirty-One

Hanalei Bay, Kauai

"Oh, Pikake! Isn't it beautiful?" Caitlin hugged her friend exuberantly as the two stood at the railing watching Kauai loom closer on the horizon. "Home at last!"

It was spring, and trees and bushes all across the island were abloom with flowers. Inhaling deeply, Caitlin fancied she could already smell them in the sunlit salty air. Even at this distance, the lush green mountains were ablaze with color, enlivening the steep, inaccessible cliffs where waterfalls were usually the only adornment for the black volcanic rock.

Still far ahead of the ship and to her right, the jutting promontory that guarded Hanalei Bay was shrouded with mist, and on cloud-draped Mt. Waialeale, it was probably raining, but otherwise, the day was splendid. Dolphins knifed the turquoise sea, and terns performed perfect arcs and swoops in the blue sky overhead. Caitlin wanted to weep with joy at the beauty she saw before her; Kauai was a rare precious gem in the endless expanse of ocean stretching between two continents and she would remember this homecoming forever.

For the past two hours, they had been sailing up the coastline headed for Hanalei Bay, and Pikake had been naming each geographical landmark as they passed it. However, Caitlin suddenly realized that her little friend had been unusually quiet since she'd pointed out Wailua, where the Wailua River joined the sea. Taking Pikake's hand, Caitlin squeezed it affectionately.

"Why are you so silent all of a sudden, Pikake? Aren't you glad we're finally home?"

When Pikake didn't immediately answer, Caitlin glanced about to see if John or Gerrick was listening, but both men were involved in the endless effort of keeping the schooner on course, despite the fickle winds.

"Pikake, did you hear me?" Caitlin pinched the girl's arm.

"What?" Pikake's dreamy eyes made Caitlin realize that her friend was off again on another daydream, planning her and John's wedding—or more likely, imagining her wedding night.

"I wish you and John were already married," Caitlin scolded, voicing the opinion she'd already expressed more than once on the long journey home. "I just don't understand why the two of you decided to wait until we got here. I know the ship isn't a very romantic place for a wedding, but if you really intend to go through with it, you ought to have done it weeks ago."

"I know perfect place for wedding, Tutu Caitlin. When we passed Wailua River, I remember a fern-filled cave up the river. It is called Mama-Akua-Lono and is a very beautiful, sacred spot, once used as a place of worship for god, Lono, who protected Hawaiian crops. The river is sacred, too, and was known as the King's Highway. Along its shores lived the *alii*, and there, they gave birth to royal children, worshipped the ancient gods, and ruled the island until they died. . . . I think fern grotto right place for me to marry John in Christian ceremony. We will blend old with new and ask Jehovah's blessing on us so nothing ever part us."

Hearing this touching explanation, Caitlin was ashamed of her mean-spiritedness. Pikake and John *did* know what they were getting into by marrying outside of their respective races, and if she still found it difficult to accept, at least she had to admire them for their determination to overcome the obstacles of disapproval and prejudice, and create a good Christian life together.

"I'll help you prepare for the wedding," she said less irritably. "In fact, I'll speak to Brother Erasmus right away and perhaps we can have the ceremony reflect the influences of both your cultures."

"Now we have arrived here, there is no more reason to wait, Tutu Caitlin. Tell him I finally ready now."

"You may be sure I'll tell him." Leaving the railing, Caitlin headed toward a group of seamen coiling lines in the stern. Gerrick's first mate was among them, and before he became too busy attending the details of their arrival, she wanted to settle not only the content of the ceremony but also the time and date for it. John and Pikake had been living as husband and wife for some time now; the sooner they legitimized their union, the better—for Pikake's slender body already looked fuller to Caitlin's suspicious eye, and she didn't want her friend to have a baby without first having a husband, even if that husband *was* a man outside her race.

Her own change of heart in the matter still amazed her, but she supposed that she was finally coming to realize that John and Pikake belonged together, just as she and Gerrick did. Acknowledging the other crew members with a smile, she called out to Gerrick's first mate. "Brother Erasmus, could I speak with you a moment?"

"Yeah . . . what is it, Miz Scott?" Erasmus separated himself from the others and lumbered toward her, his scruffy gray hair standing on end in the breeze, and his eyes squinting in the bright afternoon sunlight.

His rough ways never failed to arouse her disapproval, and she was also critical of him for not taking better care to observe the sabbath during their voyage home. Unless she reminded him, he never led the crew in prayer and meditation on Sundays, and she herself had to lead the hymns. He declared he had a voice like a bull frog's and so had never bothered learning any hymns.

"Brother Erasmus, Pikake and I have just been discussing the wedding soon to take place between her and

John. I believe it's time we pressed for a date to be set, don't you?"

"Why in hell should *I* care when they choose t' tie the knot?" Erasmus grumbled. "That's between her and him."

Caitlin quelled her rising frustration and tried to continue tactfully. "As a member of the *Naughty Lady*'s crew, you must know that John and Pikake have been sharing the same cabin, Brother Erasmus. And as a man of God, you must be as pleased as I am that they are finally going to do the proper thing."

"I don't stand in judgment of nobody," Erasmus stated flatly. "Especially not John Reynolds. I ain't just the chaplain, I'm also the first mate, and whatever John or the cap'n do or don't do is their business, not mine."

"Brother Erasmus, John and Pikake's marriage *is* your business. You will have to perform the ceremony, and that's what I want to discuss with you."

"How's that?" Eramus questioned. "You mean I'm gonna have t' marry them same as I married you an' Cap'n Scott?"

"You are the only man capable of doing so on all of Kauai," Caitlin pointed out, wondering why Erasmus so disliked officiating at weddings.

"Does John want me t' do it?" Erasmus demanded, as if actually thinking of refusing.

"Why, of course, he does. I don't know who else he could have in mind, and Pikake just told me she wants the ceremony to be held as soon as possible. She and John were only waiting until we arrived back at the island."

"Well, nobody said nothin' t' me . . . an' me and Cap'n Scott has got t' have a little talk first."

Caitlin tapped her toe in exasperation. "What has Gerrick got to do with any of this?"

"Don't ask me," Erasmus grumbled mysteriously. "You want questions answered, you better ask the cap'n, I mean, your husband."

Caitlin scowled at the fierce old man, unable to understand his bullheadedness. Something was going on here, something she didn't fathom in the slightest. Looking about for Gerrick, she saw him walking straight toward her and grinning his rakish grin. "Why are you keeping my first mate away from his duties, Cait? I thought you'd be hanging on the railing, panting with happiness to see Kauai again."

"I was," Caitlin said. "But the subject of John and Pikake's wedding came up, and I wanted to discuss it further with Brother Erasmus, since he will be conducting the ceremony—or at least, I think he will be."

Frowning and motioning Erasmus back to work, Gerrick then took her arm and steered her toward the bow, out of earshot of the others. "Cait, why don't you let John and Pikake plan their own wedding? They don't need you to help them."

"Oh, but they do! Pikake wants my assistance. I volunteered my services to help Brother Erasmus arrange a Christian service that takes into account Pikake's Hawaiian heritage."

"Cait, stay out of it. Maybe they don't want Brother Erasmus to perform the ceremony. Maybe they want someone else."

"There *is* no one else! That's what I just told him; he's the only one who can do it—unless John wants to send to Honolulu for Brother Bingham or to Maui for Brother Richards or Brother Spaulding. And if he did that, I'm not so certain one of them would come, unless it was to put a stop to it."

"Please don't interfere, Cait. This marriage is very important to John, and I'm sure he has it all planned *his* way, not yours."

"I'm not interfering!" Caitlin cried. "Since you won't believe that Pikake wants my help, why don't you ask John? I'll bet he welcomes it, too."

"I'll bet he tells you to keep your pretty nose out of it! I happen to know he *doesn't* want Erasmus performing the ceremony."

"But why not? If he was good enough for us, why wouldn't he be good enough for John and Pikake? It might take months to locate another preacher; even if

Brother Bingham agreed to marry them, their marriage would be delayed far too long."

By now, Gerrick was gritting his teeth, but Caitlin didn't care. She was as upset as he; why was he trying to stop her from arranging this marriage? Had John changed his mind?

"You're not going to back off this, are you?" Gerrick inquired hotly.

"No, I'm not. Someone must force John to do his duty by Pikake."

"Duty, hell! He can't wait to marry her, but Erasmus can't perform the ceremony."

"Why not?"

"Please just take my word for it; he can't and he won't."

"That's ridiculous, Gerrick! You're making no sense at all. Why can't he?"

"Because he's not really an ordained minister!" Gerrick exploded, his face livid. A moment later, he looked appalled. "There . . . you dragged it out of me. Now are you satisfied?"

A long, ominous moment passed before Caitlin found her tongue. "What do you mean, he's not an ordained minister? If he isn't, then how did he marry us?"

Gerrick swiped his hand through his hair in a gesture she recognized as being both angry and regretful. "I didn't mean to tell you this way, Cait. In fact, I never meant for you to find out. Erasmus is no more a minister than I am, but at the time you consented to marry me, I had the same problem as John: There was no minister to perform the ceremony. However, unlike John, I couldn't be certain you wouldn't change your mind before I found one. . . . So I invented one. I ordered Erasmus to pretend he was a minister and marry us—well not marry us, but conduct the ceremony. As far as I'm concerned, we *are* married. We exchanged vows we both intended to keep, and I don't see what difference it makes who witnessed the event. We're as much husband and wife as if Brother Bingham himself had given us his blessing."

Caitlin felt as if the wind had been knocked out of her sails. Clutching at the railing, she leaned against it and stared down into the turquoise sea, her stomach heaved with nausea, and a single thought drummed in her head: *She and Gerrick were not really married. It had all been a sham—a ploy to enable Gerrick to gain control of the sandalwood.*

Everything she had accused him of in the valley was true: The sandalwood was all Gerrick had ever wanted, and she had been his key to obtaining it. Their happiness together had been an unexpected bonus—no wonder Gerrick had been so pleased and surprised by her wanton responses in his bed! He had probably thought she was a woman like Emma Spaulding, a woman he could easily get rid of once he had achieved his goal. He'd never meant to fall in love with her; but was it love he felt?

Turning toward him, she searched his face, and the misery she saw there convinced her that he did feel something, but whether or not it was love could certainly be debated. More likely, it was lust, pure and simple. He had found it an exciting challenge to seduce and debauch a missionary. And his callous, cruel behavior revolted her.

"Cait, don't look at me like that. You know I love you. I wouldn't have chased you all the way to China if I didn't. Now that you know, why don't we repeat our wedding vows, along with Pikake and John, in front of a real minister, as soon as we can find one? As I said, to me it doesn't matter in the slightest; I regard myself as a married man. But if it would make you feel better . . ."

A complete stranger might have been talking to her; Caitlin felt she didn't even know this tall, handsome man with the windblown chestnut curls. Nor did she want to know him. Behind his beautiful face and strong body, there was nothing but a weak, selfish, amoral creature whom she despised, rather than loved. What had she ever seen in him to love?

Several times during the voyage, he'd mentioned his fear that in their absence, Chief Laanui might have relaxed his guard over the entrances to the Kalaulau Valley, and someone else might have found the sandalwood. Gerrick had no substance, no rock-hard certainty or faith in anything except money. That was all he cared about—

getting rich.

"You needn't look for a minister on my account, Gerrick," she said in a quaking voice. "I have no wish whatever to reaffirm my vows. Indeed, I'm happy to learn that I'm still an unmarried woman, free to come and go as I will. Please inform your crew to address me as *Miss* Price, not 'Miz Scott,' for when we land, I intend to become Miss Price again. And to *stay* Miss Price. From what I've seen of married life, I intend never to marry. Instead, I'll spend my days in a more worthwhile fashion than being a bed warmer for a deceitful, lying scoundrel . . ."

"Now, Cait, I know you're upset and angry, but—"

"No, Gerrick. What I am is relieved. You and I have absolutely nothing in common. We're even afraid to discuss our differences for fear of disagreeing about everything. We've never once sat down and talked about our future like two rational, mature human beings. Now, we don't have to, because you can pursue your goals, and I can pursue mine without fear of treading upon the other's hopes and desires."

"You don't mean a word of that, Cait. You know it isn't true." An angry fire blazed in Gerrick's eyes. "You and I are as necessary to each other as . . . as Celia and Mac. We fit together, we—"

"We nothing! All we have together is Celia and Mac. We've never had anything else, Gerrick. Not trust, not honesty . . ."

"A pox on trust and honesty! I love you, Cait! What else matters?"

"Everything! You don't even know what love is, Gerrick. To you, it's only two people fumbling in the dark to get their clothes off."

"Well, that's certainly part of it! Do you deny you enjoy our lovemaking?"

"Yes, I deny it! I'm ashamed of the way I act!" Caitlin suddenly realized they were shouting at each other, and the deck had gotten so quiet that only the creaking of the yardarms could be heard.

Breathing hard and struggling to regain control of her emotions, she said more calmly, "When we arrive in

Hanalei, I'm going to my parents' house. And I'm going alone. Don't try and accompany me or come looking for me there. I will not speak to you. I will not acknowledge you. I will not look at you. To me, it will be as if you never existed—I will shun you, Gerrick, just as in the old days in New England, miscreants were sometimes shunned."

"You won't be able to carry it off, Cait. When you lie down in your lonely bed at night, you'll remember how it was with us. You'll remember what my kisses could do to you. You'll remember how, even with a glance or a casual touch of the hand, we could awaken the devil in both of us."

"I won't remember; I'll make myself forget!"

"We'll see," Gerrick said, with a cold determined confidence. "And now, if you'll excuse me, I've work to be done."

"Tutu Caitlin, please come and talk with Captain Scott." Pikake entreated. "Is not right you two should be so angry. You can marry same time as me and John, can't she, John?"

"Pikake's right, Caitlin. But you already know that. You've been hiding in this house for a whole week, not speaking, not allowing visitors, and I suspect, not eating or sleeping properly. Don't you think it's time to end this rift between you? You've both suffered enough because of it. What more do you want from him than his apology? He'd do anything for you, Cait."

Caitlin was standing on the *lanai* looking out onto the sun-splashed treetops and smelling the almost overpowering odor of plumeria in full bloom. She couldn't face her visitors, especially not John. This wasn't the first time he, too, had betrayed her trust. John had known all along that she and Gerrick weren't married but had been living as man and wife. It made her feel naked that he should know how passionately she had loved Gerrick, how she had treasured every moment with him. It made her feel vulnerable, when she very much needed to feel strong.

Refusing to respond to their entreaties, she said tonelessly, "I have written to Brother Bingham, requesting that either he or one of the other missionaries come to Wailua to conduct your wedding. My letter went out three days ago aboard an outrigger making the run to Honolulu. The islanders were planning to return next week, so we should hear if Brother Bingham intends to come himself or to send someone else."

"Pikake and I thank you, Caitlin, for interceding on our behalf," John said quietly. "I must tell you, however, that if your request is denied, Pikake and I will go ahead with a traditional Hawaiian ceremony in the fern grotto on the Wailua River. You see, we believe that a man and woman marry each other, and the minister only serves as witness. With or without an official witness, we plan to say our vows."

At that, Caitlin turned. "John, the minister serves as God's representative on earth. Without his blessing on your union, you can call it what you wish, but you are simply living in sin. . . . To my everlasting shame, that is what Gerrick and I were doing."

John's dark eyes flickered in disapproval, and his full mouth thinned. "You're too harsh on yourself and Gerrick. And if you really want to make amends for what you perceive as grave wrongdoing, you'd marry him and stop this nonsense."

"It's not nonsense, John. Besides, I no longer love Gerrick, so it would be a great mistake to marry him. . . . As for yourselves, I'm pleased that at least you are waiting until I receive some response from Brother Bingham."

"If he says no, if he doesn't approve of our marrying, will you still attend the wedding? Can Pikake and I count on your presence?"

"I . . . I don't know," Caitlin confessed. "And I hope I won't have to make that decision."

Pikake let go of John's hand and pattered toward her on bare feet. Throwing her arms around Caitlin's neck, she hugged her tightly. "Please come, Tutu Caitlin! If you not come, our happiness will be spoiled."

When their embrace had ended, Caitlin smoothed back her friend's long black hair and readjusted the brilliant red *hau* blossom tucked behind her ear. "No matter what you do, no matter if I approve or disapprove, you will always be my friend, Pikake. I will always love you."

"Is that what you told Gerrick?" John inquired stiffly.

The provoking question caught Caitlin off-guard. It also angered her. "I don't remember," she said haughtily, and picking up her skirt, she hurried into the house, not in the least sorry to leave them so rudely, standing alone on the *lanai*.

Feeling more uncertain than he ever had in his life, Gerrick turned up the wick on the whale oil lamp illuminating his cabin—the cabin where Caitlin should have been sleeping that night and *every* night until he could build or buy them another home.

"What do you think? Is it worth it? Shall I stay and risk losing the sandalwood? Or shall I go and tell Kamehameha what happened to Amos Taylor and persuade him to grant *me* the rights this time?"

Gerrick studied his friend in the soft lamplight, but John never stirred in his chair. "Tell me what to do, John!" he pleaded. "I talked to the skipper of that schooner anchored off our port, and he all but admitted he was here to find sandalwood. He said he was just ahead of two more schooners headed for these waters; word has finally leaked out. Indeed, I wouldn't put it past Kamehameha himself to have sent those dogs nosing after the treasure."

John leaned back and put his feet up on the table. "Cait's not ready to kiss and make up yet, Gerrick. And I'm not sure she ever will be."

"That bad, eh? Damn!" Gerrick tossed a chair out of his way and began pacing the floor. "By now, I thought for sure she'd settle down and start to miss me. What do I do now? How in hell can I reach her?"

Wearily, John passed his hand over his face. "Gerrick,

why don't you just go to Honolulu and take care of your business with the king. Laanui can't guard the valley forever. If he does try and keep these newcomers out, he'll only make them more determined to find out what he's hiding. So far, we're still the only ones who know where to look; but that could change in a hurry. Go secure the trade rights and leave Caitlin to brood. Maybe that's what she needs—more time."

"I've given her a whole damn week!"

"A week is nothing to someone as stubborn as Cait. Go to Honolulu. Just be sure and get back here in time for my wedding. If she comes to the wedding, you can see her there, and maybe the time, place, and atmosphere will finally be right for a reconciliation."

"I was planning on marrying her when you got married." Gerrick tried unsuccessfully to keep a tremor of hurt out of his voice.

"That might not have worked out anyway." John sighed. "Caitlin doesn't know it, but I sent a letter to Honolulu along with hers. Bingham may not accept either of our arguments for why Pikake and I should be allowed to marry. I'm really not counting on it. If we don't hear from him, or if his response is negative, we'll hold the ceremony the week after next. Do you think you can obtain the trade rights and be back here in time for it?"

"I think so. Unless the king has gone to Lahaina or someplace else, and I have to go looking for him. . . . Damn it, John! I'd just as soon forget the sandalwood, stay here, and court Caitlin."

"Right now, you'd be wasting your time, Gerrick. You may not win her back. Why lose the sandalwood, too?"

Why, indeed? Gerrick wondered, and the answer quickly came to him: Without Cait, the sandalwood didn't mean a thing to him. He'd known that for a long time; but how was he to convince her of the way he felt?

"I'll sail in the morning," he told John.

"And while you're gone, don't worry. I'll look after Caitlin."

"If she lets you," Gerrick grumbled bitterly.

Chapter Thirty-Two

As Caitlin took the canvas-wrapped packet from Inamoo's outstretched hands, her heart gave a sudden, startling thump. "*Mahalo*, Inamoo. Thank you for bringing this."

Inamoo grinned his wide-toothed grin and responded in Hawaiian. "The outrigger just returned, and I knew you were waiting for it, Tutu Caitlin. Now I will go tell my sister, and she will probably run here as fast as she can to see what it says."

Caitlin merely nodded, too preoccupied with opening the packet to pay much attention to Inamoo's departure. The afternoon was hot, and she retreated to the cool of the house before smoothing out and reading the response to the letter she had sent to Brother Bingham.

"How delightful to hear from you, Sister Caitlin . . ."

the letter began.

Caitlin skimmed over the preliminary greetings and finally found that for which she was looking.

"As to your request that I or one of the other brothers officiate at a wedding between John Reynolds and your little friend, Pikake, we must not only decline, but also strenuously insist that you do everything in your power to discourage such a union. If Mr.

Reynolds is truly a pious, God-fearing gentleman, he must certainly see that his future, whether in the islands or in New England, would be better served if he chose a wife from among his own people . . ."

The letter went on to reiterate arguments Caitlin had heard before—that God did not intend for the races to mix bloodlines, that John's children would suffer from bias, and that John and Pikake themselves would have no friends except

"those already so profligate in their behavior that they care nothing for the good opinion of others, and indeed, go out of their way to flaunt society's strictures."

Crumpling the letter in anger and hurling it across the room, Caitlin shouted, "Doesn't he realize he's *furthering* the very prejudice he warns against?"

The question reverberated in the empty house. Sighing forlornly, Caitlin went out to the back *lanai* overlooking the mountains. As she gazed up at the rounded greenish-purple peaks, where wisps of cloud slithered over and around them like curling smoke, she wondered why life had to be so complicated.

Actually, she wasn't surprised at Brother Bingham's refusal; if anything, she had anticipated it. Yet even as she did so, some small part of her had clung to the hope that tolerance and forbearance would win out over arrogance. For that was what it was—pure arrogance. The missionaries believed that they, of all peoples, races, religions, and cultures, possessed the only right way of living. They believed that their beliefs were superior to everyone else's, and that anyone who didn't believe as they did was doomed to eternal damnation.

Caitlin herself had once believed this—but now she no longer did. Now she was filled with questions, doubts, and hesitations. She could no longer be certain of anything. The very foundations of her life had cracked and crumbled, and she felt terribly alone and deserted, again a prisoner in a strange, alien place . . . and this time, there was no hope of rescue.

That was what hurt the most: Gerrick had given up so easily—sailing for Honolulu after only a week on Kauai. The arrival of other fortune hunters had so filled him with fear that he might lose the sandalwood that he'd gone off without a word. Obviously, he treasured the wood over her. She may have lost sight of *her* goals, but he certainly hadn't lost sight of *his*. It did not seem fair. Loving Gerrick had turned her world upside-down, changing everything, destroying the person she had been, and leaving her a stranger to her own self.

But Gerrick hadn't changed one bit; he remained as he had always been—selfish, greedy, wicked, and charming. Were he to walk in the door and smile his old rakish, naughty grin, her heart would still twist painfully, and she couldn't be certain that she wouldn't fly into his arms.

Suddenly, she heard footsteps running up the stairs to the front *lanai*. Her breath came faster, and her heart fluttered. Whirling about, swept with a wildly spiraling hope, she waited to see who it was.

"Tutu Caitlin! Where are you? Inamoo say he bring letter from Longnecks in Honolulu." Pikake rushed into the house, ran about searching, and finally saw Caitlin standing on the back *lanai*. "Oh, there you are! What did letter say?"

Caitlin was still grappling with her disappointment that Pikake wasn't Gerrick and she didn't immediately answer. As she stood there, sadly regarding her friend and wondering how to break the news gently, Pikake guessed what had happened, and her mouth drooped in disappointment.

"They no think Pikake good enough to marry white man, do they?" she asked.

Unable to lie, Caitlin shook her head. "I'm sorry, Pikake. And worse, I'm ashamed. For years, I've scolded and harangued you . . . made you feel worthless and small. I've taught you to hide the beauty of your body beneath long dresses, to forgo wearing flowers, to go about quietly with a downcast expression, instead of laughing and playing and dancing and singing, as you were meant to do. . . . I had no right to try and change you, Pikake. And Brother Bingham has no right to forbid you to marry anyone whom you wish to marry."

Pikake appeared to consider this for a moment, and then the light flickered again in her eyes. "Does that mean that you will come to my wedding—even if I am sinning by not obeying Brother Bingham?"

"Yes," Caitlin whispered. "I will come. And if you wish, you can even have hula dancing."

"Oh, Tutu Caitlin! You make me happiest *wahine* on all of Kauai!"

As Pikake—eyes shining, face aglow once more—embraced Caitlin, all Caitlin could think of was that while Pikake was the happiest, she herself was the most miserable But she wouldn't spoil her friend's joy for anything. So she smiled and hugged Pikake and discussed wedding plans for the rest of the afternoon.

Caitlin avoided looking in the mirror all the while she was dressing for the wedding. She feared shocking even herself. For two days, she had been feverishly sewing a dress from a length of soft, vividly printed tapa cloth furnished by a friend of Pikake's. Since she had decided to attend the wedding, Caitlin had also decided to attend it dressed in a manner more appropriate to the unseasonably warm weather and her new attitudes.

The dress had no sleeves, and while the bodice adequately concealed her bosom, it did *not* hug her neck. Her throat and most of her shoulders were bare, but she hoped that the large, double-strand lei of jet-black kekui nuts she planned to wear would lessen both the appearance and the feel of being half-naked. Wriggling her bare toes in pleasure, she debated what to put on her feet. The Hawaiians always went barefoot, and shoes and linen stockings would ruin the entire effect of her half-native, tapa cloth costume.

She decided that having gone this far, she might as well go all the way; her feet would be bare, and her hair would be loose and adorned with flowers. She hadn't felt so daring since she'd been forced to wear a blue silk robe and face a courtyard of unseen men—only this time, no one was forcing her to do anything. Neither Sir Charles nor Reverend Bingham was dictating her mode of attire; she was dressing in a manner she herself had chosen and believed to be both practical and attractive.

Having finished dressing, she chanced a hurried glance in the chipped mirror over her trunk, and an involuntary gasp escaped her; the creature in the mirror was neither missionary, white woman, nor Hawaiian. Rather, she belonged to a different world altogether. The effect of her silver-gold hair tumbling down across the warm browns, creams, and rusts of the tapa cloth was both stunning and richly exotic. And furthering Caitlin's surprise and discomfiture, the ebony gleam of the kekui nuts lying across her full, high bosom served only to emphasize the contours she had hoped to conceal.

I have made a mistake, she thought, a terrible mistake.

"Tutu Caitlin! Are you ready yet?" Inamoo called from the front *lanai*. "The outriggers are waiting, and everyone is anxious to begin the journey to the fern grotto."

Caitlin stared at her reflection in growing horror. There was no time to change now; she'd have to go as she was. Spying her shawl on the foot of the bed, she snatched it up, flung it about her milk-white shoulders and neck, thereby concealing *most* of her mistake, and hurried to answer Inamoo's summons. If anyone questioned why she was wearing the garment on such a warm afternoon, she'd say it was to protect her fair skin against sunburn, though very likely, no one would even notice.

Gerrick would notice, a little voice reminded her, but since Gerrick hadn't yet returned from Honolulu, she needn't worry what *he* thought. Racing down the path toward the beach behind Inamoo, Caitlin was finally able to breathe easier remembering it was Pikake's dress, not hers, that would claim everyone's attention.

*   *   *

Gerrick and Erasmus tugged the gig up onto the riverbank, and Gerrick pointed to a trail leading through the exceptionally thick, green jungle growth.

"John said we can't miss it. We just follow the footpath, and we'll come to the cave," he told Erasmus.

"Looks like there's a big turnout among the islanders," Erasmus said, nodding toward the many outriggers already jamming the area. "This should be interestin'."

"Should be," Gerrick agreed, though his interest in John and Pikake's wedding ceremony was far different from his first mate's.

While it was true that he wanted to see John married, he wanted even more to see Caitlin. Even if she ignored him and refused to speak, he could at least feast his eyes upon her, knowing that at last he could finally take time to woo her, because Kamehameha had readily agreed to grant him the trade rights for the sandalwood.

The claim was now his, and no one else could take it. And the young king had even consented to allow Gerrick to harvest the wood on his own, in a quiet, secretive manner that wouldn't create the fortune-hunting panic Caitlin had so much feared. It had taken all of Gerrick's charm and his promise of *half* the profits to persuade the king to grant these concessions. But Gerrick didn't mind; he counted himself extremely fortunate to have done as well as he had—and to have done it in such a short time.

Had he not been so anxious to get back to Kauai, he might have delayed his return in hopes of convincing Kamehameha to settle for only a quarter of the profits. As it was, he was glad just to have made it back in time for the wedding.

"Come on, Erasmus. I hear chanting. Maybe the ceremony has already begun."

They hurried along the beaten path lined with the thickest tropical growth Gerrick had yet seen. Minutes later, they arrived at a large cave overhung with ferns and completely surrounded by heavy, fantastic greenery. A wisp of a waterfall inside the grotto helped create the mystic, unreal atmosphere of a primitive church or sanctuary, and Gerrick understood perfectly why Pikake had chosen this place as the site for her wedding; the air itself seemed drenched with mystery and alive with the presence of forgotten gods—gods who were kind, not cruel.

A mood of joyous celebration prevailed among the many gaily clad guests milling about in the cave; the Hawaiians, at least, did not seem upset by the idea of Pikake marrying a white man. On the beach at Wailua, preparations for a grand luau had been under way all afternoon. Gerrick had even ordered his crew to remain on the beach and keep watch over the *imu,* the underground oven where a whole pig was being roasted.

The islanders had all left to attend the ceremony, and while they were gone, Gerrick wanted his own surprise touches added to the wedding feast. He had purchased a large cask of rum in Honolulu, and had directed his men to bring it ashore and also to erect a tent of sorts to protect the wedding guests in case of rain.

John and Pikake would eat from rare Chinese porcelain bowls, and the mats on which they sat would be furnished with silk-covered pillows, part of the trade goods Gerrick had picked up in Canton. For the couple's first night together as husband and wife, Gerrick was having his men create a canvas bower, the inside of which was draped with bolts of silk, so that the whole resembled the private chamber on the flower boat where he and Caitlin had been reunited following her rescue.

Gerrick felt it was the least he could do for his friend. John had been disappointed but not surprised by Hiram Bingham's prejudice, and recalling all this, Gerrick wondered whether or not Caitlin really would attend the ceremony. She had told Pikake she was coming, but might she not change her mind at the last minute? Her rigid moral values had not disappeared; at any moment, she might suddenly be reminded that what John and Pikake were doing was considered grounds for expulsion from the church. Not even Kamehameha had yet succeeded in persuading the missionaries to make allowances for individual beliefs. The missionaries would no more condone John and Pikake's marriage than they would the king's with his sister.

Drawing closer to the cave, Gerrick saw that the ceremony was indeed beginning. Off to one side, two rows of men and three of women were softly chanting an ancient love song to the accompaniment of Hawaiian instruments. Meanwhile John and Pikake, attired in scant native costume, with John looking every inch a dark-skinned, dark-haired islander in his short, printed malo and flowered leis, were standing in front of an old *kahuna*, or priest.

On the other side, a beaming, happy Chief Laanui sat cross-legged on his own pandanus mat, his cape of bird feathers glistening beneath the torches that illuminated the dark shadows of the cave. Heedless of order, the people pressed closer, the better to see, and Gerrick lost sight of Pikake's small figure clad in a tapa cloth skirt and leis, much the same as she had looked on the day of the auction.

Eagerly, he studied the crowd for Caitlin, expecting her to stand out because of her long sleeves, high-necked gown, and brightly shining hair. The silver-gold color finally caught his eye, but as Gerrick started toward her, he noticed something astonishing: the way Caitlin was dressed. Her vividly printed gown, her unusual leis, and the flowers tucked in her hair were a great shock; never had she looked so lovely and natural, as if she had finally found the style and manner that most became her blond beauty. Only one thing marred the overall effect: the shawl clinging to her slender white shoulders. Gerrick wanted to go over, grab it, and tear it to pieces; to him, the shawl symbolized Caitlin's inability to accept her own beauty as God-given and therefore right and good.

Passing behind and around the islanders blocking his path to her, Gerrick came up behind Caitlin, who as yet was unaware of his presence.

"Take off that damn shawl, Caitlin," he growled in her ear.

She jumped and half turned, but he slid his arm around her waist and held her imprisoned against his chest.

"It's too hot for it, and if you think it becomes you, you're crazy. The dress, however, looks perfect, and the beads are likewise perfect, and so are your bare arms, your loose hair, and the flowers tucked behind your ear. You're the most gorgeous, sensual creature I've ever seen, Cait . . . and if I can't enjoy your nakedness, I'd rather look at you dressed as you are now than in anything I've yet seen you wear—even that Chinese robe."

"Let go of me, Gerrick . . ." Caitlin hissed, her body rigid but unstruggling as she tried not to draw attention to herself. "Let go of me at once! Everyone is staring at us!"

"Not one person is even looking this way. Why, they can't even hear us for all the singing and drum beating. They're too busy watching the ceremony—a ceremony *we* should be a part of, just as John and Pikake are a part of it."

It was true. The music had increased in tempo, and John and Pikake had turned to each other, smiling into each other's eyes, as the *kahuna* draped a large tapa cloth cloak about them.

"Gerrick Scott, your behavior is indecent! And I could *never* marry you in another fake, heathen ceremony such as this. Just because I decided to attend and am dressed like this doesn't mean I can forget all I've ever been taught."

"I'm not asking you to forget your upbringing; I'm just urging you to temper your beliefs with tolerance and love. Why don't you sail away with me tonight, and we'll find a real preacher and marry, and then come back here and live happily ever after."

"We can't. We're too far apart, Gerrick. We're too different."

"We can work it out, Cait."

"It's impossible. If you want to stay in the islands, you'd be far better suited to someone like . . . Ilima. She wouldn't try and change you—or try and change the way the islanders think and live."

"What in hell is so wrong about the way they think and live? From what I've seen of them, the islanders are gentle, peaceful, kind, playful, generous . . . wait a minute, and I'll think of some more attributes. Even old Laanui isn't such a bad fellow; as you pointed out, he learned his greed from us. We're the sinners around here. I'd take Laanui over Amos Taylor or that sanctimonious Hiram Bingham

404

any day."

"Gerrick, stop it!" Caitlin pleaded, finally squirming away. Facing him with a wrathful glare, she warned, "If you don't stop, I'll be forced to leave, and John and Pikake's wedding will be spoiled. Is that what you want? Must you heedlessly trample *everyone's* feelings, not just mine?"

"Your feelings are the last ones I want to trample, Cait. Please, won't you at least talk to me?"

Her blue-gray eyes were wintry. "I've nothing to say to you. It's finished between us. The sooner you accept that, as I have, the happier you'll be."

He couldn't resist a last jab. *"Are* you happy, Cait? Can you look me in the eye and swear you're happy?"

Her chin trembled, and tears filled her eyes. "No, I can't—at least not yet. But I'm trying, Gerrick, and I'm going to go on trying. Somehow, some way, I'll learn to live without you. And I'll also learn to like myself again and to . . . to know where I'm going. I . . . I hope you also find peace within yourself."

"God's teeth!" Gerrick exploded, but anything else he might have said was drowned out by the sudden clapping of hands and happy shouts of the Hawaiians.

Gerrick glanced toward John and Pikake, who were throwing off the tapa cloth and rising from the ground where they had apparently lain down beneath the cloak for several moments.

"I would have thought you'd have found something more . . . gentlemanly to say," Caitlin remarked sadly. "Please excuse me while I go and congratulate the bride and groom."

Enraged and feeling helpless, Gerrick watched her go. If he couldn't reach her here, he couldn't reach her anywhere. Her mind and heart were closed against him, and nothing he could say seemed capable of opening them again.

What you need is a good tot of rum, old boy, he thought to himself, and leaving Erasmus to find his own way back to the luau, Gerrick turned on his heel and headed for his gig.

Chapter Thirty-Three

Caitlin picked at the pork, tasted the poi, and finally sat back and gave up on eating any of the abundant food provided for the wedding feast. She still felt guilty over attending the wedding, though every time she looked at John's and Pikake's radiant faces, she knew that the marriage was right and good, no matter what Brother Bingham said.

She wanted to leave but had no way of getting home, since none of the Hawaiians were as yet ready to depart in their outriggers. Her transportation problem was a complication she had not foreseen—nor had she guessed how difficult it would be to be near Gerrick again, and watch him sullenly sit and drink rum, all the while staring steadily in her direction.

She wondered if he realized how much he was drinking, and how, every time he lifted the cup to his lips, he was only increasing her certainty that they did *not* belong together. Half of Gerrick's crew were already loud and rowdy, a result of too many toasts to the bride and groom, and many of the Hawaiians—men, women, and children—were acting strangely, too, though Caitlin hadn't seen any save a few of the men quaffing the liquid from the barrel. She thought everyone seemed too bright-eyed and feverish, too bent on having fun and celebrating, but then perhaps, it was only because she herself was so gloomy and depressed, and also so unaccustomed to such frivolity.

Night had fallen several hours previously, and beneath the smoking torches, the faces and bodies of the Hawaiians seemed flushed, their eyes black and shining, some almost vacant-looking. Such primitive enjoyment of food, drink, and dancing made Caitlin feel uncomfortable; why must the islanders do everything to excess? she wondered.

The Hawaiian musicians began beating out a frenzied rhythm on their gourd drums, or *ipu hekes*, and almost as a single body, the islanders leapt to their feet and began dancing. Some were tripping and staggering as they did so, increasing Caitlin's suspicions that Gerrick's crewmen had been freely sharing their rum. She was disgusted and overwhelmed with guilt. Her father would have stopped this carousing long ago, but here she sat, mute as a stone, allowing the wedding feast to degenerate into an orgy. Before the night was over, Gerrick's sailors would probably be falling upon the women before her very eyes.

Caitlin peered through the smoke, looking for John, and finally saw him and Pikake, still seated in places of honor upon mats piled high with silken Chinese pillows. Leaning close to Pikake, John was whispering in her ear, but Pikake appeared half-dazed, as intoxicated as everyone else. John's florid face and too bright, heavy-lidded eyes gave evidence that he, too, had been drinking rum.

Caitlin bit her lower lip, uncertain what she ought to do. Perhaps she should appeal to Chief Laanui to call a halt to the celebratoin and bid everyone return home, if they were even capable of sailing their outriggers back to Hanalei. Caitlin spotted the chief lounging on the mats and his indolent, drunken appearance shocked her almost as much as John's and Pikake's. Laanui's face was red and puffy, his eyes vacant.

A spasm of alarm shot through her; what was going on here? Why did everyone seem so . . . so feverish? Even as her mind fastened on the word "feverish," several laughing islanders, arms about each other, staggered down the beach toward the water's edge.

"I am so hot—I am burning!" one woman cried, and tearing off her *pau*, she plunged into the surf.

It was not unusual for the islanders to go swimming, anywhere, anytime. Nonetheless Caitlin arose, her heart suddenly hammering. Weaving her way through the remaining throng of dancing, laughing, staggering Hawaiians and sailors, Caitlin made her way to John and Pikake.

"Pikake!" she cried, falling to her knees beside her friend.

"Tutu Caitlin! Is that you?" Pikake grinned lopsidedly. "I feel so . . . so funny. And my head hurts."

"Too much excitement," John said, grinning at Caitlin. "I think it's time my new wife went to bed, but she doesn't want to leave the *luau*."

"John, wait. Are you sure she isn't ill?" Caitlin placed her hand on Pikake's forehead. Her friend's skin was ominously warm. "When did this start, John?"

"When did what start?" John took a swallow from a gold-rimmed, porcelain cup and smilingly held it out to Caitlin. "Have some, Cait. Maybe it will soften that stern, disapproving look on your face. And maybe, if you get a little drunk, Gerrick can finally talk some sense into you."

"Put down that cup and pay attention, John! Your wife appears ill. Her forehead is hot enough to burn my palm, and she . . . she . . ." Caitlin grabbed Pikake's arms and carefully examined the flesh on the inside crook of her elbow. "Look at this! She's breaking out in a rash."

"A rash?" John peered at the small red spots dotting Pikake's inner arm.

"I'll bet her stomach is already covered with them. She must lie down, and you must keep her quiet."

A look of concern crept into John's eye. "It isn't serious, is it? Why, an hour ago, she was perfectly fine."

With growing panic, Caitlin studied her little friend. Pikake seemed to be growing sicker by the minute. Suddenly, her head tilted to one side, and she said thickly, "Tutu Caitlin? I want go swimming. The ocean will make me cool again. I am so hot, so very hot."

As she slumped to one side, John caught her, his eyes opening wide, as if he'd been shocked into sobriety. "Good

Lord, what's wrong with her? What's happening?"

Their attention caught onto the sounds coming from the darkened beach. Amid much laughter and groaning, more islanders were flocking to the sea and throwing themselves into the surf. To some, it would appear only an impromptu swimming party on a warm moonlit night, but Caitlin was so frozen with dread she could hardly answer. "John, I can't be sure, of course, but I think we've got an outbreak of measles on our hands."

"Thank God," John breathed in relief. "Measles aren't very serious. . . . Hell, I had them myself when I was a boy, and so did Gerrick. He got them first, and shortly thereafter, so did I."

"Not for *us* they aren't serious. But for the Hawaiians, measles are devastating—often fatal. I've heard of outbreaks that sweep through villages in a matter of hours, leaving hundreds dead and dying—so weak they can't help themselves or anyone else. Many die from drowning because the only way they know to relieve their fever is to go swimming. And all too quickly, they weaken and cannot even summon the strength to leave the water."

Horror spread across John's face as he protectively cradled Pikake in his strong arms. "But where does the outbreak come from? How does it start? And if this *is* measles, what can we do to stop it?"

"Strangers . . . the disease always starts with strange white men who come here, not realizing what they are bringing with them. Perhaps someone among the fortune hunters brought it. . . . Only now they are gone and will never know what they started. As for stopping it, there's not much we can do except keep the islanders calm and quiet—and *away* from the ocean. I do know of some local remedies for fever if we can find the plants at night . . ."

"Swimming . . ." Pikake pleaded, struggling in John's arms. "I want go swimming!"

"No, Pikake. You must lie down and stay quiet," John told her. "Don't worry. We'll take care of you. By God, *you* won't die from this awful thing."

"Have you seen Tutu Caitlin?" a woman's voice suddenly asked, and looking up, Caitlin saw Ilima swaying on her feet before them. "T—Tutu Caitlin, where is she?" The girl's hand went to her head. "Oh, it hurt so much. And I am so hot. If she comes, tell her I go swimming."

Caitlin scrambled to her feet. "Ilima, you have a fever, and you must *not* go swimming. Do you hear me? Stay away from the sea. Come lie down on the mats, and I will find something to ease your pain."

"No," the girl said stubbornly. "I go find Tutu Caitlin. She know what to do." Ilima lurched away before Caitlin could stop her.

"Get Gerrick," John commanded, rising with Pikake in his arms. "Tell him what's happening. . . . Lord in heaven, they're flocking to the sea like children on a holiday. The whole damn lot of them will drown."

Caitlin wasted not another moment. Gerrick looked startled to see her dashing toward him and shouting his name, and he was even more startled when she told him the cause of the sudden pandemonium and break up of the wedding celebration. At first, because of his expression of incredulity and astonishment, she thought he was too drunk to take charge. But within minutes, he began shouting orders for his men to gather. "Erasmus! Get down to the beach and tell those jackasses among the crew who've gone swimming with the islanders to get the hell out of the water and drag every last islander out with them—if they have to grab them by the hair to do so."

"Yes, Cap'n! Right away!" Erasmus bolted toward the beach, shouting at the top of his lungs. "Henderson! McIver! Get outa that water!"

"We'll clear away the food and have the sick lie down on the mats," Gerrick suggested, and Caitlin could have wept with gratitude that she wasn't facing this crisis alone. Gerrick seemed unaffected by the amount of rum he had drunk, and under the lash of his tongue, his crew members quickly sobered and began gathering up the remains of the feast.

"What do you suggest to lower their fevers?" His green

eyes probed her face. "Tell me what you need, and my men will get it, if we have to go up in the mountains with torches to light our way."

"Awa root," Caitlin replied promptly. "It's the easiest thing to find and is even cultivated. Chewing the buds will make them sleepy and bring down their fevers."

"Awa? Won't it also make them drunk?" Gerrick's question reminded Caitlin of the heady concoction made from the same plant and called by the same name.

"I wouldn't know about that," she sniffed. "The remedy for fever is chewing the buds. The awa plant grows in damp places in the forest. We should also look for ti leaves. I have seen these dipped in cold water and placed on the forehead to relieve headaches and elevated temperatures."

"I'll mount a search party at once."

"And I'll speak to Chief Laanui and have him place a *kapu* on swimming in the ocean until this is over. In time of crisis, the islanders may be more likely to obey the old ways than the new ones."

Along with Gerrick, Erasmus, John, and the crew of the *Naughty Lady*, Caitlin labored most of the night to check the outbreak of measles. As one islander after another broke out in a rash, her diagnosis became more certain. High fevers, sudden debilitating weakness, and delirium either preceded or accompanied the rashes. The treatment she devised consisted of encouraging the victims to lie down on the mats and chew awa buds, while she, Gerrick, or Erasmus placed damp ti leaves on their fevered foreheads and held gourds of fresh water to their parched lips. Gerrick's crew members, meanwhile, patrolled the beach and riverbank, keeping the victims from suddenly jumping up and dashing into the ocean or river.

Despite their diligent work, many of the islanders grew steadily weaker—and some became panicky, crying out their fear of dying and begging for the *kahuna* to come and drive away the evil spirits, the *unihipili*. Caitlin comforted them as best she could, for the *kahuna* himself was ill, as was Chief Laanui. She knelt beside the most frightened natives and prayed with them, reminding them of their

Chrsitian teachings—but not everyone would pray with her. One old man called continuously for Lono, and another begged for Pele's help. Yet another demanded sacrifices be made to Ku, whose wrath had surely fallen upon his once-beloved, but now wayward, children.

Caitlin's sense of failure and disappointment ran deep; after all the teachings of her father, herself, and even Amos Taylor posing as her uncle, the Hawaiians had slumped back into the dark beliefs and superstitions of their culture before the arrival of the missionaries. Even Pikake, over whom John hovered like some hulking, protective angel, murmured constantly of some god or goddess whose name Caitlin did not recognize.

Near dawn, the first death occurred. It was a child, and Caitlin wept as she closed the child's eyes and pried open the tiny fingers that had been tightly clutching her hand. Minutes later, a fat old woman breathed her last, and then a skinny, bony old man. Blinded by tears, Caitlin knelt beside a young woman who was having difficulty breathing. Recognizing Ilima, Caitlin gasped. The girl's lovely face was contorted in a grimace, and her lips mouthed a soundless plea.

Caitlin could feel the approach of a cold, fearful presence, and the hairs prickled on the back of her neck. Trembling, she burst into prayer. "Father, forgive this young woman her sins. Remember that she's just a child, with little knowledge of right and wrong. Spare her, please, so that she may live and learn more about You. Don't call her to account for her life before she's scarcely had a chance to live it."

Sitting down beside Ilima, Caitlin lifted the girl's head and cushioned it in her lap. She smoothed back Ilima's long, heavy, black hair. The scarlet blossom behind Ilima's ear was crumpled and dying, and Caitlin removed it and tossed it aside. She adjusted the ti leaf on Ilima's forehead and wished she knew what else to do for her. But Ilima's fate was now in God's hands, not hers; she had already plumbed the depths of her small store of knowledge.

As the sun rose behind the mountains, Gerrick came to

Caitlin and knelt down. "Cait, there are two outriggers headed this way—fishermen, I think. You'd better come and warn them not to venture ashore. If they do, they may fall ill—or even worse, carry the illness back to their own villages. I've already ordered my men to patrol the area and keep everyone on land away. If we're lucky, we can confine the outbreak to Wailua."

"Of course, I'll come. Will you look after Ilima?" Caitlin moved to rise, taking care to gently deposit Ilima's head upon the pandanus mats. "The next thing we'll have to do is move the sick under the palm trees, so the sun won't be beating down upon them. And food—we'll have to prepare food for those well enough to eat."

"You won't have to prepare anything for this one," Gerrick observed, feeling for Ilima's pulse. "She's dead, Cait."

"Dead!" Caitlin stared at the girl in shock. "No! She can't be!"

"Poor creature. I'll have Erasmus remove her body to the burial pit we've dug."

"Gerrick, no!" Ilima's laughing, voluptuous image filled Caitlin's mind; how could so vibrant a young woman have died so quickly?

Gerrick touched her hand, his green eyes sorrowing but compelling her to listen. "Cait, we've got to hurry before those fishermen come ashore. Forget Ilima. She's only one of many who will die this day. Now we've got to try and save others who as yet haven't been exposed."

"I'm coming," she said, wiping her eyes with the back of her hand. And rising to her feet, she followed Gerrick down to the beach.

The islanders in the canoes offshore apparently thought a party was still in progress, and they obviously wanted to join it. Grinning widely, they sent their outriggers skimming toward shore. Caitlin held Gerrick's hand so the surf wouldn't knock her down and waded out into water up to her waist. Then she cupped her hand around her mouth so her greeting wouldn't be blown away on the fresh morning wind.

"*Aloha!*" she called.

413

Demonstrating the typical Hawaiian expertise in handling watercraft, the men drew abreast of her and balanced off their oars and sails to hold the outriggers almost stationary.

"You mustn't come any closer," Caitlin warned in Hawaiian. "The islanders have all fallen sick, and some have died. It is the spotted sickness; you must stay away so you don't become sick yourselves."

The Hawaiians exchanged fearful glances, plainly having heard of the spotted sickness. News of any disaster or calamity spread rapidly throughout the islands, occasioning much gossip and speculation. Caitlin knew this and was counting on the islanders' fear to outweigh their curiosity and desire to witness the phenomenon with their own eyes.

Then one of the younger men spoke up, his voice carrying a note of belligerence. "If my brothers and sisters at Wailua are sick and dying, how is it that you *haoles* are not affected?"

His glance swept her and Gerrick accusingly, as if he suspected them of some treachery. Surprised by his hostility, Caitlin took careful note of his broad, attractive face, square shoulders, and hard, muscular body which his malo did nothing to hide. Beneath the shock of black hair sweeping his shoulders, his black eyes flashed anger and contempt; somewhere, sometime, he'd run afoul of white men and decided to hold it against all whites.

"Many of us *haoles* have already had the disease," Caitlin delicately tried to explain. "And those of us who haven't won't get as sick from it as you islanders do. Indeed, I doubt we'll even come down with it for another week or two."

She was reminded to take precautions for this possibility; after the outbreak had been brought under control, any among Gerrick's crew who had *not* had the disease must be quarantined. She herself must go into hiding, for *she* had never had measles.

The fishermen began talking among themselves, debating whether to ignore her warnings and go ashore, or hurry away as fast as they could. Most of them were craning their necks to see the beach, and looking back over her shoulder, Caitlin saw Erasmus and one of the other crew members carrying a limp body to the pit Gerrick had ordered dug.

When Erasmus and his companion tossed the body into the pit, the men all began talking at once, and the canoes rocked with the commotion of them standing and pointing fingers.

"Tell them again how dangerous it is for them to be here," Gerrick said. "Tell them they must go up and down the shoreline warning everyone to stay away."

"I'll have to scream to make myself heard," Caitlin observed.

"Then scream," Gerrick said. "I wish to hell I'd brought my pistol. Somehow I never have it when I really need it."

His mention of a firearm firmed Caitlin's determination to keep the situation under control. Again cupping her hands around her mouth, she shouted Gerrick's instructions.

When she had finished, the same belligerent young man leaned forward and studied her intently. "Aren't you the daughter of the Longneck who used to live at Hanalei?"

Caitlin nodded, thinking her admission would add more weight to her commands. "My father was Brother William Price. We have lived, worked, and taught among the islanders for many years."

"Then your uncle is *Makuakane* George," the young man noted with a curling lip.

Again, Caitlin nodded, at a loss to explain the true nature of her relationship with Amos Taylor. "*Makuakane* George is now dead," she informed the young man, who was looking angrier by the minute.

The man—or boy, as was more likely despite his stockiness—turned to his companions. "I once attended services conducted by *Makuakane* George. He said if the islanders did not bring him trade goods or help him find sandalwood in the mountains, he would ask the Christian God to punish us, to send disease and famine among us. He said the Christian God was already angry because we had not built Him a church of wood."

415

"He *never* said that!" Caitlin cried, deeply shocked. "If he had, I would have heard of it and stopped him."

The boy turned back to her, his black eyes scornful of her denial. "I did not see you there. But as the god, Kane, is my witness, that is what he said. I heard it with my own ears. The people were much afraid, especially after he warned us to tell no one of his threat or our suffering would be even greater. After that, many stopped coming to hear him preach, and now, his threat has come true. Either that, or the old gods are so angry with us for allowing the *opala haoles* to turn us away from them, that *they* are punishing us."

"You mustn't believe *any* of that nonsense!" Caitlin held out her hands entreatingly to the other men in the canoes, but their dark, suspicious glances betrayed their willingness to believe the worst. "The spotted sickness is a disease that can infect anyone. Whites, too! I believe it was white men who brought it here in the first place."

"So you *admit* you caused this to happen."

"No, I didn't say that; I only said—"

Before she could explain further, the young man interrupted, pointing at her wrathfully. "If my brothers and sisters are dying, it is *your* fault. You, too, wanted a church built of wood, and so did your father, as well as your uncle. Like the wicked *kahunas* of old, you have prayed the people into sickness, because they would not do what you wanted."

"What are you saying?" So upset by what she was hearing, Caitlin could not pause long enough to explain the accusations to Gerrick. Ignoring his questioning, alarmed expression, she argued hotly, "My father and I have always *loved* the islanders and wanted only what was best for them. If you do not believe me, ask Chief Laanui."

"Where is the great chief?"

"He . . . he is lying ill on the beach."

"While *you* remain healthy." The young man faced his companions, his face etched with bitterness. "I propose that we destroy these *haoles* and thereby destroy the spotted sickness they have caused."

"But Boki, we have not brought weapons, and if we go ashore, we ourselves may die," one man protested timidly.

The name "Boki" meant boss. It had once belonged to an early governor of Oahu, and Caitlin trembled to hear the young man called such, for it was a name commanding respect and obedience; the islanders would be much swayed by what Boki said or did.

"I swear to you we did not cause this calamity," she insisted. "Before the sickness broke out, this was a wedding feast, and everyone was celebrating. We aren't enemies, but dearest friends. The new husband is a white man who at this very moment is caring for his wife, a Hawaiian as close to me as a sister."

Caitlin had thought to reassure Boki, but the news of a mixed marriage had the opposite effect. Boki's nostrils flared in disapproval. "We will return to Hanamaulu and consult with the *kahuna* there. He is an old man, still true to the ancient ways and anxious to preserve them. He will say prayers to Ku for our protection against this wickedness, and we can then return and avenge the deaths of our brothers and sisters. Just as the first Kamehameha slew his enemies and lay them upon the altars in the old *heiaus*, we will slay all of you and offer your bodies in sacrifice."

"If you so much as step on shore, you will become infected with the spotted sickness," Caitlin warned, hoping their fear would yet win out over their hatred.

"Prepare yourself, daughter of the evil one. For *you* will be the first to die."

And having promised that, Boki signaled both canoes to sail away, which they quickly did. As the outriggers retreated, tacking against the wind, Gerrick took Caitlin's hand and led her toward shore.

"Thank God, they listened to you, Cait. For a while there, I thought they were refusing to leave."

"Oh, Gerrick . . ." Caitlin sighed. "How much you still have to learn of our language!"

And she then explained exactly what had happened.

417

Chapter Thirty-Four

After Gerrick had a chance to think about the situation and discuss it with John, he was adamant they should gather the crew, load Pikake into a gig, row out to the schooner, and leave Kauai until the epidemic had abated.

"If we aren't here, they can't attack us and may not even come ashore," he argued, his green eyes blazing, and a lock of chestnut hair falling across his forehead.

Caitlin longed to smooth back the wayward curl and cuddle in Gerrick's arms until she fell asleep; every movement reminded her of how tired she was, but she pushed these temptations aside and struggled to think rationally.

"Rather than flee," John was saying, "why don't we stand and fight? A few rounds of canister from the ship's long gun would blow them out of the water. Actually, we don't even have to hit them; one round just *short* of their outriggers might be sufficient to scare them away."

"Please don't talk of firing cannons at the islanders," Caitlin protested. "And don't talk of leaving either—unless it's without me. Someone must stay and convince Boki and his followers not to land. If we just leave, there will be no one to stop them. And the chances of the disease spreading will be greatly increased."

"You'll leave here if I have to clout you over the head and carry you aboard the *Naughty Lady*." Gerrick glared at her, his jaw set determinedly. "You were uncon-

418

scious the last time I rescued you in China, and frankly, it saved me a lot of trouble. I didn't have to ask your permission and risk having you refuse to come away with me."

Caitlin's cheeks flamed. She and Gerrick were speaking now because they had no choice. But that didn't mean all was forgiven and forgotten. She mustn't allow him to reestablish familiarity and communication. Pointedly giving her attention to John, she said, "I'm going to speak to Chief Laanui. If he isn't so sick he can't think, perhaps he'll have an idea of how to avert bloodshed besides running away and leaving the islanders to die unattended."

"Don't brand me a damn murderer!" Gerrick shouted. "I'd be willing to stay here and help them, but I refuse to put the lives of you, me, my crew, John, Pikake, and Erasmus in danger. And that's what we'd be doing if we stayed. What if they bring back more outriggers and outnumber us? That's how Cook died. Or don't you recall how the first white man to discover these islands was killed when he inadvertently aroused the tempers of these heathens?"

"I am well aware of how Captain James Cook died," Caitlin said stiffly. "This, however, is different."

"Like hell it is," Gerrick retorted. "I never before realized how primitive and superstitious these people really are."

"I thought you always considered them perfect—gentle as children, also sweet, innocent, and playful," Caitlin jibed.

"Trust you to remind me of that!"

John held up his hand in a conciliatory gesture. "By the time you two quit arguing, we could have a whole army of vengeful Hawaiians descending upon us in their outriggers. I've changed my mind; Gerrick's right. We should leave while we still can. They might take it into their heads to set fire to the schooner while we're still here on the beach; then we'd really be in trouble. . . . Besides, I think we should sail for Maui. There are plenty of isolated places there where we can hole up until we make sure none of *us* are going to get measles and pass the disease on to others."

"I had been worrying about that," Caitlin conceded. "I myself should be quarantined."

"And knowing that, you still want to stay here—so you can sicken and die alongside of your precious islanders."

Gerrick's voice dripped sarcasm, and Caitlin couldn't take it any longer. "What happens to me is my affair, not yours, Gerrick Scott! I'm not your wife, thank God, and I never will be . . ." Pausing to still her shaking voice, Caitlin turned to John and continued more calmly, "John, I'm going to see Chief Laanui now. I'll return shortly and help you prepare something to eat for Pikake. I'm pleased that her fever seems down this morning, but if she doesn't eat or drink, she'll only grow weaker and suffer a relapse."

"Thank you, Caitlin, I'd appreciate that. In the meantime, though, I'll have Erasmus and the crew prepare a store of fresh food, water, awa buds, and ti leaves, so that if we do have to make a fast escape, the islanders won't be entirely helpless. The stronger ones can help the weaker."

"As I said, *I* won't be leaving—but anything you do before *you* leave will be appreciated."

Ignoring Gerrick's scowl, Caitlin turned and marched down the beach. Each step away from Gerrick helped restore her equilibrium, and by the time she found Chief Laanui, her breathing was almost back to normal. To her amazement, the old chieftain was propped in a sitting position against a stack of Chinese pillows and anxiously surveying the scene of devastation and sorrow around him. Caitlin knelt down beside him, took his plump, clammy hand in hers, and said, *"Aloha,* old friend. How are you feeling?"

Laanui's cloak and helmet were gone, torn off in the throes of delirium that thankfully had now abated, and gone also was his proud authority and sly good humor. His childlike face and heavy body were covered with the measles rash, and his small, puffy eyes, encased in sagging flesh, were the saddest she had ever seen. "Not good, Tutu Caitlin, but I think maybe I will live. Not like so many of these other poor children. Why are my people so weak, and your people so strong? Why do we lose our way and die, while you live and prosper?"

Caitlin realized the old chief wasn't thinking only of the destruction caused by the measles, but of the collapse of his entire culture and civilization. He was old enough to remember how it had once been, before the coming of the missionaries, whalers, and traders, and even before the abolishment of *kapu* and the ancient ways. He could remember the first Kamehameha and Kamehameha's favorite wife, Kaahumanu. Caitlin recalled Laanui once telling her of his great friendship with Liholiho, or Kamehameha II, who, along with his wife, Kamamalu, had died of measles on a visit to London in 1824.

In the course of his lifetime, Laanui had witnessed the destruction of everything he had ever known. It wasn't a downfall caused by war or battles, but by something far stronger: new ideas. The foreign ideas accompanying the influx of strangers to these shores had been more powerful and compelling than the beliefs his people had always cherished, and now, he, too, had fallen victim to a strange disease against which he had no way of coping. So he sat silently upon the beach, his eyes filled with sadness, and his mouth slackened in defeat.

"I'm so sorry, Laanui," Caitlin said, and in that moment, she *was* profoundly sorry she had been a part of the changes the old chief had witnessed. "I never dreamed this could happen, and I fear the outbreak is not yet over. Some fishermen drew near the shore, and when I warned them away, they threatened to return and kill me—and all the whites who are here. They believe we are responsible. In a way, we are, but we have never meant any harm. And if those fishermen do return, they will also become ill and die. Can you think of any way to stop them?"

"Yes, Tutu." Laanui sighed regretfully and picked at the gold tassel on a red silk pillow. "You must sail away before they come."

"I meant some other way, Laanui. I cannot leave you to cope with this alone. If I did, and more of you died I'd never forgive myself."

"We will not all die, Tutu. I myself am now recovering, and soon, others will be well enough to help look after the rest. If you are worrying about how we shall manage, you must cease. I have been lying here watching all you've been doing, and I now know what must be done."

Caitlin tightly gripped the old man's hand. "Chief Laanui, I feel it is my duty to see you through this. You are my family, my brothers and sisters. I have no other. Don't send me away when I can finally repay you for the affection I've enjoyed all these years . . ."

"You are a very special woman, Tutu Caitlin. I think of you as a daughter, and if it pleases you to remain, then of course you must. But I do not think your husband will allow it."

"Gerrick is *not* my husband. I am ashamed to tell you that the ceremony in which I thought I had married him was no ceremony at all. It wasn't binding upon either of us."

Laanui's eyebrows lifted. "Did you not promise to cleave to him always, as the whites always do when they marry? And did he not promise to cleave to you?"

"Yes, but . . . but the promises meant nothing, for they were not made before a minister of our faith."

Looking confused, Laanui shook his head. "I do not understand how a promise can mean nothing. But then there is much about your beliefs I do not understand."

"One day, when this is all over, perhaps I can explain things better."

"Yes, and maybe this time I will be more ready to listen." Laanui slanted a questioning glance in her direction. "Captain Scott has not forgotten his promise to give me his ship, has he? Was that also a false promise? I guarded the Kalaulau Valley well, and no one has set foot in it."

"I'm certain he hasn't forgotten it, and no, it wasn't a false promise. If it was, I'll do all in my power to see that you get your ship."

"Good. Then let me rest awhile and think upon the

problem of the fishermen."

Laanui closed his eyes, and Caitlin left him. She spent the remainder of the morning with one eye on the horizon, watching for outriggers, and the other on Gerrick and his crew, who were making preparations for departure. She nursed Inamoo, the *kahuna*, and many others, prepared a soft mash of fruit for Pikake, and then searched the area for fresh coconuts to provide a nourishing, refreshing drink for others who might be ready for more than just water.

About midafternoon, Caitlin heard a distant pounding sound, carried by the wind from the direction of Hanamaulu. It was the sound made by wooden mallets pounding tapa cloth on a log. She was used to such constant pounding in Hanalei, but this time, a feeling of dread crept over her. None of the missionaries had yet figured out the code for how messages were transmitted through the tapping of the mallets, but it was a well-known fact that somehow, important news and messages *were* transmitted.

She had little doubt of what messages were now being sent; even before Chief Laanui called for her, she knew the pounding had something to do with the pending attack. A young woman informed her that Chief Laanui desired her presence, and she hurried to him and knelt down.

"What is it, old friend? What is happening?"

"You and your friends must go now," Laanui said. "Wailua will soon be under attack—both by land and by sea. All of Kauai has been informed of the sickness here, and *you* are being blamed. If you don't leave, they will kill you."

"Laanui, I don't care what happens to me. What is more important is that all those who come here will carry the sickness home to their own villages. Every man, woman, and child on the island is in danger."

"You must not worry, Tutu Caitlin. I have thought of a way to keep them from coming too close. But it will only work if you yourself are not here to tempt them with your presence."

"What is he saying?" Gerrick asked from behind her.

Caitlin turned to see his tall figure looming over her, his face creased with worry and grim foreboding. "He . . . he's saying we must leave at once."

"My opinion, too. And also John's. We don't like the sound of those drums."

"They aren't drums," Caitlin said. "They're tapa mallets beating on logs. But you're right about the messages they're sending. The entire population of the island is being urged to come here and destroy us."

"Then we're leaving now, Cait. This very minute. Say good-bye, and let's get the hell out of here."

Caitlin hid her face in her hands. It had become impossible even to rise to her feet. Grief and hopelessness had rendered her immobile; the sudden onslaught of despair sweeping over her was even worse than it had been when she faced a lifetime as the concubine of a sadistic mandarin. "I won't leave them, Gerrick. I'd rather die than leave them. They are as helpless as children. While I still live, I might be able to warn those fishermen away, to make them understand the danger . . ."

Iron-hard hands suddenly seized her and hauled her upright. "You're coming with me, Cait. And you're coming *now*."

"No!" she screamed, fighting to break free.

"Take her . . ." Laanui said plainly in perfect English. "And do not return to Kauai until you see my feathered cloak and helmet flying from a staff atop the mountain at Hanalei."

Caitlin's astonishment at the chief's linguistic ability, heretofore unknown to her, was overshadowed only by her rage as Gerrick began dragging her away. She dug her heels in the sand and resisted with all her might. "I won't go! You can't make me!"

"Forgive me, Cait, but you don't give me any choice."

Calmly, Gerrick drew back his fist. Caitlin saw the blow coming, but couldn't duck fast enough. The lower half of her face exploded in pain, and her head snapped back. Stars whirled in the sudden blackness before her eyes. She knew she was losing consciousness, and with her last breath of awareness managed to gasp, "You *bastard!*"

And then she felt herself crumpling and slipping into a deep black void.

"At least, I didn't break her jaw," Gerrick reminded John and Erasmus. "If I hadn't punched her, she'd be dead by now and probably lying on some old stone altar as a sacrifice to one of their bloodthirsty pagan gods."

"Her face is still black and blue," John reminded him, his dark eyes cold.

"And she ain't smiled once since it happened," said Erasmus. "We been anchored here for more'n a week, and she hardly even talks, not even t' Pikake."

By "here," Erasmus meant off the shore of Maui, along one of its wildest, most uninhabited coastlines. A jagged coral reef separated them from the island, but occasionally, Gerrick would send a few men in a longboat through a narrow channel to the rocky beach where they could gather fruit and water. Neither Caitlin nor any of the crew had come down with measles, but her mental and emotional state had him greatly worried.

"Why don't you tell me something I don't know, gentlemen?" he asked his friends. "Better yet, why don't you tell me what I can do about Caitlin's unhappiness?"

"I ain't got the foggiest notion," Erasmus admitted. "But I sure wish you'd do somethin'. It ain't right for a lass as sweet and kind as she is t' be so miserable."

"I suppose I could always jump overboard and feed myself to the sharks. That might please her." Gerrick leaned on the ship's railing and surveyed the ever-sparkling depths of the ocean. In the distance, Maui's lush green beauty beckoned, the cloud-kissed summit of Haleakala serene and mysterious beneath the rose-tinged morning sky.

"Why don't you take her ashore, Gerrick? Take her somewhere the two of you can be alone. Talk to her. Tell her you love her." John's voice was gentle, not nearly as condemnatory as his eyes. "She's lost so much. The people for whom she and her family sacrificed themselves nearly killed her. And *you* haven't treated her very well either."

"I've tried talking to her and telling her I love her," Gerrick protested. "But thus far everything I say has fallen on deaf ears. I doubt she can think of anything except what's probably been happening on Kauai."

"We couldn't help what happened there," John said. "Remind her of that. If those damn fool fishermen showed up with their friends, they're likely dead by now. And if they are, it's their own damn fault. . . . We'll never know what happened until we go back. But I say it's still too soon. Pikake's been worried to death about Inamoo, but I've told her we have to wait at least another week before we dare return to Hanalei and see if the old chief has hung out his feathered cape and helmet."

"You're right, me boy. It's way too soon to go back," Erasmus agreed.

Gerrick listened to his friends discuss the situation, but he never took his eyes from the summit of Haleakala. He had wanted very much to climb the dormant volcano the last time he'd been here; something about it awed and excited him. He felt irresistibly drawn to its majestic heights. What revelations awaited him there? What scenic vistas and heart-stopping beauty?

"Pack me a couple blankets, a water skin, and some food, Erasmus," he heard himself say. "I've just thought of the perfect place to take Caitlin."

"Where's that?" John asked.

"To the top of Haleakala," Gerrick replied. "If she can't discover peace of mind there, I doubt she can discover it anywhere."

"But what if she won't go, lad?" Erasmus inquired, frowning.

Feeling suddenly hopeful, Gerrick grinned. "Well, I punched her once; I suppose I could punch her again. Or at least threaten her with it."

"You punch her again, and I'll pound you into a bowl of poi," John muttered.

"Relax, John. Just worry about keeping Pikake well

and happy. Leave my stubborn Caitlin to me."

Caitlin paused in her climbing to catch her breath. She hadn't wanted to accompany Gerrick on this exhausting trek up the side of Haleakala. But he had threatened and browbeaten her into it. Now, they had been climbing for two whole days and had spent the previous night shivering beneath their thin blankets. The higher they climbed, the colder it became. Of course, had she been willing to allow Gerrick to hold her in his arms all night, she might have been warmer. But she hadn't been willing. Physical intimacy no longer attracted her. She felt dead inside and could not imagine anything or anyone ever again fanning a spark of life or desire in her.

"Look at that view, Cait! It's magnificent." Seeing that she had stopped, Gerrick had walked back to her and was pointing down the mountainside.

Behind and below them, the island lay spread like a chief's cloak of such fantastic design and color that it defied words to describe it. On either side of the narrow neck of the island, the sea was a burning blue—the same color as the sky, except that the sky was filled with luminous, puffy clouds, some drifting below them as well as above.

"Yes, Gerrick, the view is magnificent," she agreed obediently, but in her heart, the stunning view barely touched her.

She had no wish to stand exclaiming over it and turned away long before Gerrick left off admiring the sun-dappled landscape of greens, oranges, reds, bronzes, and blacks. A gray and white striped, black mottled bird, the size of a chicken, darted past her feet and disappeared between some rocks.

"What was that?" Gerrick asked, falling into step beside her.

"I believe it's called a *nene* bird," Caitlin said, offering no more information than absolutely necessary.

"I've never seen a bird like it, but there must be hundreds

of them up here; something is making that chirping sound."

Caitlin trudged on in silence, Gerrick adjusted the pack strapped to his broad back and followed. "The air is so thin and cold, it's getting difficult to breathe," he observed. "And walking through wisps of clouds is quite an unnerving experience."

They were approaching a puff of cloud now, and for several seconds, Caitlin felt entirely alone. The cloud wisps snaked around her ankles and her skirt, and she was suddenly chilled and extremely glad of her old, long-sleeved, high-necked gown that had been stowed away in Gerrick's cabin—and glad also for her shawl. For the first time in the islands, she really needed it.

Gerrick grinned at her as they exited the patch of fog. "It feels as if we're trespassing in the domain of the gods, doesn't it? What does Haleakala mean?"

"The House of the Sun," Caitlin replied. Unwillingly, she remembered the story of the god Maui, who lassoed the sun, using one of his sister's pubic hairs, and held it prisoner in Haleakala crater, so that his mother might have more hours of daylight in which to pound tapa cloth.

If Gerrick did not remember the story from Pikake's telling of it to John during their first trip to Maui, he would enjoy hearing it now. But Caitlin clamped her lips together, loath to share anything with Gerrick. There was no sense in it when they had no future together, and as soon as she could, she would leave him and return to the missionary life in Hanalei.

"Soon we should be at the crater," Gerrick said, tilting back his head and looking toward the summit.

Then he reached down, plucked some buttercups growing in a rocky crevice and held them out to her. At the lower elevations, the bright flowers had been everywhere, providing a yellow carpet to walk upon, and besides these, there were trees abloom with every color in the rainbow.

"No, thank you," she said. "If I want flowers, I can pick all I need on the way back down."

Gerrick crumpled the buttercups in his hand and let

them fall. They continued walking, each lost in his and her own thoughts, as they passed through another patch of cloud. Their footsteps echoed eerily on the crunchy ground. The reddish, rocky soil was giving way to black cinder, and the landscape was steadily becoming more barren and desolate. A vast silence now enfolded them, and clouds drifted so low they brushed the tops of their heads.

"Cait, stop." Gerrick grabbed her arm. "Look behind you."

Sighing her irritation, she turned woodenly. The view was even more breathtaking than it had been before. The sun shafting the clouds had created a heavenly spectacle in which *they* were the god and goddess looking down upon the distant earth. Below them were endlessly changing patterns and colors as the clouds swept majestically across the island of Maui.

Despite herself, Caitlin breathed in sharply, awed by nature's sumptuous display. Nearby, she spotted a strange plant—a spiky, silvery-looking ball she had seen nowhere else in the islands. Gerrick saw where she was now looking and commented softly, "Incredible, isn't it? It feels as if we're standing at the very top of the world. Even the plants are different. *I* am different . . . exalted and at the same time humbled. I wish we could stay here forever."

Caitlin started to say, "Me, too . . ." but then snapped instead, "Don't include me in your plans. If you want to stay, you'll have to stay by yourself. I believe we've finally reached the top. There's the crater over there. That means that tomorrow *I* can start the climb down again."

She left Gerrick looking much chagrined and walked toward a jut of rock from whose height the crater could better be seen. But when she had climbed it, she discovered that though the crater *was* visible, cut into the mountain-top like a huge depression made by a giant's thumb, it was also filled with clouds—an ocean of fluffy white clouds. Caitlin was reminded of piled goose feathers stretching for miles and miles.

When she tired of standing and staring, she climbed down from the rock and helped set up camp. In silence, she ate the dried meat and fresh fruits Gerrick handed her. And in silence, she drank from the water skin and then wrapped herself in a blanket and lay down upon the hard cinders. The air was cold, still, and quiet, and she hoped it would stay that way through the night. At this elevation, a wind would be cutting, making sleep impossible and possibly freezing them where they lay.

The sun was dropping low on the horizon, and aching with weariness, she closed her eyes; by the time the sun had set, she intended to be fast asleep.

A short time later, Gerrick suddenly said, "Caitlin, for God's sake, come watch this sunset. You'll never again see another like it. The colors! Red, orange, purple, violet . . . Open your eyes and at least look at the sky. If you want a sense of God and religion, this is as close on earth to Him as you or I or anyone will ever get."

Caitlin squeezed her eyes tightly shut. Now was a fine time for Gerrick to finally discover God—and how dare he presume to introduce *her* to the Almighty!

"Caitlin, please . . ."

Caitlin rolled over on her side, causing a great crunching of cinders. Extending one hand, she tugged the edge of the blanket over her head. "Leave me alone, Gerrick. I'm exhausted."

"Cait, damn it! Come and watch this. Come share it with me."

"Good night, Gerrick," she said firmly, and he did not ask her again.

Chapter Thirty-Five

When Caitlin awoke, it was still dark and icy cold—too cold to go back to sleep. Looking for Gerrick, she sat up. He was still rolled in his blanket a short distance away. The stars were fading, and the moon had almost set; she guessed the hour to be shortly before dawn. Glad to have a few moments of privacy, she arose and attended to her personal needs. With her hair brushed and her clothes straightened, she wrapped the blanket around herself and climbed the jutting rock to await the sunrise.

Below her, lustrous clouds still filled the volcano's huge crater. Stars hanging near its rim winked with jeweled brightness. The silence stretched into infinity, but Caitlin did not feel alone. As Gerrick had done, she sensed a divine presence. The barren, beautiful landscape bore the imprint of a Being whose attributes and personality she could only guess at and wonder about. She had thought herself close to her Creator, and as knowledgeable as anyone about Him.

Now she realized she knew nothing; she was but an ignorant, struggling, insignificant particle in the grand order of things. How dare she presume to teach or preach to anyone? How dare she judge Gerrick and find him wanting? Here, atop the world, her vision was the clearest it had ever been. She could see the earth and all the universe: the land, sea, stars, and moon. She could look into her own dark heart and finally understand its most secret yearnings . . . yearnings that were all for Gerrick. No matter what he had done or how he had hurt her, she loved him. And he loved her. When all was said and done, what else mattered?

Along the eastern horizon, a faint smear of purple heralded the dawn. Waiting, Caitlin held her breath. The purple heightened into a deep rose color, and the nearest clouds blushed the same vivid hue. That was all the warning there was. Suddenly, a stiletto-thin line of gold cut the eastern sky. The line became a thick, bright wedge splitting the blackness. In its radiance, it was blinding.

As the sun soared over the crater's rim, the clouds assumed fantastic shapes and colors, as if a playful god had splashed paint all around. And as the clouds slowly drifted apart, Caitlin saw the rich and varied coloration of the crater itself, revealed in brilliant splashes of yellow, black, gray, red, brown, and purple. Dazzling light bathed the House of the Sun, and Caitlin counted nine tall cinder cones rising from the crater floor.

Wisps of cloud played hide and seek among the cones, and then the cloud masses rolled together again, constantly shifting and changing, snaking across the crater toward her, fleeing the reach of the rising sun. Caitlin felt a mist on her face, finer than rain, yet pervasive enough to dampen her cheeks, hair, and clothing. She closed her eyes a moment, and when she opened them, a rainbow was arcing over the crater, each color shimmering and pure.

In the center of the rainbow stood a solitary figure, a wavering apparition. When Caitlin moved, it moved. She blinked in disbelief, and the figure disappeared—but the rainbow lingered several moments. At last, the glorious reds, greens, blues, and purples began to fade, and tears rolled down Caitlin's cheeks. Even to herself, she could not explain why she was crying, except that the beauty of the sunrise and the rainbow had stirred something deep inside her that had been lying dormant and half-dead. Now her love for Gerrick was once again a vibrant, living thing—and she knew what she must do to gain the happiness so long eluding her.

A slight sound behind made her turn. Gerrick was

standing there. How long he'd been there, she didn't know, but he came toward her, holding out his arms. She never hesitated, but flew into his embrace. He was trembling as he hugged her; long shudders wracked his frame. He, too, was weeping, overcome by emotion and the joy of their reunion. Their tears mingled and ran together.

At the same moment, they leaned back and gazed into each other's eyes. Caitlin could not have spoken if her life depended on it. But no words were necessary. She read Gerrick's feelings as plainly as if they were written in ink on his forehead. He loved her. He was sorry he had deceived her. He wanted to marry her. He yearned for her love.

"Forgive me," was all he said, and they were the two sweetest words she had ever heard.

"Only if you can forgive me," she whispered. "Oh, Gerrick, I've been such a fool . . ."

"Hush," he said, placing a finger on her lips.

He took her hand and began leading her down the face of the rock. The morning sun was warm on their shoulders, its golden light a blessing and a benediction.

Three days later, they were married in the front room of Clarissa and William Richards's house in Lahaina. The Spauldings had neither been informed of the wedding nor invited, and in addition to the Richards family, John, Pikake, and Erasmus were the only witnesses. The ceremony was quiet and subdued, partly because Caitlin and Gerrick wanted it so, and partly because everyone involved felt the awkwardness of the situation.

Afterward, Clarissa Richards took Caitlin aside and said in a mothering tone of voice, "This time, my dear, you are truly married. I just hope you haven't made a mistake like your little friend, Pikake. You know she has erred most grievously and will doubtless have to suffer for her foolishness and sinfulness."

Despite her own inner happiness, Caitlin bristled. "I know you do not approve of their marriage or the manner of it, Clarissa, but John and Pikake will have a wonderful life together. As will Gerrick and I. None of us needs your approval; the love we have for each other is all we really need. Remember the Bible admonition: "And now abideth faith, hope, and charity, these three; but the greatest of these is charity."

Clarissa had the grace to look ashamed. "Yes, well, I hope everything works out for all of you. We will pray for you, Sister Caitlin."

"Pray also for all my friends on Kauai. If only I knew they had survived the measles epidemic, I could relax and enjoy my wedding night."

At the mention of the night to come, Clarissa's mouth pursed. Primly, she looked away. Smiling at the woman's inability to acknowledge reality, Caitlin hugged her. "Before I crawl between the sheets on our cabin bed, I'll say my prayers, Sister Clarissa."

"The Lord did command us to be fruitful and multiply," Clarissa said tentatively, struggling not to frown when she said it.

"Then we'll try very hard to obey that command."

"What's so funny, Cait?" Gerrick asked, coming up and slipping an arm around her waist.

"Oh, nothing. I'll explain it later."

They took their leave of the Richards as soon as they could escape Clarissa's belated hospitality. The plump smiling woman and her lean, proper, serious-faced husband provided tea and cakes in apologetic abundance, urging John and Pikake especially to eat heartily.

"I must learn how to make cakes!" Pikake trilled as she went out the door, unabashedly stuffing her mouth with her fourth one and then licking her fingers.

Owing to John's solicitous care, Pikake had completely recovered from her bout with measles and was once again so radiantly happy and so obviously in love with her new husband that Clarissa's face softened whenever she looked at them—despite her misgivings.

"Next time you come to Lahaina, you must come visit me, and I will teach you how," Clarissa said. At a disapproving glance from her husband, she added, "Well,

I don't give a fig what anyone thinks, William. If the girl wishes me to teach her domestic skills, I shall do so. After all, maybe it's time we reconsidered our policy against mixed marriages."

It was a small victory, considering the opposition that remained, but Caitlin felt greatly heartened. She did not have to fake her fondness for Clarissa as she bade her a warm good-bye. "Thank you for everything!" she cried, waving as Gerrick took her other hand and all but dragged her toward the waterfront and the ship.

"Will you please hurry, Mrs. Scott?" he growled under his breath. "Mac is so impatient to get you alone at last, that I fear I can no longer control him."

"Counsel him to patience," Caitlin whispered back. "For we still have many things we must discuss before I can once again consider us a married couple."

"What? We're *already* a married couple; this time, I've got the papers to prove it."

"The marriage isn't yet consummated," Caitlin corrected, mimicking Clarissa's primness. "And before it is, we need to reach some understandings."

"What understandings?" Gerrick glared at her suspiciously, but Caitlin only walked faster.

"You'll see," she promised. "Just as soon as we reach the privacy of our cabin on the *Naughty Lady*."

Erasmus and the crew cheered when Caitlin and Gerrick arrived on board the ship and Gerrick announced, "We've really done it now, lads. We're as married as married can be."

He ordered the ship to set sail immediately, and also allowed a cask of rum to be broken open. But he didn't linger on deck to sample any himself. Caitlin heard him speaking quietly to John and Erasmus. "Look after things, will you? My new wife and I are going to our cabin now, and any man who disturbs us will first be keelhauled and then made to walk the plank."

"Rather harsh punishment for such a minor offense, isn't it?" John commented.

"Not as I see it. Keelhauling and walking the plank perfectly fit the crime." Gerrick winked at John and hurried to Caitlin's side. "Come along, sweetheart. I'm anxious for our *discussion.*"

The way he emphasized *discussion* made John and Erasmus roll their eyes at each other, and Caitlin entered their cabin with her cheeks aflame. Before the door had even closed behind them, she rounded on Gerrick. "You think this all very amusing, but to me, it's deadly serious. The last time I married you—or thought I had—I made the mistake of leaving our future entirely to chance. I asked few questions, and the ones I did ask, I allowed you to set aside. Now, I demand some answers!"

"Why, what answers are you looking for?" Gerrick came toward her, divesting himself of jacket and shirt as he did so.

The sight of his bare chest, carpeted in chestnut curls, distracted Caitlin, but she crossed her arms in front of her breasts and eyed him sternly. "I want to know what you intend to do now that we're married."

"Do? Why I intend to kiss and fondle every inch of your soft, silky body. I intend to ravish you—tenderly but thoroughly—from head to foot."

His words unleashed a flood of erotic images in Caitlin's mind: Gerrick sliding his hand down her naked back. Gerrick burying his face between her breasts. Gerrick poised above her and parting her thighs.

"I meant do with our lives," she said shakily. "I presume you've obtained the trade rights to the sandalwood. What are your plans for harvesting it? How do you intend to spend the profits? Where will we live in the meantime? And what will we do when you've finished?"

Sighing, Gerrick pulled a chair out from the table and sat down on it. "Come sit on my knee," he invited. "At least you can be comfortable while I explain everything to you."

"I . . . I think I had better remain standing," Caitlin said, afraid that such proximity to Mac might make Celia clamor for attention.

"All right. I'll make it brief but accurate. I *did* obtain

the trade rights from Kamehameha, but he demanded half the profits in exchange—"

"*Half!* Why that's outrageous. I'll speak to him and demand he take less."

Gerrick grinned and shook his head. "You can try, my love. I certainly won't stop you. I also convinced the king to allow me to harvest the wood in my own quiet, secretive way, so as not to create a panic and cause hundreds of fortune hunters to invade the island—bringing with them their diseases."

"Oh, Gerrick, that's wonderful! Perhaps Chief Laanui can help with that."

"I'm hoping so. With the profits we make from selling the wood in Canton, John must receive his share and pay back my father's friend who put up the money to purchase Pikake at the auction."

"Of course," Caitlin agreed. "That would only be fair."

"And after that, I intend to spend what's left building a school on Kauai—so the islanders can all learn to read and write, and hopefully, overcome their ignorance and superstition."

Caitlin took a step closer to Gerrick, so stunned she could barely speak. "Do . . . you really mean it, Gerrick? You would use your share of the profits to build a school?"

"I don't plan to teach in it though, Caitlin. That's your job—which you may pursue with my blessing, provided it doesn't interfere with our family life. When our own children come along, you'll have to find someone else to take over—or at least, you'll have to reduce the number of hours you spend there. I wouldn't want my children neglected while their mother teaches someone else's children. . . . Oh, hell. I'll leave all that to you. I know you won't deprive our babies."

"*Our babies . . .*" Caitlin murmured, savoring each word. "But, Gerrick . . . what will *you* do? You can't be a trader anymore. You promised to give the *Naughty Lady* to Laanui."

Gerrick tilted back his chair, neatly balancing it on two legs. "I do intend to give the ship to him—but not quite yet. First, I need it to transport the sandalwood to Canton.

While in Canton, I'll fill the hold with trade goods for the return trip to the islands. I filled it this time—with tea, silk, porcelain, and so on."

"But where are these things now?" Caitlin remembered the silk pillows and chinaware at Pikake's wedding feast.

"They were all unloaded yesterday. This morning, a fellow named Nate Hampstead began making the arrangements to have them shipped to the mainland—for a small share in the profits, of course. He is also arranging for me to lease three other ships to accompany the *Naughty Lady* to China with the sandalwood. Using my father's contacts there, I can procure the finest goods at the lowest prices and earn myself and John a tidy sum for investing in a business opportunity we have in mind."

"What business opportunity?"

"Sugar cane," Gerrick said calmly. "We think Hawaii might have a great future in raising and processing cane into raw sugar."

"G—Gerrick . . you seem to have done a wonderful job figuring all this out."

He smirked triumphantly, preening like a cat beneath the compliment. "One thing I've never lacked is the ability to think big. One day, the Scott-Reynolds Sugar Company will be a well-known name in the islands and around the world."

"Oh, Gerrick . . ." Caitlin breathed softly, for suddenly she had a vision. They would raise sugar cane near the Hanalei Valley, atop a gently rolling hill, and live in a long white house with a *lanai* going all the way around it. Below them, nestled in the valley, would be the school—and the church with a white steeple. Fields of cane would surround the house and gardens, behind them would rise the mist-shrouded mountains, and below would lie the turquoise sea—sparkling in the sun.

"Yes, I can picture it," she said, the dream growing ever more vivid.

In her mind's eye, the door to the white house opened, and children ran out and raced down the hill. Their chestnut curls were blowing in the tradewinds, and they joined other children from another house nearby. These youngsters had black hair and black eyes; they were island children—no, they were the children of John and Pikake, playing together and growing up together, in a land where the color of one's skin, hair, or eyes had ceased to matter.

Caitlin hurried to Gerrick and almost knocked him over, throwing her arms around him. "I can picture it all, Gerrick . . . the house, the cane fields, the school, the church . . ."

"I never said anything about a church." Gerrick gazed up at her, his expression half-alarmed.

"Oh, but there *must* be a church, a place to worship on Sundays, where all the islanders from miles around can come and pray and sing together. And what about your family in New England? They must come and visit us. They must be here when the church is dedicated."

"I *had* wanted to send for my father," Gerrick said. "To live with us."

"He can have his own private wing in the house!" Caitlin bubbled. "And we'll have a nursery wing, too . . . and you and I must have our own suite of rooms. And we need a place for guests—yes, a special guest house! And small, pretty houses for the workers who will help us in the cane fields."

"My God," Gerrick muttered. "Do you realize how much all of this is going to cost?"

"We can do it, Gerrick!" Caitlin went down on her knees beside him. "I'll help you plant and harvest cane and do whatever it is one does with cane to make it into sugar. We can plant rice, too—and taro, and bananas . . ."

"Aren't you forgetting mangoes?"

"Oh, of course, mangoes!"

Gerrick reached over and grabbed her, hauling her into his lap. "But, of course, we'll never be too busy for *this* . . ." He pressed his lips against her smiling mouth.

Laughing, she turned her head. "You're right, Gerrick. I'll always have time for this . . . time set aside especially for Mac and Celia."

He reigned kisses down upon her face, neck, and shoulders, tearing at her dress to bare her flesh to his seeking mouth. "You'd better have time for Mac right now. Because he can't wait another minute, Cait."

Cradling her in his arms, he rose and carried her to the bed. But before he lowered her upon it, he paused and gazed impishly into her eyes. "Before we consummate this marriage, is there anything else you wish to discuss?"

"Yes," Caitlin whispered. "I wish to say I love you, Gerrick Scott, and I'm going to spend the rest of my life loving you."

"And I love you, Cait. God, how I love you! You know I'm not a religious man, and I probably never will be. . . . But when I hold you in my arms, I know exactly what the Creator intended for me—it's loving you. And to make sure I do what He wants, He's given me an early taste of heaven, a teaser as it were, to keep me on the straight and narrow."

"Heaven? You've had a taste of heaven? You've never told me this, Gerrick. Why, what is it like?"

Gerrick gently deposited her on the bed and lay down beside her. "Close your eyes, sweet wife, and you'll find out for yourself. I'll *take* you to heaven."

She did close her eyes and then teased smilingly, "Well, I'm waiting."

He rolled over on top of her and began kissing her relentlessly. The journey began, and Caitlin wrapped her arms around Gerrick and surrendered herself to his expert leadership. Heaven did not seem far; indeed, she suspected it was just around the next twist in the path. Ahead of them, on either side, the jungle's depths beckoned. Ferns and orchids lined their way, and a tinkling waterfall could be heard in the distance. The scent of plumeria drew them onward.

This was a journey she would take many times, she realized, as she had already taken it before . . . but each time would be new and different, special and exciting. That was how it was when you loved someone as much as she loved Gerrick. The journey would always be magical . . . and it would never, ever end . . . not until the end of time. Not until the end of eternity.

Epilogue

As the *Naughty Lady* nosed into Hanalei Bay, Caitlin stood anxiously at the railing. Their homecoming both thrilled and terrified her. She did not know what to expect. Would they be greeted as old friends—or as enemies who had caused death and sorrow? How many of the islanders were still alive?

On shore was a group of fishermen mending nets. Already, they were looking up and pointing to the ship. Their excited voices carried across the water, but individual words and phrases all ran together. Gerrick, John, and Pikake came to stand beside her.

"Well, they know we're here. They're running for their canoes," John informed everyone unnecessarily. "And now someone is blowing a conch shell to alert all the villagers."

As the mournful sound echoed over the pounding of the surf, Pikake entwined her fingers in Caitlin's and squeezed them. "Don't worry, Tutu Caitlin. My people all love you. They only wish to welcome us, not do us harm."

Behind them, the crew was silently gathering, weapons at the ready. Caitlin had objected to this, but Gerrick had been adamant; they must take precautions—just in case a mood of fear and hostility still prevailed.

"Here comes Laanui." Gerrick nodded toward the tall, portly old chieftain lumbering down the beach and entering a canoe. "Where's his cape and helmet?"

441

"There!" Caitlin pointed to the items they had all forgotten in their excitement. The crimson-feathered cape and gold helmet were fluttering in the breeze from the top of a pole planted on the nearest mountaintop.

Joy swelled in her bosom; now she knew it was all right. They were welcome. And the islanders' happiness at seeing them was readily apparent in their smiling faces and shouted greetings.

"*Aloha!*"

"Tutu Caitlin, *aloha* and welcome home!"

"Pikake, is that really you beside that handsome *haole?*"

"Look over here, Tutu Caitlin! It's me—one of your old students. Have you returned to resume teaching us?"

"Where have you been, Tutu Caitlin? We have missed you so much!"

It was as if the measles epidemic had never taken place—or was so minor as to be easily forgotten. Emotion clogged Caitlin's throat as she smiled and waved back at everybody. In every direction, canoes and outriggers were racing toward them, their inhabitants laughing, singing, and calling out to others to join them. In one of the canoes was Inamoo, madly waving to Pikake.

"Hide those weapons!" Gerrick barked as the first canoe bumped into the ship's bow.

Three men and two chattering, half-naked girls wearing flowers began climbing up the rigging. "Tutu Caitlin! Tutu Caitlin is home!" they cried.

Arriving on deck, they all ran to Caitlin, and there was much hugging and nose-rubbing. Others, including Inamoo, soon reached the ship, and the deck began to fill with bodies. Gerrick's crew members circulated among the lovely island women, trying out their awkward Hawaiian. After a long embrace with her brother, Pikake chattered nonstop in Hawaiian, and Caitlin lapsed into it also, forgetting that Gerrick and John could understand only if the language was spoken slowly.

Finally, Gerrick elbowed his way to Caitlin's side. "Laanui is here," he whispered.

Immediately, she broke away from the crowd around

her and went to the old chief's side. "Laanui, my dear, dear friend!"

Tearfully, they embraced.

"It is good you have returned home, Tutu. We have done nothing but play like children and watch for you, ever since we returned from Wailua . . ."

"The spotted sickness . . ." Caitlin began, but then she stopped, diverted by an even more pressing question. "Laanui, why have I never heard you speak such perfect English before? You just spoke it again, now . . . but prior to the last time we were together, you always pretended you spoke and understood very little."

"Ah, Tutu . . ." Laanui's childlike face creased in apologetic smiles. "Forgive an old man his tricks. It is only that I discovered I would learn much more about the whites if they thought I could not understand them."

"You were very naughty to have deceived me so."

"I beg your pardon, Tutu. Now that my speaking ability is no longer a secret, you must continue teaching me the *palapala*, for I do not write as well as I speak."

"I'll gladly teach you the *palapala*—in the new school my husband is going to build."

"The new school? Your new husband?" Grinning widely, Laanui turned to Gerrick. "I knew as soon as I met you that you were a kind, good man—and the right *kane* for this *wahine*."

"How did you know that?" Gerrick questioned, one eyebrow lifting.

"This I never tell. This is another secret. And I also know that you will have many long, happy years in Kauai. You will live here always and be part of the island's new beginnings. Your children and grandchildren will be born here. They will play with *my* grandchildren and great grandchildren. And you will teach us *haole* ways so that we are not confused and destroyed by new ideas that come to the island."

The chief's predictions were so close to Caitlin's and Gerrick's own plans that they exchanged glances of amazement. Laanui laughed heartily at their surprise.

"We have prepared a great luau to welcome you home. Come feast with us. Come celebrate . . . and while we sit upon the mats, I will enjoy watching my ship riding gently upon the waves."

"Wait a minute!" Gerrick hollered. "How did you even know we were coming today? And what happened at Wailua? I'm not going anywhere until you come up with some answers."

Laanui's grin turned sly. "Maybe you wish to learn a few of *my* ways, eh? Last night, I study the stars and tradewinds, and they tell me today is good day for return journey home. It is very simple; one night I will show you how to read them. If you had not returned today, you would have had to wait long time, because channel will soon be too rough for safe passage. You came just in time."

"But Wailua . . ." Caitlin interrupted. "How did you keep the spotted sickness from spreading to those fishermen and their friends?"

"My people's minds were confused that day, Tutu. They were remembering old ways, not new. So I, too, remembered the old ways and used them to control my people's fear. . . . All along the beach and near the trails to Wailua, I had Inamoo put up *kapu* sticks."

"*Kapu* sticks?" Gerrick asked.

"Tall wooden sticks topped with feathers, dog hair, or white tapa. In days of old, the sticks warned the people that a place was *kapu*, or forbidden, and they must not enter on pain of death. When the fishermen warriors returned with many outriggers, they saw the *kapu* sticks and stayed away. And as soon as we were all well again, we returned to Hanalei."

"Were there any more d—deaths?" Caitlin asked, her voice quivering.

"No, Tutu. Thanks to you, we knew what to do. Had you not been there, and everyone went swimming in the sea, many more would have died. I myself would be dead. Your name is holy upon our lips, Tutu. We will remember you always in our chants and stories."

Determined not to spoil this glad occasion with tears,

Caitlin swallowed the lump in her throat and smiled. "Now that I'm home, Laanui, I intend never to leave again."

"Never?" Gerrick possessively linked his arm through hers. "I don't think I like the sound of that word. I'd hoped you had planned to make the journey to Canton with me—and also to sail to New England to fetch my father."

"Well, maybe not *never*," Caitlin backtracked.

Gerrick tilted her face to his and rubbed his nose alongside hers. "That's better. . . . Now, are you ready to go ashore?"

Caitlin glanced toward the curving, white beach where the frothing surf was kissing the sand. Back from the water's edge, the palm trees were waving their lacy green fronds in the gentle, scented wind. She breathed deeply, her joy overflowing.

"Yes," she said. "I'm ready."

"She's ready," Gerrick repeated to Laanui.

"I ready, too!" Pikake trilled.

John grinned. "Well, if everybody's ready, what are we waiting for?"

Inamoo helped Caitlin climb down into an outrigger festooned with flowers. Everyone else then clambered aboard, and as the light, graceful craft skimmed toward the jeweled island, Caitlin thought how fitting it was they should be using an outrigger, instead of a gig.

"You and I are going to have to learn how to maneuver one of these damn things," Gerrick said beside her. "It would be ideal for exploring hidden beaches."

Caitlin only nodded and smiled; she'd had the same exact thought. They had all kinds of beaches to explore—and a whole lifetime in which to do it. This time, they were really home.

Afterword from the Author

Many of the secondary characters described in these pages are borrowed from actual Hawaiian history. The missionary era was a time of tumultuous change, when ideas and attitudes clashed. I have tried to present these clashes as accurately as possible. But in as much as Gerrick and Caitlin are fictional characters, their conversations with missionaries and members of Hawaiian royalty and officialdom are also fictional.

The settings, however, are not. They are as true to life as I can make them. Should you be so fortunate to journey to lovely, enchanting Hawaii, you will find the islands of Kauai, Maui, and Oahu much as I have described them. Beneath the layers of modern-day civilization, and away from the guided tours and merchants, lies a timeless, exotic beauty that deeply touches one. The sun still shines as brightly, the sea is as pure a blue, and the clouds still drift low across the luscious mountains.

Lovers still stroll the white and black sand beaches, sunrise over Heleakala is still a spectacular, mystic experience, and the Kalaulau Valley remains as shrouded with mist and mystery as it ever was. Rainbows are commonplace. In the land of eternal *aloha*, love awaits all those who come in search of it with open hearts. May you one day experience all that Hawaii has to offer; and before you leave, don't forget to say a silent prayer to the island gods so that one day you may return.

Aloha and *mahalo*.

<u>FREE</u> Preview Each Month and $ave

Zebra has made arrangements for you to preview 4 brand new HEARTFIRE novels each month...FREE for 10 days. You'll get them as soon as they are published. If you are not delighted with any of them, just return them with no questions asked. But if you decide these are everything we said they are, you'll pay just $3.25 each—a total of $13.00 (a $15.00 value). **That's a $2.00 saving each month off the regular price.** Plus there is NO shipping or handling charge. These are delivered right to your door absolutely free! There is no obligation and there is no minimum number of books to buy.

TO GET YOUR
FIRST MONTH'S PREVIEW...
Mail the Coupon Below!